A HEAVY BURDEN TO BEAR

by

Emmy Culley

Grosvenor House
Publishing Limited

All rights reserved
Copyright © Emily Culley, 2012

This novel is entirely a work of fiction. The names, characters and incidents portrayed in it are solely the work of the author's imagination. Any resemblance to actual persons, living or dead, events or locations is entirely coincidental.

A Heavy Burden to Bear copyright Emmy Culley published in 2012 by Grosvenor House Publishers.

The Author asserts the moral right to be identified as the author of these works.

All rights reserved. No part of this publication may be reproduced, stored in a retrieval system, or transmitted, in any form, electronic, mechanical, photocopying, recording or otherwise without the prior permission of the publishers.

This book is sold subject to the condition that it shall not, by any way of trade or otherwise, be lent, re-sold, hired out or otherwise circulated without the publisher's prior consent in any form of binding or cover other than that in which it is published and without a similar condition including this condition being imposed on the subsequent purchaser.

Book cover photography copyright Simon Walden - FilmPhoto, Cheltenham, UK

Models; front and back cover Rob Berning and back cover only Paul Winters

Websites: www.filmphoto.co.uk www.emmyculley.com

ISBN 978-1-78148-795-2

Glossary

Ague – Elizabethan term for malaria

Ambergris – whale vomit, a food delicacy popular in Elizabethan times

Ballast – Heavy material placed low in a vessel to improve stability

Bauble – a mock staff/sceptre carried by a court jester

Bawd/bawd house/bawdy den – procuress or madam/brothel

Bing a waste – Tudor slang meaning 'go away' in a rude manner!

Bit – Elizabethan slang for a cob (see below for definition)

Blackjack – a leather tankard with a tar-coated interior, used to hold ale

Bodhrán – a Celtic handheld, framed, shallow, goatskin drum

Bollocks – English slang word for testicles

Bosun – Boatswain

Bubbies – Tudor slang meaning breasts

Buboes – sublingual lymph nodes, hence the term 'Bubonic Plague' which caused inflammation of the buboes

Cacklefruit – Tudor slang meaning chicken eggs

Cat o' nine tails – a whip made from three ropes each separated into three strands with knotted ends. Used to flog British sailors in Elizabethan times

Caulking – stopping up the seams of a ship to make it watertight

Cavies – guineapigs

Clapperdudgeon – a beggar born

Clenchpoop – a clown

Cob – term used for a 'piece of eight'; a silver Spanish 8 reales coin in Ireland and the British colonies

Cockshut time – Elizabethan slang meaning twilight

Codso! – a Tudor swear word

Comfit – a sweet/candy in Tudor times

Consumption – Old English term for tuberculosis

Costiveness – Elizabethan term for constipation

Cunnie/cunt – a vagina… derived from the Latin 'cunnus'. Used as an everyday, inoffensive word in Tudor times.

Cur – dog; a bestial insult

Doublet – a close-fitting jacket worn by men in Tudor times

Duffy – the West Indian term for 'ghost'

Dumpish – a made-up word used by Queen Elizabeth I referring to her sad mood. Her jester would 'undumpish' her

Eanlings – Elizabethan word meaning 'lambs'

Fain – Elizabethan word meaning 'gladly', 'willingly'

Fanny – Old English slang word meaning vagina

Filching – thieving

Flummery – an early form of jelly made by straining boiled oatmeal or flour

Forsooth – Tudor word meaning 'Truly'

Garderobe – a toilet where clothes were kept as foul odours deterred moths

'Gardy loo!' – Tudor slang adapted from French expression, 'Guardez l'eau!' meaning 'Watch out for the water!'

Gong farmer – a man who removed excrement from cesspits and privies in Tudor England

Gun loop – an opening for a gun in a wall or parapet

Gunwale (Slang - gunnels) – the upper edge of the side of a ship

Hautboy – Elizabethan wind instrument similar to an oboe

Hie – Elizabethan word for hurry (pronounced 'Hi')

Hippocras – spiced mulled wine

Hogshead – a large cask to hold a specific measure of liquid (usually ale, wine or cider)

Hue and cry – In common law, a hue and cry (Latin; hutesium et clamor, 'a horn and shouting') is a process by which bystanders are summoned to assist in the apprehension of a criminal who has been witnessed committing a crime

Jags – a slash in a garment exposing material of a different colour (popular during the Tudor times)

Jigmaker – a writer of ballads

Jordan – Old English term for a chamber pot or 'piss pot'

Jings – Scottish exclamation

Ken – Scottish word meaning 'know'

'To let the cat out of the bag' – An idiom meaning, 'to reveal a secret unintentionally' stemmed from the use of the cat o' nine tails used to flog ill-disciplined Elizabethan sailors. It was kept in a bag to prevent it from becoming stiff from exposure to sun and sea salt

Madrigal – a song for two or three unaccompanied voices, developed in Italy in the late 13th and early 14th centuries.

Marchpane – marzipan

Merkin – a pubic wig

Nappy – (when referring to ale) strong, heady, tendency to cause sleepiness

Nipper – slang for child (usually male)

Oakum – loose fibre from ropes used to caulk ships

Pardy – Elizabethan oath usually used by women and children

Pillicock – penis

Poitín – (Irish Gaelic meaning 'little pot') alcoholic spirit distilled from potatoes

Pipe Down – the last signal from the bosun's pipe each night meaning 'lights out' and 'silence'

Pottage – Tudor word meaning stew

Ratlines – a series of small ropes used for climbing rigging

Quiver – Tudor slang for vagina

Scrofula – also known as the 'King's Evil' was a form of tuberculosis

Scuttlebutt – a water barrel on a ship

Shakes – Tudor slang for the sections of wood from barrels that had been 'shaken' down to store

Shift – a loose shirt-like undergarment worn by women in Tudor times

Skink – a sand lizard

Spondulicks – old English slang word for money

S'truth – a strong Tudor curse meaning 'God's truth'

Sweating sickness – also known as 'Sudor Anglicus' (English sweat) an epidemic that occurred six times during 15th and 16th century England then disappeared

Swive – Tudor slang meaning 'to have sex'

Tapuya – old Tupi word meaning 'foreigner' – (person who does not speak the Tupi language)

Tenterhook – a hook that holds cloth that is stretched to dry

Tincture – medicine made by dissolving a drug in alcohol

Truckle-bed – A small bed on wheels

Verily – Tudor word meaning 'indeed, truly or really'. Similar to 'forsooth' (as above)

Virginals – a musical instrument of the harpsichord family

Vihuela – a type of early Spanish stringed musical instrument

Wahala – Pidgin English (Nigerian) meaning 'problem' or 'worry'

Wherry – a small row boat (river taxi) typically used on the Thames in Tudor times. 'Wherrymen' or 'watermen' took passengers in their wherries

Winchester Goose – Elizabethan term for a prostitute working in Southwark (the domain of the Bishop of Winchester)

Zounds – (Pronounced 'zoons') a strong Tudor curse meaning 'God's wounds'

Bibliography

Poem Source: Elizabeth I: Collected Works, by Leah S. Marcus, Janel Mueller and Mary Beth Rose, eds. Chicago: University of Chicago Press, 2002. 302-3

The Progresses and Public Processions of Queen Elizabeth Volume I
(J. G. Nichols, 1823).

Sweet Robin: A Biography of Robert Dudley Earl of Leicester 1533–1588,
by Hamish Hamilton. Wilson, Derek (1981)

Staffordshire library copy of STC2 11627: The ioyfull receyuing of the Queenes most excellent Maiestie into hir Highnesse citie of Norwich, as repr. by EEBO.

Southwark: Old London Bridge, Old and New London: Volume 6, by Edward Walford (1878)

The Lady in the Tower: The Fall of Anne Boleyn, by Alison Weir:

Ballantine Books; (2010)

Sleepless Souls, by Michael MacDonald and Terence R. Murphy:
Clarendon Oxford, (1990)

The Country Justice, by Michael Dalton

Printed by William Rawlins and Samuel Roycroft, London (1655)

Electronic access: EEBO Early English Books Online

Acknowledgements

I dedicate this book to my precious son, Tadhg Culley, who I love beyond words. Hopefully someday we'll see our work reach and entertain the masses. I'll never stop dreaming! Our wee clan has been through so much lately and I've not coped well but I need you to know that I'm very proud of you. No matter what, you'll always be my best friend and wee bro! Liebe x

'The more you love your art, your calling... the more important its accomplishment to the evolution of your soul, the more you will fear it, and the more resistance you will experience facing it.' Steven Pressfield

Abundant thanks to my Mum and Dad; the most supportive, kind and loving parents ever. Despite numerous difficult times coping with dreadful illness and constant pain you've both always been there for me. I don't know what I'd have done without you! I hope you know how much I love and appreciate you.

Huge appreciation goes to my sweet Nan and soul twin, Micky, and her beloved Pat, my Granddad, for playing a huge part in my upbringing and life, always encouraging my creativity and interest in history. May their souls have reunited to forever rest in peace. My Granddad will always be my hero and role-model. My Nan was the most beautiful woman I've ever known. 2010 was a sad year when she died the day before my 44th birthday. I miss them both very much.

A big 'mercre dis!' to my God Father and uncle, Dave Brown, who is still my loyal proof-reader. Thank you for your patience, valuable advice and precious time. Once again, sorry about the naughty bits and 'fulfy' words!

Many thanks to my friend and talented photographer, Simon Walden, who took some great cover shots. Not forgetting my two cover models, Rob Berning (front and back cover) and Paul Winters (back cover) for doing a great job.

I also extend my gratitude to Paul Dolmen/Kemp for building my website, adding the text to the book cover and offering sound advice and constructive criticism but, most of all, for being a beautiful friend.

Big hugs to Ifor Griffith and Rita Kemp, two very precious friends. Thank you for abundant laughs and always being there for me.

Last but not least, thank you to my friend, Mark Carter, for caring and encouragement.

Without my son, parents and extended clan I might as well not exist. I am lucky to have you all in my life. Never forget that I love you all.

Emmy (proud descendant of the MacNichols clan of the Scottish Highlands and the Culley clan of Ireland)

Be safe and happy always!

'We can easily manage if we will only take, each day, the burden appointed to it. But the load will be too heavy for us if we carry yesterday's burden over again today, and then add the burden of the morrow before we are required to bear it.'

John Newton 1725-1807

Chapter 1

Beauty Was Her Curse

Little sound could be heard along the winding rows save for the dull thud of the hunchback's footfall as he ran free inside the town boundaries. As he navigated the narrow, well-trodden, cobbled streets of Plymouth, the young man mumbled to himself. Hopping clumsily over uneven pebbles and flints, this ungainly character appeared to be stricken with madness, bursting into a maniacal, high pitched cackle every so often. Any passer-by would have turned a blind eye to the filthy pauper who had suffered from birth with a debilitating bone disease causing his body to become twisted and warped. Dry, pain-wracked bones had become enlarged and fused in places making his appearance even more grotesque. The makeshift hessian garments that he wore had actually become part of the wretched monstrosity. Over many years, coarse body hairs had knitted themselves into the rough fabric that he had never taken off. He simply added extra pieces of scrap as his body expanded. Areas of skin had grown over cloth where neglected wounds had formed scabs that bonded fabric and flesh, with new layers growing as they fell away. Onlookers often found it difficult to believe that this piteous soul had once been some unfortunate woman's baby! Mud and dried animal shit had built up on rags bound around the man's swollen ankles and misshapen feet forming footwear that had never been removed. On closer inspection, thick, yellowy-brown toenails had formed claws that had grown into the material; their curves helped to keep the 'boots' in place. A club foot did not slow his pace but a huge hump protruded from torn cloth revealing the filthiest skin imaginable. This odd, heavy-set being had adapted to his environment, his entire appearance becoming camouflage, allowing him to blend so well into the wattle and daub buildings.

Misfits, cripples and freaks were usually encouraged to stay away from well-populated areas so as not to offend ordinary folk. Today was an exception to the rule for it was a public holiday. The hunchback was in a hurry to claim his spot at the hanging. He was determined to make his painful journey well worthwhile! Empty streets beckoned as the outcast began to fumble beneath his tunic, touching his hardening member at the thought of all the women he could accidentally bump into at such a crowded event. He cursed as he stuck his best foot into a firm, but slippery, turd that had recently been flung out into the gutter along the middle of the row. A pig squealed at the sudden appearance of the unwelcome creature. The hog had previously been unconcerned by the stranger's approach, as he had padded upon the scene softly with an uneven gait. This was so unlike the noisy, confident humans the pig was used to. Confusion set in as dogs, cats and pigs scavenging amongst the debris in search of rotten food all turned their attention to the odd invader that they sensed to be a threat.

The man continued to limp and hop comically along, zigzagging his way around angry beasts with dangerously large teeth, trying his best to fend off their snapping jaws. He was pestered by the vicious animals until he produced a short, thick stick with a cruel-looking knob on the end. With an accurate swing, the wielder embedded the club into an unfortunate hound's skull, its impact making a nauseating crunch. Yelping as it collapsed on the ground, the animal was cut off mid snarl, twitching as its jowls relaxed to emit a steady stream of scarlet liquid. The scent of blood enraged the pack of hungry creatures and they turned their attention to the freshly slaughtered carcass. It was a hideous sight as frenzied, desperate animals tore away meat from a dog they had been running alongside only a few minutes earlier. The beggar tucked his makeshift weapon back into his belt. Letting out a crazed burst of laughter he continued on his way. Nothing would deter this social exile from reaching his chosen destination. Feeling an achingly pleasant sensation in his groin, he neared the huge, rowdy crowd that had gathered in the town square.

Slathering and panting, the new addition to the seething mass was able to craftily worm his way towards the gallows. Luckier folk held handkerchiefs to their noses in an attempt to stifle the vile stink that had suddenly crept up on them. Some were too late or still looking for the source of the reek by the time it had faded. Steadily pushing his way through the gathering of eager, sweaty people, the monster paused for a moment to press his impressive erection against an attractive young woman who was totally oblivious of his actions. Muttering false apologies, and gurning hideously, he continued to force his way through a crowd that made way for a reject who would have been lynched for his blatant nerve had it not been such an important event. Gloating over his coveted place amongst the lucky few in the first four rows, the hunchback watched as Captain Sushana Culley was roughly pulled up the wooden steps to the gallows. 'Yeeeeesssss!' he grunted to himself with glee. His hard-on had been spent after copping a feel of the breasts of an unfortunate girl who had been unaware of his presence. Nevertheless, he felt his aching groin immediately stir at the sight of the sensational pyrate queen. She stood brave and proud as the executioner's coarse hands groped and tugged at her breasts. The vile creature that placed a noose around her neck forced her to relive the brutal rape she had endured the previous night. The ugly voyeur below sighed with perverse pleasure, satisfied that he had already been rewarded for risking such a challenging journey. Then, it all happened in an instant...

As the sickening wretch stood squeezing his stiffening penis, the condemned closed her beautiful blue eyes tightly. Shana felt a sharp prod in the small of her back. 'Stand on the stool!' the executioner commanded as he took her by the elbow to hurry her up. 'Aaaahhhh', her witness groaned as he feasted his greedy, bulbous eyes on the pyrate wench's body. Trapping spiteful shards of glass firmly between her tongue and the roof of her mouth, Shana silently thanked her lover for providing the eyeglass which she had painfully broken down. As she tasted her own blood, a rush of adrenaline hit, giving her a sudden burst of energy.

The insignificant cripple who had spent over two hours climbing and hopping over obstacles, and hobbling along twisting rows to finally stand before the notorious woman, had actually caught her gaze! Unable to contain his excitement, he let out a whoop followed by an unearthly gargling and foul-stinking breath. The people around him tried to move away in disgust as they suddenly discovered the source of the diabolical stench. Displaying his loathsome grin, raising his eyebrows impossibly high and stretching his chin until it almost touched the tip of his crust-riddled nose, the hunchback had managed to steal some attention from the star of the show... for a few seconds at least. Breaking eye contact with the misshapen character, Shana took in as deep a breath as possible. With impressive force and accuracy, she spat the glass needles as hard as she could directly at her captor's face.

Olaf Hickford, the Queen's High Executioner, yelped like an injured hound, relaxing his grip on Captain Culley's breasts. He stumbled around, frantically clawing at his bloody, lacerated eyes. Shana held her head high, smiling in triumph as she felt the roughness of the rope tighten against the delicate skin of her neck. As she focused on the azure blue eyes of a handsome young man nearby she felt a warm glow inside, remembering her beloved son Patrick... their eyes were so similar! Hickford grabbed blindly at the fine silken material of her blouse, ripping it and exposing her ample breasts. Yelling a Banshee cry, the pyrate queen gave her audience a performance that would be difficult to forget. Clinging to the memory of her son, and knowing that he was safe on foreign shores, she jumped as high as she could. The crowd jeered and yelled with shock and excitement at the entertaining but horrific scene playing out before them. Some watched, transfixed with morbid fascination, whilst others covered their eyes in disgust at the botched execution. Hickford would not learn the full extent of the occurrence until later when he had been exiled in shame. He would go down in history as the High Executioner who had used a rope that was too long for the hanging of the most wanted pyrate in England.

It had all happened so fast. One minute Anthony, the blacksmith's son, was watching his beautiful heroine being molested by an abusive lout. The next, he witnessed her head hurtle towards him as the full extent of the vile event dawned on him. Confusion reigned and the crowd went wild! People screamed as they were pushed to the ground and trampled underfoot. Some tried in vain to reach the gallows but others turned to flee. A full riot ensued and shots were fired in an effort to control the heaving, panicked mob.

Despite the numbing effects of opium, Sushana imagined the agony as she heard her shinbones snap like dry twigs when her feet hit the ground. Blood splashed into her eyes as her head was torn from her neck. She felt a hot, stinging sensation as she struggled to focus on vague swirling images. Anthony could have sworn that he had seen Shana's lips move as her head flew high above the hysterical crowd. Her blood spattered the shocked faces of her adoring fans as some looked upwards, not quite believing what they were witnessing. The last images to pass through Shana's mind were of blue skies, white clouds and so many faces whirling around in a confusing kaleidoscope of blurred colour. Then, complete darkness. Her dying sense was one of security as large, warm hands held her head with care, covering her ears and calming her mind. Anthony had been right. The dying woman's lips had formed an involuntary smile. Shana had managed to accomplish the final revenge that she had craved. The last sounds that Captain Culley heard were muffled screams and cries of complete turmoil. At last able to relax, she closed her sightless eyes in the knowledge that the coward Hickford had been beaten at his own sick game.

Instinct commanded Anthony to run yet something deep within his soul urged him to do the unthinkable.

He grabbed the warm head of the executed victim and quickly tucked it under his doublet. Covering the conspicuous bump with his hat, he forced his way through the milling crowd. To the blacksmith's amazement, not a single person had noticed what he had done. Most were trying to escape after muskets had been fired. The crowd was out of control and the noise was unbearable. Violence had broken out in places and many were acting in an unruly and destructive way. Some young men had managed to climb onto the gallows, tearing down pieces of timber and cutting rope to sell as souvenirs. A mob ripped away pieces of clothing from the headless corpse and hacked off fingers for expensive rings.

Anthony spotted a hunchback pushing his way through the masses and grabbed him by the neck of his thick hessian tunic. People would soon get out of the way for a stinking freak. With eyes bulging in disbelief, that someone had actually touched him, the repulsive man blurted something incoherent in a guttural gargle. Leaving the riotous mob behind the fit, young blacksmith was soon able to pick up his pace, half carrying, half dragging his new companion beside him. The crippled pauper continued his garbled protest, yet seemed in no hurry to escape the grasp of his tall, handsome kidnapper. Anthony managed to run quickly through the narrow streets despite his awkward new burden. Everywhere was deserted as everyone from miles around had gathered at the square to witness the execution. Heavy footsteps echoed as Anthony jogged down Grope Cunt Lane. He turned sharply into Rotten Row. The hunchback twisted his thick neck around to see faded, weather-worn signs swaying above. Rusted chains creaked as a warm breeze stirred them gently. Dogs snarled, cats hissed and pigs squealed and grunted as the young man thudded past with his wriggling load. Shana's dark blood had begun to seep through Anthony's garments, its metallic stench pungent. At last he felt relief when he saw the entrance gate to St. Xavier's churchyard.

A slight wind carried the odour of freshly dug earth as the two men squeezed through the lych gate with some difficulty. Although the hunchback remained quite relaxed considering the circumstances, Creppin, as he was commonly known, added considerable width to Anthony's broad frame. On entering the graveyard, the blacksmith dropped the hunchback on the soft turf. 'Ww... what dost tha' rrrequire frrrom Crrreppin, sire?' Anthony was surprised to hear a high pitched, rather unnerving nasal voice as the odd man asked a question that he had no intention of answering. Despite a protruding chin and a few rotten teeth loose in diseased gums, Creppin formed his words well, apart from rolling his r's annoyingly. Sweat dripped from his captor's brow as they made their way together over to the freshly filled grave of Isaac Bromley.

Isaac had been buried earlier that afternoon, so hastily that a spade had been left nearby. Carefully taking Captain Culley's bloody head out of his doublet, Anthony wasted no time. Creppin stood drooling at the sight of the woman's pretty face; a gob of spittle appeared on his floppy lower lip and dribbled over his enlarged jaw. The unfortunate soul shook his head in confusion, mumbling to himself as if conversing with another person. Anthony was amused at the pathetic sight of his companion knocking away some earth that had stuck to his dreadful garb as if he had actually dressed for a special occasion! Wiping accumulated snot from his bulbous nose, Creppin dropped clumsily to his knees and rolled himself onto his back, to stare at the sky above. Then he spoke between shallow, rasping breaths. 'What has yon strrrong young man in mind for Crrreppin? He haths need of us but willnay tell whyforrrr!' Again, Anthony found it quite amusing to watch the strange man talking to himself but decided to put the wretch's mind at rest. 'Would tha be courteous 'nuff t'elp me dig? I shall make it well worth tha while.' Snuffling and snorting like a hungry hog, the disfigured man turned over onto all fours and scrambled up to face his addresser. Head bent awkwardly, Creppin stared with bulbous eyes that were set way too far apart. The left was much lower than the right and muddy brown with a large pupil that seemed to be staring off into the distance, over Anthony's right shoulder. The right was smaller and piercing, greyish blue with a pinhead pupil that was firmly fixed onto Anthony's own eyes. Heavy diagonal eyebrows met at their highest point, giving the man a rather pathetic expression. Anthony could not help but feel pity towards this weird, deformed creature as his moist eyes rolled upwards. 'Accept thine offerrr I shall, kind sirrreee! Crrreppin is all'ays glad ter' make some pennieeees!' Creppin had the knack of spitting his p's as if blowing a pea shooter. Again, this added to the eccentric character's curiously gruesome charm. Anthony was sensible enough to take a quick step backwards to avoid the spray of spittle.

It took no time at all for the blacksmith to gain Creppin's childlike trust and sworn loyalty after offering the rogue a groat in reward for his help. Grimacing as he wiped his ever-dripping nose on the back of a filthy, shiny sleeve, he hobbled over to the shovel. It had been left lying next to the mound of earth that covered the coffin of Isaac Bromley, a local shoemaker. Despite his disability, Creppin was a strong man and wasted no time digging great damp sods of worm-riddled earth until his spade struck the wooden coffin. 'Yi!' he yelped as he dropped the tool and scrabbled at the sides of the earthen walls to pull his hefty bulk to freedom. Anthony slapped his helper on the back and noticed how he moved his heavy brows in quick succession, as if his face was being manipulated by unseen fingers. Creppin's brows danced above animated eyes yet, within a split second, those same odd eyes became cruel, dark, slanted slits. He displayed the most unnerving sneer. Hideously ulcerated gums appeared above filthy, discoloured teeth. If the whole event had not been so bizarrely macabre, Anthony would have been unable to suppress his nervous laughter but time was of the essence. Quickly, he placed the severed head on the ground, took off his bloody doublet and covered the evidence. Jumping down into the gaping pit onto boards that creaked under his weight, the muscular man grabbed the discarded shovel and began to prise open the coffin lid. As iron nails, fashioned by his own skilled hand, tore out from the best walnut the undertaker could offer the smell of the bloated corpse filled the blacksmith's nostrils. A spray of vomit covered the face of the deceased, knocking carefully placed pennies from paper-thin eyelids that had been sewn together with dark cotton thread. The shoemaker's family had certainly given their loved-one a burial with no expense spared!

A memorial stone bearing the dead man's name had not yet been set in place. The experienced gravedigger was waiting for the earth to settle to ensure stability. Composing himself, Anthony reached up and grabbed the severed head with one large hand, holding the other over nose and mouth trying to inhale as little as possible of the ghastly smell of the cadaver. Thankfully a fresh breeze carried away some of the odour as he took a final look at Sushana Culley's pale, yet still beautiful face. He noticed an exquisite, golden necklace covered in fresh blood that was congealing fast. The point of a star-shaped pendant had become embedded in the skin under Shana's chin. Anthony winced at the thought of the noose tightening around the poor woman's neck. Grabbing the star, he pulled it free and was struck by a compelling feeling that he had to take the treasure to its rightful owner. Wiping the blood from the jewel revealed an impressive ruby. Everyone knew of the captain's immense love for her only child, Patrick, who was awaiting her return on faraway shores. Anthony had heard of the pyrate's hatred towards the English Queen who had offered the highest bounty ever for her capture... all because the outlaw had refused to give a percentage of her loot to the Crown! He felt deep respect for Shana and the way she had planned her own death in defiance of the Queen.

Looking up at a painfully beautiful sky, its hue somewhere between coral and deepest crimson, the blacksmith noticed a few weak wisps of cloud lingering lazily before a hazy, pearlescent crescent moon. No longer able to stifle pent up tears, he wept silently. Luckily, the summer night was slowly drawing in and the first of many unpleasant tasks was almost complete. Anthony felt extreme loneliness as he placed Shana's head next to that of Isaac Bromley. Strangely, he felt no guilt as he was sure that the old man who lay lifeless before him would have seen the funny side of sharing a grave with the head of the notorious pyrate queen! The blacksmith's mind was spinning as he concealed the valuable necklace beneath his linen shirt. He tightened his belt and carefully replaced the coffin lid, driving the nails back in with the wooden handle of the gravedigger's spade. Creppin and Anthony worked with muted efficiency until the grave was refilled. Grabbing his blood-stained doublet, Anthony left the graveside with the hunchback following a few paces behind him.

That fateful night of Saturday the twelfth of July 1578, Anthony emerged from St. Xavier's Churchyard with his accomplice. Together they had concealed a secret that would have made Queen Elizabeth's blood boil and seal their fates as the next victims of her unforgiving noose. The Head of the High Church of England, who claimed to be directed by God Himself, had forbidden Christian burial for any executed criminal. Some of the bodies were given to relatives for disposal depending on the severity of their crime. Children hanged for stealing a loaf of bread were occasionally granted the honour of a Christian burial service on condition that it was held outside hallowed ground. This offered little comfort as their tiny, broken bodies were handed over to distraught parents. Most victims of the noose were placed in iron cages, their sorry carcasses left to rot inside, littering the main coach routes to deter others from the temptation of crime. Anyone who committed high treason would have their head displayed in a prominent place as a warning to others. The fact that Anthony had been able to bury the head of a notorious terrorist in hallowed ground would certainly be punishable by death. He now believed that he was fated to play a significant part in Patrick Culley's future. From the moment their eyes had met, as Shana stood on the gallows to the time he gently laid her head to rest, he had felt a strong affinity with the extraordinary woman. A barn owl hooted nearby and leaves rustled softly above as the two figures left the small graveyard. No-one would notice that the earth had been disturbed a second time that day and Anthony could not have planned a better way of hiding Shana's head if he had tried!

The following morning began with a dramatic sunrise and Peter, the old gravedigger, smiled as he felt the warmth ease his aching back. He was happy with his lot, thankful for a full belly every night and a comfortable straw mattress to sleep on in the gatehouse. Peter earned no wage but acted as caretaker of the church and grounds, responsible for overseeing all burials. He was often trusted as a spare pall bearer if a family was one short. A friendly, quiet soul who kept himself to himself, he ensured that all burials were carried out with utmost respect for his dead… for that is how he regarded the dear departed friends who he looked after in the graveyard. With a pensive look on his face, the old man stooped to pull a small piece of hessian from the mound of earth that he had dug only the previous afternoon. He rolled it between thumb and forefinger before throwing it aside. As he watched where it landed he looked at the good, sturdy shoes that he wore and said a silent prayer for the soul of his newest friend who had spent his first night in the tidiest graveyard in England… or so the old man liked to think. Humming a peaceful hymn, Peter began his first daily inspection of the grounds of St. Xavier's and smiled in the knowledge that all was as it should be.

CHAPTER 2

Patrick's Premonition

On a remote beach on São Vicente, one of the Cape Verde islands off the Western coast of Africa, Patrick Culley looked out at a beautiful clear blue sea. The young man took his short knife and sliced off a succulent piece of mango. Closing his bright blue eyes, he savoured the taste of his favourite fruit. Fingering the soft leather pouch that he always wore on a thong around his neck, he began to think about his mother. She had earned the nickname 'Captain Culley the castrator' and coveted title of 'pyrate queen' for her daring, ferocity and bravery. Many feared the hardened warrior woman who took trophies from her unfortunate victims, not caring whether they were alive or dead when she sliced off their testicles. She made them into pouches like the one that her son was wearing.

As a young lad Patrick had claimed his own trophy from his first kill whilst serving aboard his mother's ship. Although he had taken the life of the bastard who had murdered Irish, the man who had become his surrogate father, he would never get over the loss. Feeling nauseous as he brought to mind the face of the man who had caused so much pain and misery in his life, Patrick spat a curse into the sand. If only he had made him suffer more. Death had been too kind a penalty for such scum! Patrick displayed an over-protective nature towards women, especially his mother. A mistrust of most men was ingrained in his being. After all, his very existence was the result of a brutal rape. His mother had managed to kill her attacker but not before he had released his sorry seed into her womb. Self-hatred plagued Shana's only child and although she loved him more than her own life, nothing would take away the cursed reality of his conception. Pausing briefly before he cut another slice of fruit, Patrick felt a sudden dread. Surging heat rushed through his veins. His heart skipped a beat. An inexplicably unnerving sensation made his whole body shudder. Mouthing a silent wish that his mother was enjoying a happy fortieth birthday, his gut instinct told him that something awful had happened. If anyone dared harm her, Patrick would make sure that they suffered a fate worse than death. He often imagined ways to seek revenge on the bitch Queen if his mother was ever captured. Stabbing his blade deep into the sand, he began to grind his teeth together hard. He had a horrible feeling that it would not be long before he would be seeking retribution. Something terrible had happened to his mother; he just knew it! There was nothing he could do but await news. A hardened character, Patrick put aside the bad feeling and looked down at the words tattooed on his wrist. Alea iacta est. The die is cast. As his mother had always told him, 'Everything is in the hands of the fates.'

Patrick tried hard to ignore the presence of the tall, dark man who sat patiently servicing his pistols under the shade of a nearby palm tree. Although his silent guardian always gave him space and never bothered him, Patrick still felt as though Moses was being over-protective. It was understandable that the sole heir of the infamous pyrate leader had to be safeguarded but Patrick believed that a teenaged Culley descendant deserved more freedom! True, his mother had dared to lead a fierce anti-slavery campaign and made no secret of her disrespect for the Queen of England, who longed to see her worst enemy hanging from the gibbet. Even so, Patrick believed that he was perfectly capable of looking out for himself. Since he had lived a life of pyracy for as long as he could remember, he could fight better than most. He seriously doubted the need of a warden in his mother's absence but despite his reluctance he respected her wishes and fears; fears which were actually not unfounded.

Shana Culley had become a living legend. Stories of her ferocity in battle, daring heists and slave freedom missions had already made history earning her the title 'Most wanted person in England'. The bounty on her head was the highest ever recorded. The captain's strong alliance with Irish pyrate queen, Grace O'Malley, caused the English Queen great concern as their combined forces posed a serious threat against Tudor reign. Patrick knew the risks that his mother was taking on her rescue mission. He also trusted that she had known best when she left him in São Vicente with her lover, John Hawkins, and trustworthy friend, Moses. As soon as Shana had received word of Grace's capture, Patrick had understood that his mother had to risk returning to Ireland where her friend was being held in Dublin Castle. She had taken a sturdy, well-armed, manned and equipped vessel and loyal trusted crewmember, Remando, who Patrick knew would defend his captain with his life.

Admiral John Hawkins had been working for the Crown by proxy since he had fallen in love with his feisty pyrate lover and they had to keep their relationship secret. With his slave trading days behind him, Hawkins planned to help Shana and Grace O'Malley plot against the English Queen. John's cousin, Sir Francis Drake, had replaced him as one of the Queen's favourites at court and, for the meantime at least, was able to help keep her mind off his absence. Regular messages between the two men enabled them to convince the conceited monarch that Hawkins was performing his duty as Naval Treasurer; although, unbeknownst to her, he was enjoying life with his new woman. Recently, Hawkins had helped introduce a new warship that was far more manoeuvrable than any before. Back in Plymouth his shipyards were busy producing these much improved vessels whilst he waited in São Vicente for Shana's return. He hoped that his innovative design would keep the grasping monarch content for a good few months.

Inviting waves of a sparkling ocean beckoned Patrick's company. Removing his fine linen shirt as he ran barefoot through the warm, shimmering white sands, he welcomed cool, crystal-clear waters. Strong arms took him on a vigorous swim. A school of flying fish soon joined him, silver fins flashing brightly as they caught the dying rays of the setting sun. Although he missed his mother, Patrick always made the most of his days spent in the paradise she had chosen as their home base. He swam strong and fast against the current, heading out towards Mount Cara. Face Mountain, as it was aptly called, boasted a striking silhouette that looked like the profile of a man's face staring up at the gold and tangerine streaked skies.

The group of ten islands that made up Cape Verde were of volcanic origin, one of them still having a live volcano. Each had a uniquely majestic, arid landscape and was beautiful in its own way. São Vicente was not the most aesthetically pleasing but it had other more important features that would appeal to any pyrate captain. Staying hot all year round the island enjoyed short tropical storms that were over very quickly. Dry and barren with a flat, desert-like landscape and stretches of sand dunes, drought and hurricanes made it difficult to grow anything. Fortunately, excellent northeasterly trade winds meant that fish were abundant in surrounding waters. The constant wind pattern around the Verde Isles meant that ships sailing between Europe and the New World made obligatory stops at São Vicente's deep water port of Mindelo for repairs and provisions. This enabled Shana and her gang to keep in touch with the outside world yet remain incognito amongst the friendly Cape Verdean inhabitants who had no interest in English law.

Monte Verde was the highest mountain on the island and one of the few places that stayed green all year round due to the humidity of the clouds. The island's network of caves, subterranean lakes and crevices, formed over many years of volcanic eruptions, provided numerous hiding places for stashes of booty. Sheer, jagged cliffs rising from the sea hid a labyrinth of tunnels that now held treasures from around the world. Shana had ensured that a fair portion of bounty from her years of pyracy stayed close at hand.

Loyal Moses had kept his word to his captain and friend and had watched out for her son since she had left the island. The tall, dark-skinned man owed his life to Shana's close friend, Grace O'Malley. Moses was a Moorish pyrate who was thought to have been captured by the English. When his broken body had been washed ashore on Grace's land, she had taken him in, nursed him and severed a gangrenous arm. Grace was an Irish noblewoman, a Celtic queen who was fiercely defensive of her lands and a steadfast ally of the Culley clan. Moses had chosen to serve Captain Culley, pledging his loyalty to the pyrate queen who he now regarded as his own kin. A gentle giant who had known Patrick since he was a baby, the picturesque character could not have been mistaken for anything but a pyrate. Standing head and shoulders above most men with a solid, sturdy build, Moses was a mute. His tongue had been torn out as punishment for crimes of pyracy. Unsightly scars remained where clumsy stitches had sewn his lips together. Yet despite his disabilities, Moses always managed to perform most sailors' duties and fought like a true warrior. He did not take his responsibility lightly and cared for Patrick in his mother's absence. Ironically, although Queen Elizabeth and the Irish noblewoman were sworn enemies, each held a deep respect for the other's strength and power in a male-dominated world. Despite this, the two powerful women would never call a truce. Shana was loyal to the Irish pyrate queen and their bond was strong. The stubborn woman had left her only son, her lover and her friends to rescue Grace who had made it clear that she should stay away. Patrick swam faster. He yelled aloud in frustration and anger towards the mother he adored.

Expertly whittling a piece of driftwood as he sat silently in the shade, Moses took in his surroundings. Incredibly dextrous despite having only one arm, the burly pirate held the bleached wood firmly between his knees. His only hand was huge and strong fingers worked his knife, skilfully carving an intricate frigate bird native to those shores. He welcomed the gentle breeze and July climate that followed the drought that had brought destructive eroding winds. Locals were glad that the blasts of hot wind that swept across the island carrying unwelcome brown dust had finally passed. Farming techniques were poor. Goats were allowed to roam and graze freely so short violent rainfalls washed away loosened topsoil into the sea. Moses' mind was troubled as he tried to focus on the job at hand. He pondered the fate of the ward he had grown so close to and feared for his future. Everyone knew how close Patrick was to his mother and his friend felt inner turmoil as he imagined the consequences if anything was to happen to her. Years of pent-up anger was boiling in the lad's veins. His hatred towards Queen Elizabeth had only been refuelled when she had raised the bounty on his mother's head. Woe betide the monarch if she ever felt the wrath of Patrick Culley.

A familiar chatter interrupted Moses' thoughts as a tiny monkey leapt onto his lap. Flint, of all creatures, should have known better than to invade a hardened pyrate's space without warning! With a flick of the wrist, instinct took over and Moses swiped the monkey with the back of his hand before he had even managed to land. Yelping as he flew through the air Flint landed, dazed and confused, between a pair of ripe coconuts. Hawkins' deep, loud laugh made Moses feel a little less guilty as he scooped the shivering creature up into his palm and sat beside his friend. Flint's little belly was swollen, no doubt full of food, and he looked up at the two men with wide, pitiful eyes. The mischievous critter had been in the company of pyrates as a ship's pet for longer than Moses could remember and he was amazed how he would never learn! Flint's son, Tripod, came bounding towards them, face contorting into a comical grimace with faux concern for his over-dramatic single parent. The pyrates had named the baby monkey after a well-loved fallen comrade in arms. Idly scratching the soft pink skin on his stomach, Flint showed no concern or pain from the incident but was clearly out to milk it nevertheless! The smaller monkey began to groom his Dad and the pair watched as Moses hacked a coconut in half with one strike of his cutlass. Both monkeys helped themselves to the sweet milk and all was peaceful again on the idyllic tropical beach.

As Patrick swam faster, the riddle that his mother had taught him came to mind. 'Season the bald one's gift wi' great care'. He had managed to decipher the first line of the riddle a while ago. 'The bald one' referred to Grace O'Malley, who had been nicknamed 'bald Grace', as she had cut her hair very short ever since she was a young girl. She had often been mistaken for a boy. 'Seasoning, hmm', the young man thought harder as he remembered that Grace had brought lil' Flint back to Ireland as a gift for a lover. The pet's renowned addiction to valuable Aframomum pepper suddenly dawned on him! If the correct dosage was given this miraculous spice could enhance and sustain erectile function. When 'seasoned' with the spice, the wee tyke would have an erection that he would show off, entertaining himself and others for hours! As for the next line, 'It may ignite so, pri'thee, beware!' Well, if Patrick was correct in guessing that any friction in that area would inflame the organ, 'Peel gently back and do not tear,' probably referred to the unfortunate ape's delicate foreskin. 'Then ye may take it if ye dare!' would therefore be a warning that Patrick would be a fool to take lightly! Flint could inflict a nasty bite with his sharp incisors and there were a few who could attest to that. Sedating Flint should not be a problem. Shana had taught her son the medicinal and therapeutic properties and uses of herbs, spices and essential oils extracted from plants and leaves. She knew that Patrick would be more than capable of mixing the right ingredients to put the monkey to sleep and take whatever was hidden beneath his foreskin. He could not help being amused by her shrewdness. After all, who would ever think of anyone concealing something important in a pet's penis! Ever amazed by his mother's wild imagination Patrick decided to relieve the poor creature of his uncomfortable burden that night. He turned smoothly on a frothy wave and headed back for shore.

Some Tupi tribesmen had joined John and Moses on the beach. The group sat around a healthy, crackling fire. Patrick recognised the delicious smell of giant skink meat being slowly cooked over steady flames. A familiar voice called him to join them. It felt good to see another loyal friend, a small man who had always been known as Shrimp. When Patrick was a baby, the Lilliputian pyrate had been amongst his mother's crew when they visited São Vicente. During their stay, he had fallen in love with the chief's daughter and married her. Now they had two healthy children. Realising his hunger, Patrick took a place next to his friend, Jaeci (meaning 'moon' in the Tupi language). The young men were always pleased to see each other and often went exploring and hunting together. Everyone welcomed the newcomer and they were soon sharing a substantial meal of boiled shrimp and sweet potato stew with succulent pieces of skink. As the moon cast an eerie iridescent shadow onto the secluded sandy beach, the party gathered their few belongings and went their separate ways. Jaeci and his companions made a picturesque sight as they stood on the sands as still as statues, their bronze tattooed skin lit only by the light of the watery moon and its shimmering reflection on the calm waters.

Patrick stood at the edge of the sparse forest under a gnarled dragon tree. He observed the skilled hunters thrusting their sharp spears into a good number of turtles that had struggled ashore. Yearly, between the months of May and September, both leatherback and green turtles paid a visit to the island beaches where they would make nests. The luckiest amongst them returned to the ocean after burying around forty whitish eggs safely beneath the sand. These would hopefully hatch in about eight weeks' time. Then the beach would come alive with tiny turtle hatchlings, breaking free from their shells and instinctively stumbling their way towards the sea. However, many of the eggs would be collected for food. The Tupi people believed that eating turtle meat could prevent and help recovery from leprosy. They were clever enough to preserve a good amount of the fresh meat in salt, which they sold at a fair price to visiting sailors who were always keen to buy a stock of imperishable food for long voyages.

Patrick stood for a while watching the group of skilled hunters. He envied their uncomplicated existence. Simple survival; hunting, fishing and fighting was all they knew. They had chopped down trees and burned brush to make small clearings for the tribeswomen to harvest their crops. They would plant corn, pumpkins, beans, cassava, squashes and peanuts to later gather, prepare and cook as a staple diet for the tribe. Frequently moving their villages to take advantage of fresh hunting territory and new farming land, possessions were limited and could be packed easily in times of tribal migration. The Tupi tribesmen were distinguished looking characters. Like tonsured monks, they only ever left a ring of hair on their heads. They shaved off their eyebrows and pubic hair and each had their lower lip and cheeks pierced as young boys. As they grew, their piercings were stretched until they could wear larger jewellery. Shell and fish bone pendants rattled together as they leapt forward now and then to spear their prey with speed and accuracy. Patrick enjoyed watching his friends work. They made intriguing subjects to draw with polished plugs of green jadeite through their lips and cheeks, and elaborate belts of colourful feathers and shells about their waists. The short, stocky warriors gained a stripe tattoo with each enemy kill. Their appearance and behaviour that night was benign in comparison to times of war between other local tribes. Cannibalism was common in those parts and Patrick's friends captured prisoners from enemy tribes for ritual slaughter. When they devoured their enemies it was believed that they would also inherit their strength. Their ways were not all that different to those of his pyrate clan.

Captain Culley was well-known for her ferocious temper and vengeful spirit and her son had certainly inherited those traits. Another surge of inexplicable fear for his mother's safety rose inside him, giving way to scalding anger. Involuntarily clenching his jaw tightly and grinding his teeth painfully, Patrick punched the tree trunk several times as hard as he could. His enraged yell alerted his group of friends but they soon went back to their culling when they realised who it was.

With bloody and swollen knuckles, Patrick decided that it was time to go home, seek out Flint and find out what he was concealing.

Untying his trews to take a piss, he heard a loud gunshot. He refastened them quickly and ran back onto the beach to join Moses, who had already strapped four loaded pistols onto his belts. Passing his young friend three more guns, the mute signed expertly with his only hand. Patrick reacted immediately and the two ran through the sand towards the source of the commotion. Several more shots had been fired so the pyrates picked up speed, feeling their leg muscles strain as the shingle shifted beneath their bare feet. Passing a cluster of arrows, the men felt pleased that their Tupi allies had already reached the skirmish. Large areas of dark, blood-spattered white sand reassured them that the warriors had hit their targets. The beach was deserted so Patrick and Moses headed into the fringe of palm trees. Zigzagging their way through sun-bleached tree trunks, they reached a jagged cliff. The sound of more shots cracked, their echoes reverberating loudly in the gaping gorge. 'Almost on 'em', Patrick whispered. He had heard the Tupi bird-call; a signal that the tribesmen used when closing in on their prey. Heaven help the assailants now. Patrick's friends belonged to the most dominant tribe in the area. Anyone who dared breach their boundaries would be slaughtered.

The two men were relieved to see the thin waterfall trickling down the rock-face into a picturesque lake. Refilling leather flasks and then scooping fresh, cool water into cupped hands, they drank thirstily before ducking under a vine-leaf curtain. The natural screen concealed the entrance to one of their many hideaways.

Beneath tranquil, sweeping valleys, a network of basalt shafts and caves concealed more treasure than anyone could possibly imagine. It took a few minutes for their eyes to adjust to the darkness. Patrick located a metal box filled with tapers and torches. Taking his tinderbox, he produced a flame and lit a couple. Moses spotted them first. Huddled together in a nook, two black men shivered, staring wide-eyed at the pyrates. Their dark skin was battered and bleeding. It was clear to see that they had been whipped and beaten. Swollen flesh was shredded with deep, open wounds. Shivering with exhaustion and fear, one of the African men spoke in his native tongue. Shocked to find out that Patrick not only understood their language but could speak it too, the men looked at each other in relief. Having made many African friends over the years, Patrick had learned a few of their dialects and spoke them well. Moses stood tall and threw his water vessel over to the fugitives. They gulped down the welcome fluid and smiled nervously. Moses offered his hand to help the injured run-aways and they struggled to their feet. The two men were in a wretched state. It was only when they stood that the extent of their injuries could be seen. Patrick had established that they had been slaves working for a Portuguese family who owned a nearby sugar plantation. They told Patrick how they had been given one hundred lashes each when caught eating sugar cane.

Tomi and Manu had made a break earlier that day after retaliating against their cruel tormenter. Their story enraged their rescuers and made Patrick all the more determined to continue the fight against the horrific business of slavery. Tearing his shirt into strips, Moses began to dress as many of the escapees' wounds as possible whilst Patrick translated the newly freed slaves' story; 'Brother, these men have endured agony over at Fazenda's place.' Moses' anger brewed inside as he listened to his friend relay the horrific tortures that the slaves had suffered. 'Manu, the shorter one, was caught chewing cane an' was dealt one hundred lashes. I can scarce believe 'twas one o' his own who gid' him a whippin'!' Tomi winced with pain as Moses applied a simple tourniquet above four bleeding, mashed stumps that had once been fingers. Patrick continued, his voice low and stern, 'Then a bastard overseer took Manu t' their boss who wasna' satisfied wi' the punishment. By their word, he even 'as a gaol an' whippin' posts on his land. Bastard oft kills slaves s'if they were animals.' Tomi screamed in agony as Moses tightened a bandage around his ribcage to hold in protruding bones. Moses looked back at Patrick and shook his head. The men had both sustained such terrible injuries that he did not hold out much hope for their survival.

Outside the shelter of the cave, the normal sound of birdsong and croaking frogs could be heard once again. Patrick reassured the petrified men that their hunters had been captured. The one called Manu broke down in tears. His translator continued the morbid account of his abuse; 'This one was shoved into a hogshead wi' long nails driven in, so's the sharp ends protruded inside. Fazenda ordered one' o' his arse-lickin' boss-slaves ter toss it o'er a hill into the valley. Cask wi' slave inside plummeted half a mile downhill. Tomi an' another were told to fetch the mess that was left of this poor wretch. They all made a run for it, in the knowledge that there'd be more cruelty awaitin' 'em back at plantation… musket shots we heard were Fazenda's men on a man hunt. Third lad didnay make it.' Pausing briefly to pass his water bottle to his patient, Moses' eyes narrowed as he tried to imagine the ordeal that these two runaways had been made to suffer. Subconsciously, he raised his hand to his hideously scarred lips as he noticed that the wounded men had been branded. A large letter F had been scorched into each of their left cheeks. This identified them as Fazenda's property.

Patrick and Moses looked at each other and nodded in silence, acknowledging a pact that they had made long ago. Fazenda had sealed his own doom. His abusive actions would have dreadful consequences. The Culley pyrate clan believed in the threefold law; whatever you do to others will be done to you in return, only thrice over. However, before this matter could be dealt with, Patrick and Moses had to get the casualties to the Tupi village as quickly as possible. There, the skilled medicine woman would apply pastes that would hopefully heal their wounds and help prevent infection.

After dropping the African men off, the two vengeful men wasted no time at all. Nothing was going to keep the pyrates from joining their Tupi friends to watch the execution of their captives but they planned to add their own donation to the macabre ritual. Although the prisoners would all be cooked that night, no-one would be feasting on that day's catch. The man-eating tribe often consumed meat taken from the bodies of Tupi warriors from rival tribes. Their stock was replenished when they made captures during frequent intertribal battles. These victims would be slain during an honourable ritual sacrifice to their god. Tupi people believed that cannibalism enabled them to take on the persona of their victims and absorb the deceased warrior's spiritual essence. According to Patrick's Tupi friends this would boost their strength, power, bravery and knowledge, hence the reason why they preferred to eat fellow warriors. They even took on the names of their victims. The longer their name, the higher they were regarded. It had always been made very clear to Patrick and the other pyrates that they should never eat anyone who they did not respect. It would certainly be no great triumph to eat the flesh of the sadistic, cowardly bullies who had preyed on innocent slaves. The Tupi tribe kept large pigs. Nothing would be wasted after the feast as unwanted meat and bone from unworthy prisoners would be fed to the hungry hogs.

It had been decided by the tribal council to kill the captives who were unfit to eat in a viciously cruel manner. As a gesture of etiquette, they awaited the arrival of their pyrate guests before they began the executions and sacrificial rituals. When Patrick and Moses finally arrived, the shaman was delighted to see that they had brought him a gift. Hog-tied but ungagged, Fazenda yelled his protests. His eyes were almost popping out of his skull as he fought in vain to free himself. Moses was grinning in a particularly unnerving manner as he and Patrick dropped their snivelling offering in front of the wooden cage housing the rest of the prisoners. The two pyrates paid their respects to the tribal elders who had prepared an area within the sacred section of land. This was where the ceremony would be carried out. Patrick noticed that two pit fires had been prepared outside the hallowed perimeter. An inward shudder made the hairs on the back of his neck stand on end. He saw the glow of the red-hot stones that lined the burning pits. A third pit was soon dug for the late-comer and a fire quickly lit.

A lone drum beat a steady rhythm as a line of brightly dressed warriors snaked into the consecrated area. The shaman invited Patrick and Moses to join them in the circle. This was a great honour. Having stripped off their clothes, the pyrates took their places where they were permitted to watch the revered ceremony. Soon losing themselves in the passionate beat of the drum, they fell into a trance-like state. The hypnotic sound waves of a bullroarer sent the audience into a hysterical frenzy. The ancient ritual instrument, consisting of a blade on the end of a cord, was whirled around a warrior's head. With great skill, the wielder varied the pitch as he span the blade high above him. The blade wound itself around the strong cord then the warrior reversed the spin to make it unwind to produce a different noise. Fazenda's screams added to the eerie whooshing, whining sounds. Two women took a cudgel each and smashed the captive's legs and arms. This prevented him from running away when they untied him. Without the use of his arms Fazenda would not be able to retaliate. For added humiliation, his bloated, sweaty body was stripped bare by the giggling tribeswomen. When he began to beg and whimper, they gagged him in disgust.

More drummers joined in and the tempo quickened. Three Tupi prisoners were brought out of the cage. They stood insolently before their enemies. Their expressions showed their loathing. Pride and anger had been deeply ingrained into their hearts. They had been allowed to live for a few months to mull over their impending fate. Patrick translated so that Moses could follow the ceremony. One of the sacrificial victims spoke first, 'Thou shalt kill us and devour our flesh but there are still many of our tribe who will avenge us!' The shaman pushed a spear into the warrior's flesh, just above the man's heart and replied to his taunt, 'Thou shalt become one with us when we devour thy flesh!' Ornately dressed warriors matched their pace with the pulsating beat of the drum. Their eyes rolled up into their heads as they chanted to their god. Bright robes swirled around the warriors' naked bodies under the pale moonlight. The soft, yellow glow of dancing flames illuminated their dark, glistening skin. Beads of sweat on smooth brown flesh glittered like thousands of tiny diamonds as the tribal dancers ducked and twisted in a frenzied rave. The drums beat louder as they whirled and stomped around wildly, faster and faster, to the rising rhythm.

Fazenda and his two men shivered with fear. Their horrific screams were ignored as each was dragged over to his own makeshift oven. Sitting on the ground with their children, the tribeswomen writhed in hysterical frenzy as their spirits soared. They craved the taste of consecrated human flesh. The two foreign captives' legs and arms had been broken hours earlier. They were suffering excruciating pain. Both were forced into a seated position, feet tucked beneath injured thighs, keeping their hands in front of them. Two tribeswomen rebound their naked bodies and gagged them. Fazenda's men were then lifted by the strongest warriors who lowered them, still in a seated position, onto the red-hot stones. Their cries were blood-curdling as they felt their backsides burn. Fazenda passed out. Next, some women covered the victims' bodies with leaves and sat around the pit whilst they roasted alive. Now, it was Fazenda's turn.

A man-child was given a small cauldron of boiling water that he slowly emptied over the unconscious man's face. In his shocked state, Fazenda was carried over to his allotted fire pit. To his horror, he noticed that the hole contained a blazing fire but no heated stones lined its walls. Instead, two sturdy pieces of wood had been lodged firmly into the ground, one opposite the other. The branches had been chosen especially for their v-shaped ends. The shaman approached holding a long metal rod that had been sharpened to a point at one end. Bloodshot eyes widened with terror as hysteria set in. Fazenda's muffled pleas were ignored as the drumbeat matched the beat of his racing heart. Religious folk might believe that divine justice was served when excessive pain shot through the condemned man's chest just as the enormous skewer was rammed into his anus. The shaman, however, viewed the torture that he had chosen as a fitting penalty to pay for the brutal anal rape of many African slaves. Fazenda's heart did not stop beating until a good five minutes after he had breathed in the aroma of his own flesh as it slowly roasted on the spit. The shaman invited Patrick over whilst the pathetic bully was still alive. The pigs could be heard squealing wildly in their pen as the smell of meat filled their dusty nostrils. Patrick found great pleasure when he whispered right into Fazenda's ear, 'Th'art nay good 'nuff fer anyone t'eat. Hark at the swine whose bellies thy flesh shalt fill when thou art cooked to perfection!' Patrick spat on the man's red-raw face. His spittle landed on the bubbling, blistered surface of Fazenda's cheek. It hissed in the intense heat before vanishing.

    The two pyrates were finally able to relax and look forward to the night ahead as they watched the shaman turn the sadistic brute's body. The skin on his front had begun to char. Patrick's only regret was that the many slaves who had suffered whilst under his ownership had not been present to witness his slaughter. When he had cooked right through, Moses had the pleasure of hacking his carcass up into pieces. The pigs slathered at the mouth when large chunks of cooked human flesh were thrown into their pen. Each had their fill and not a trace was left. A woman presented Patrick with a souvenir of Fazenda's skull and ulna bones. They had been wrapped in a piece of white linen torn from the dead man's shirt. His bones had been stripped clean and had whitened well during the roasting process. They had not suffered a single crack.

The slaughter of the rival tribes' warriors was deemed far more civilised and honourable according to Tupi tribal law. Whilst on sacred ground, the victims' throats were all slit consecutively from behind. Their blood was caught in bowls. The shaman took the first drink then it was passed around. The bodies were thrown onto a large fire and left for a few minutes to heat up. When they were sufficiently warmed, they were dragged out with long hooks so the women could scrape off any unwanted hair. Each cadaver was washed then laid on its back ready for butchering. Firstly, the shaman tore out the windpipe and esophagus from each. A large portion was crudely sliced from each stomach and intestines and organs were pulled out. Everything but the liver was chopped into equal parts to be washed then cooked on skewers over the fire. When they were well enough done, they were passed around for people to eat whilst the main course was being prepared.

Each empty carcass was filled with hot stones, covered with plantain leaves and all orifices were stuffed with herbs. The prepared bundles were then lowered into separate pits that had been lined with more hot stones. Each victim's liver was placed next to the correct torso and plenty of vegetables were also added. Branches were laid over the top of the roast and then a layer of banana leaves. This was all covered with earth to keep in the steam. The meal only took an hour to cook and the shaman was delighted that the roast meat from the slain warriors was particularly succulent and tender. There was plenty to go around and the children enjoyed the most select morsels, chewing on the fingers and toes until the bones were clean.

Everyone agreed that the feast had been exceptional that night. Patrick and Moses felt invigorated and alive. Patrick's mother had always encouraged him to respect and honour other cultures and native religions so he had been practicing cannibalism since childhood. Western societies thought the tradition abhorrent and nauseating; the ultimate taboo. Patrick had always found this particularly ironic as his own ancient Celtic ancestors had sacrificed and eaten people too. Before going to war, the Celts believed that they had to offer their gods human lives to enable them to take the lives of their enemies. They differed from the Tupi people only because strong, healthy men were never sacrificed as they were needed to fight. Criminals and cripples would be killed instead. Their death would ensure victory.

Feeling perfectly content, with bellies full of food, Patrick and Moses slept soundly amongst thirty Tupi families that night. A cool midnight breeze carried the scent of smoking meat as thin strips of spiced human flesh dried out above a slow fire. The spine-chilling howls of a wolf pack could be heard as they caught a hint of the distinctive aroma.

Chapter 3

Anthony's Destiny Unfolds

A cockerel crowed at dawn as Anthony lay on his comfortable straw-stuffed mattress. His sleepy eyes registered the attic room walls of the terraced house that his father, Arthur Brown, had built before he was born. Arthur was a widower and lived with his only child on the outskirts of town. It was not too far from the forge that he had built himself, following his allotted time as an apprentice blacksmith. The two men were very close and worked well together. Anthony got up and looked down at the hunched form lying on the floorboards at the bottom of his bed. Creppin snored loudly and was oblivious to the wakening world around him. Walking over to the small window, the tall man stooped as he tried to open the shutters which instantly jammed. The ruddy, grinning face of the local butcher peered through the narrow gap as he hastily threw out the contents of his piss pot. 'Mornin' young feller!' he bellowed, before closing his shutters so Anthony could open his. Picturesque but ramshackle homes rose unsteadily above the shady, dank pebbled street that was aptly named Rotten Row.

Times were hard for traders who were forced to pay heavy taxes, dues and ground rent to the Crown. In highly populated places like Plymouth, where land was very expensive, traders had found a canny solution to at least one financial problem. By building their homes in close proximity to those of other traders', they were able to get away with larger upper rooms. Substantial 'overhangs' were constructed with adjacent buildings or props providing support. These extended storeys allowed much more living space without paying hefty ground rent. The overhangs would often almost touch those of neighbouring buildings which meant that the narrow, twisting streets that had formed below saw little sunlight.

Hearing a grunting sound from behind him, Anthony thanked his neighbour before passing the empty piss bucket to his bleary-eyed houseguest. 'Thanking ye kindly marrrster', Creppin managed to mumble before hauling himself up onto swollen knobbly knees and urinating heavily into the wooden pail. Sniggering childishly at the length of time it took to expel the contents of his over-sized bladder, Creppin managed to unnerve Anthony for the first time since fate had literally thrown them together. An arc of amber fluid still sprayed into the container but every few seconds Creppin stopped the steady flow to turn and check his roommate's reaction. Not knowing whether to leave the room or pretend not to notice, the blacksmith began to gather some of his tools and clothes together to lay them on his bed. A sudden loud fart broke the awkward silence and both men roared with laughter. Even then Creppin managed to continue to piss for a full minute longer! Anthony made a mental note to visit the apothecary and buy plenty of lavender, to help disguise the foul smell of the man who he planned to keep in his company for a good while.

Anthony filled two decent sized backpacks with enough preservatives for the long journey ahead. He wrapped Shana's precious necklace in cloth and strapped it to his body, along with enough money to pay for room, board and travelling expenses. Ensuring that he and his odd escort were well-armed, he chose light, hardy weapons. Two of the finest longbows and arrows, a double-edged sword and several knives with cruel-looking blades were amongst his armoury. Although his son's hasty departure came as a surprise to Arthur, no questions were asked. The work-weary blacksmith had raised his son well and never expected him to stay with him into old age. He had always believed that the best thing you can give your children is independence. Anthony had learned his father's trade and was a hard worker but Arthur had always known that the day would come when he would want to see more of the world. Sadly, his son had never known his mother who had died during childbirth, so the two of them had lived together for many years. 'Tha'v done tha' 'ole Da proud, me lad', the old man whispered. Passing his son a heavy leather pouch he pulled him close with strong muscular arms. 'Ne'er ferget tha roots but dunna fret 'bout me... I've 'ad more years than many in these parts an' dunna 'spect to last much longer.' 'Thank ye, Dar', Anthony replied with a lump in his throat. '.. fer e'erythin'.' The two men embraced each other heartily and Anthony left the home where he had spent many good years.

Creppin did not stop babbling away as he limped enthusiastically alongside his new 'master'. 'Tha'll ne'er rrregrrret hirrring me marster! Crrreppin's the most loyal servant tha could e'er 'a met.' Anthony's mind raced as he mulled over the tasks that had to be carried out quickly if his plans to find Shana Culley's only son were to succeed. Casting a quick sideward glance at his over-enthusiastic companion, he made a mental note to design some sort of contraption to help Creppin get along easier. They had many long treks ahead of them and he did not want to put the man through unnecessary pain. Equally he could not afford to be hindered by the lame individual, so this challenging problem would have to be addressed as soon as possible.

Dusk was fast approaching. A waning moon cast an eerie dim light that occasionally disappeared when clouds covered its watery crescent. Anthony was amused that Creppin had stopped talking since night shadows had invaded their tracks. His breathing remained heavy and rasping as he stumbled along with great determination. Had it not been for Creppin losing his footing on uneven cobbles, Anthony would never have seen the hidden figure crouched in a darkened alley a few yards away. Stooping to help his crippled companion to his feet, he noticed the vague outline of a man and managed to whisper a warning before the outlaw realised he had been spotted. Acting on a purely protective instinct and with incredible agility for such a twisted form, Creppin pulled himself up into a crouch and leapt forward to grab their would-be assailant. An unearthly, guttural growl grew to a crescendo as the hunchback smashed his bone club deep into the other man's skull. Pulling a cruel looking weapon from beneath his make-shift tunic, a skilful swipe of the jagged blade caused a fatal wound. Slipping in the entrails that had spilled from his victim, Creppin lunged forward clumsily managing to grab a second attacker who had emerged from another dark hiding place.

Anthony was fighting two well-built vagabonds who had joined the skirmish but their weapons were no match for the double-edged sword that he had tempered himself. A sickening sound of metal grazing bone was heard as the blacksmith drove the lethally sharp blade through an unprotected torso. Before he could withdraw his weapon, he took a nasty stab to a shoulder. Thankfully his opponent had aimed too high, missing any vital organs. Bringing his head back as far as possible before smashing his bony forehead into the face of the stranger, Anthony grabbed his hunting knife and drew its sharpened blade across the thug's throat. A splatter of warm blood sprayed his own face before the body slumped at his feet. Feeling light headed, Anthony staggered over to steady himself against a wall before dropping down onto cool cobblestones. He managed to make out Creppin's figure bent over one of his victims, and was quietly relieved that he had invited him along. The faint sound of distant voices brought fresh hope. Anthony called out, 'Creppin! Need help t' stand… been injured… s'that an inn nearby? Canst tha' hear folk talkin'?' When he realised that his friend had been injured, Creppin gasped dramatically, a bit over-concerned for Anthony's liking. Although the blacksmith found the clumsy oaf's fussing quite disconcerting, he was still glad of his company and inwardly admitted that he was fast becoming fond of the strange character. The poor fellow had, without a doubt, been dealt a bad deal in life. As if the pain caused by his disability was not enough to cope with, his appearance had become particularly hideous. Yet so far Creppin had shown nothing but loyalty. Quickly tearing a piece of clothing from the corpse that he had already stripped of weaponry and loot, the hunchback bounded over to his injured master and pushed it into the bleeding wound. Seeing that Anthony's sword was still in the villain's chest, he grabbed the helm and, using one foot to steady himself, heaved the deadly weapon out of the carcass. 'Tha'll surely 'a need o' this beauty aginn marrrster!'

In no time at all, the two men had reached the Welcome Inn. They sat in front of a blazing fire that was being tended to by an attractive, buxom landlady. Dolly Fletcher had taken an immediate fancy to the muscular, young stranger and Anthony did not protest when she had insisted on cleaning and dressing his wound. Sipping warm broth and tucking into a generous board of bread, cheese and a thick slice of meat pie, he was careful not to give out any personal information. He held the hostess' interest by telling her that they had come from Plymouth. Anthony was all too aware of the danger of look-outs in taverns. For a decent tip, they would tell local outlaws which travellers were on long-distance journeys, poorly armed or carrying valuables. Despite the notoriety of gangs of thieves who made their living preying on vulnerable travellers, he was often surprised how many people were still naïve never dreaming it could happen to them. Many visitors would vanish without trace after leaving an inn with a belly full of ale. Ironically, it was local crime and folklore that allowed the small community of Ivybridge to thrive as inn employees were kept busy by the steady stream of passers-by. Stories of werewolves and vagabonds preying on people who travelled through the territory provided locals with gruesome tales to frighten visitors into staying the night, parting with more money than they had originally planned.

The Welcome Inn was a popular coaching inn on the Exeter to Plymouth road. Ivybridge was a staging post on the well-travelled London route, as its bridge was the only way to cross the River Erme. The bridge that spanned the river was only wide enough for pack-horses and riders. Regular traffic kept the majority of villagers in work, which meant that most were friendly, pleasant folk who loved to exchange gossip with strangers. Anthony and Creppin were no exception and word soon circulated that Dolly was hosting first-hand witnesses of the most talked about spectacle that year; the execution of Captain Culley. Nearly all the villagers had taken advantage of the most lucrative trade opportunity in a long time and stayed to attend to the hundreds who had stopped on their way to Plymouth to watch the infamous execution. As only a few amongst them had attended, many were keen to hear every last gory detail, as the crowds journeyed home.

The two new-comers settled in comfortably, ready for a long night in front of a well-tended roaring fire. They readily welcomed free mead and food courtesy of the landlady. Dolly was extremely grateful to Anthony for entertaining a full house. His elaborate and descriptive account of the pyrate queen's dramatic death kept punters morbidly fascinated, whilst musicians played lively folk music during breaks. Creppin sat in the sawdust at his chosen master's feet, amongst dogs and children, snarling at anyone who would dare make a noise whilst Anthony was in full flow. Pitchers were refilled well into the early hours. The atmosphere grew more intense as each tale of Captain Culley's daring life of robbery and rebellion on the high seas became more gripping and dangerous. By the end of Anthony's heroic account of the life and death of the feisty female pyrate, the audience were in awe. Even the local healer, old Annie, had offered her skills free of charge. She stitched part of the storyteller's wound whilst the local blacksmith fetched a heated iron rod to cauterise the deepest gash.

An abundance of fine mead and spiced rhum numbed Anthony's senses and his pain had dulled. The lamps had gradually been extinguished as the exhausted landlady bolted the heavy studded oak doors behind the last customer. He had hung on long enough to force her to lose her temper and prod his nether regions with her broom. 'Be gone with thee, Marster Trumpston!' Dolly yelled. 'Tha've an 'ome ter go to so dunna be pesterin' moy guest nay more, tha' hark?' Still grumbling, she pulled out a handful of dried bacon-strips from a barrel and placed them under the fire hearth. Guests who had paid for lodging liked to 'chew the fat' when they got up. 'Ne'er in moy days 'ave oy witnessed a man able ter prattle as much as Tom Trumpston! Tha'd think e'd gi' 'is mouth a rest on occasion!' Eyeing her young lodger from head to toe, Dolly winked and raised her eyebrows before she hitched up her heavy skirts and walked up the stairs.

Anthony felt his cock begin to harden as he imagined Dolly's soft, plump, naked body lying in wait on a bed upstairs. A sudden foul stench hit him and instantly ruined the thought. 'Feck, Creppin!' he slurred in annoyance at the proximity of his servant's face. 'Tha breath stinks like a rottin' corpse! Be gone and find tha'sen' some salt n' a birch twig ter clean what teeth tha has left.' With a snarl, Creppin snatched a lantern and scuffled off into the darkness. He found a room where ropes had been secured for punters who were too drunk to find their way home. Lines of bodies slumped over tightened rope that held them in place under their armpits. Squashed together in three rows they filled the small room. Without cleaning his rotten teeth, Creppin took his short gutting knife and prodded an unconscious woman in the ribs to rouse her. He shoved his heavy bulk against her to make room on the line, throwing his long arms over the small section of rope that he had claimed. As his newfound neighbour was in such an inebriated state that she fell straight back to sleep, Creppin decided to take advantage of her. He reached a gnarled but dextrous hand over, slipping it beneath her shift. Drool gathered on trembling lips as he manoeuvred his free hand down between his legs to satisfy himself. He was determined to make the most of this unmissable opportunity. Sliding his thick, calloused hand between the woman's sweaty thighs he quivered uncontrollably as he pawed at the mound of thick hair. He thrust a filthy finger inside her slack, sticky wetness. If the unfortunate wench had known who was fondling and poking her cunnie as he masturbated vigorously, her blood would have curdled within her veins without a doubt!

Anthony's face contorted when he felt a pulsating squeeze around his hard shaft. Letting out a loud groan, he exploded inside the satisfied woman beneath him. Creppin was not the only one to strike it lucky that night at the 'Welcome Inn'!

CHAPTER 4

The Burden Shared

The journey to Teignmouth was not as bad as Anthony had expected. Although his companion struggled a little more at night, he proved to be quite fit and energetic. Despite his lumbering gait, the hunchback matched the smith's pace and became a reliable companion. The more time Anthony spent in the eccentric character's company, the fonder he became of him. Wherever the pair went, they were welcomed and accommodated, their performance entertaining many as they became more enthusiastic in telling their popular, gruesome tale. Creppin soon became an outstanding jester and definitely earned his keep, although he insisted on keeping his 'clothesies' despite Anthony's frequent offers to buy him new garments. Since their paths had crossed due to bizarre circumstance, Anthony and Creppin had built a strong rapport as they became accustomed to an extreme change of lifestyle. Neither man had ever ventured far from his birthplace yet both had adapted well to life on the move. Anthony became more at ease with the whole adventure and when he finally saw Mary Maggy's, the orphanage that Sushana Culley had founded as a young woman, he felt an overwhelming feeling of relief and true purpose.

The mismatched travellers stood before the simple gated entrance to Sushana Culley's estate. Anthony admired the craftsmanship of the well-made iron gates. As he pulled up the heavy latch, a wave of anxiety washed over him. He was about to enter the place where his deceased idol had been raised. It dawned on him that he was actually going to meet people who had known the infamous pyrate queen intimately, those who had loved the woman that had become a world-renowned legend. A sense of humility hit him and he stood in silence for a few minutes. Awkward eager shuffling interrupted Anthony as Creppin stood slack-jawed awaiting his master's next move. An excited whimper brought a smile to the blacksmith's face. For some unknown reason, the fates had chosen them to embark together on this gallant mission in respect of a brave woman. As usual, Anthony's sidekick interrupted his thoughts. 'Prrrithee tell me marrrrster, does tha' have need o' Crrreppin o'er yonder orrr…' Before he could finish his sentence, Anthony took him by the elbow and led him through the gates. 'Come wi' me. We daresen't lose any more time, matey!' It seemed that the fleeting feeling of apprehension had been mutual. Since it was he who was responsible for the hunchback's involvement in this predicament, the blacksmith took charge and led Creppin across the field. 'Whyforrr artst we in this palace, marrrster? Crrreppin 'ainst used ter such 'scrrrumptulous' places an' ainst drrressed prrroper t'enter neither.' Skipping alongside Anthony nervously, keeping his head low, he stumbled on a rock and fell clumsily. Having second thoughts about the ugly man's presence at the orphanage, Anthony ordered him to go back and wait by the gate. He continued on alone.

After hearing many tales of the lucrative smuggling trade that went on over Culley land he was not surprised to see such an impressive building in the distance. The first set of stables Anthony passed in the enormous field housed eight immaculate stallions. Well-used to working with horses, his benign nature immediately put the animals at ease. Two of the horses were older than the others and he could not help imagining that Shana might have ridden them as a young woman. Patting the nearest on his velvety muzzle, he whispered, 'Let's pray the younguns'll nay be afeared o' Creppin, eh lad!' Nuzzling his large head against Anthony's thick woollen doublet, the horse snorted and blew out of his nostrils, nudging the newcomer playfully. When the other horses began to whinny for attention it was clearly time to leave. The walk across the field took Anthony past a derelict building that showed signs of once being a monastery. Its grey stone walls had been destroyed during King Henry VIII's reign. Arched Gothic window frames still stood strong amidst overgrown thickets of hawthorn and bramble. Stopping to grab a few plump, ripe blackberries, the blacksmith noticed how quiet and peaceful it was. The therapeutic sound of the River Teign and occasional birdsong added to the tranquillity. A delightful mosaic of sloping pastureland, divided by ancient hedgerows provided the most exquisite view. Anthony reached the entrance to Mary Maggy's. He pulled the rope that rang a bell inside the building. A few minutes passed. Hearing the sound of light footsteps he was pleasantly surprised when a pretty young woman opened the door. Removing his hat, Anthony introduced himself, 'Gi'ye good day, Miss. Pri'thee, can tha' allow me ter make tha' 'quaintance. My name is Anthony Brown. I come on a merciful errand on b'half o' the late Cap'n Sushana Culley.' The woman's face paled. Grabbing the visitor by the arm, she hastily ushered him inside. 'Word of Shana? By God 'a mercy!' The young woman crossed herself and stood still, looking into Anthony's eyes. 'Oh! Forgi' me fer lack o' manners. I'm Shana. Me Ma' named me after the cap'n. 'Tis a pleasure ter make tha 'quaintance. Come, meet the others.'

Anthony hardly had time to take in the surroundings. The woman rushed him through a substantial courtyard that had been built around a small, tidy stable block. He noticed that the place was well maintained and each time they came across any staff or children they were greeted with a polite curtsy or bow. 'We 'urd 'bout Shana's execution… 'twas a dreadful shock t'us all.' The woman was clearly fighting back tears. 'We were all so fond of our founder n' all'. Shana's words were hurried. She seemed breathless at times but Anthony was smitten by her youthful charm and homely good looks. He listened intently, taking in every word uttered by this woman who had once known Captain Culley. 'Father McGillacuddy's nay long sung Mass for her precious soul, so tha picked tha timin' well… what did tha say's tha name sir? Pri'thee, forgive me poor mem'ry at this woeful time.'

They reached a narrow, nail-studded oak door which looked heavy as Shana had to push it fully open with her shoulder. As she struggled, she bent forward, her light linen shift dropping slightly to reveal more of her pert breast. Anthony felt aroused and did not notice the elaborate chair immediately inside the wood-panelled room that they had entered. A muffled 'Hmmmumm' alerted him just in time. He managed to avoid sitting unceremoniously on the woman seated in the armchair by nimbly performing an impressive last-minute sidestep. He arched his back, regained his balance and found himself facing a large table. Children giggled and a deep, booming male voice was heard, 'Simmer doyn moy wee darlin's. 'Tisnay' der royt manner ter welcome a new guest, d'yers nat tink?' The Irish priest's delightful sing-song lilt put Anthony at instant ease. Introducing himself with a huge, red-faced smile, the pleasant old character heaved himself up to shake hands. 'Moy neeyum is Farder McGilacuddy. Noy what can we do fer yers, moy dear feller me laaad?'

The room fell deathly silent. Anthony stood with his mouth agape and was speechless in the company of the Catholic priest. He was dressed in a traditional cassock and hat and wore a large obtrusive crucifix. The wooden floor had been strewn with fresh rushes, flowers and fragrant herbs. The combination of scents smelled divine. Working alongside adults, the children resumed their craft making. Some whittled, some carved intricate designs whilst others strung ornate wooden beads together to make Rosaries. The place was a hive of industry, like nothing Anthony had ever seen. The pyrate queen's name-sake could contain herself no longer, ''E's brought word of our Shana, Father. Let's all take a break an' 'ark at what 'e 'as ter say.'

The pupils were immediately dismissed and went outside to play, leaving the adults alone to discuss the important matter in private. Remembering that Creppin was still waiting for him out in the field, Anthony panicked and babbled on incoherently about his companion who might scare the children. A young woman poured a generous cup of mead. She gestured to Anthony to take a seat next to an older man, who smiled considerately at their unexpected guest. Robert introduced himself and then stood to acquaint everyone else in the room. When he had finished he went over to join his wife, Flo, who was the woman Anthony had almost sat on when he had first entered the room. Now it made perfect sense! The chair that Flo was sitting in had wheels on its legs. Her husband moved her next to Fr. McGillacuddy so she could be included in the impending meeting. As conversation began to flow, Anthony learned that Robert and Flo's only daughter, Louisa, was the young woman who had poured the mead and Shana was their orphaned niece. Shana's mother, Abi, had been Flo's twin. Abi had become a pyrate soon after her husband had died. Shana spoke highly of her mother who had led a short but adventurous life abroad with Captain Culley. A heavy set, stocky man with tanned skin and a nervous disposition leant over the table to shake hands with Anthony. He quietly introduced himself as Josh, the stable hand. 'Gi' it away, son!' Robert piped up, 'Thou art more than a stable 'and 'round 'ere!' Everyone nodded and spoke in agreement as the shy man blushed modestly, averting his gaze to the table top. Josh's humble nature boosted Anthony's confidence so he began to explain the reason for his untimely visit. 'Now e'ryone knows 'oo's oo an' the like, I 'ave urgent need o' tha help in important matters concernin' the late Captain Sushana Culley.' Anthony's audience was captivated, hanging onto his every word. Out of respect for her close friends, he began to recount an accurate but less disturbing report of Shana's execution than the one he had told his previous listeners. By the end of his story, not a sound could be heard. Anthony could see clearly how his traumatic testimony had distressed these kind people. Fr. McGillacuddy was the first to speak after a few minutes of sorrowful reflection. His words could not have come sooner for the bearer of such depressing news. It was devastating enough that Shana's loved ones had been denied the chance of giving her a proper wake and burial without the added shock of being told about her severed head.

It was clear that the priest and Shana took the news hardest, by the angered expression on their faces. Despite Anthony's intention of goodwill, his innocent actions had unsettled these strangers. In their eyes, a Protestant churchyard was not the place for any Catholic to be laid to rest. Just as he was beginning to wonder whether he had made the wrong choice by coming to Shana's hometown, the door burst open. A heap of writhing, energetic children piled in. As Robert and Josh prized each child away from the main mass, Anthony was amazed to see that the source of all their excitement was none other than Creppin! Grinning from ear to ear, or as near as possible considering his lop-sided facial features, the weird character stood with chin jutting forward, smiling hideously at the party of adults. Anthony groaned and mouthed a silent prayer of thanks for having such a loveable rogue on his side… who would ever have believed that the pair would have become friends?!

Although Creppin was totally oblivious to the fact, his timing had been impeccable! Anthony was beginning to love him for that uncanny trait alone. A small, sickly-looking boy with a crutch stepped forward and took hold of the hunchback's large hand. 'May I intwo-j-j-j-juice', the boy stuttered. A snigger from the other orphans made him step back, blushing. 'C'mon children, let Charlie speak', Louisa urged encouragingly. The boy continued, '…t-ter-ter-tis Master C-cer-wer-weppin 'oos come a v-ver-ver-visitin' us.' Creppin pulled off his hat and began wringing it in his hands nervously. 'Pardy m'intrrrrupshun' gentlyfolks', he whimpered. Another child piped up, 'Can we sow our new fwiend awound Marewee Maggie's peweeeease, father?' Nodding his permission, the children thanked the priest before grabbing their new friend and leading him out of the room.

Without a mention of the lingering stench that Creppin had left behind, Louisa and Shana immediately set to work de-odourising the room by throwing fresh herbs and dried lavender onto the floor. Embarrassed by his companion's lack of hygiene, Anthony asked the young women if they could try to persuade Creppin to take a much-needed bath and consider the option of fresh, new clothes. Without a single derogatory remark about his dreadful unkempt state, the two smiled and reassured their guest that his friend would leave the orphanage a changed man.

By the end of the lengthy meeting, Anthony felt confident that he had made the right choice to seek help from these good people. Robert and Fr. McGillacuddy advised him to go directly to Grace O'Malley. They told him that it was important for her to hear the news. Word had been spread on the grapevine that she had been set free following Shana's death. Without a doubt, the Irish pyrate queen would want to help Anthony take the heirloom to its rightful owner. Crossing himself before he announced that he was going to offer up abundant prayers over the next few months, Fr. McGillacuddy silently hoped that Grace would gain revenge on the witch Ann Boleyn's Protestant daughter.

By nightfall the two strangers had been shown all around Mary Maggy's orphanage and had met everyone who lived there. Creppin had become fascinated by a beautiful African woman called Princess. Shana Culley had rescued the dark-skinned beauty along with her sister, Kia, from a slave ship. Kia had managed to escape with her baby, Taru, and an angry looking young man called Gift. By some miracle, Princess persuaded her new admirer to bathe. Creppin even allowed Josh and one of the older orphan boys to help with a well-needed grooming session. Apparently, it took the stable hand's best set of nippers, a hoof pick and a rasp to clip and file down toenails as strong and thick as bone. And that was after a full hour of soaking in a tub of steaming hot water. It was after midnight when Princess re-emerged with the hunchback shuffling timidly behind her. Everyone found it difficult to supress their laughter as he constantly tugged at the clean woollen tunic and leggings that he had been given to wear. He kept scratching frantically at his freshly scrubbed, new skin. Like an inquisitive animal, Creppin sniffed at the cloth and then his own hands and fingers. He appeared to be puzzled as he was unable to recognise his own familiar stink. Reluctant to leave Princess' side, the hunchback fetched her a chair and sat at her feet. When she had been grooming him, he had noticed that two of the African woman's fingers were missing on her left hand. This had concerned the hunchback greatly but he had been too shy to ask how she had lost them. He kept looking up at her and smiling devotedly. 'Thankin' thee kindly m' lady. Crrreppin sssmells as frrresh as newly borned lambykinsies!' he remarked proudly. Anthony knew that it would not be very long before the grime collected and foul smells returned. Thankful for small mercies, he wondered how the peculiar fellow would fare at sea. Then he noticed that the cripple was wearing a pair of sturdy leather boots. With a weary sigh of relief the tired man felt pleased that his odd companion should at least be able to get around a lot more comfortably from then onwards. All that had to be done now was to prise Creppin away from his new idol, Princess. There was much to learn about Captain Culley and Anthony was eager to absorb every little detail about this remarkable woman.

CHAPTER 5

A Mere Taste of Queen Bess's Wrath

Elizabeth was beside herself with fury. She had been in a foul mood since receiving word of the idiot Hickford's awful botch-up of an execution. 'Nooooooooo!' she yelled aloud clenching her delicate hands into fists. Well-manicured nails painfully pierced the soft, pale skin of her palms. The Queen had not managed to sleep a wink in four nights! Visions of her greatest rival, the popular pyrate queen, making a laughing stock of the High Executioner constantly plagued her thoughts. Nothing could take her mind off this recent disaster, even riding her prize stallion, 'Red', who she had fondly named after her father.

As her father had done when her own mother, Queen Anne Boleyn, was executed Elizabeth had ensured that she would be away from court on the date of the well-known pyrate's hanging. Although she had loathed the insolent, thieving bitch she also respected her for daring to fight for a cause that she had believed in so strongly. Elizabeth was not pleased that the pyrate queen had gained immense admiration and infamy amongst ordinary English folk. O'Malley's capture had done the trick and lured her most prized prey as planned but the Irish noblewoman had been released soon after Sushana's death. Elizabeth knew full well that she would soon be out for revenge. Captain Culley's hanging would have been a welcome relief had it gone smoothly. Elizabeth grew very bitter whilst Sushana Culley lived and now that bitterness would linger long after her death. All because of a fool whom she had trusted with an execution that should never have gone wrong; the result should have been a triumph not a farce! Ridicule was not something that the Tudors took to kindly.

The Queen had vowed not to return to London until the severed head of the rebellious pyrate had been rammed firmly onto a spike. By now, it should be displayed on London Bridge for all to see, providing choice pickings for ravens and crows but oh no! The latest news was that the bloody thing had gone missing! 'Curse the incapable buffoon…!' Elizabeth roared out an unfinished sentence that ended with a blood-curdling scream. Her favourite pets, two tiny pocket beagles whined nervously and snuggled closer together on their silk cushion. Her face glowed scarlet in her frantic state despite heavy white make-up that her lady-in-waiting had meticulously applied that morning. Small pox had left the Queen's face badly scarred with deep pock marks. These could only be disguised by a heavy application of ceruse; a thick white paste that her Royal Apothecary mixed, from scratch, every morning. The camouflage make-up consisted of the popular base ingredients white lead and vinegar with a few extra secret additions. Having insisted on being left alone for the day Elizabeth had been out riding in the grounds of her own Palace of Havering, all morning. There were still extensive renovations being carried out on the medieval building. Extra rooms had been added and were taking longer to finish than initially expected. On return from her ride, Elizabeth had refused lunch as she had lost her appetite. She found it impossible to focus on anything since she was constantly plagued by vivid visions of 'that wretched, filching cur's missing head!'

Back in London, hushed whispers spread word around the palace of the Queen's unquenchable fury on hearing news of the botched hanging. The disappearance of the throne's most notorious antagonist's head had become a standing joke in court. The story spread quickly across the country, providing welcome entertainment in taverns, crossroads and market squares. Many a ribald ballad writer earned a pretty penny at Elizabeth's expense. Servants and courtiers dreaded her return. Ever wary of their notoriously temperamental monarch, they pitied the party who had been chosen to accompany her on the Royal Progress. Now it would all be down to Robert Dudley or Francis Drake; the only people who had ever been able to tame her anger. Francis was good at feeding the monarch's renowned ego as he had often done before when she had faced ordeals during her reign. Robert Dudley was the Queen's long-time lover who had been summoned immediately. Thankfully, his presence was imminent. Whenever possible, he would be forewarned about the situation at hand and the source of the hot-headed woman's rage. He could then plan a suitable way to console her. His canny methods involved a lot of flattery and exquisite gifts but the most effective therapy of all was sexual gratification! More often than not, all of these methods were required to satisfy the needy, greedy sovereign. Elizabeth was definitely her father's daughter, as everyone who had known him well would agree. Anyone in court who displeased her would be banished immediately and she was never afraid to sentence those close to her to death.

Suddenly tearing the beautifully beaded lace collar from her dress, the furious woman paced up and down her finely decorated apartment like a caged animal. Eventually she sat at her writing desk, snatched a quill and parchment and began to write a warrant for Hickford's arrest. She was determined to order the dungeon master to inflict the most degrading and brutal torture upon the idiot who had managed to diminish her popularity amongst many of her subjects. She would have him branded on the forehead so he would be forced to beg on the streets and never be able to work again.

Elizabeth craved the love and respect of her people. So much so that she had sacrificed her own happiness to please her citizens. For years she had been in love with her childhood friend, Robert Dudley, who she fondly called her 'sweet Robin'. She had granted him the title Earl of Leicester, a position which enabled him to spend more time with her at court without suspicion. She had chosen to live a single life and encouraged her nickname, Virgin Queen. Back in 1560, Robert's sickly wife, Amy, had died when she broke her neck falling down a short flight of stairs at Cumnor Hall in Berkshire. Vicious rumours began to circulate around court. It was a trying time for the Queen and her lover who had been enjoying a secret affair for years. Although Robert was with the Queen at Windsor Castle when the accident happened, many had their suspicions about his wife's sudden death which conveniently left him free to marry. Without a doubt, Elizabeth would have married him in an instant, had public opinion not been so against the match. She had vowed to him that she would marry no other man. Ever since the unfortunate event, that had not actually had anything to do with Robert or Elizabeth, they had no other choice but continue their clandestine love affair. The whole situation was ironic because Robert's deceased wife had breast cancer. According to her physician, she would have been dead within months had the unfortunate accident not occurred. Over the years, Robert became the most hated man of his time and for him to become Prince Consort would certainly have spurred rebellion against the Queen. This was something that she was never prepared to chance.

Elizabeth's few confidants knew how much stress her affair with Dudley had caused her. The latest reports of his overzealous attention to the recently widowed Lady Essex, Lettice Knollys, only added to her concerns. There were rumours of Robert's involvement in the Earl of Essex's death especially since they had been renowned enemies. Suspicions of foul play were rife even though the Earl had died of dysentery in Ireland. It was common knowledge around his estate that Robert visited the Earl's wife, Lettice, regularly whilst her husband was away. The latest gossip was that they had been enjoying an illicit affair for many years. The fact that two of Lettice's sons' bore an uncanny resemblance to the Earl of Leicester fuelled malicious allegations of adultery. As her husband had been overseas at both times of conception, everyone knew that he could not possibly have fathered either child.

Inwardly Elizabeth cursed herself for becoming less guarded. Her numerous public outbursts only confirmed that she had inherited her father's uncontrollable jealousy. What grieved her most was that Lettice had been her close friend since childhood and one of the few women she thought she could trust, especially in matters of the heart! Letty and Bess, as they affectionately called each other, had always been very similar in appearance. Over the years, they had felt a mutual sisterly bond. The Queen seethed with anger at the thought that she had shared such intimate details of Robert's firm, fit body and virile sexual appetite with the wanton whore. An all too familiar throbbing pain in her left temple suddenly made her wince. She closed her eyes tightly and willed it to stop. Elizabeth had suffered from excruciating headaches since her teenage years; yet another unwelcome inheritance from her father! The searing ache behind her eyes made her feel so nauseous that she threw herself onto her bed, moaning and pulling at her thin, greying hair. She was finding it so much harder to cope with heartache as she grew older. Her lover had made things so damnably difficult, it was almost becoming unbearable… but she could not let him go. Her love was too deep. 'How dare she! How dare THEY! Arrogant, devious fools!' Elizabeth hissed between gritted teeth, her jaw aching from muscles that had not relaxed for days.

Those who spent any time with the Queen could recognise discontent or rage merely by looking into her eyes… if they were brave enough to do so. Cruel brown eyes were exaggerated against alabaster white skin which gave her the same fearsomely stern look of her father. Like him, Elizabeth was a romantic, as passionate as she was ferocious. Inspired to write, she took up parchment and quill. She began to pen a poem. Her immaculate steady handwriting showing no sign of her rage but the words from her tormented heart were plain:

I grieve and dare not show my discontent;
I love and yet am forced to seem to hate;
I do, yet dare not say I ever meant…

An ink splash spoiled the word 'meant' which brought on another frenzied fit of yelling and cursing. Tearing the thick parchment in two, Elizabeth grabbed a fresh piece and tried to steady her hand before she began to write again. Servants continued with daily chores needed to keep the Queen's home-from-home running flawlessly. They occasionally shot each other nervous glances, not daring to make too much noise should they irk their mistress more. No-one wanted to give the Queen reason to blame them for her foul mood. They were all well-used to her bursting from her private chambers without warning and taking it out on the nearest scape-goat. Each room in her living quarters had been meticulously prepared for the royal visit and laid out exactly like the royal apartments in her numerous homes. All hangings, furnishings, ornaments and equipment had been brought from the Royal Household by a preceding party of ushers whose job was to ensure that the Queen's suite was exactly as it was everywhere she stayed.

Every few months, Elizabeth would move homes so that each of her fourteen palaces could be aired and repaired in turn. She would also visit numerous stately homes owned by noblemen and gentry. The Royal East Anglia summer progress was large to say the least. It consisted of courtiers, Chamber Officers, Privy Councillors, the Yeomen of the Guard and Gentlemen Pensioners, not to mention all the servants of each. It had taken months of planning and entourages travelled ahead of the royal party to prepare everything for the Queen's arrival. As always, Elizabeth had been shrewd with her plans to visit some of her wealthier subjects' homes at their expense. One of her reasons for choosing to visit Norfolk and Suffolk was to relieve at least a few of the many wealthy and obstinate Catholic families of some of their savings. It always cost those chosen to accommodate and entertain the Royal Progress a small fortune. 'Good Queen Bess', as many fondly called their monarch, would be sure to make the most of their hospitality by encouraging each family to out-do the previous hosts.

A scroll had arrived the day before and Elizabeth had been thrilled to see Robert's golden wax seal. He had been taking the waters at Buxton Spa in the hope that it would help ease the pain in one of his legs. Withdrawing to her bedroom where she could read without being interrupted, the lovelorn woman traced her index finger across two neat ink circles with small marks above each. She could not help herself and allowed a secret smile. She had nicknamed her lover 'two eyes' and their secret symbol always amused her, despite her current mood:

My precious Bess, my heart!

I hope now ere long to lay next to thee to enjoy that blessedly beautiful sight which I have been so long kept from. A few of these days seem many years and I am determined to hie me home and rejoin my Queene, my truest love once again.

Elizabeth decided to lengthen her stay at Havering by a few days and have word sent to Audley End House that her party would be later than expected. To have been in a mood of total amorous bliss one day, then absolute despair the next would have shaken even the hardest of hearts. The emotional influence that Robert had over his Bess was powerful enough to prompt her to start a war! This was one of the many reasons why few were in favour of any relationship between the two head-strong characters. Worried, angry and upset, the Queen folded the expensive French paper and placed it in a box where she kept all of her private letters from Robert. A foreboding shudder wracked her body and tears welled in her deep amber brown eyes. There was one thing of which she was certain… she would rather perish than lose her truest love.

CHAPTER 6

Voyage to Meet the Sea Queen of Connaught

Anthony had always thought himself lucky to be skilled in such a lucrative trade as blacksmithing but secretly, he had always fancied a more exciting life at sea. He had paid to be taken to Connaught where he hoped to meet with Grace O'Malley and was relieved to find that neither he nor Creppin suffered with sea sickness. According to many a hardened sailor, there was no better way to test the strength of the stomach than a voyage from England to the treacherously unpredictable Irish coast. As he stood on the deck of the merchant ship, Anthony now understood exactly what they had meant. Seas were notoriously savage when gale force winds came rushing down the narrow channel between England and Ireland. The cool summer's day when the new band of adventurers set sail aboard a merchant vessel had been no exception.

To Anthony's pleasant surprise, he had managed to gain four new recruits following his visit to Mary Maggy's. They had managed to convince the captain to take extra passengers as none of them were sailors. Josh, Shana, Gift and a burly, tough sixteen year old orphan called Saul, had all been keen to join forces with Patrick Culley. There was nothing they wanted more than to help him gain vengeance over the Protestant Queen responsible for his mother's death.

A dying sun hovered above the horizon as the experienced crew cast anchor in O'Malley territorial waters. Tired sailors took advantage of the short break before they continued on their way to the port of Galway. There they would sell on their cargo. Spirits were high as the crew settled down to eat a simple meal of hard biscuits and salted meat, washed down with plenty of ale. Anthony stood on deck awaiting the arrival of the Sea Queen of Connaught, Gráine Ní Mháille or Grace O'Malley as she was called by the English. Her shores offered a dramatic view of a landscape so hauntingly barren yet indescribably beautiful. It was a feeling of absolute enchantment that affected Anthony most as he gazed out over choppy grey waters. Immediately captivated by this mystical isle, he felt an inexplicably strong sense of belonging.

It did not take long to spot the three galleys that had been lying in wait just out of sight, tucked behind the soaring cliffs of Clare Island. The light vessels were approaching at an impressive speed and Anthony's pulse quickened in eager anticipation. O'Malley's light, speedy craft were renowned for pouncing on slower merchant vessels bound for Galway, close to Grace's territory. If any dared refuse to pay protection money, they would be boarded and plundered. Long used to paying the levy that Grace demanded to ensure safe passage through her waters, the crew had already set aside five large barrels of sugar as payment. A rumble of thunder accompanied heavy spots of cool rain. The creaking vessel rocked in steady rhythm on agitated waves. Even at this early stage of the storm, Anthony could see how mercilessly the Celtic Sea would treat those not courageous or skilled enough to navigate its savagely volatile waters. Dangerous reefs surrounding the jagged cliffs of Clare Island meant that heavy merchant ships could easily run aground. As angry waves beat against the grey rock face, Anthony squinted trying to gain a clearer sight of the blurred scene in front of him.

A tall, broad-set warrior woman stood proudly astride her ship. She had given the other vessel a wide berth to avoid collision as they swung with the wind. Shouting obscenities as she urged the men to hurry before the storm worsened, the Irish noblewoman called out to the cargo ship's captain, 'Garrrd awmoity! Whatchyers ahll awaitin' aaarn? Haul us a loin an' we'll take yer load off yers!' Some friendly banter ensued between the two captains whilst their crew transferred barrels on a rope and pulley. During the exchange, Grace agreed to take Anthony and his group back to her castle. Soon they were below deck on the Irish craft as the disciplined crew expertly manoeuvred her into the mouth of a small inlet opening onto Clew Bay. Laying anchor, crew and passengers disembarked. Soaked to the skin, everyone was relieved to see the grey stone structure looming before them.

Rockfleet Castle was Grace's favourite of five fortified homes. The others; Belclare, Cathair-na-Mart, Carrowmore and Murrick were situated at intervals along the O'Malley coastline providing an excellent line of defence against invasion. Clare Island was the perfect place for monitoring all ship traffic in and around Clew Bay and further along the western coast. Secret passages led from Grace's castles to the mainland where her men would light beacon fires to alert her fleet. Over two hundred pyrates were now under her leadership.

Much smaller than Anthony had expected, Rockfleet was nothing like the impressively majestic Norman castles back in England. He was amazed to see the relatively small-scale, medieval style construction which was no more than a single defensive tower. Despite its meagre proportions, the foreboding square stone structure before him had so far proved impenetrable, defying both man and the elements. The cold wind and stinging rain had numbed his skin. His eyes were dry and sore. Fascinated by the simplicity of Rockfleet's design, he watched as the day's plunder was hauled up into the castle and passed through a small arched doorway high up on the east wall. Feeling a heavy pat on his shoulder Anthony turned to see Grace O'Malley standing next to him. Their eyes were almost level; hers a penetrating green, afire with vitality. The woman's energy was contagious. With a sudden roar of deep laughter, Grace grabbed her visitor by the arm and led him through the small door into Rockfleet Castle.

Well-used to living amongst men, Grace peeled off her wet woollen trews and changed into a dry chemise and simple green kirtle. Her guests were offered clean, dry clothes and soon felt their benefit. The dim torchlight flickered and the wind howled outside. Creppin stood trembling in his wet new clobber that he was reluctant to change. He muttered to himself, 'Crrreppin shall nay de-clothe. Prrrincesssss's finerrry shall stay on me bones, so be it, sez I!' The pyrate queen's distinctly noble features made her stand out from the crowd. Despite weather-beaten skin, her complexion appeared healthy. A deep tan and newly grown dark hair made her pretty green eyes look so bright. A born leader, Grace oozed confidence and had the air of royalty. Anthony could see how this remarkable warrior woman had gained her reputation as a feisty hell-raiser. He felt instantly at ease in her presence and the feeling was mutual. Grace had sensed Anthony's loyalty as soon as they met and knew that he was a compassionate man when she observed him with his crippled servant.

Shana looked small and delicate standing next to Grace. Despite her frail, feminine appearance she soon showed her tough side. Noticing one of the men gawking at her whilst she undressed, Shana decided that she was going to have to make a stand early. She was not going to allow anyone to disrespect her. Taking one of the knives that she kept tucked inside a stocking top, she lifted its point to her chin then threw hard and fast. Her aim was perfect and the sharp blade hit its target. The knife pierced the barrel that the voyeur was sitting on, right between his open legs. Shana had managed to catch his leggings with the blade so when the young man jumped up in embarrassment, the sound of tearing cloth made everyone laugh. Grace gave the smaller woman a hard slap on the back, almost knocking her flying. Shana felt good that the pyrate queen had openly shown her a sign of respect. Ever since he had been taken in at Mary Maggy's, Saul had been fond of Shana and he did not like the rude Irish man's attitude. Danny was a cocky lout and, to make matters worse, Shana's sharp rebuff had encouraged him even more. Saul was livid. Something had to be done to deter this halfwit's unwanted attention. Danny took the knife back over to the feisty wench. Showing off, he flexed his well-developed muscles and wiped the blade slowly on his shirt sleeve before returning it to Shana. He finished with a low mock bow. The Irish men all laughed at their friend but Saul's face reddened with anger at Danny's bare-faced cheek. The fool was clearly very popular amongst his peers. As Grace's men chatted away in their foreign tongue Saul found his friends, Gift and Josh, and advised them to stick together. He wanted to make sure that Shana would not be bothered anymore. 'Dunno 'bout thee but I dunna trust this Irish crew s'far as I cud 'url the 'unchback.' Neither man commented but the expression on their faces said enough. Josh took Shana by the arm and told her to stay close. The pretty woman smiled at her new guardians and felt pleased that they cared about her. Nevertheless, she felt confident in her ability to defend herself. She had always taken weaponry training seriously and was keen to put her skills and tactics into practice. Shana had more than one reason for embarking on this very personal mission. Like Abi, her brave and free-spirited mother before her, Shana was a natural born fighter determined to stand for a worthy cause.

Looking around for Creppin, Anthony noticed him cowering against a stack of shields and a pile of fishing nets. The large room was used as an armoury. Highly polished surfaces of different metals gleamed brightly in the torchlight, throwing glistening reflections against dancing shadows on the surrounding walls. Creppin looked pale and frightened. He was still mumbling to himself and threw an occasional nervous glance at the Irish pyrate queen. When Grace invited everyone to join her to eat, Anthony watched the cripple scrabble behind one of the larger shields to hide. He approached Creppin with caution as he had seen the damage he could do with a cudgel when caught unawares. A look of relief spread across the hunchback's ugly face when he noticed his companion. 'Oh pardy, pardy, marrrster!' the hunchback contorted his face into an expression of sheer despair.

He kept his voice low, 'Crrreppin's afeared muchly o' yon pyrrratical giantesssss. Od's pittikins, her grrreen eyes put us in mind of a witch, marrrster! Crrreppin smelllt one rrroasssting, September laaaarssst.' It was hard not to laugh at how pathetic the hunchback had become as he wrung his hands in despair. It took a while for Anthony to convince him that he would be safe in Grace's company. Eventually, Creppin scrambled after him to join the others upstairs.

The glow of a roaring fire made a welcome sight and everyone helped themselves to delicious beef pottage. For the rest of the night, Creppin's mistrustful eyes bolted back and forth between his newfound protector and the pyrate queen. His beady eye twitched nervously and he whimpered whenever she spoke. Grace and her men's hospitality knew no bounds. Once Anthony had explained the reason for his visit, the Irish noblewoman swore an oath that she would do anything she could to help him reach Patrick. She was convinced that he would want to continue his mother's fight against the English sovereign.

The English had been gradually changing Ireland's traditional laws and had outlawed the election of clan chieftains. The O'Malleys had long reigned over Connaught and were determined that things stayed that way. Grace still held a royal position over her lands and swore that no Englishman, or woman, would ever take that away from her. She and Sir Henry Sidney, the Lord Deputy of Ireland by appointment of the English Queen, had spent many hours discussing Ireland's issues with England. Grace was a shrewd politician who could hold her own in such matters. Many a preserved body of a disagreeable Englishman was buried deep in peatbog graves surrounding her castles. The hardened warrior Queen vowed that the bloodshed would not cease until Ireland was ruled by her rightful clans once again.

Over the years, Grace had recruited fighting men, and occasionally women, both from Ireland and Scotland. She would transport the 'Gallóglaigh' or gallowglass mercenaries, a class of elite warriors from the Norse-Gaelic clans of the Scottish Highlands, to and from her lands. During clan wars, Irish chieftains would employ this well-armed, highly trained aristocratic infantry who guaranteed strong resistance under enemy attack. Grace often sailed to Scotland, picked up the mercenaries and brought them back to Ireland for a decent fee. Her crew would plunder Scotland's outlying islands on their way home. Over the years, she saw many a successful battle won by clans whose chieftains had hired the mighty mercenaries. Naturally, she soon followed suit. Grace used her own team of Gallóglaigh to train lower class Irish foot soldiers. She provided them with the best weaponry and armour, far superior to that of the ordinary fighter. A large part of O'Malley's bounty was put towards training her 'Fianna Fail' or 'Soldiers of Destiny'; an army that she and Sushana had formed. Together, they had hoped to lead them someday to defeat Elizabeth, putting an end to her Protestant rule. Shana's war had been against the supremacist's disregard for basic human life in her support of the slave trade, anti-Catholicism and mistreatment of the country's lower classes. Despite her premature death, many of her comrades would ensure that the war would not end. Grace was confident that Patrick would carry on the fight.

After an hour of listening to Anthony explain his story to an attentive host, Creppin needed to take a shit.

He had never defecated in a garderobe before and was keen to give it a try. No-one noticed him creep out of the room and he was soon investigating the rest of the castle. Childlike in manner, he limped down worn, winding stone steps, stopping occasionally to peer through narrow slit windows. With an imaginary bow, he fired invisible arrows down on make-believe attackers. Whistling as he went, the crooked man hopped happily from room to room in search of the privy. Rockfleet was very warm that summer night. There was an earthy, comforting smell of burning peat in the air. Every room had a fireplace which was stoked with fresh turf all year round. Thick stone walls absorbed heat well and radiated it back into the building. A light, blue-grey smoke lingered in the air, permeating leather wall hangings, and adding an unusual aroma to the furniture. It was surprisingly pleasant to inhale and held a moist pungency that seemed to help open the airways, making it easier to breathe. Whatever it was about the ambience within Grace O'Malley's fortified home, Creppin was beginning to like it. Tapping the toes of his new boots on every step as he descended the narrow spiral stairs, the hunchback explored every nook and cranny of the four storey fort. Every now and then, he stood on tiptoes to look up through the gun loops at the clouds racing through the dark skies. As heavy rain pelted down, he could just make out the rectangular shaped timber building under the watery light of the moon. For safety, the kitchens and main banquet hall had been constructed well away from the main structure.

Smirking to himself as he sat contentedly, leggings around ankles, Creppin passed wind loudly as he sat on the wooden bench in the garderobe. Giggling hysterically at the echo of his fart, he soon forgot how unnerved he had felt when he first set foot on Irish soil. Leaping up quickly to avoid getting too cold, he re-tied his leggings just in time. Two of the biggest dogs he had ever seen came bounding towards him along the narrow corridor. 'Yi!' Creppin yelped in shock. Instinctively, he reached for his cudgel. He scarcely had time to swing the cruel weapon that he had used to bludgeon many a mangy mutt to death. The massive beasts were on him, pinning him down with huge paws. Licking his face and head with their soft, wet tongues, the hounds soon covered Creppin with slobber. He was laughing so hard he began to cry. 'Ooo ooo ooo! Pardy, pardy me!' he snuffled as he petted the dogs. Never in his days had the deformed man been fussed over as much as he had been since meeting Anthony. Having spent his whole life being branded an exile, Creppin was not used to being treated so kindly. Lately, he had been experiencing unfamiliar emotions and it was all beginning to overwhelm him. It did not take long for Colm, one of Grace's best sailors, to go and see what was causing all the commotion. He called off the dogs immediately and went to help their quarry. Although Creppin had managed to gain confidence since he had been in Anthony's company, he was still very uncomfortable around strangers. He would rarely communicate with anyone. Before Colm could check whether the crippled Englishman had been harmed by Grace's wolfhounds, Creppin had scrabbled back to his feet. He darted off, eager to continue exploring. The two hounds licked their tall, skinny friend as he petted them. 'Did yers foind anudder mate dare me laddies?' Grace's two favourite dogs, Merlin and Mistlytoes, slumped their great bodies down next to each other to guard the narrow corridor as Colm staggered drunkenly into the garderobe to take a well needed crap.

Most of the men had succumbed to the effects of a belly-full of ale. Many had fallen asleep to the therapeutic sound of constant rainfall, gushing winds and a healthy, crackling fire. A chorus of loud snores reverberated through wooden floorboards and Grace took Anthony and Shana up to her private chambers on the top two floors. Luxurious fur rugs and sturdy, ornate chests spilled over with treasures accumulated from her lucrative trade.

Although Shana had been used to relatively high living at Mary Maggy's, she had never seen so much finery gathered in such a small area. When the late Sushana Culley had become orphaned as a baby, her guardian old Albert, managed her inheritance. Sensibly, he used her late father's and maternal grandfather's accumulated wealth to buy more land on behalf of the child. Over the years, Albert and Shana, (when she became old enough) allowed regular passage of contraband through their land. The path leading from the landing point on the River Teign up to the orphanage became known as 'Culley's Cut'. Smugglers brought desirable wares to be stored and later traded on the black market, thus avoiding the heavy import tax added by the Crown. The orphanage provided plenty of storage space for contraband and Culley's Cut soon became the most successful black market business of the time. Its prosperity had continued until the present day. Business was also still good for Culley's Spiceland (the legitimate company that Shana had left Robert and the others at Mary Maggy's to run). Substantial tax dues from the spice business were paid regularly to the Crown and, consequently, provided a smoke screen for the far more profitable underground trade.

In awe of her surroundings, Shana stared at Grace's glittering treasures. Delicately embroidered tapestries, coffers containing the finest silk and lace dresses, exquisite jewels and elaborate trinkets made her gasp with delight. Nothing could ever have prepared her for this treasure trove. Grace smiled at the young woman's joy and was pleased by her open admiration. 'Moy daaarrrlin', feast yer oys arn some o' der most valuable pieces in d'world.' Mesmerised by the wonderful collection of prize booty, Shana was delighted when Grace allowed her full access to the valuables during her stay. 'Oy hate ter see such foinery put ter waste. As oym farrr too old t' be prancin' aroind in such blazon attoyer, oy invoit yers ter be moy guest m' pretty. Dress as a queen t' yers heart's deloight!' The young woman jumped up and down with excitement, then threw her arms around a surprised Grace who blushed coyly, 'Awww! Away widjers noy!'

Anthony and the kind-hearted noblewoman smiled as they left Shana in her absolute element. Walking through her elaborate bedchamber, Grace noticed her guest eyeing the heavy chain fixed to her bedpost. As she led him through the gate, up a few more stone steps and out onto the ramparts, she explained how she had devised a perfect anti-theft device. When mooring at Rockfleet, Grace would always fasten the other end of the bedpost chain to her favourite ship on the coastline. That way, if anyone dared try to steal the vessel, she would feel her bed move across the stone floor and 'May Gaaad have morcey on d' soul of d' fee-und who dare teev moy praaarperty!' Grace looked down on her well-maintained ships with pride.

As they swayed on choppy, rolling waves in the distance, Grace announced that it was high tide. Anthony noticed flecks of copper in the older woman's hair. She was a natural beauty. He could not help looking at her but she did not seem to mind. A cold gust of wind caught her dark locks, stirring the long, coiled strands as she looked up at the stars. Clouds occasionally shrouded their brilliance but every now and then, a faint comforting glow flickered back into life. Out in the open elements, Grace allowed pent up tears to flow. Despite the quaver, the sound of her deep voice felt soothing to the man who suddenly felt far from home. 'Didst yers know yers the double t'arrr handsome young Paddy?'

A comfortable silence was appreciated between two virtual strangers who differed in so many ways yet both felt a rare and wonderful rapport. Many an artist and poet have struggled to portray the instant, intimate feelings felt between kindred souls. There was no need for Anthony to reply. Deep in his heart, he already knew what Grace was telling him. From the very minute when Sushana Culley had stood before him, with rope around her neck, looking down into his eyes, he had known that there had been some sort of attraction. Male ego and virility had misled the naïve young man into believing that the brief moment of affinity that they shared had been of a romantic nature. A mutual soul attraction, spiritual bonding or whatever the bards and playwrights choose to call it. Yet now it was painstakingly obvious! Shana had noticed Anthony's deep blue eyes and held his gaze, melting his very soul, just minutes before she took the final leap to her death… all because they had reminded her of her son, Patrick's eyes. Despite the revelation, he was well aware of the impact the remarkable woman had already had on his life and, still, he felt inexplicably comfortable with it. A total stranger, mere seconds from committing suicide, had managed to make an incredible impression on a grounded, sensible man who was content with his comfortable life. He had embarked on a potentially dangerous, daring mission. Anthony truly believed that the fates had to have something of great importance in store for him. Closing his eyes, the blacksmith threw back his head and took a deep breath before re-opening them to see the starlit night anew. ''Tis uncanny, moy lad. Ye could be our Paddy, I tell yers nay loy'

The sound of waves lapping at the foot of the castle grew louder as the wind changed. As Grace stood with Anthony on the pinnacle of her fortress, she allowed him to see another side of herself, baring a truly vulnerable soul. Her followers believed that this woman's aura could be felt from miles around and that she would be remembered long after her death as a heroine in a man's world. Grace O'Malley was incredible in so many ways. Yet on that stormy, unsettling night, the simple blacksmith's son saw an aging, world-weary woman. She felt trapped within a seemingly unending cycle of deep mourning. So many people had given their lives for their beloved Eire and she never had time to grieve before another pile of bodies lay lifeless before her. Grace missed some of her friends and comrades in arms dearly but she also envied the peace of their departed souls.

Anthony's heart pounded violently in dreaded rhythm against the walls of his chest. He realised that, very soon, he would experience the danger and brutality of battle first-hand. Aware that she had allowed a complete stranger a glimpse of her over-burdened, exhausted soul,

Grace stepped away from Anthony. What on earth was she thinking? She was old enough to be his mother! She wiped away warm, cleansing tears to feel the icy sting of reality as a tempestuous wind raged, whipping the ends of her hair against sore cheeks. Anthony's mind raced. All of a sudden, he felt very humble and inexperienced in this powerful woman's presence. His head dropped as the Irish noblewoman edged away. He had led such a sheltered life compared to these people. Drawn away from a simple existence, by a force too complex to comprehend, he realised how these hardened pyrates had witnessed the loss of too many lives. Lives wasted in mindless wars; pointless feuds to gain wealth and power. These wars fed an imperial greed so obscene that even churches turned a blind eye to profiting from trading in human life. These times were being hailed as Elizabeth's 'Golden Age'; an era that inspired national pride, yet her nation was surrounded by sea beds made up of human bones; bones still shackled, man to woman; woman to child. Bodies seen as natural wastage, surplus cargo; no point in feeding livestock no longer fit to trade. The atrocious truth hit Anthony as a sudden bolt of lightning forked overhead. It was accompanied by a loud boom of thunder.

Stripped bare of any previous inhibition or concerns, a sudden surge of uncontrollable passion overtook the couple. Throwing themselves together, they tore away each other's clothing, desperate to feed the most basic human need. Energised with a mutual appreciation of simply being alive, two bodies became one. Their sex was rough, bodies thrashing together violently within the squall. Flesh was torn, leaving blood smears as their limbs banged against the wet rock. Grace fucked like she fought, with no mercy or remorse. She was dominant, shamelessly lustful and greedy for more. Grace would not allow Anthony's release until she had been satisfied by her own final climax. Yelling aloud a guttural growl, she came over and over again. As her cunnie gave way to contracting bliss, the Irish pyrate queen's whole body shook with ultimate satisfaction. Piercing green eyes drained Anthony's very soul and he gave in to her wiles... pushing deeper into her... the horny bitch was not going to allow him to cum until she had had her fill! As the warrior woman dug her large, strong fingers into his shoulders, Anthony could bear the pleasure/pain no longer. He would have to force her to stop her tricks before he gave way to fury. Grabbing her roughly by the throat, he began to squeeze hard. Thighs tightened their grip around his waist. He felt her feet push his buttocks forcing his hard cock so deep inside her that he found it difficult to release. Despite danger of losing consciousness, Grace still fought to prolong the frenzied animalistic fuck. Closing his eyes, Anthony imagined being inside Sushana Culley. He released his murderous grip to feel Grace's body respond in a thrashing fit of undisputable ecstasy. Finally, he released his hot lifeseed into her and a mutual sexual craving was spent. Grabbing the clothing that they had shed before the unexpected act, Grace and Anthony ran inside her castle to shelter from the storm.

CHAPTER 7

Afflicted Lovers Reunite

It was a beautiful, sunny day when the Queen and two of her closest friends, Ladies Catherine Carey-Knollys and Anne Russell-Dudley, sat giggling like young girls in her bedchamber. The source of their excitement was news that Robert Dudley was now only a few hours away. He had sent messengers before him with his first reunion gift for his lover; four fine Irish stallions. Elizabeth was delighted when she saw the horses. They were far stronger and faster than any mount she had ever owned. Robert knew her so well. Her passion for horses had no match. They had both been extraordinarily skilful riders since childhood, riding together for hours on end. No-one could ever keep up with them and they were always first to the kill on their regular hunting expeditions. Elizabeth had made Robert Master of the Queen's Horse shortly after her coronation. The role suited him perfectly and enabled them to spend more time together planning her public appearances and organising progresses and personal entertainment. Adventurous and daring in everything they did, they were a match made in heaven. However, their combined destiny always seemed doomed.

'Oh Ma'am! I lay a wager to say that Robert shall surely die when he realises thou know'st of his fancy for Lettice Knollys. Of all the women to choose from. Heaven forbid, the lady hath nerve!' Catherine rolled her eyes at Anne's bluntness. Never one to mince her words,

Anne meant no malice. She was very naïve. The older lady-in-waiting felt ashamed, 'I warned my scatter-brain daughter to discourage his advances. As e'er, she paid no heed. My only hope is that thou shalt forgive me for her appalling behaviour, Ma'am.' A stern expression spread across the aging Queen's semi-painted face. Elizabeth loved Catherine like a surrogate mother. She would never allow Lettice to ruin the close bond that they shared. Shifting position in her seat, Elizabeth reassured her faithful and valued friend that she lay no blame on her head for her daughter's disrespect. Lettice was a grown woman after all.

The Queen had been suffering with face-ache for months. The oil of cloves recommended by her physicians had numbed the pain for a while. Kathryn had rubbed it into her gums every few hours but the pain had soon returned. No-one dared tell Elizabeth that she should have a rotten tooth extracted. Lately, she had been feeling gloomy about her age and such news would have made her feel even worse. Thankfully, her make-up artist was used to the Queen's unpredictable moods. She paused patiently to gauge her temperament before continuing to apply more white paste. Elizabeth sipped her daily tonic and seemed quite calm as she gave a servant girl a menu of her choice of food for the day. She was insistent that the cooks were given strict, detailed instruction on how to prepare and present the food for that evening's banquet. A young, newly-trained costumer swallowed nervously as she tightened Elizabeth's corset. Unlike the beautician, she had not long been in attendance to the Queen. Pulling the cord as hard as possible, she breathed a sigh of relief as she managed to squeeze Elizabeth's small frame into a perfectly stiff posture. The Queen did not flinch and her beautician winked reassuringly at her colleague who reached for the next item of clothing to be fitted. Her mistress nodded her approval and the girl attached the richly embroidered sleeves with a little more confidence.

Anne let out a playful titter. Her big, brown eyes sparkled with mischief at the idea of her friend having sex in that very room! Blushing at the mere thought of another man's naked body, she wondered whether Robert was as good a lover as his brother, Ambrose. A shiver of pleasure spread through her body, making every nerve-end tingle. It felt as though her skin was being gently blown by the warmest sea breeze. She desired nothing more than to be satisfied by her husband again. Her moist cunnie twitched involuntarily at the mere thought of it. Catherine couldn't help but tease Anne, 'I wonder who our sweet 'Amys' is calling to mind... or quiver?' Suddenly realising that her friends had been watching her fantasise, Anne put her hand to her face in shame. She blushed deeply before she burst out laughing. 'Amys' was her husband's pet name for his pretty, young wife. Ambrose was totally devoted to her and everyone knew how besotted they were with each other. 'Ohhhhh, do let us have Blanche give us all a Tarot reading tonight!' Catherine pleaded. Lady Blanche Parry was another close friend and confidante of the Queen's. Blanche had helped care for her since childhood, when she had accompanied her aunt, Lady Troy, as Lady Mistress to Court. Her cousin and close friend, Dr. John Dee, was a true cosmopolitan. He was a genius, having a seemingly endless field of knowledge. A gifted mathematician, he was the Queen's favourite astronomer and valued consultant in both state and personal matters. Elizabeth had even consulted Dee on the best day to hold her coronation. Sadly, theirs was a relationship that had to be kept under wraps as he had been accused of sorcery in the past. The Queen dared not take any chances of being accused of the same crime that had led her mother to the executioner's block.

Well educated in the subject of the Magical Universe, Dee had always fascinated Elizabeth. He was a keen alchemist and travelled all over the world, often using magic as a cover for espionage. He had become close to the head of the Queen's secret service, Sir Francis Walsingham, who had strongly encouraged him to become a successful spy. Dee regularly smuggled invaluable astronomical instruments back to England, including two of Mercator's world globes. With these, he was able to train the first great navigators. He would regularly update the maps that he had collected on his travels. His skills as a special agent and cartographer had helped England expand her empire and gradually gain rule of the seas. Elizabeth and her Imperial Geographer would sit together and talk for hours on end. She even took his medical advice more seriously than that of her numerous physicians. She was delighted when Dee came up with a new ethereal title of 'Gloriana, Queen of the Faerie Realm'. It really pleased her when she heard her subjects call her by that name.

Both Catherine and Elizabeth were strong believers in mysticism, sharing an interest in astrology and numerology. The two women had many other things in common, including their royal bloodline. Catherine and the Queen had both been fathered by King Henry VIII. Their mothers, Anne and Mary Boleyn, had been sisters. Elizabeth had always respected Catherine and acknowledged her as her half-sister. However the relationship could never be made official because sadly, she was one of many of Henry's bastard children. This actually made Catherine's daughter, Lettice, Elizabeth's blood niece! The two had been best friends for years. This made Catherine even more ashamed of Lettice's recent behaviour, especially since the Queen had always been so kind and empathic towards them both. She could quite easily have chosen to reject them especially since her mother Anne Boleyn's relationship with her sister had not been good during her final years.

When Anne Russell-Dudley heard mention of a possible Tarot reading, her face lit up. Her childlike enthusiasm always touched her two friends. Each of the women found it difficult without their men around and missed them terribly, especially poor, childless Anne. She was keen to find out whether she had become pregnant at long last. There was nothing she wanted more than to give her husband a child, preferably a son. Robert Dudley had arranged for Anne to marry his older brother when she was sixteen. She had been very happy with the match despite their twenty year age gap and had been fond of her brother-in-law ever since. 'My dear ladies, thou shalt surely find much delight in the jollities that I have arranged for this Midsummer's Night. Of course, we shall consult Lady Blanche if time permits. Now, make haste. We have little time before mon amour arrives.' Smiling contentedly, the Queen passed a bowl of fresh thyme and peppermint to her friends before they left. She took a pinch herself to freshen her breath. Elizabeth had a strong sense of smell and always insisted that everyone in her presence chewed the fresh herbs to hide any foul odour. She washed her fingers in a bowl of rosewater then called for her musicians.

Everyone felt relieved that Elizabeth's mood was improving now that Robert was on his way. He was always full of life and immense fun to be with. The couple knew each other so well that it felt uncanny at times. They had grown up together, attended the same Royal classes and shared an unquestionable mutual trust. Elizabeth and Robert had also been through some difficult and dangerous times and always looked out for each other.

Finally, when the Queen was alone, she gazed at her reflection in a looking glass. 'Oh God's truth!' she cursed bitterly under her breath. Displeased with what she saw, she lifted her long fingertips to touch her face lightly. Thick white make-up concealed her damaged skin but made her look old and drawn. No longer plump or full, her painted ruby lips gave her a stern appearance. The wig that she wore was immaculate and youthful in stark contrast to the face that it framed; only the best for the sovereign. Made with real, curly, red locks, the hairpiece was a near-perfect match to Elizabeth's own hair before it had thinned and become grey and dull. Little did she know, or care, that wig-makers often bought hair from desperate mothers who traded their daughters' tresses for money to buy food. Despite the soothing sound of music that echoed through the room, Elizabeth began to feel apprehensive about her lover's visit. She was determined to find out where Robert's loyalties lay. Taking a deep breath, she stifled tears of sheer dread. Inspecting her costume in the mirror, she picked up a small bow and pinned it into the curls at the base of her neck. 'Ahhhhh, perfect!' Her spirits lifted slightly when she saw the results of her efforts. Dabbing her wrists and the back of her neck with her exclusive perfume, she was ready to play her trick on Robert.

The Royal Perfumer, who happened to be Parisian, had mixed the Queen a unique fragrance. He had blended her favourite essential oil of lavender with musk and added oils from a variety of roses and ferns taken from the Royal Garden. It had taken him months to find the perfect blend to her satisfaction. It smelled divine.

On hearing the familiar sound of jingling bells and a soothing hum, Elizabeth smiled. Her favourite court jester's cheerful voice brought on a sigh of relief. Standing outside her door, Richard Tarleton began to sing, 'Me-rrry meet moy 'faerie-vorite' queen…', he paused just long enough to hear Elizabeth chuckle. A thick west country accent never failed to amuse. '…Thoin luvverrr-'s so nearrr an' thoin quiverrr's sooo keen…' he knew how the Queen enjoyed spicy lyrics, 'Pri-thee moy dearrr booty, treat thoin luverrr welllll…' Like a young child Elizabeth sat listening, beaming all over her face, eagerly awaiting delivery of the final line, '…sooooo 'is pillicock stays 'arrrd an' 'is 'umourrrs stay welllll.' With a burst of much needed laughter she clapped loudly and went out to meet 'Laughing Dick', as she fondly called him. Dick was the leading comic actor in her personal band of performers, The Queen's Men. Always happy to see him, Elizabeth gushed, 'Let me see my wonderful undumpisher!' For as long as she could remember, Dick had always been the one to cheer her up when she felt down. It was ironic that, despite his jolly profession, the poor man suffered with bouts of melancholy himself. No-one realised his grief and he often retired to his room feeling exhausted and alone. His wife had died not long into their marriage, after she had given birth to a healthy baby boy. Although Dick often referred to her in jest, he missed her terribly.

He vowed never to re-marry but ensured that his only child was well cared for.

Everyone at court loved the crazy bard who had long reigned as England's funniest man. Dick was squint-eyed with a large, flat nose. He only had to peep around the curtain to make an audience laugh. His funniest character role was a 'local yokel' who was a complete idiot. Bowing so low that his nose almost touched the floor, Dick continued to serenade Elizabeth in a broad Somerset accent, 'Ooooohhhhh moyyy, oooohhh moyyy! Thoinnn bubb-ieees be so rowwwsey, so roipe an' so perrrrt. Two booootiful peaches undr'our good Queen Bess's shirrrrt.' Grinning madly at his muse, Dick wiped drool from an over-protruding bottom lip before dancing excitedly on the spot. He produced a bunch of fresh lavender tied with purple silk ribbon. Elizabeth insisted that her chief gardener, Anthony Corbett, send freshly picked lavender every day, all year round. This put him under tremendous pressure since the English climate was as temperamental as its monarch!

Elizabeth was pleased to have Dick's company, 'Oh, my jolliest jigmaker! Thou shalt someday make me laugh so hard that my sides shall surely split!' Lowering her voice to a whisper, the Queen continued, 'Robert knowst not what I have in store for him. Once again, I find he hath deceived me. Methinks his pathetic pillicock doth rule his mind! He hath neglected to tell his queen of his acute fondness for Lettice.' Deeply pensive and concerned for his jealous friend, Dick rolled his eyes and answered softly, 'Pri'thee, do tell what in 'eaven's name 'as the imperrrtinent raaaarrrscal been up to wi' our little Letty?' He was astonished to hear of the Queen's supposed best friend's disloyalty. Elizabeth responded, spitting venom, 'Our little Letty? Swiving, brazen-faced strumpet, more-the-like!' Being extremely fond of Elizabeth, the wee jester always felt uneasy when she was having relationship problems. This latest conflict was even more distressing to hear, especially since the third party involved was someone who had always been close to the Queen.

Although she could often be annoyingly stubborn and self-centred, Elizabeth was devoted to her lover. She had done everything she possibly could to try to persuade the Privy Council to support her in her wish to marry Robert. There really was nothing more she could do yet he refused to believe it. After all she was Queen, and furthermore, head of the Church of England. Dick sympathised deeply with his frustrated friend and could see how this stalemate situation was tearing her apart. Since he had become a Groom of Her Majesty's Chamber he was the only man, other than her lover, who was allowed to tell Elizabeth her faults. Anyone else would never dare criticise their monarch for fear of being sent to the tower. Many a man had lost their head for less! The Queen often confided in Dick over personal matters and admired him for his brutal honesty. Elizabeth stated coldly, 'Since Lettice has become widowed, Robert has been overly attentive. It shall all cease, lest they regret their foolery.'

The Queen preferred her male courtiers to be single. If they really wanted to marry, they had to ask her permission beforehand. She often refused, giving various lame excuses. The bare truth was that Elizabeth wanted all male courtiers to give their complete attention to her. Dick listened patiently to her latest ploy. He did not understand why she had to set a trap rather than simply confront her lover. His advice was to leave well alone,

'Moy beauty, thou knowst moy thorrrrts on thoin mischief! Thou'llt fall from great 'oyts if tha fiddlest wi' fate. Take 'eed, nay good'll come o' tamperin'. 'Ow many toyms 'ave oy warrrn'd thee? Play wi' foyer 'an thoy fingerrrs shall burrrrn!' Wrinkling her nose playfully, Elizabeth chose to ignore Dick's wise words giving an abrupt retort, 'Utter poppycock! A lesson needs to be learned!' Quickly changing the subject, the irritable Queen asked her jester to play his pipe and tabor later that night. 'Thou shalt attend my bed chamber at twilight. Now be gone!' she added. Fluttering his eyelashes and ducking a dainty curtsy, Dick gave a feminine giggle and tip-toed backwards out of the room. 'See thee at cockshut toym, moy deary!' came a squeaky high-pitched voice as he hurried away. Elizabeth grumbled in fake annoyance but could not help smile. The cheeky man had a knack of goading her, just enough to vex her, only to make a joke at the perfect moment so she would burst into laughter. Clapping her hands in glee, the excited Queen called for her chambermaid. It was time to try her disguise out on her Robin.

'Lettice! What a pleasant surprise.' Robert exclaimed as he put his arms around the waist of the woman with her back to him. Nuzzling his face against the nape of her neck, he kissed her delicate skin and breathed in the scent of lavender and... roses! He pulled back instantly. There was only one person permitted to wear the most expensive perfume with such a good measure of pure rose oil! 'Zounds! What in Heav...' His words were cut short when Elizabeth swirled around so quickly that the long strings of pearls around her neck hit him straight in the face. 'Soooo! Two Eyes also hath two faces!' She struck him on the head sharply with her closed fan.

He winced, smirking and acknowledged her with a half-hearted bow. Elizabeth knew that Robert was sure to fall for her trick when she had transformed herself into his 'fancy piece'. Her maid had dropped her tray on seeing who she thought to be Lettice Knollys. The Queen's disgraced friend always wore a silk bow pinned to her wig, at the base of her neck. That was often the only way people had been able to tell her apart from Princess Elizabeth when they were younger. They were so alike in both looks and manner. However, Lettice's temperament was much more mild and placid. Elizabeth seethed, spitting as she screamed, 'To think… when I read your fickle words telling how sorely you missed your love!' Robert felt flattered by his Bess's angry reaction on hearing word of his pursuit of a new love interest. Naturally, doubts about the Queen's devotion had plagued him since she had rejected both of his marriage proposals. 'My beautiful Bess, if thou shalt breathe in deeply f…' With tightly clenched fists, Elizabeth's voice dropped a tone. She spoke through gritted teeth, 'How darest thou patronise thy Queen!' Robert bowed before her and had to stifle a smile. His lover raged with jealousy. Now he felt certain that he still held the highest place in her heart. And, oh how good it felt to know that!

Robert adored the strong, independent woman who had captivated his heart from a very early age. He could not help himself. He also aimed to make Bess suffer for refusing to marry him; 'Soooo, I take it that thou hast received word of my amorous advances toward Let…' Robert was cut off mid-sentence. 'How darest thou maketh a mockery of thy monar…' Elizabeth was angered further by yet another interruption. Robert could not help but react to her haughtiness. He laughed loudly at her attempt at superiority. 'A mockery?! Remember who thou art accusing, my lovely!' Robert was, and always had been, the only man able to bring his Bess down to earth. Admittedly, sometimes it would take a little time. Nevertheless, she would always come around to his way of thinking in the end. Elizabeth's combined superior authority as monarch and head of the Church of England meant that she demanded the utmost respect to reflect her magnificence. Yet, to Robert, her arrogance and egotism was simply too much to bear at times. This was one of those times. His patience was quickly wearing thin.

'Aaaaaggghhhh!!' Bess howled an enraged battle cry that faded into a deep, guttural growl. Robert kept his dulcet tones calm and steady, 'How pretty thou art when fuming, my precious jewel.' He gazed at the woman he loved and went to take her long, gloved fingers in his hand. Immediately snatching her hand free the stubborn Queen frowned deeply. Standing solidly, with legs astride under her sumptuous gown, she crossed her arms and hunched her shoulders. She looked exactly like her father, Henry, used to when he was annoyed. Elizabeth stomped her silver-slippered feet. Robert refused to give in to this ridiculous, belligerent eruption. He knew full well that she had missed him as much as he had her. Although he was disgusted with her for setting a trap, which admittedly he fell for, he was flattered that she still wanted him above any other man.

Robert untied an embroidered pouch from his belt and dangled it in front of his lover's face. Bess's eyes narrowed and she pouted her red lips. Her bottom lip trembled as she seethed. 'Enough of this bribery!' Without any warning, the Earl grabbed her by the waist. He lifted her, kicking and squealing, and hauled her nimble body over his shoulder. Being a tall, strong and very fit man he managed to stay upright but not for long. Robert suffered a flurry of punches and his feisty lover even bit him on the face at one point. She struggled like a mad woman in an attempt to free herself from his firm grasp. Finally, he managed to wrestle her against a wall. 'Unhand me, or…' Robert forced his lips against Elizabeth's, kissing her firmly and passionately. Every fibre of her being tingled with pleasure; she felt like she was melting. She could feel the heat exude from his body as he pressed firmly against her. A familiar scent of musk-like pheromones made it impossible for her to resist his sexual power. Her legs felt weak as she gave in to the most incredible kiss.

No longer able to contain his desire, Robert took hold of Bess's delicate silken bodice and tore it apart. Roughly, he pulled her onto his lap and began kissing her throat. When Elizabeth felt him squeeze her exposed breast, she could not help herself. Groaning with pure pleasure, she parted her rosebud lips once again and went to bite his ear. Well-used to Elizabeth's mischievous ways, Robert had been waiting for a trick like this, 'A, a, ahhh, my brutal Bess! Methinks thou shalt surely be punish…' He struggled with the strong woman as, once again, she tried to break free. The Queen's muscular body twisted and writhed against his. Feeling his cock grow hard beneath restrictive clothes he pulled off her neck ruff and used it to bind her wrists together. Once they had been secured, her protests lessened. Robert knew that his sexual dominance aroused her deeply. Running a hand under her skirts, he felt her strong thigh muscles tighten as his captive's body responded. Bess held her breath as she eagerly awaited his next move in helpless anticipation. Robert forced her supple body over his knee, face down. He took his time lifting each of her heavy skirts until finally the bare cheeks of her backside were completely exposed. Savouring every minute of her state of submission, Robert took his time stroking, caressing and squeezing every inch of flesh until she began to squirm. Now, she was desperate for him to force her legs apart and enter her. The Queen was not used to waiting for anything... ever. That fact alone made the tantalising game all the more gratifying for both lovers.

Low, muffled voices could be heard nearby; undoubtedly the servants busy preparing the hall for the evening's festivities. The danger of being caught at any moment heightened Bess's aroused state. She could only begin to imagine the commotion if her secret need to be sexually dominated was ever discovered. Biting her lip, she tried hard to steady her erratic breathing. Her heart raced as she felt fresh wetness seep from between her legs onto the flesh of her milky-white thighs. Robert denied her the pleasure of feeling his fingers touch her wetness but it excited him to see her so turned on. It came as a complete surprise. Bess flinched as she felt the first hard slap. Burying her face into her lover's crotch, she let out a quiet moan. The vibrations from the sound made Robert even more erect. He spanked her pretty arse cheeks until she shook her head wildly, her eyes squeezed tightly shut. She would not, she could not yell aloud! A submissive woman now whispered between clenched teeth, 'Pri'thee, sire, show mercy! I apologise for displeasing thee.' She felt herself break into a hot sweat. Her whole body flushed pink with wanton desire. Sliding dextrous fingers beneath fine silken stocking tops, Robert knew exactly which areas to touch to further stimulate his lover. 'Mmmmm', Bess let out a groan. 'Shhhhhh, my pretty wench! Take thine punishment in silence!'

Now Bess showed total submission under Robert's command. The spanking continued until the soft, pale skin of the Queen's buttocks had turned dark pink. He kept checking the amount of red hand-marks until he was satisfied that she had been punished enough. Only then did he lift her up by the hips to turn her over to face him. Some of Bess's make-up had rubbed away. Robert found her reddened, tear-stained face appealing as she looked seductively into his eyes. In a blissful state of arousal she parted her lips slightly, and closed her eyes, hoping to be rewarded with a kiss. Denying her even the slightest amount of control, her Master untied the cord on his trews and pulled out his large, erect cock. He pushed her down onto her knees. She dropped forward onto all fours so he could enter her from behind. Robert fucked Bess hard and fast. Her passivity gave him a mind-blowing sexual high. She tried hard to stifle moans of pleasure as she felt him pounding into her. After a few minutes, he could no longer hold back and ejaculated inside her.

When he was finished, Bess turned around and knelt before the Earl, surprising him with the embroidered pouch that she was holding. She had managed to free her wrists and grab hold of it during the scuffle. Bending to kiss the sensitive head of his penis, she looked up at her satisfied man, 'Let me see if my 'Eyes' hath chosen a fitting gift for his naughty wench.' Robert burst out laughing as the crafty woman untied the ribbon and took out the beautiful diamond necklace that he had commissioned to be made for his queen. The jewellery was exquisite; its centrepiece had been made to resemble an eye and was set with mother of pearl and a sapphire. It was Elizabeth's turn to laugh when she saw that the gift had been chosen with her pet name for him in mind. This confirmed that their uncanny bond was as strong as ever. Robert looked into her eyes as he removed her gloves to place a matching ring on the middle finger of her left hand. 'Bess, thou art my true love. I am devoted to thee, e'er have been and shall be fore'er'more.' A clock chimed six times as the lovers parted. They each went to their separate chambers to dress for the festivities. The night was still young and the first guests were arriving.

The banqueting hall looked magnificent. No expense had been spared. Everyone was in awe as they stepped into the enchanted world that Elizabeth had designed and her skilled servants had created. They had certainly done her proud. White Romanesque columns, brought in especially for the occasion, had been erected around the edge of the grand hall. Branches of sweet-smelling blossom coiled around pillars from floor to ceiling. A canopy of ivy had been interlaced with garlands of jasmine, adding another divine perfume to the room. Large mirrors with gilded frames surrounded a long table. The table top was covered with white silken cloth, fringed with gold and embroidered with silver stars. Ornate silver plates and salvers were filled with culinary delights. The Queen had ordered sweet dishes to satisfy her well-known sweet tooth. Huge fondant icing sculptures had been covered with sugar to make them sparkle in the candlelight. In the centre of the table was a sugar sculpture of a white, winged stallion. Its mane and tail had been covered with 24 ct gold leaf. Pieces of gold leaf had also been added into glass dishes of flummery that surrounded the centrepiece. It was obvious that this royal feast had been planned with much thought and care. Delicate sugar cages had been suspended from chains above the table. Guests were delighted when they looked up to see brightly coloured sugar birds inside. Each had been placed on fine wire so they trembled gently whenever the cages moved. Guests had been asked to dress to suit a faerie theme. Everyone had made a great effort with their costumes. Ladies wore sparkling, pastel-coloured gowns. Some wore wigs shot through with threads of silver or gold to match fragile, bejewelled lace wings. Amongst the courtiers were two horned likenesses to the satyr, Pan, several elves and numerous nymphs. Court musicians were dressed in green and played from the Minstrels' Gallery, a balcony high above the grand hall. Singers from the Chapel Royal sang madrigals as the guests took their places.

Once everyone was seated, Laughing Dick entered, making everyone howl with laughter at his chosen garb. Dressed as a leprechaun, he balanced a small, black pot on his nose and held a bauble with the head of an open-mouthed faerie carved at its top. His big belly swelled against the cloth of his outfit and spindly, bandy legs made the character look hilarious. As the fool tumbled around the room, he expertly balanced the cauldron on his head, occasionally faking the odd stumble. His act enthralled guests as golden coins spilled from the pot's brim. It was certainly no coincidence that most of the treasure fell into the laps of the prettiest women present. Whilst Dick performed, the wine flowed until it was time for the Queen to make her grand entrance. When the time came, the jester pulled off his leprechaun attire to reveal a second costume beneath. Everyone gasped in horror. Ladies covered their eyes and most of the men sat speechless at the vulgar sight. The music grew louder, then an eruption of spontaneous laughter soon filled the room when everyone realised that Dick was wearing a flesh-coloured outfit that made him appear naked in the soft candlelight. A leaf had been perched on the end of a huge, upturned codpiece with a bright pink end. The purr of the drum-roll on his humble tabor was drowned out by a fanfare.

Six tiny people, some of them dwarves some midgets, all dressed as faerie folk, emerged from the layers of shimmering silk hangings. They were pulling a huge white swan on a rope behind them. The magical bird was complete with real feathers, sparkling glass eyes and bejewelled golden crown. A shrill, piercing sound of a hautboy created an eerie, almost supernatural atmosphere as the miniature entourage led the ethereal creature around the room. When they reached the head of the table, they secured the swan to the floor. Two of the tiny faeries pulled back its huge wings. To everyone's amazement, Laughing Dick jumped out of the bird. He was greeted by a crescendo of cheering and applause. Pressing an index finger to his lips to ask for silence, the jester, in cupid's guise, lifted his silver bow. Aiming above the heads of the audience, he shot a swift arrow. It hit its target, splitting an inflated pig's bladder perfectly. A cascade of silver streamers spilled from inside. Amidst the shimmering shower, ladies Anne and Catherine lifted their glasses in honour of their friend. Elizabeth had certainly put on the spectacular show that she had promised. Stupid Cupid did a perfect somersault over the little people then pulled back the curtains to reveal a stage, its set, a faerie realm. Real water trickled from a masterfully painted mountain scene to create a realistic miniature waterfall. As Dick removed his leafy crown he took a low bow. 'Pri'thee, moy deloitful, dreamy faerie folksies.' The crowd clapped loudly and musicians began to play. 'Welcome thine 'ost, 'er majesticly, magnificent queeeeen of all faerieeees, Glorrrr-iana!' A big bang made the jester jump like a frog before he vanished behind a screen of blue smoke.

The music became softer as guests gasped in anticipation. Some women had been scared by the sudden explosion but everyone's spirits soon lifted when Lady Catherine noticed that the Queen was sitting at the head of the table. The swan's body had lost its feathers and become a golden throne but the neck, head and wings had remained intact. All of this conjuring had been done whilst Dick had everyone's attention. Elizabeth had entered the room via an underground tunnel, through a trapdoor. Then servants had passed the throne up to the little people who re-arranged the swan for the Queen to be seated. Her costume was fantastic. She wore a golden gown covered with infinite jewels and huge silver wings that had rows of tiny glass beads that trembled with her slightest movement. Robert sat next to her, dressed as an elf with pointed ears and a green doublet made entirely from silken leaves. 'Let us begin this revelry of delight! Eat, drink and be merry. Presently, we shall be entertained by my players.' The Queen lifted a glass of hippocras and everyone toasted their hostess.

The food tasted delicious. The chefs had used a quarter of a ton of sugar to make all of the delicacies. Elizabeth had ensured that there was plenty of Robert's favourite dish; sweet sausage made with ambergris, the most coveted therefore most expensive food in the world. This rare delicacy was also arguably the most disgusting as it was actually bile from the sperm whale. Referred to in the colonies as 'floating gold' it could be found washed up on the shore after years at sea. When mature, the natural excrement has a sweet smell and, apparently, tasted delicious.

Down in the servants' quarters, everyone was disappointed by the meagre amount of left-overs at the end of the banquet. As usual, gossip was rife and the young serving girls were all of a fluster. They were fussing over their hair and pinching their cheeks to make them rosy in hope of catching the eye of a handsome actor. A pretty blonde girl hitched up her enormous breasts and swayed her hips seductively as she talked, 'Ooo that one wi' pointy ears an' a black beard can gi' me a good, 'ard swivin' after ladies av' 'ad their pokes'. The young male servants were always put out when the all-star company were around. Orgies were popular amongst the upper classes. Some of the lords even paid actors to have sex with their wives whilst they watched. Besotted women and homosexual men would leave extravagant gifts for their favourite players. If the actor was that way inclined, he would sometimes service his male admirers in a secret location. These rendezvouses were extremely risky for the men. If caught during the act, they would be arrested and executed for performing illegal sexual activity. Women swooned over the prestigious and popular actors. The most popular star at that time was John Bentley, a leading player in the Queen's private acting troupe. A skilled swordsman and a complete rogue, John always played the hero. He had a hell-raising reputation and was renowned for his ability to service three or four women in a single night. Apparently, he had been blessed with an extremely long member with a substantial girth that could satisfy the slackest of cunnies. Regrettably, Bentley also had a reputation for having a temper that was even hotter than his sexual appetite. Most men loathed him because of his expert carnal skills and, subsequently, he was often getting into fights over women. Once, he had been imprisoned for stabbing a man who had blankly refused to pay to watch a play. It came as no surprise when the Queen's well-loved actor was freed soon after.

The Queen charmed her guests by playing the virginals before the performance. Dick made everyone laugh in his lead role as 'Stupid Cupid', who kept missing his targets and pairing dreadfully mismatched lovers. Elizabeth was relieved when the night passed without a single derogatory comment or disapproving look aimed at Robert. In fact, the carefully chosen courtiers had been surprisingly discreet, even courteous, towards the Earl. They had all thoroughly enjoyed a celebration that would take a long time to forget. Most important of all, word would soon spread of Elizabeth's extravagant hospitality. Even during the interval, everyone enjoyed alcoholic cordial, marchpane gems and small pieces of heart-shaped toast with a choice of honeycomb, milk and rose, or the Queen's favourite lavender jam. To everyone's delight, Elizabeth let her two miniature dachshunds out of their richly embroidered pouches. Little Jack and Jill had been named after the naughty rhyme. They made everyone laugh when they jumped out and started to chase each other around the table. They dodged obstacles and zigzagged skilfully between the porcelain until

Elizabeth called them. Obediently, they scampered over to her immediately and jumped up to lick her before she put them back into their pouches.

Most of the guests had gone home by the time Lady Blanche began her Tarot readings. Sadly, there was no news of a future pregnancy for Anne but she was satisfied with the promise of undying love from her husband. Elizabeth's reading reflected her wisdom in sweetening the acid tongues of vipers who wished nothing more than to see Robert Dudley's downfall. On hearing this, Robert was the first of the group to retire. He had already been disappointed by Blanche's prediction that he and the Queen would be lovers until his death but would never marry. When he bent to kiss Elizabeth goodnight, she told him to wait for her in her bed chamber. Before he left the room, Blanche told him to have a light chainmail garment made. She advised him to wear this under his normal clothes at all times. When the Queen, Catherine, Anne, Blanche and her cousin, John Dee, were left alone, Dee produced Elizabeth's weekly astrology chart. He gave her a serious warning that someone close to her would deceive her before the year was out. As Blanche turned over several cards, she spoke gravely, 'Ma'am thou shalt have several threats on thy precious life over the next two years. Foreign hatred brews... the cards tell of an explosion and someone seeking hideous revenge.'

Inner turmoil scorched Elizabeth's heart with fear of the terrifying predictions. She tried to make light of the doom, 'Should each of mine enemies be a Tarot card, thou wouldst need several sets to include them all. Many treasonous worms turn the soils of England, Ireland and Scotland afore we even begin to venture into warmer climes where other sods lie!' Elizabeth broke the uneasy silence with her witty pun. The small group were well aware of the danger of being accused of witchery. Extreme care was taken when conducting their spiritual meetings, ensuring that they were always in a secure, private environment. So many people believed that Elizabeth's mother had been a witch and it was commonly accepted that her daughter had inherited her ethereal powers. Hence the less educated citizens' common belief that their Queen really did have rule over Faerieland as well as England. Elizabeth and Dee often took psychotropic drugs and used flying ointment and opium which enabled them to go on astral journeys. If they were ever caught doing this, it would be their end without a shred of doubt.

Back in her quarters, Elizabeth was cross with herself for giving in to Robert's charms so easily. Every time they were together, she found it impossible to resist his sexual magnetism. Suddenly breaking away from a passionate kiss, Elizabeth ordered her lover to leave. He smiled at her with entrancing eyes. She could not help but return a flirtatious grin. The man was incorrigible. He had an innate magnetism second to none! Soon after he had left, Elizabeth's servants arrived with bowls of refreshing rose water. She allowed herself to relax, feeling rejuvenated and satisfied. Once again, she had Robert to herself and knew exactly what he was up to. When they had been apart for any length of time, the Queen felt terribly insecure. She needed constant confirmation of his undying devotion and although he sent letters and gifts regularly, nothing could ever match intimate contact. As her maids gently cleansed her face and body, Elizabeth's skin tingled at the memory of her lover's touch. She looked forward to Laughing Dick's arrival so she could share her delight.

As always, the cheeky jester made perfect timing. The welcome sound of his pipe and tabor made her smile as Dick approached her bedroom. With a wide grin, he made Elizabeth laugh as soon as he set foot in the door, 'Well, ourrr Bess, thou 'ast bin bless't! Oy lay a big fat wagerrr that tha's 'ad a good ol' swoyvin' from our ol' cuddly Dudley.' Waving a hand to dismiss her grooming maids, Elizabeth sighed deeply. She was relieved to be left alone with her comical friend. The long night of celebrations had taken its toll. The Queen felt weary. However, Dick managed to renew her excitement as they began to chat about that night's many events. Feeling a new burst of energy, Elizabeth told her friend all about her trick that had worked perfectly and Robert's initial angry reaction. She spared no details when describing the intensely passionate encounter that had followed. Her graphic account was accompanied by plenty of 'oo's' and 'ahhh's' from Dick. The pair chatted excitedly, well into the early hours. When the jester reminded his friend that she should get some beauty sleep, the tired but contented Queen reluctantly bid him good night. Laughing Dick always managed to reassure Elizabeth and put her at ease. He was a good man, a devoted servant and, most importantly, a true and trustworthy friend. After listening to a comical goodnight ballad, the Queen was left alone. She knelt to say her nightly prayers, then added two drops of pure essential lavender oil to her pillow. Not yet ready to lie down, Elizabeth's mind began to buzz with fresh inspiration. She sat at her writing desk and, dipping a fresh swan's quill into ink, added another verse to her poem:

> My care is like my shadow in the sun -
> Follows me flying, flies when I pursue it,
> Stands and lies by me, doth what I have done;
> His too familiar care doth make me rue it.
> No means I find to rid him from my breast,
> Till by the end of things it be supprest.

The Queen yawned, smiling happily as she inspected the immaculate detail on the beautiful ring that her Robin had given her. He was such a generous soul and an incredible lover. It felt good to have him close again. She sipped the tonic that the Royal Apothecary had prepared before she climbed into her comfortable four-poster bed. It was not long before Elizabeth fell into a deep and peaceful slumber.

Chapter 8

A Voyage with Pyrates

On hearing Anthony's eye-witness account of her beloved Shana's brave act of suicide in defiance of the English Queen, Grace had been beside herself with rage. The time was fast approaching for her Fianna Fail to make its military presence known to the power-hungry cur. She was determined to do it right this time and make sure that the royal bitch suffered a fate worse than death. It had taken a few days to finalise plans of action that would be put in place whilst Anthony travelled to São Vicente. It had been a difficult decision to make whether to accompany him or not. Since Grace was sure that nothing could ease Patrick's pain over his mother's death, she had decided to stay in Ireland. She could do a lot more from home by preparing her men for the forthcoming war.

Determined to make the most of the little time she had before Patrick's return, Grace had already sent word to Spain. She knew that she could rely on Spanish support. They were eager to join ranks against the Protestant English Queen and would be pleased to hear of the movement's new recruit, Admiral Hawkins. As an infiltrator, he would certainly be able to give Elizabeth's enemies a unique, invaluable advantage. Having control over the movements of English fleets, Hawkins could use his power to weaken England's naval defence lines without the Queen's knowledge. If the English were led to believe that they were under Spanish attack, they would most definitely retaliate. Hawkins could then order the Royal fleet to attack and pursue enemy vessels leaving their shoreline defenceless. O'Malley then planned to move in to destroy the remaining vessels. Eire's New Model Army would finally be in a position to wreak long sought after revenge. Grace's proposal for Patrick's assassination attempt was a simple one; to play on Queen Elizabeth's vulnerability. Always keen to please her citizens, the Queen would plan spectacular public celebrations at various times in the year. Ironically, despite the nation's terrible treatment of ordinary folk, she prided herself in being 'the peoples' monarch'. One of the ploys that she used to help boost her popularity was to mingle amongst her common subjects. Although tight security measures were put in place on these occasions this was, without a doubt, the best time for the cut-throats to strike.

Standing high on the parapet of Rockfleet, Grace confided in Anthony, 'Oy propose dat our Paddy blows de toyt-arsed darter of a witch outta de water. Yer see, her conceit shall be her downfall, oy tells yers!' Anthony only had to look at the strong, Irish noblewoman to rouse a rush of adrenalin within his veins. The soured, dismal expression on her face made the hatred and bitterness that she harboured all too clear. Grace despised Elizabeth more than ever. Anthony listened intently as she schemed, 'Der's nuttin' dat pleases de haughty, crusty-cunted ol' prude more dan a party fer her fickle subjects. Imagine 'dis...' she paused mid-sentence. A cool wind made Grace shudder as she gazed far out over choppy, grey seas. Gulls screeched unsettling laments as they hovered above. A feeling of doom suddenly spread through Grace's body. She closed her eyes and tried to hold back bleak emotions. Something told the spiritual noblewoman that the fine, young man beside her was fated to suffer. Although she had not known Anthony long, they shared an uncanny connection. He felt it too. Almost 'hearing' her thoughts Anthony spoke out, 'What troubles thee?' He felt genuine concern for the wild woman who he respected so much. ''Tis nuttin'.' Grace lied. Completely out of character, she grabbed Anthony's hand and squeezed tightly. She continued, 'Yers should all stroyk when she puts on one of dem fancy shows. Dat would be de best toim ter blarrst de proddy whore's whoit-warshed arse ter kingdom come!' Anthony laughed aloud at Grace's insulting description of Elizabeth. Part of him wished that he could stay with this captivating woman. She carried on her spiel, totally oblivious to his thoughts, 'Oy have skilled men ready fer yers arl. Dey'll deal wid explosives. Arl yers need now is a big set o' bollocks!' This last statement made them both burst out in laughter. They embraced each other firmly, as comrades in arms do.

It had come as a surprise to Grace that she and Anthony had become firm friends in such a short space of time. The pyrate knew that she would miss her intriguing new ally and she aimed to do everything possible to help ease his heavy burden. She had already had word sent to the Cimarrones, a rebellious group of escaped African slaves who Shana had helped when they decided to settle near São Vicente. Grace was confident that they would join forces with Patrick to fight for their cause. She had chosen two of her best men to accompany Anthony. Danny, her top helmsman, was incredibly loyal and a skilled swordsman. He was also an expert with gunpowder. Although he was an insatiable flirt, who was always in fights with jealous men, Grace was certain that he would protect Patrick with his life. A born fighter, who had the gift of the gab, Danny would not have any qualms about joining the group of assassins. A devoted son of Eire, the young Irishman would want nothing more than to be amongst Patrick's gang fighting against the English Queen. Colm was Grace's second choice. He was another reliable man who would lay down his life for his beloved Eire. Shana Culley had been very fond of the kind hearted pyrate who had a love for all animals. As Grace had expected, Colm had been the first to volunteer to escort the Englishman on his mission. 'I'm afeared, Gronyer. 'Tis all new to me', Anthony spoke with brutal honesty. Grace took his face in her hands and looked deeply into his blue eyes. 'Yers shalt nat fail, my 'andsome. 'Tis' nat an aption ter allow t'enter yer moind. Besoids, ye'll have der spirit o' der pure drap insoid yers tonoight. Dat'll surely help yers on yer way.' 'The pure drop? What poisons dost thou have in store for me?' Anthony joked. Without another word Grace gave her suspicious friend a thump on the back and led him back into her castle.

Creppin was still having fun exploring Grace's home. He had found many a secret nook and cranny during his stay. Grace's wolfhounds, Merlin and Mistlytoes, had become so attached to their new houseguest that they followed him everywhere. The hunchback's new clobber had become flea-infested once again and was now covered in coarse, grey dog hair. 'Yi... Yi... Yi... yowooooo!' the crazy little man yelled as he bounced clumsily down the stone steps to take the hounds on their daily run. He had adapted his usual high-pitched call to a bellowing howl. He believed that this helped him to communicate with 'Crrreppin's pupplypetsieees', as he now called them. Smashing their bodies against the arched, grey stone doorway in their struggle for freedom, the trio lurched outdoors en masse. Creppin took an abrupt nosedive into the mud. He struggled to get back up. The excited dogs did not help as they pawed at him, licking and slobbering all over his head. Colm whistled loudly to call them off so the hunchback was able to stand. 'Thankin' yeeee!' Creppin shouted happily as he heaved his bulk up clumsily and limped away as fast as he could. He was determined to gain some distance before the hounds caught him up.

The huge dogs had helped the odd little man to gain confidence. He had become way more outgoing during his stay at Rockfleet. He was a little less wary and, on occasion, was even able to communicate with strangers. Young Shana watched as the dogs were released and bounded off after the excited man. She had been out with some of the others cutting turf for much of the day. Her back ached from digging. The constant dampness seemed to seep into the bones as it had back in her homeland. She was looking forward to warming them in front of a well stoked fire. The prospect of becoming a crewmember on the forthcoming voyage was thrilling. Having met Grace's hand-picked crew a few days before, she felt much more comfortable about taking on the demanding role of sailor's mate.

Initially, the idea of learning the ropes had been daunting for the young woman until Grace had encouraged her to go out to sea on one of her patrol galleys. Shana had proven to be as competent as her fellow mates of the opposite sex when it was her turn to handle some of the ropes and pulleys. Danny, the cheeky Irish pyrate who had a thing for her, had been especially impressed. He made an example of Saul who had been loud and cocksure on boarding the vessel. The robust lad had managed to get in the way during the patrol and was soon replaced by Shana who had initially been wary of being a burden. She listened intently to instructions and acted without any hesitation or fuss. In fact, on their return, the crew reported back to Grace that she was the best recruit of the bunch. Blushing deeply, she felt pleased that she had managed her first experience on the ropes well and knew that her mother would have been proud. Although they lacked Shana's natural aptitude as sailors, Anthony, Gift, Josh and Saul had all proved themselves to be eager learners which pleased Grace's crew.

Pyrates were tough, hardy seadogs who had no choice but man their vessel through all kinds of severe weather and hazardous conditions. They had to be ready to defend themselves against enemy attacks at all times, no matter how exhausted they might be. Grace's crew were a courageous and skilled bunch of experienced sailors who could count on each other through thick and thin. Together, they had endured long, hard days and nights at sea, without sleep and with rations so low that they had been forced to kill and eat the ships' vermin to stay alive. Many had died in sheer agony when battle injuries had become infected and gangrenous. Tropical diseases, poxes or scurvy were rife and also took their toll. Despite these miserable and dangerous ordeals, the Irish crew had managed to survive and sustain a healthy amount of camaraderie.

A wailing northerly wind whipped its way around Rockfleet Castle. A blanket of dark cloud sped across the skies. Unrelenting rain pelted the fortress walls. Inside, the atmosphere had become tense with a mix of pre-battle angst and enthusiasm. Although spirits were already high, Grace was determined to send her small but valiant force away with an extra special soul boost. She was going to give Anthony's new crew a leaving party that would hopefully take them away from their troubles... for a while, at least.

The centuries-old tradition of brewing poitín, an occasionally lethal alcoholic drink, had long played a part in rural Irish folklore. One of the most potent concoctions known to man, poitín was the subject of many a ballad and limerick. This traditional Irish booze was especially popular at wakes and marriages. Brewed in total secrecy by clans along the windswept coast of Western Ireland, 'potcheen' (as the English call it) had been Grace's favourite drink since her first sip as a child. Its production process was laborious, requiring patience and skills that had been passed down through many generations. Widows often learned the distillation process so that they could earn a steady income. With every new batch of poitín, 'the pure drop' is created. This coveted first tot from the vat is renowned for its magical healing benefits. Only a select, lucky few have the opportunity to taste the sacred elixir. Unbeknown to him, Grace planned to let Anthony drink the precious pure drop that night. She believed that if anything was to help save the lad, then this would be the most hopeful bet.

When everyone had returned to Rockfleet that evening, Grace made an announcement. She addressed Anthony and his newly formed crew, 'Moy hearties, I shall bid yers all a fond farewell wid a party aflow wid nuttin' but der best 'mudders' milk'. Everyone but the clueless English cheered at the news and the send-off celebrations were soon in full swing. Irish folk ballads were sung to the heavenly sounds of the harp. Grace had stowed away a few of the valuable Celtic instruments when the English Queen had passed a law that all Irish harpists be executed and their precious harps burned. She had also tried to forbid Gaelic speech, in an attempt to subjugate the inhabitants of Eire. The English monarch's attack on the very core of Irish Celtic culture had made the people even more determined to continue to play their traditional ancient airs. The history of their entire culture had been composed by their ancestors in these cherished folksongs. Each had been passed down from generation to generation and told of battles, defeats and victories, murders, forbidden love, births, deaths and marriages. Celebrations of new friendship, solidarity and fond farewells went on for hours within the walls of Grace's castle.

Old Séamus was a blind man who had distilled the 'quare stuff' as he called his intoxicating mountain dew. The distilling process was done over a peat fire using crystal clear waters from the mountain stream, then fermented in bog holes. He believed that he was able to trap nature's magical purity from the elements and, during a time-consuming process, produce a concoction to cure all ills. When anyone made a drop-off, it was tradition to invite them in for a few drinks. They would often stay for days until they had slept off the effects. Séamus had lost his sight long ago due to over-consumption of his famous fiery tipple. Although Anthony and the others were aware of the possible dangers of the Irish booze, they were ready to experience its potency.

The earthy aroma of a healthy turf fire filled the crowded room and everyone had gathered around to listen to the old expert tell his tales. Séamus enjoyed talking as much as drinking. Grace joked, 'Be Jaysus, Shaymus! Anywan 'ud tink yer'd swallowed the blaaarrrny stone, nat just kissed de' fecker!' The old man gave a rasping chortle and lit a taper from the roaring fire. His Gaelic words fascinated Creppin and even the wolfhounds pricked up their ears at the mention of 'uisce beatha', meaning 'water of life'. 'Dis is de' strongest wee dram dat'll e'er pass yer lips... oy'm tellin' yers arrrl de troot, so oy am.' As he spoke, he poured a little of his home-made alcoholic brew into a ladle. To the English visitors' surprise, he then set fire to the liquid which produced a pretty purple flame. 'Dis test proves dat me' likker is fit fer consumption... Some rogues out dere 'av bin cart addin' pure shite ter de' sacred tipple! Gaaaad 'ave mercy arn d' hopeless souls t'ave messed wi' d' drink dat der bless-ed Saint of our oisle, Saint Paddy his Holy Self, was de' forst ter distill. De' brew dat is unfit ter swig burns as red as blood, so avoid it loik an Englishman... present company excepted o' carse!' There was a tranquil hush. Nothing could be heard but the sound of a crackling fire and the eerie wail of the wind. Unperturbed, old Séamus continued his demonstration. 'I'm tellin' yers arl dese secrets so's ye'll ne'er allow a poisonous batch ter pass yers lips.' Gnarled fingers gripped the handle of the ladle and Séamus' hand began to shake as Grace guided him over to a pail of milk. Very carefully, he added a little to the remainder of the poitín test sample. 'Noy, yers are arrrl able ter see dat de milk doesnay curdle. If e'er it does, den yer ditch der batch an' bury de' barrrstards who distilled de' bad stuff. Had oy learned de art o' testin' afore oy drank an entoyer wee pat to meself, oy'd be able ter sees yers arl now!' The wise man's milky, sightless eyes looked sad as they stared uselessly from sunken sockets. He reached into his pouch to bring out a small medicine bottle. Feeling for Grace's hands, Séamus handed her the treasured tonic... the first dram, the pure drop.

With a loud cheer, everyone encouraged the guests to start drinking. Taking a good swig from his own leather bottle, Séamus waited for the noise to drop before he continued his lesson. 'Moy mudder n' farder... mayzer' good Larrrd bless der dear zzeparrrted souls...' he began to slur his words as the alcohol instantly took effect, 'dey'd bathed in dizz an' rubbed it inter eashhudder's achin' jointsh...' he hiccupped before continuing, 'ash a medishinal shreatment wid nay udder ter beat itsh blessshhhhhed power.' The old man carried on rambling for a good hour, sharing countless uses for this miracle spirit. He claimed that poitín could cure, heal, stimulate and invigorate every part of the human and even animal body! Apparently, lacklustre race horses would gain a tremendous energy boost after consuming a generous dose from the wee pot. Séamus was able to name a few well-known winners that had secured race after race before they were dragged off to the knacker's yard at a fine old age. When drank in moderation, poitín could help to maintain a man's virility and by becoming intoxicated on a regular basis it was believed that a person could prolong their life. An excellent indigestion aid, the miracle liquor could cast off melancholy and, according to the expert distiller, 'quicken de moind and relieve de wind by bringin' arn der farrrrts.' Highly explosive, it could even be ignited to blow up rocks! On the rare occasion, Grace and her pyrates made lethal missiles by lighting a soaked rag in a bottle of the potent tonic and hurling it at enemy ships.

Creppin had only needed a couple of wee drams before he curled up to sleep with Merlin and Mistlytoes who had both drunk their fair share of poitín. He lay in piss-soaked clothes because his legs had given way beneath him when he had tried to get up and make it to the privy. A hardened drinker, Grace was able to entertain her guests by dancing, singing and sword-fighting well into the early hours until exhaustion finally overtook her. Anthony managed to hold his own but his English friends had passed out soon after their first few tots from the little pot.

When everyone else had fallen asleep, Grace took Anthony by the hand and pulled him to his feet. Although he was unsteady, he managed to stumble alongside his hostess up through her private quarters and out onto the ramparts. The friends stood together silently and watched the sun creep over the horizon. No words were needed. Deep down, they were both well aware that they might never see each other again. A bloody sun cast its deep scarlet reflection onto retreating waves. The sound of an ebbing tide echoed Anthony's melancholic feelings. He gazed out over the wet, green wilderness that the sea had deserted for a while. As if sensing his unease, Grace pulled him close and kissed his forehead. 'She's been moy loyf for years, m' hearty and hasnay let me doyn.' Referring to the ocean that she had loved ever since she had stowed away on her father's ship as a child, Grace wondered how her friend would cope with its volatility and unpredictability. She believed that he would surely become addicted to the lure of the waves once he had tasted a life at sea. His fascination was already clear to see. 'Look after tha'self', Anthony whispered as he looked deep into Grace's emerald green eyes. They had as much allure as the sea itself and he felt glad that he had come to know her so well in such a short space of time. Feeling suddenly sober, they embraced and kissed each other before going back into the castle to get some well-needed rest.

Everyone woke to the delicious smell of lamb pottage. They were soon tucking into a hearty meal. Old Séamus lay by the fire and reached for his large stick. He struggled to his feet. Creppin laughed aloud as he felt two sloppy, wet tongues licking his face as Grace's hounds tried to rouse him. Suddenly realising that he had soaked himself in his own piss, he grumbled at the prospect of having to change his treasured trews. Their galley was ready to take them on a journey to distant shores and he had managed to piss himself! 'Miiiihhh!' Mistlytoes cocked his head comically at the gurning hunchback as he grumbled to himself, 'Typical t'is that Crrrreppin's swig o' pochyneenin...' Séamus chuckled to himself on hearing the Englishman's mispronunciation of his beloved nectar. The grotesque little man was a natural-born comic without even knowing it! He continued, '...parsed rrrright thrrrough Crrreppin's berladder afore we even felts its magickins'!' Coughing and spluttering from inhaling too much of the thick smoke that filled the crowded room Creppin stretched his body as far as his crippled bones would allow. He hauled himself up. Both dogs sprang nimbly up onto their hind legs. They tussled to be the first to gain a grip of the hunchback by plonking their great paws on either side of his shoulders. Laughing wildly as he tried to calm the lively beasts, Creppin swayed with them, back and forth in a clumsy dance. Once again, Colm came to his rescue, only to be told that he could cope without any help. The sensitive man left the cavorting trio. He felt pity for Creppin. He knew that the strange character would be devastated when the time came to leave Rockfleet and his new canine companions. Helping himself to another bowlful of delicious pottage, the boatswain looked forward to the voyage ahead.

After everyone had eaten their fill, Grace took Anthony down to check over the vessel that would soon take them on the voyage to São Vicente. The pyrate queen stood tall and gave Anthony a serious look, 'Oy had der lads have her freshly careened, so she's good n'ready fer her langest voyage yet. Noy, ye shalt have some o' moy finest men ter aid yers.' She turned her head away, trying her hardest not to show her feelings. Anthony sensed her sadness and pulled her close. He was surprised to see that she had been crying, 'My beautiful warrior queen. Thou must nay fret 'bout me. I'm a big lad tha knowst!' Grace smiled and Anthony startled her with a firm kiss on the lips. 'Thank 'ee.' he said looking straight into her sea-green eyes. The Queen of Connaught pulled away from his grasp and ran. She ran barefoot, fast and hard against the chilling wind. Her copper tresses danced behind her like waves on the erratic breeze. A dark stallion sensed its mistress's approach and turned on its heel. The magnificent beast began a slow trot as if preparing for a long ride. With a warrior cry, Grace leapt onto the horse's back and grabbed a bunch of coarse mane hair in each hand. Digging her heels into the stallion's sides, she squeezed her strong thighs hard against its responsive body. Grace rode her favourite horse off into the distance. She did not return to Rockfleet until she was sure that Anthony and his crew had left Irish waters. Her feelings for the valiant young man were far stronger than she had realised.

Chapter 9

Remando's Return

Remando was amongst the crew that disembarked from the Portuguese trade ship at Mindelo port in São Vicente. He took in the familiar scenery that he had missed since he and Sushana Culley had left the tranquil island. Thankfully, it was early morning so the harbour offered a calming ambience. The exhausted pyrate was thankful for that blessing at least. A local fisherman spotted the stocky, muscular one-eyed man and waved, shouting a 'welcome home' greeting in his native tongue. Usually full of life and keen to stop for a chat, Remando flicked his hat in polite response and quickened his pace. Due to his flashy style of dress and memorable appearance, Remando was a character who would be difficult to miss. Half Spanish and half Portuguese, he had a dark complexion and spoke both languages fluently. He loved to wear gold jewellery, especially rings which he had mounted with the best quality diamonds that his ill-gotten gains could buy. His normal, self-assured gait was replaced by a clumsy stomp as he felt unusually flustered. The dread of telling Patrick that he had left his mother to face her doom alone troubled him deeply. He had thought of nothing else since he had witnessed the sinking of the Emaleeza. The events that followed the disastrous event were brought to mind.

Amidst the commotion of the onslaught of heavy artillery, Remando had obeyed his captain's strict command to abandon ship. The only reason he chose not to disobey was because Sushana had insisted he took word to her son. Loyal and brave, he would never have deserted the friend who he had known since she was a wee child. Some of his fondest memories were of the days when he had used Culley's Cut to drop off contraband goods. The striking pyrate had always been kind to the inquisitive child who was polite but keen to hear about his perilous adventures at sea. Sushana had been fascinated by his accent so Remando had taken time to teach the intelligent girl some of her first foreign words.

Remando recalled every last detail of the events that followed Sushana's order. He had no other choice than to save himself. As he dived into the cold, unwelcoming sea his conscience had already begun to play havoc with his mind. Remando only just managed to swim away from their doomed ship before she was blasted to smithereens by cannon fire. When he had reached a safe enough distance away from danger, he trod water long enough to witness the burning hulk disappear into the ocean's depths. The Catholic seadog prayed aloud to Our Lady before he continued to swim. Not knowing whether Sushana had been pulled down with her ship, escaped, died or been captured, the fugitive pyrate swam for his life. Luckily, the tide was with him so he was able to make it to a small fishing village. It seemed like hours before he emerged from the sea worn out, shivering and soaked to the skin.

An elderly widow sat alone outside a tiny fisherman's cottage. Surrounded by empty wicker baskets, she had been selling cockles and mussels earlier that day. Unperturbed, the woman observed the stranger as he staggered ashore. Patiently, she continued lacemaking, occasionally looking up from her craftwork to watch

Remando's approach. Knobbly, arthritic fingers skilfully looped and twisted fine silken thread to form pretty floral decorations. The pyrate untied a leather pouch from his belt and walked up the steep cobbled path towards the industrious woman. When he stopped a few yards away, she yelled out, 'Come hither lad! Moy oysoyt's nay as good as it used to be an' dusk's settin' in.' Remando obliged and stepped closer until he was standing right in front of her, at the old woman's feet. His soaking wet clothes dripped onto the cobbled street. Unconcerned by his sodden state, she invited him to sit beside her. He plonked his heavy body down on a rickety stool, hoping that it would not collapse beneath his hefty bulk. He was glad to take the weight off his feet. 'Does't thou know where I can purchase food and fresh clobber, my dears?' The foreigner spoke clearly in almost perfect English apart from his quirky habit of adding an 's' to the odd noun. Despite his unsavoury choice of vocation Remando oozed politeness. The short-sighted woman narrowed her milky eyes to try and see the stranger more clearly. A blurred image was all that she could muster but her imagination was good. She sensed a roguish character with a good spirit, not unlike her late husband.

Finding his unusual accent attractive, the lacemaker began to engage in small talk. She had guessed correctly that the stranger was not as young as she had initially thought. Taking time to introduce herself, she put down her lace and hook to allow him to kiss the back of her gnarled old hand. Giggling like a young girl, she responded to his affectionate greeting, 'I'm Esmeralda. We'd be glad o' some extra coinage to 'elp feed the young'uns.' Remando dropped the heavy purse into the old woman's wicker basket. She smiled gratefully.

The pyrate was well aware that there was a substantial amount of coinage inside. Its contents were, most likely, far more than the old widow could have possibly imagined. Esmeralda continued, 'My son does 'is best to bring in full nets but 'tis ne'er easy in wintertime. We 'as ter preserve what we can and sell some o' the daily catch too. Can be 'ard at times but we manage.' The old woman looked thoughtful. ''Is wife's with child again so's I'm a-makin' some extra collars for 'er ter take ter' sell at market. I does what I can fer me room n' board. I'm thankful t'ave a family oo cares 'bout an ol' codger 'nuff to 'elp 'er out in 'er twilight years.' Stretching her bent back as much as her arthritic bones would allow, she went to stand. Remando offered her his arm and she smiled again and accepted, grasping on tightly to steady herself. The unpleasant sound of dry, creaking bones made her groan as she turned around painfully. 'Come inside, lad. I think I might 'ave just the thing for thee.' Still holding his arm for support, she mounted the steps that led into the tiny cottage. Remando noticed a sign that read 'Cockle Cottage' and wondered whether it had been built by her late husband when the couple were young.

As if she had read his mind, Esmeralda began to tell her visitor her life story. Remando felt relieved to have happened upon such a friendly host. Often judged by his rogue-like appearance, he was well-used to a hostile reception wherever he travelled. His dark, scarred skin, bright expensive attire and foreign tongue made it quite obvious that he was a pyrate. As he followed Esmeralda into Cockle Cottage, he crossed himself and thanked God for His mercy.

The old woman's son and daughter-in-law were also very kind people. They gave the fugitive everything he needed to continue on his journey. They were extremely grateful for the generous sum of money that he had given them. They asked no questions and Esmeralda had been right with her initial speculation. Luckily, Remando was the same build and height as her late husband had been. His clothes fitted almost perfectly. Esmeralda fed her guest well and insisted that he slept in her small bed that night. Her grandchildren were delighted when they learned that their grandmother would be sleeping in their room. The following day, the fisherman sold Remando a horse for a fair price and he felt quite sad to have to leave the hospitable clan. The children had quickly warmed to him as he had always been good with youngsters. The previous night, the whole family had gathered together in front of the fire. Everyone had been captivated by the intriguing stranger's exciting stories of the New World.

As luck would have it, on arrival at Plymouth docks, Remando had managed to sell the horse for a tidy profit. As always, he had a strong craving for ale so he went into the nearest inn to lighten his purse. A pretty serving wench took an immediate shine to him. He tipped her well so she made sure that his blackjack was never empty. When the pyrate could drink no more, he stumbled outside to piss. As he relieved himself, he heard people speaking Portuguese. Staggering towards the group of men, he heard them talking about the unpleasant lumps that had appeared on one of the sailor's cocks. Introducing himself in their language, the drunken pyrate was able to diagnose and suggest a remedy for the unsightly sexually transmitted disease. Grateful for his advice, the captain of the Portuguese trade ship promised him free passage to São Vicente if he would join his crew. As they were sailing to the New World, the Cape Verde island would be an ideal place to restock supplies and carry out any necessary repairs.

Remando shook his head and was brought back to reality as he continued on his way to take news to Patrick. He was even oblivious to the characteristic call of a red-billed tropicbird. Usually, he would be delighted to hear the bird that he nicknamed the bosun bird because its whistle was exactly like a boatswain's. The striking creature swept high above the ocean, occasionally diving to catch a squid. Its two white, streaming tail feathers floated elegantly behind the exotic bird as she took some of her catch back to her hatchlings. She had nested high on a rugged cliff side.

Hurrying along, Remando began to rehearse what he was going to say to Patrick. Disturbing thoughts raced through his mind: How on earth do you tell a lad that you abandoned his mother in her most desperate time of need? Convinced that Patrick would react violently to his news, Remando imagined himself being run through with one of the blades that Shana had given to her son. There was no way that he was going to retaliate so all that he would be able do was defend himself. Patrick was a skilled swordsman so he would have to be quick. Remando was no spring chicken and his reactions were much slower than they used to be. He usually relied on his flintlock pistols that were always loaded and ready to fire... but that would not do in this situation. Wiping sweat from his brow, the distraught pyrate kept his head down. He began a steady jog as the island was gradually waking up. All he wanted to do was to deliver his dead captain's message and then, if he managed to stay alive, he would go straight over to his African friend's home.

He could not wait to buy a barrel or two of his home brewed grog. The ex-slave distilled the strong spirit from sugarcane. As the morning sun crept higher in a speckled peachy sky, Remando felt the soft sand become hotter, burning the soles of his bare feet. He slipped his boots back on and disappeared into the cool shade of the palm trees.

Sushana and John Hawkins had set up their first home together on the tropical paradise island, far away from English shores. They lived in a simple, one storey villa with enough rooms to accommodate their pyrate clan. Patrick shared a room with Moses and Remando came and went as he pleased. Sushana would always keep a few extra rugs and blankets in a spare room in case any of her crew needed to stay overnight. The humble home had soon become a popular place to visit and there was never a shortage of food or alcohol. The captain's absence had left a big void and the place had not felt the same since her sudden departure. Patrick would always rue the day when he had allowed his mother to leave without him. As every day passed with no news, everyone feared that Sushana would never return. John had sent word to his cousin, Francis Drake, but had yet to receive his reply.

Sushana's parrot, Micken, missed her desperately. He thought that she was his mother and pined for her night and day. The wee bird had been off his food for a few days and was not responding to anyone, even Patrick who he usually tolerated in his Mama's absence. The poor little creature had not even wanted to venture out with Flint and Tripod for a while. Patrick was becoming very concerned. Completely devoid of energy, the colourful parrot's head lolled to one side. He kept his delicate eyelids closed as he stood with one leg tucked up into his soft, fluffy white belly feathers. No longer having the strength to stay balanced on one leg without support, the clever creature had wrapped one of his thin, handmade rope toys around his beak. This trick ensured that he would not fall off his branch. No matter how tasty the treat his miniature monkey friend offered him, the grieving bird kept his beak firmly closed. He refused to touch a single morsel. Not a drop of water had passed his bill in days. Patrick and Moses were convinced that Micken would surely die if he never saw Sushana again. Morale was low in the little home and a depressive air had quickly replaced the usual pleasant, welcoming atmosphere.

Moses was out collecting eggs from the henhouse when he spotted Remando walking along the dry dirt path towards him. The pyrate's brightly coloured flamboyant outfit belied the sadness and regret that he felt that day. He coughed when a cloud of dust circled his head as a donkey and cart passed by, full of sweet corn kernels. A happy little African boy shouted a greeting and tossed the picturesque pyrate a ripened kernel. Lifting his hat in thanks, Remando bowed low making the young lad laugh as he bounced on the back of the cart, eating raw sweet corn from the cob. As Remando continued to trudge his way towards the chalet Moses disappeared inside to alert Patrick. Patrick ran out to meet him. Relieved to see his friend, he grabbed him in a tight embrace and they both held onto each other. It was all Remando could do to muster a smile at such a warm welcome. Pulling away, he took Patrick by the shoulders and looked up into his eyes. His voice quivered as he began to explain, 'I was afeared I'd ne'er set eyes 'pon thee again, brother!' He paused, swallowing deeply. 'Tis dreadful news that I brings, my lad.' Patrick was not surprised to hear Remando's words. He waited with baited breath for his friend to confirm his worst nightmare. Remando kept his account to the point, short but sadly not so sweet, 'They captured her.' Patrick felt his stomach turn over as his worst fears were confirmed. Although he tried hard to stifle his tears, Remando sobbed as he delivered the dreadful news. Shana's final message had proved the uncannily close bond that she had shared with her only child. When she was alive, the connection had been so strong that they often sensed each other's pain, even when miles apart. Patrick reassured his loyal family friend that he had been given no other choice but to obey his stubborn captain's command. Remando broke down when he was told not to feel any guilt.

Subconsciously, Patrick touched the Spanish coin that poor Flint had been carrying around under his foreskin for... he dreaded to think how long! For safe-keeping he had carefully threaded the silver cob onto a woven thong that he wore around his neck at all times. When Patrick had first seen the coin he had instantly recognised the shape of Lundy Island that his mother had engraved on its face. She had always encouraged him to draw maps wherever they went and he would mark areas where he had spotted a new species of animal or bird. A minute hole had been drilled in the miniature map of Lundy. Patrick guessed that it marked the spot where his mother had buried something for him.

The moment Patrick had been dreading had arrived. He was devastated and had never felt so alone. His instinct had been right when he had felt his mother's anguish on the day of her execution. Leaving Remando to tell John and Moses the terrible news, the young man ran fast and hard. He was stricken with the agony of grief that wracked his entire body, spirit and soul. The pain was far greater than any physical pain that he had ever endured. He would gladly suffer death rather than feel such despair. All that he could think of was revenge. Charging through the forest, he pushed his body to the limit. Bounding through the undergrowth, he hurdled over any obstruction in his path. When he banged himself against an obstacle, pure adrenalin kept him going, faster and faster, until he reached the top of a high cliff. Patrick shuddered as he stood at the verge of the cliff and looked down at the relentless waves crashing against the rocks. The sea had gradually eaten away a gouge in the rocks that sheltered a tiny beach. Patrick remembered his mother taking him there when they had first settled in São Vicente. They had spent many happy times together on that beach. As far as he knew, no-one else was aware it was there. It was neatly tucked away, well hidden behind two outcrops of stubborn rock that had miraculously withstood all of nature's force. Since his mother's departure the tranquil hideaway had become his favourite retreat. Hell he missed her! Blood seeped from gashes all over his body where he had stumbled into rocks and trees. In his desperate hurry to reach the secluded place where he needed to be alone, he had been unusually careless. As the warm rays of an afternoon sun highlighted the utopian scene below, Patrick's sense of mortality intensified. Usually welcomed, a fresh sea breeze irritated the distraught man.

Patrick spotted a tiny wild flower at his bloodied feet. It had somehow managed to root inside a rock crevice.

Bending to examine its delicate petals, he lost himself in deep thought. The vulnerable bud reminded him of his mother. Despite having to endure a terrible existence, the woman had never given up her fight for survival. As her only child, he owed it to her to carry on in her stead. Taking several steps backwards Patrick took a long, deep breath then made a sudden sprint towards the edge of the towering cliff. He leapt into the air and felt the harsh wind stinging his unprotected wounds. A small group of seals recognised the sound of their friend's diving style as his body broke through the cool frothy surface of the water. Immediately, the excited sociable creatures left the shaded coral reef to join him.

Remando felt alive and optimistic as he viewed the island in a far better light than he had done only a few hours earlier. John and Moses had listened patiently to his story of escape and the witness accounts of Sushana's execution. As expected, they both took it hard but neither blamed him for doing as he had been told. Remando wondered whether Hawkins would return to the Queen's Court to seek revenge or revert back to his old ways. Love could do strange things to people and John had been smitten with the pyrate queen since their very first encounter. Only time would tell whether the admiral's loyalty to Shana's cause would continue after her death. The suspicious pyrate had an inherent mistrust of the well-bred. He guessed that, once again, Hawkins would allow himself to be manipulated by the fickle Queen.

Whistling as he walked, Remando appreciated nature's beauty once again as he observed the enchanting scenery. He could hear the sound of sea birds calling as he glimpsed a beautiful mosaic of laurel trees in a distant forest. The island boasted many magnificent land and seascapes that could be seen from various places and Remando knew where to find the most spectacular of each. Enjoying a newfound peace of mind, the pyrate made his way down a steep ravine and approached a narrow opening in the rock. This would lead him to one of the many underground lava channels. Disappearing out of sight, the one-eyed pyrate took out his tinderbox, grabbed a torch from a bracket on the wall and lit it quickly. A steady breeze blew the flame and it hissed and flickered as Remando wound his way through the labyrinth of tunnels. Each would eventually lead to a cave amongst many that were dotted along the island's seashores. Still shocked but relieved by Patrick's surprisingly amenable reception and reaction to his news, Remando gradually allowed himself to unwind. He felt pleased that he had managed to deliver his dead friend's final wish. Now, he looked forward to drinking a toast to her memory. Wiping a tear from his good eye, Remando stopped to mop his sweat covered brow. He had reached a sharp bend where the passageway narrowed considerably. He squatted to peer under the gaping hole that led to the cave that he was looking for. Crawling on all fours, Remando said a silent prayer of thanks that his belly had not expanded too much to prevent him from wriggling through the small gap. Breathless and thirsty, he emerged on the other side to be met with a fine sight.

The large cave was packed full of treasure, leaving hardly any room for much else. It did not take Remando long to locate the large secure chest that contained well-earned booty that he had stashed away over many years of robbery on the high seas. He lit more torches from the plentiful supply that had been left in a large container.

Placing them in the hoops of metal stands, he gasped at the wondrous plunder that glittered and sparkled before him. Treasure never ceased to impress the materialistic man. Unlike many others who had swung from a noose after a short career, Remando had been lucky. Despite his fortunate knack of avoiding captivity, he had suffered many a near-fatal wound. His body was criss-crossed with thick purple scars from injuries sustained in far too many brutal brawls to remember. Taking a flaming torch, Remando stood still for a few minutes. He felt sad to think that his late friend would never set eyes on their bounty again. Letting out a deep sigh of regret, he tied several jam-packed pouches onto his belt and crawled back into the dark hole.

Chapter 10

Patrick's Legacy Delivered

Anthony and his crew finally sighted the port in São Vicente. It was September and well into the rainy season. The blacksmith and his friends had adapted well to life at sea. Their first decent length voyage had given them ample opportunity to learn the ropes under the instruction of Grace's men. Their galley had weathered well and the crew had bonded quickly. Even Creppin had made himself useful by slaughtering and butchering livestock for food. Shana had managed to avoid too much contact with her Celtic admirer, Danny, so Saul did not have to intervene.

Grace's men could not resist a few raids on the way over so Anthony and the others had their first taste of pyracy. Shana took to it like she had been marauding for years and Anthony felt a rush that he could easily become addicted to. With enough Spanish gold to buy three more galleys, the temporary crew split their prize equally with exception of the captain and quartermaster who received two shares; the master gunner and boatswain took one and a half shares each. The others were more than happy with their helping of loot and looked forward to spending it at the busy port of Mindelo.

After anchoring, Grace's men began to carry out necessary repairs on their ship ready for the return voyage to Ireland. Danny, Colm and Cathal worked with them but had volunteered to stay with Anthony and Patrick. Josh, Shana, Gift and Saul all disembarked and were keen to explore. Shana had decided to dress in men's clothing like her late mother, Abi, had done when she was a pyrate. She looked totally convincing as a young man and even caught the eye of a group of native girls who sat on reed mats gutting fish. The Irish crew were to await Anthony's return before they left for Ireland. Grace had assured him that her men would not leave until they were satisfied that the Englishman had found Patrick Culley. Anthony felt apprehensive as he hugged little Shana and said farewell to the others before he made his way to the plantation where he hoped to find Patrick, John and Moses. Grace had given him a map to make it easier to locate Patrick's home.

The island was like nothing he could have possibly imagined. It was a completely different world to the one that he had left behind. The wildlife was incredible and the young man could not help but stop and study every new creature that he came across. It took him longer than he had expected but he finally recognised Grace's detailed description of Culley land. Farm workers laughed and chatted happily as they tended the crops of sugarcane. Anthony had never seen the crops that were planted, harvested and processed to produce the 'white gold' as his fellow country folk had named the addictively sweet taste of sugar. This popular product was fast becoming the most lucrative oversees commodity and ships docked daily to stock up with the luxury treat. As he walked amongst the tall rows of sugarcane, he noticed that there were native islanders, white settlers and African people amongst the employees. Long, graceful, sword-shaped leaves were teased by a calm breeze to produce a calming, rustling sound. The blacksmith was relieved to see that none of the labourers wore shackles and there was not a single whip-yielding overseer in sight. Everyone looked healthy and content which reassured the foreigner that he was definitely in the right place.

The unique plantation language of Pidgin English had evolved over time. This enabled all nationalities to communicate and understand work requirements during daily plantation life. Some of the workers stopped to wave at the good looking stranger who observed them with interest and admiration. Their toil was backbreaking yet freedom had obviously given them the incentive to work hard for a fair boss. Two pretty, darkskinned young women carrying crude buckets of water walked towards Anthony. They giggled when he tipped his hat politely as he passed them by. The foreigner was sweating profusely, unaccustomed to such oppressive heat. He felt relieved when he saw large spots of rain darken the dry earth. The sudden downpour sent the labourers running for cover. Very soon the dry, dusty ground became flooded with rushing water. Fields that had been full of life only a few minutes earlier were deserted as sheets of persistent heavy rain poured down.

Lightening flashed in darkened, threatening skies above and Anthony made for the building that he could just about make out further along the now muddy track. Filthy streams of water rushed downhill yet, despite such heavy rain, the blacksmith still felt warm. When he reached the small porch, he noticed three rickety wooden chairs. Their white paint had peeled badly in the heat of the sun. A small wall gecko scurried into a crack under the basic roof and the smell of tobacco smoke lingered in the humid air. He knocked loudly at the front door and waited. It looked as if the seats had only recently been abandoned since someone had left a basket of half peeled shrimp next to one of them. No answer. The sky lit up followed by claps of thunder. The storm was right on top of him.

Anthony tried the door of the humble home and found it unlocked. It creaked open on unoiled hinges and the visitor called out loudly, 'Is Patrick Culley home?' Anthony had not expected to hear such a comically high-pitched reply, 'Micken yeeeeeaaaahhhh!' The sound of heavy footsteps could be heard and a young man appeared, his blue eyes wide with astonishment. Both men stood and stared at each other. They were so alike it was uncanny. 'Who art thou?' quizzed Patrick as he held out a hand to greet the stranger. Their handshake was firm. Micken's reaction and his own gut instinct had already told Patrick that the visitor posed no threat. 'Come hither', he beckoned before he had given Anthony the chance to tell him his name. Following his double into a small, basic kitchen, he smiled when he saw a beautiful, brightly-coloured little bird standing on a branch in a makeshift cage. 'Pri'thee, do try to take him...', Patrick said encouragingly, pausing long enough for Anthony to introduce himself. 'Anthony Brown, blacksmith, well... I was a blacksmith', he gave his polite belated introduction. Patrick unlatched the small cage door to allow the mystery guest access. Anthony reached inside with his large hand, two fingers extended. Micken stretched a leg and spread out a bright green wing. He yawned widely and blinked his pretty orange eyes. 'Well I never!' exclaimed Patrick as the parrot stepped onto one of Anthony's fingers. 'I'd 'a ne'er believed this had I nay seen it wi' my own eyes! He's nay e'en opened his eyes since...' Patrick swallowed and turned his head away. Anthony sensed the other man's deep grief. 'I was afeared that I'd ne'er make it o'er ter thee Patrick.' Micken had started rubbing his black feather-capped head vigorously on the rough skin of the blacksmith's hand. The two men laughed as the multi-coloured bird started to whistle loudly. Then he mimicked their laughter.

Patrick gave his visitor a small cup of water to offer the parrot. Without hesitation, he dipped in his beak and drank eagerly. 'Poor critter's been in misery since my mother's departure. He's nay touched a morsel nor drunk a drop since she left,' he explained as he grabbed two empty wooden tankards. He poured Anthony and himself a generous amount of mead and swilled his back straight away. He refilled his tankard and the two men chatted casually about Micken who seemed instantly cured by the stranger's presence. The parrot ate everything that Anthony offered him and was soon settled back inside his cage. At last he appeared to be quite content with his leg tucked up under soft, white belly feathers. He did not stir even when two mischievous monkeys bounded into the room screaming at each other as they fought over a large piece of coconut.

Skidding to an abrupt halt right in front of the birdcage, Flint swiped his son around the back of the head as if their bad behaviour was due to him alone. Pressing his face up close to the bars of the cage, he checked on his miniature companion. Patrick explained how worried everyone had been about his mother's pet black-headed caique. Even the Tupi medicine woman who reared the native breed of parrot had diagnosed severe depression due to bereavement. She feared the worst for Micken. Shaking his head vigorously and beaming an exaggerated smile, the elder Tamarin monkey spontaneously reached up a tiny hand to hold the stranger's. Sensing his father's trust of Patrick's guest, Tripod leapt up onto the tall man's shoulder and began to chunter away like a little old man. Politely, the young monkey offered Anthony a bite of coconut. The guest declined, so he began to nibble away at its sweet, succulent flesh himself. In a brazen show of dominance, Flint sprang up onto the blacksmith's arm and grabbed the shell to take his share. Another loud clap of thunder made the comical pair jump. Micken yelped in fear and began to tremble on his perch. Anthony comforted the animals with soothing words and stroked the top of Flint and Tripod's heads. The gentle man poked a finger through the cage bars to rub the soft bright yellow and coral-coloured feathers of the parrot's neck. Patrick was amazed how the animals had bonded with the unfamiliar man, especially Flint and Tripod since they were usually very wary of strangers.

The blacksmith had made such a positive initial impression that both men had become side-tracked. Patrick swigged back more mead and became curious, 'What brings thee here?' Heavy rain still pelted down onto the roof so Anthony had to answer loudly, 'I have important news fer thee'. He left it at that, feeling that the time was not yet right for him to elaborate. Patrick did not press him further for information. He felt comfortable with this new company and trusted that the man had good reason to withhold information until a more appropriate time. Helping himself to another mugful of mead, he invited his guest into the main living room. John Hawkins and Moses were sitting at a table engrossed in a card game. John puffed away on an elaborately carved ivory and walnut pipe. The blacksmith noticed that the ominous looking pyrate sitting opposite the serious man had an artificial arm. Moses had only recently commissioned a local craftsman to make a basic prosthesis for him. The wooden limb had a cruel-looking three-pronged hook attached to the end. Moses was using it well. He had wedged a neat fan of cards between the sharp metal claws. Anthony knew that he could make a better job of the hook and began to think about designing a gripping claw similar to that of a crab's. Neither man looked up from their game as they were well-used to visitors who often dropped by.

The sound of rain striking the thin roof almost drowned out the voice that called from outside. A clap of thunder accompanied an almighty crash that came from the kitchen. Remando appeared, swaying in the doorway. The pyrate stood there for a couple of minutes with a large, soppy grin spread over his face. He looked ridiculous in his floppy, wet hat that had collapsed during the storm. A limp, wet feather had stuck to the side of his face. The drunkard began to chat away to no-one in particular. He was slurring so badly that his words were difficult to decipher. Everyone knew that he was inebriated after drinking too much cachaça.

The old seadog had paid a visit to an islander who produced the finest, most potent alcoholic drink in the area. Cachaça or 'aguardente', roughly translated, 'burning water', as the African slaves who had originally produced the spirit liked to call it, was one of Remando's many weaknesses. Since their masters had forbidden slaves from drinking any alcohol, they had begun producing their own potent brew in secret. It was concocted from fermented sugarcane syrup, the process similar to the one their Irish counterparts used to produce poitín. Remando fell over a stool, stumbling into Micken's cage, as he tried and failed to locate his room. Almost falling off his perch, Micken just about managed to tighten his grip but squawked his severe disapproval. Irritated by Remando's behaviour, John's frowning red face peered over his playing cards to express utter contempt. Despite his obvious disapproval, he did not move a muscle until he had decided which card to discard. Refusing to rush his hand he took another card from the pile. Then he spoke loud and clear but did not turn to look at the man he addressed, 'God's nails! Get thee to bed, thou heavy-headed rudesby!'

Remando stepped closer and stood wavering before the two seated men. He bent forward and held up an unsteady hand. Pointing a finger and waving it around in front of John's face, he struggled to focus not even recognising his complainant. Before he had the chance to say a word in his own defence, Moses stood up and drew a machete from his belt. The peace-keeping warrior had sensed serious trouble brewing. Since hearing news of his lover's death John had not been himself. The last thing that Moses wanted was bloodshed amongst allies. With a menacing expression on his badly scarred face, the intimidating pyrate pressed his weapon against Remando's throat. He could only hope that the harmless fool would understand his actions as a silent warning to back off. Flint squealed with sheer panic and grabbed his son by a skinny arm. Swiftly, he leapt out of the room with his infant in tow. The adult monkey harboured an intense fear of conflict. Whenever he sensed danger the wise animal had learned to head for cover as quickly as possible. Luckily Patrick intervened just in time grabbing his drunken friend by the arm. With a quick jerk of the head, he signalled for Anthony to help him take Remando to out of harm's way.

As the two men manhandled the intoxicated pyrate his face turned ashen and, without warning, he spewed a large arc of foul-smelling vomit over the floor. When some puke splashed onto his clothes, John saw red. In a flash, he leapt up and punched Remando square in the jaw, knocking his head backwards at a nasty angle. Instantly losing consciousness, the victim's body slumped down clumsily. 'John! Thou hadst nay need ter strike him!' This was the first time ever that Patrick had challenged the ill-tempered man. He had tolerated his mother's partner whilst she had been alive solely out of respect for her. Now it was time for confrontation as he had decided that he was not going to put up with the conceited oaf's arrogant behaviour anymore.

John Hawkins had been in love with the pyrate queen but Patrick had always been suspicious of his motives. The wealthy admiral, who had long been one of Queen Elizabeth's favourites, had been mesmerised by his mother's beauty, bravery and guile. He had quickly become infatuated with her and longed to be part of her adventurous, exciting and perilous life. Patrick always felt that John had wanted to possess his mother as if she was a trophy. Despite many impressive characteristics that Shana Culley had displayed as the most wanted pyrate in the world, on the inside she was still an extremely vulnerable woman. The standoff between the two men lasted a good few minutes, neither of them wanting to back down. Moses had his flintlock pistol at the ready but Patrick waved a hand for him to disarm. He had decided to defuse the situation. He wanted John Hawkins alive. Whatever he thought of the man, there was one thing for certain; John had come to resent the English Queen almost as much as he did.

Patrick expected the Naval Commander to return to the Queen's Court in the next week or so. Since Remando had brought news of Shana's death John had become withdrawn. His mood swings were even more erratic than usual. The drunken pyrate's arrival had been the straw that broke the camel's back and had prompted the admiral to revert to his old bullying ways. Scarlet faced and unable to express well-buried grief, John unclenched his bloodied fist and sat back down. It had been ingrained in him since he was a boy that men should never cry. He could not resist adding a hefty hint of sarcasm to his stern tone, 'Pri'thee, do tell. Who do we have here in our humble abode?' Anthony glanced at Patrick, silently questioning whether a response would be a good idea. Patrick shook his head slowly and gestured with his hand to Anthony to help him guide Remando into his bed chamber. No-one responded to John's question. Surprisingly, he let it go.

Remando's loud snores were a sure sign that he would be fine after the assault so he was left to sleep off the effects of the alcohol. Patrick gave Anthony some clean, dry clothes. He offered his doppelganger another drink before he left him alone to change. When he emerged from the bedchamber, Patrick was pleased to see how well the clothes fitted. Grace had been right; the two young men could have been twins. The downpour of rain stopped as suddenly as it had started and they walked out onto the porch. A light vapour rose from the damp ground. Patrick invited Anthony on a private tour of the plantation.

The strangers chatted casually as they approached some single-storey structures in the process of being built. Men mixed clay, vegetable fibres, oxblood, dung and horsehair to make 'taipa de pilão', the local term for 'rammed earth'. A simple wooden framework had been constructed and the men were filling in the wall cavities with the mixture. It was then patted down firmly to make it compact. Patrick explained how this process ensured that the finished walls would be strong. The taipa de pilão would be left for a couple of days to dry naturally, then another layer added. In the meantime, it was the women's task to make the roof tiles. These were made by moulding red clay on their upper thighs. This primitive but perfectly effective method gave the tiles a slightly curved shape. Once they had been laid on the roof, both interior and exterior walls could be whitewashed. Traditionally, doors and woodwork were painted with pastel colours. Patrick wanted the plantation labourers to have welcoming homes to go back to at the end of a hard day's labour. He explained that all original slave shacks had been burnt to the ground soon after his mother had given the African slaves their freedom. As far as she was concerned, they were not even fit for animals to inhabit. Shana Culley had promised everyone who chose to stay and work for her that they would never be maltreated again.

A hazy sun emerged from departing clouds and Anthony was surprised to notice how quickly everything dried after such a heavy storm. He walked beside Patrick along the earthen track and was surprised to see that the sugarcane field had been set on fire. The blacksmith learned that the fire would only burn the dry leaves and repel any poisonous snakes that could be lurking amongst the sugarcane stalks. Apparently, the flames would leave all stalks and roots unharmed and the field snake-free ready to be harvested. Patrick covered his mouth and nose with a damp cloth and passed one to his guest as they continued the tour. When they were clear of the smoke, the knowledgeable man continued to describe the whole sugar-making process. After the labourers had used machetes to hack down the long, leafless cane the women would tie them into bundles to be carried away. The cane would be crushed in a wooden press during the sap extraction process. Water and lime juice would then be added and the mixture taken to be boiled. This process was particularly dangerous and many plantation owners still forced their slaves to work in horrendous conditions.

Countless slaves had died as a result of severe burns when they had been forced to work too many hours using poor equipment. The thin clothes that they were made to wear offered no protection from the scalding liquid. Patrick ensured that teams working in the boiling huts on Culley land were rotated regularly, dressed appropriately and paid the highest wage. When the blacksmith visited the boiling huts he felt right at home with the furnaces and relentless, sweltering heat. Patrick was impressed to learn that Anthony had such valuable skills. Not being able to resist lending a hand, the metalworker stoked the fire and removed unwanted ashes. The furnace was a crude rectangular box that had been made from cut stone similar to that of his father's back home. An opening at its base allowed access to stoke the fire. Above the furnace were several copper tanks that reduced in size so became hotter the nearer they were to the blazing furnace. Cane juice was poured into the largest kettle to be heated. Lime juice was then added to remove any impurities. As the fluid passed through each kettle it became more and more refined until it reached the smallest. By this time it had turned into thick, dark-brown syrup known as molasses. A fair amount of this liquid sugar was drawn off for distillation to produce cachaça. Unbeknown to Remando, Patrick and a couple of African workers had set up a distillery and had already produced three successful batches of the potent spirit. The remainder of the syrup was poured into a cooling trough and crystals of raw sugar would soon form. These were transferred into hogsheads to be sold or stored.

The two strangers learned a lot about each other that day. They walked for hours and Patrick showed his new friend some of his favourite haunts. Anthony enjoyed a visit to the local market where traders insisted that he sampled everything they had for sale. The polite stranger was persuaded to try all kinds of seafood and even dry-cured turtle meat before he managed to move on. He and Patrick left with a whole basketful of tasty morsels that they took to the beach to eat. When they sat on the rocks to share the meal Anthony began his story. His pyrate host sat in silence, listening intently to every detail as the blacksmith explained why he had left his whole life behind to seek out a complete stranger. Finally, Patrick had the missing pieces to complete the puzzle of events that had occurred since his mother's departure. He sat still and silent for a while before he said anything. 'Swim with me.' It was hardly an invitation but more of a demand. Anthony complied and stripped off his linen shirt. They left their valuables hidden in a secure place and raced into tepid waters.

Patrick was a strong swimmer but his new friend managed to keep up with him as they dipped and dived through a natural underwater maze. Brightly-coloured fish cast dappled shadows onto pristine coral reefs as they swam together in synchronised shoals. Streams of light shone down from a lazy afternoon sun, catching their tiny luminescent scales. The blacksmith had never experienced anything like it before. He marvelled at the wonders and treasures of the spectacular ocean bed. Returning to the surface to take a deep breath, Anthony noticed several grey fins approaching. Patrick's head bobbed up beside him, 'Follow me', he said and re-submerged.

A friendly pod of dolphins welcomed the swimmers. They were inquisitive about Patrick's new friend and nudged Anthony gently with their smooth noses. Patrick's marine companions took the swimmers on an underwater tour of their territory. Leading the men through narrow tunnels and crevices of solidified lava, they showed them where to resurface for air in small coves and larger caves. Occasionally, a curious creature would venture out of its hiding place then disappear in a flash, back into one of many cracks and crevices. Anthony was amazed at the amount of wildlife that he had been introduced to since his arrival on this marvellous isle. Bands of sunlight danced on the backs of the playful dolphins as smooth waves rolled gently above. The beautiful, affectionate creatures swam in zigzags with their human playmates then rose briefly, just long enough to fill their lungs with fresh sea air before diving back down into the depths. Keen for adventure, they tossed seaweed to one another and played chase, gliding quickly through the underwater labyrinth. Fins brushed bodies and hands held fins as the pod swam in unison with Anthony and Patrick. Two dolphins swam belly to belly for a while before rising to the surface. The men followed suit and laughed at the mischievous mammals as they teased them by slapping their tails on the water's surface.

This was an unusually care-free time for Patrick. Whilst amongst these therapeutic, loving marine creatures, he was able to forget his troubles... for the time being at least. A vermilion sun teetered above the horizon, its reflection adding a slightly darker, agitated hue to the blue waters. Nudging their friends to signal farewell before returning to the depths, the dolphins had given Anthony a wonderful memory that would stay with him until his dying day. The men swam back to the beach where Patrick lit a fire. They sat a while to reflect over the day's events. It had been a long time since either of them had managed to relax. Having only met a few hours earlier, they shared a rare mutual trust. Both fatalists, they knew that wherever their destinies were to take them, they would always remain firm friends.

Anthony decided it was the right time to give Patrick his mother's gold and ruby necklace. He soon learned that the precious piece of jewellery had been John Hawkins' gift to Sushana on the day of their hand fasting ceremony. As John was still married to a wealthy woman back in England, the lovers had made a commitment to one another in a traditional Celtic pagan ceremony. After jumping over a broom, they had promised to be with each other for a year and a day. Their hands were bound together with a silken scarf. It would be up to them whether they would recommit or part ways after their allotted time had passed. As fate had decreed, they would not have the chance to make that choice now that Shana was gone.

Although Patrick had already heard word of his mother's death he was grateful to hear Anthony's eye-witness account. He was delighted that the blacksmith had visited Grace O'Malley who had sent word that she was preparing for an attack on England. He was sure that the Irishwomen knew that he would crave vengeance. Patrick felt reassured that she had already begun to set the wheels in motion. He would not rest until the Queen of England had been murdered and had already begun to plan her assassination. Impressed by Anthony's initially blind commitment, Patrick decided to take him back to meet the others. News from Ireland had to be relayed to Hawkins, who he hoped would want a hand in betraying the self-absorbed, bitter Queen.

Back at the plantation, Remando had sobered up and was eating fresh mango out on the porch. John was brooding inside so Patrick took the opportunity to tell him and Moses Anthony's news. They all agreed that something had to be done about Queen Elizabeth. John had been pondering over the best time to leave the island and return to England. He vowed that he would do all that he could to help avenge his lover's execution. Patrick had to ask, 'On what day dost thou plan to leave?' By absolute coincidence, a messenger had brought word from John's cousin, Francis Drake, that very afternoon. His news was grave and short and he wrote of the Queen's ever-growing paranoia. John turned to look at Patrick, 'We shall take advantage of this time whilst the venomous whore is absorbed in her own melancholy. I shall return to court anon as she is most vulnerable during these times.' Moses gave a sign to show his allegiance to Patrick and he and Remando agreed to take the blacksmith back to the port to fetch the others. Micken screeched in protest as Anthony walked past his cage. Moses took the parrot out and he flew over to settle on his new friend's shoulder. 'Looks as though thou hast formed a permanent bond.' Patrick shouted as Anthony and the others walked out of the door. 'A wager that thou shalt be covered in bird shite by tha return!' they heard John add just as the wee parrot bent forward, wriggled his tail feathers to expel a splat onto Anthony's white shirt. 'Hmmmm, thankye kindly, master Micken!' he said and everyone was pleased to hear the parrot's high-pitched voice repeat his name.

Anthony was amused to see that Creppin had taken up a permanent position on deck eagerly awaiting his return. When he sighted the three men approaching the ship, he shouted loudly, waving his long arms above him. Shana surprised the blacksmith with a hug. She was excited and eager to tell him all about her new discoveries since she had ventured into Mindelo. Remando instantly recognised her as Abi's daughter and began to weep. The young woman felt rather awkward in the emotional stranger's presence and instantly put up her guard. The pyrate and her late mother, Abi, had been lovers during the last few months before her death. No matter how much alcohol the broken man consumed, he could never banish the terrible memory of her fragile, mutilated body. He had been unable to go anywhere near the beach where her corpse had been found.

Abi's daughter reminded Remando so much of his beautiful soul mate. The pyrate embraced her warmly, 'We finally meets my dear Shanny. Thy mother spoke well of thee.' Despite her initial feelings of discomfort with the stranger's over-familiarity, she allowed him a long hug. When Remando released his grip she looked up at him thoughtfully. 'I may keep the name Shanny, it pleases me well,' the young woman told him and she did exactly that. From that day onward, she became known as Shanny. Anthony introduced the rest of the crew to Moses and Remando who were glad to see some of Grace's men amongst them. After they had said their farewells to the crew who were sailing back to Ireland, Patrick's band of followers returned to the plantation. Micken took an instant shine to Shanny and hopped onto her shoulder.

Creppin scurried nervously behind the gang, mumbling away to himself. He loathed being in another new place and was ready for the worst to happen. He had made sure that he was well armed with his cudgel and knives. When they reached Patrick's home, everyone was given a place to sleep and to store their belongings. Patrick was impressed with the blacksmith for gathering a small band of supporters but not very keen that the hunchback had been brought along. He viewed the crippled man as a burden and seriously doubted that he could be of any use to anyone. Laying his concerns to one side for future debate with his new ally, he was pleased to be re-united with some of his Irish friends. They soon updated him on news from the Emerald Isle. Patrick could not wait to return and trusted Grace to prepare what she could until his arrival which he hoped would not be long.

Anthony lay on a hammock listening to night sounds that he was unaccustomed to. The Irish lads' snores were keeping him awake but he was not too concerned. His mind raced with excitement as he was now sure that he had done the right thing. Already, he felt like he belonged to a group who had the opportunity to change history.

He brought to mind his father and simple life back in England and was lost in thought until he felt a sharp jab in the ribs. Rolling his eyes, he wondered who would be able to convince Creppin to have his fingernails and toenails trimmed, as they were getting very long and sharp again. 'Maaarster, Crrreppin needs ter take a shite.' Anthony sighed deeply and felt another prod from the nuisance beneath him, 'Maaarrrster! Wherefore shalt I shite?' he asked. Anthony gave a snappy reply, 'Zounds! Enough o' thy proddin' feller! Follow me.' Dropping down from his hammock, Anthony stretched and stepped over the sleeping bodies until he reached the door. The hunchback managed to stomp on Danny's fingers and took a swift punch to the back of his calf before regaining his balance. Groaning loudly, he stumbled out of the crowded room.

'Methinks 'tis me nerves playin' havoc wi' me bowels, marrrster.' Creppin whined before letting out several short farts as he managed to pull down his undergarments just in time to defecate. Moses was sitting out on the porch where he often slept overnight in a hammock. Even the slightest unfamiliar sound would wake the worldly pyrate so he always took the night watch. When he had heard Creppin's urgent pleas he had found it amusing. Scowling at the man who still squatted barely an arm's length in front of him, he stood up in mock anger. The mute mimed the action of digging a hole. Anthony snorted as he tried not to laugh, knowing full well that the pyrate was teasing the hunchback. Flickering flames highlighted the raised criss-cross scars on the tall man's lips which made his appearance even more sinister than usual. With eyebrows raised higher than ever, a fretful Creppin cowered before the stern-looking pyrate who loomed above him. Quickly pulling up his braes but not lingering long enough to tie them, the hunchback made it onto the porch in a single leap. Whimpering, he hurried back through the door. He had been wary of the dark man with no tongue since he first saw him, believing that he was some kind of demon. 'Crrreppin shalt surely avoid yon devil's spawn!' he mumbled to himself as he trod on Saul's leg and stumbled onto the floor. Fortunately, he landed right on his sleeping spot. Covering his eyes with grubby hands, he tucked his swollen knees up into his chest and tried to calm himself so he could fall asleep.

Moses smiled at Anthony who winked before he went after the terrified hunchback. The tall, dark pyrate took a long swig from a bottle of spiced rhum. He chuckled silently in the knowledge that he would have a lot of fun teasing the strange white man with a twisted form and disgusting odour. He breathed out a long sigh and wiped his scarred lips with the back of his hand. Moses was deep in thought. The time had come for Patrick to continue his mother's fight against a powerful empire. It was not going to be an easy feat but he knew for definite that Patrick was ready. He was sure about something else too... with Grace O'Malley involved, Patrick Culley would have the backing of the largest pyrate militia in history.

CHAPTER 11

A Son's Deep Grief

One of Irish's finely detailed drawings of Sushana Culley hung on the wall of the small, simply furnished home. The words that he had written with his quill beneath her likeness read, 'Dum spiro spero' their translation, 'As long as I breathe I hope'. The previous year, Shana and John Hawkins had decided to set up home in a small village near the Tupinambá tribal land. The couple had taken over two coconut, two sugarcane and three corn plantations shortly after their arrival. The land had once been owned by a merciless lout who used African slaves for free labour. On Sushana's first visit to his neighbouring homestead, she had witnessed atrocious things. Appalled by the emaciated state of the slaves working the land, the freedom fighter had already decided that she would not be walking away without their master feeling her wrath. She had been appalled to see pregnant women working the fields doing the same manual hard labour as their male counterparts. It was plain to see that one of the women was almost full term. Her large, swollen belly strained against the cheap cotton material of her flimsy dress as she struggled with a heavy scythe. Two children carrying water into the field dared to look over at the visitor. Their screams urged Shana to quicken her pace, as she counted the lashes that the overseer dealt to the inquisitive young boy and girl. Neither of them could have been more than eight years old! Livid at the African man's actions against his own people, Shana called out for him to stop the lashing. He did not even turn to see where the voice had come from. By the time she had reached them they had already suffered more brutality than infants should ever have to bear. They cowered on the ground, their small backs lacerated with deep wounds from the bullwhip.

With a bloodcurdling scream, the pyrate queen leapt high, kicking her leg out with such force that the crunch of smashed vertebrae could be heard as her foot hit the brute's spine. He yelled, spinning around to face his attacker who had pulled a boarding axe from her belt. Red-faced with sheer rage, Sushana shrieked a war cry as she swung the weapon at his face, burying the blade into his cheekbone. The coward bellowed as he took the heavy blow that knocked him sideways onto the ground. Sushana stamped her foot into his chest and yanked out her axe leaving a bloody hole in his face. Not satisfied that the snivelling bully had suffered enough pain for striking mere babes, she stood astride her victim. Bending her knees, she jumped up as high as possible and landed back on the shocked man's ribcage. One of the children who he had punished hurled a spray of vomit as he watched the unexpected attack. Sushana felt such satisfaction when she felt her victim's ribs crack under her weight and pierce his lungs with sharp broken bone. A familiar rasping, gurgling sound escaped his throat as his eyes grew wide in terror. The brutal swine grabbed his neck as he struggled to breathe. Sushana bounced again, only lighter this time until frothy, bright red blood began to seep from his mouth. She spat down on his face and grabbed her gutting knife. With a satisfied smile, the vengeful pyrate queen looked into the man's eyes and took great pleasure as she hacked her trophies from his loins. Shoving his severed testicles into her belt pouch, she left him alone between the cornrows with a hole where his manhood had once been. At last, the lazy, sadistic overseer had the potential to be of some use to the land. Fresh blood from his gaping wound seeped slowly into the earth to help feed the new crop.

With her hands still covered in blood, Sushana ran as fast as she could to the plantation owner's house. There, her worst fears were confirmed when she found him sodomising a beautiful young African girl. She pulled the sweating beast off his victim and pressed the barrel of her flintlock pistol into the base of his spine. Before she squeezed the trigger, she pulled the naked child close to her. Calmly reassuring the traumatised girl that, from that day onwards she would be alright, the captain fired. The sound of the shot was muffled slightly but the damage would lead to fatality… eventually. Splinters of vertebrae and chunks of flesh and sinew splattered against the walls and all over the two women. They stood together, both staring down into the terrified eyes of the helpless rapist. He was unable to move as the damage from the single shot had caused paralysis from the neck down. 'May thee rot in the depths of hell!' Shana growled venomously as she kicked the dying man hard on the bridge of his nose in absolute disgust. As the tyrant lay dying, he even had the nerve to beg his killer to deliver a final shot to his brain. When she would not oblige, the despicable creature screamed a final command to his female slave to put him out of misery!

The cold expression on Shana's face revealed her disgust and contempt for the revolting rapist as she untied a large silk scarf from her waist. Stroking the newly liberated woman's face, she wrapped it around her shoulders. The woman knew full well that it would take years for the brute's victim to get over the harrowing incident. That was IF she ever managed to come to terms with it at all. Sushana realised all too well the physical and mental pain and degradation that continual sexual abuse had caused her. Swallowing back the tears, she understood exactly how filthy and worthless the poor wretch felt at that moment. Cradling the smaller woman's face close to her heart, Sushana led her away from the crime scene. When the plantation owner's religious wife saw the state of the poor slave, she broke down in tears. Apparently, she too had endured years of her husband's abuse and violence and was thankful that he had finally been punished for his many sins.

Having offered freedom to the slaves on the plantation together with a decent amount of money to help them start a new life, Sushana Culley had laid claim to the dead man's land. She moved in immediately with her clan and extended family who all pulled together to improve the neglected home. Some of the African people chose to stay and work as free men and women. John Hawkins and Sushana had always ensured that they were all paid fairly and treated well. Even the deceased owner's wife and children were happy about the new ownership. They asked to stay until they felt ready to return to their homeland. Some of the Tupi tribe helped manage the plantation whilst the new owners were away on raids and voyages. Sushana and John had plans to expand the plantation and develop others to provide decently paid work for liberated slaves who wanted to build a new life. The pyrate queen had been very happy to empower the native people. She soon encouraged the

Tupi tribe to learn the process of sugar extraction. A mill was built and they were soon exporting the valuable commodity to Europe. Sushana gained much pleasure when she learnt that some of the sugar produced from cane grown on her plantation had become Queen Elizabeth's favourite indulgence and had also caused her teeth to rot!

Following a good night's sleep, Remando rose early and took Shanny, Saul, Gift and Josh to visit the college that Sushana and John had founded. As the only natural port of São Vicente, Port Grande had been an ideal place to build their language college. The first year of the project to educate local tribal people teaching them English and simple maths had been very successful. Alberto College encouraged and empowered its students, giving them an opportunity to begin new ventures in their community and beyond. Shanny's mother, Abi, had been passionate about the project and had taught there for a good while before her unfortunate death. Having gained an excellent reputation, wealthy merchants gave regular substantial donations towards the running of the successful establishment. It was an emotional day for Shanny. She had finally been given the opportunity to visit the place where her late mother had worked. Abi had helped set up and run the college and Shanny was impressed by the whole scheme. Something told her that she would someday return and offer her services. Two of the original students who Abi had taught had taken over the teaching. More than fifty pupils were now in attendance. They planned to expand the venture over the next few years by using donations to build more classrooms.

Throughout the day, Remando and Shanny became better acquainted. The young woman began to warm to the attentive pyrate. She was beginning to understand why her adventurous mother had fallen in love with the intriguing character. Remando felt so proud being with the intelligent woman whose mother had made a huge impact on him during such a short time. Shanny was totally oblivious to the fact that he had already decided to take on the role of her protector. Before Remando had met the woman who he had never dreamed would come into his life, he had been on a mission of self-destruction. Not caring whether he lived or died, he had been drinking as much alcohol as he could keep down to mask his deep grief. That day, Remando made a silent vow that he would take his new responsibility seriously and protect his precious Shanny with his life. He had failed to save her mother and believed that God had given him another chance to make amends. Smiling to himself as he listened to his guests repeat the Tupi words to the students' delight, Remando felt like a new man. He had not touched a drop of alcohol that day and felt more alive than he had in a long time.

Earlier that morning when Moses had seen his good friend sitting eating a hearty breakfast with the newcomers, he had felt pleased for him. Before he had lost his lover, Remando had been known as the craziest, most care-free member of the crew. Always dressed to impress, he was the man who everyone wanted to be around during bad times. No matter how hopeless a situation became, Remando could raise the lowest of spirits. Despite his villainous trade, he had maintained his staunch Catholic faith and carried his rosary beads everywhere. He always wore a chunky, elaborate gold crucifix around his thick neck. During a crisis Remando would have a biblical quote at the ready to help boost morale and give hope. He would deliver God's word with such finesse that even the most hardened atheist had been known to take a moment to stop and reflect. Even when dressed to the hilt in his flamboyant pyrate attire, his infectious smile would surely melt the heart of an angel.

Even though he was unable to speak, Moses always managed to gain respect from others. Despite his foreboding appearance, he could be gentle and was always fair amongst his pyrate brethren. He and Patrick had mastered the art of signing with their hands. When their hands were occupied, they even used facial expressions to communicate. Patrick had asked his guardian to take the rest of the group to visit the Tupi tribe so Anthony, Danny, Colm and Cathal were all eager to find out more about the island's native people. Creppin was not so keen. In fact, it had taken Anthony a while to find him after breakfast. After a quick search, Moses followed his nose and found the hunchback behind one of the new building sites, standing with a spade in one hand, his other scratching his sore backside. The poor creature had been suffering from severe diarrhoea since arriving in São Vicente and was becoming very concerned. Taking pity on him, Moses nodded his approval of the little mound of earth that Creppin stood next to. He reached into a pouch on his belt and took out a small vial of clear liquid. Taking a small sip of the medicine to reassure the simpleton that it was safe to drink, Moses passed it to him. The hunchback's stomach growled and burbled as if grateful for a potential remedy and he bowed low before Moses. 'Thanking ye kindly, Mosiah', the hunchback responded. Lifting his hand to indicate that it was no big thing, the pyrate watched

Creppin swig back the Tupi medicine woman's remedy before signalling that it was time for them to leave.

A seemingly ceaseless downpour of rain began as Moses led his group on a challenging trek that took them along an undulating cliff ridge path until they reached a spectacular waterfall. Passing through the noisy rushing water Moses showed them dens and hideaways that they would never have guessed existed. Creppin was relieved that his stomach had calmed down so he was grateful to the Moorish pyrate. He had begun to feel a little more at ease with Moses but was still wary. Filling their water bottles with fresh mountain spring water whenever possible, the men continued on through forests as the relentless rain poured down. Moses pushed on until the rain ceased just as they reached the swollen, muddy banks of a rapid river. Here, they stopped to eat some fruit that their guide had brought along for the demanding journey. As soon as everyone had relieved themselves, he urged them on.

Pockets of mist hovered above the rushing waters and the trekkers were thankful for a refreshingly cool wind. Still unused to the humid tropical climate, the foreigners felt uncomfortable in the oppressive heat. Moses was well-used to it and had never been bothered by the drones of blood-sucking insects that pestered the poor Irish lads. He pointed out a grey-headed kingfisher that was taking advantage of the sweet-smelling human bait that had ventured into its territory. Sitting on a branch, the colourful bird had managed to catch several insects, their limbs sticking out of its bright red beak. Anthony had been bitten a few times but every inch of Danny, Colm and Cathal's exposed skin was covered with raised pink bumps. You could not put a pinprick between each one. Their blotched faces had swollen so badly in reaction to the insect bites that they were finding it difficult to see. Moses showed little concern as he knew that the Tupi medicine woman would apply salves to reduce the swelling. He would have to get Patrick to mix them some essential oils to wear to deter the pests in the future. Creppin struggled along behind the group but did not slow them down. Predictably, not a single insect was brave enough to pierce his tough, grimy skin. Anthony piped up, 'Any insect mad nuff t'even attempt to pierce Creppin's skin'd have a crooked proboscis ferrr its trrrouble!' Everyone laughed except for the confused hunchback, 'Whyfore crrrooked Bob's kiss marrrster?' The poor man hobbled alongside the blacksmith trying his hardest to understand his joke but only managed to make everyone laugh more in his efforts!

Glad to feel the gentle breeze grow stronger as the riverbed widened, Moses' party left its banks to enter a forest. There was a magical ambience amongst the cool shade of the leafy canopy. As the hiss of rushing water diminished, the tranquil sound of birdsong could be heard. Moses pointed out a family of green vervet monkeys sitting in a tree quietly observing their approach. They chattered away unconcerned, their young springing playfully from branch to branch, chasing each other's tails. Anthony and Creppin fell back for a while to watch the attractive primates who were just as interested in them. Having unusual green tinged golden-brown fur on their backs and white fur on their bellies, brows and cheeks, their faces, hands and feet had contrasting black skin. The hunchback found it hilarious when he noticed that the male monkeys had blue testicles and bright red penises. The animals appeared to be offended by the hideous human's ridicule. In a mocking retort they screamed a piercingly loud mimic of his mirth. Quickly moving on, Creppin suddenly felt an unnerving sensation. He warned his companion to stay alert. Crouching in the undergrowth, the two men waited in silence, weapons at the ready. Anthony spied a small lake ahead of them. Surrounded by swaying palm trees and crowded with tamarisks it was a pleasant sight to behold. A colourful lizard eyed the intruders as it scurried by.

A small dog came bounding through the tangled undergrowth towards Creppin. Wagging its white-tipped tail frantically as if welcoming a long-lost master, the tribal hound sprang up into the air and landed straight on the hunchback's knees. Losing his balance, Creppin tumbled backwards onto spongy moss. The dog whimpered with excitement and licked the ugly man all over his face. Appalling singing could be heard, 'Hark hark de daaags do bark; de beggars are coming to town. Some in rags and some in jags and one in a velvet gown!' Danny emerged from behind a bush. 'Fie! We thought thee were foes!' Anthony chastised the cheeky-faced Irishman who seemed in far better spirits than he had been not so long ago. 'What's smothered all over tha' chops?' the blacksmith asked sarcastically, knowing full well that it was balm to calm his irritated skin. The dog responded to a high-pitched whistle and raced off into the forest. 'Hark at this', the Irishman winked and beckoned the men to go closer, 'S'truth, ye shallnay believe dese wee folks! De kiddies are chewin' on dead men's fingers an' toes!' Anthony did not know whether to take Danny seriously. A slight breeze carried a delicious scent of herbs and Creppin sat bolt upright, his nose twitching like a hungry animal. 'Ooooo! What kinds o' fingies n' toesies?'

he asked. Anthony looked at his companion quizzically, not quite believing that he had heard the simpleton correctly. Recognising his master's disapproval, the hunchback stood up and started to shuffle his large feet uncomfortably. 'Come, Creppin. Let us join t'others and find out fer ourselves.' The flapping of large wings caught Creppin's attention. He pointed towards the water and spoke softly, 'Look o'er yonder. 'Aint ne'er seen a purple birdie afore.' It took Anthony a couple of minutes before he spotted the elegant, long-necked heron standing motionless at the shallow water's edge. Its purplish-brown plumage provided excellent camouflage against the reeds. The solitary hunter stood in wait. Then its long, white, snakelike neck formed an S. As quick as a flash, the patient predator shot out its powerful neck and snapped up a lizard in its slim, yellow bill. Swallowing the fish whole, head-first it waded a little further then let out a loud 'kar-kar-kar' before taking off.

Danny was completely oblivious to the magnificent bird's presence and would have shown no interest even if he had seen it. The Irish pyrate was very much a man's man who enjoyed drinking alcohol, fighting, women and more women. Fiercely patriotic, he lived to fight for freedom for his country. He despised the English but made an exception where Patrick and his friends were concerned. They were loyal to Grace so that was all he needed to know. Keen to return to the Tupi village that was only a stone's throw away, Danny was looking forward to staying there for a few nights. He hoped to sleep in one of the longhouses after being serviced by a native girl. The Irishman had always wondered what it would be like to have sex with a wild tribal woman. He only hoped that the rumours he had heard at

Mindelo Port were true. A local fisherman had told him that the Tupi chief always offered his best women to 'entertain' honoured guests.

It was a pleasant surprise to see the Tupi people doing chores and activities in such an idyllic setting. Anthony had almost expected to come across severed heads on spikes displayed around the outskirts of the village. No witchdoctors came out to meet them. He had imagined the medicine men with pure white eyeballs and teeth that had been filed to points making it easier to rip human flesh from bones. In fact, there was not a single cooking pot in sight large enough to hold a whole person. The scene before him could not have been further from those that he had conjured up in his wild imagination. The blacksmith felt ashamed of himself for believing the ridiculous horror stories that he had heard over the years. Several domesticated dogs padded around the Tupi village. Children played happily outside well-constructed longhouses whilst most of the women sat together pounding corn. The wee tribal dog that had pounced on Creppin only a few minutes earlier pricked up his large pointed ears when he saw the hunchback approaching the clearing. He wagged his long, upturned tail so enthusiastically that it thumped both sets of ribs at high speed. Mostly black with brown and white spots, his face had a white muzzle and a long nose. The mutt had white eyebrows that were comically expressive just like Creppin's. It was clear to see his delight when he saw the hunchback enter his territory.

Making a beeline for his target, the dog kept jumping up to bite the crippled man's clothing. Creppin felt a little easier now he had the mischievous little mongrel as company. A young woman shouted the animal's Tupi name, 'Sykyîé!' which meant 'to be afraid of'. His name had been chosen to match the brave hound's fiery and aggressive nature. A natural guard dog, Sykyîé had always been particularly protective of children, being instinctively aware of their vulnerability. Creppin attempted to pronounce the dog's Tupi name but the woman frowned each time, repeating it louder. He soon became frustrated with himself and stomped his large feet, squeezing his eyes tightly shut. He spoke aloud, addressing no-one in particular, 'Pardy pardy me! Crrreppin has trrrouble wi' yon shnufflepup's name. Methinks frrrom now on, this crrreature shall be called 'Skips'. The friendly pet responded to his new tag with several licks of Creppin's filthy hand. A group of children decided to introduce themselves to the crippled man who their pet had instantly bonded with. Surprisingly, the language barrier was not an issue as everyone used simple sign language to communicate. The hunchback joined in with the youngsters and they all used sticks to draw in the damp earth. Creppin felt much more comfortable in the company of children who soon convinced him to join them. As he hobbled off with his new friends he shouted back at Anthony, 'Pardy me marrrster. I's takin' leave an' goin' with these young'uns. I shall rrrreturn anon.' Skips barked his approval and sped excitedly around his heels.

The blacksmith felt relieved that his ward had been welcomed so warmly. He had been feeling rather claustrophobic of late. Creppin had become more and more dependant since they had left home. Although Anthony was far more patient than most men of his age and era, he found himself becoming less tolerant of the needy character. Despite this relatively minor qualm, he accepted sole responsibility for the unfortunate soul. If Anthony had not grabbed him after Sushana's hanging the poor man would not be miles away from his home! More importantly, without Creppin, he might not even have made it out of England alive. He had to accept that he owed his life to his unconventional companion and that was something that he would not take for granted or ever forget.

The tribe slept on the ground or in hammocks inside the communal longhouses. Although men visited the women's home for conjugal purposes, men and women lived in separate accommodation. Children lived with their mothers. Boys were taken away to live amongst the male warriors at an early age to avoid being mollycoddled. Chief Araribóia came out to meet Moses and his party and was very pleased to hear their story. He welcomed each visitor separately but made a big fuss of Anthony. Summoning the whole tribe, he explained the blacksmith's bravery for taking on such a challenging mission. He presented him with a traditional tribal shell necklace. An English midget called Shrimp was happy to translate for the chief. The former pyrate's mixed-race children were being raised to be bilingual so he encouraged his oldest son to say a few simple words. To his father's delight, the boy spoke clearly. Shrimp oozed with pride when he addressed the strangers with such confidence.

Moses presented the chief with gifts of sandals made from vegetable fibre, tobacco and several knives. As a token of gratitude the chief invited his sons to offer their wives to attend to the men's sexual needs. Danny's green eyes widened, 'Wahoo!' he exclaimed. Anthony gave him a sharp jab in the ribs for his discourtesy.

The chief's eldest son offered two of his four wives to Moses and Anthony who nodded their gratitude. Other Tupi warriors offered their wives to attend to the foreign visitors. The men stood in line wearing big grins on their faces. Creppin froze on the spot with mouth agape when a Tupi woman approached him. She showed total respect and smiled at him politely. He began to tremble at the mere thought of a female allowing him any kind of consensual sexual contact... a female of the human kind that is. The odd stray animal had offered no resistance in the recent past but even the hunchback did not expect them to be counted as any real conquest. His voice quavered as an involuntary 'Ooo...o...oo' escaped his drivelling lips. His hardness was plain to see; a wet patch was seeping through the cloth of his trews. The soiled material strained against an impressive bulge.

As always, Chief Araribóia offered an open invitation to anyone associated with Patrick Culley or his late mother. The visitors were free to stay as long as they wished. Shrimp told the exultant men that the chief wanted them to stay for at least three days. That would give them time to prepare for a sacrificial ritual. He turned to Anthony, 'Sacrifices will be offered to our God to ask that his divine power give you the victory you crave.' Two of Patrick's closest Tupi friends, Jaeci and Serijipe, stepped forward. In broken English, they told Moses that they would fight with him in honour of Patrick's dead mother's spirit. Moses knew that these flint-hearted warriors were determined to kill and devour the flesh of the English Queen. Shrimp translated the chief's sincere but solemn speech, 'We mourn the death of a brave and true warrior woman. We shall avenge her wasted spirit. We must gain the powers of the bravest warriors. I decree that we shall invade the most ferocious of our enemy tribes, the Temiminó.' On hearing mention of the most feared and revered tribe, the women gasped and the men stiffened their stance. Jaeci took a large stick over to the chief who carved another notch into the red wood to mark that day's passage before the planned attack. Women and children squatted on their haunches, elders sat on wooden stools and the warriors stood surrounding the chief. Shrimp translated Chief Araribóia's closing words, 'We shall attack on the morrow.'

Tobacco was brought out for the men to chew and women tended their children and prepared food. Creppin and Danny had to be warned not to stare at the barebreasted women; especially those who wore no garter. An unmarried Tupi woman wore one of these on her right leg until she took a husband. Then she would be permitted to remove it. The men did not take kindly to anyone ogling their wives. Rules were very strict within the community. If a woman committed adultery she would be gang-raped by every man in the tribe and then executed. The male offender would be made to beat her to death with his war club. If married, his wife/wives would be given to the cuckold.

Proud warriors took turns to demonstrate to the visitors how they made their weapons. Bows were used in war and for hunting. Their arrows were tipped with a poisonous paste that contained deadly venom extracted from brightly coloured, harmless-looking frogs. A mere scratch from the tip would mean certain death. The visitors were shown how to make blow pipes, long fishing spears, wooden war clubs, two-handed wooden swords and shields. Knives were made from sharp rock. All weapons were decorated with patterns to match those painted on the warriors' bodies when they went to war. The tribe often attacked at night in canoes that they called 'piragas', each holding up to fifty men. They fought mainly on the water but would often invade other Tupi villages. Firing arrows to set thatched roofs alight, they would capture warriors to take back to their village for sacrifice. There, they would be awarded 'caracolis' for each triumphant battle. These were crescent-shaped copper pendants that would always be worn with great pride. The visitors made themselves fishing spears and a weapon of their choice. Before sundown, the men went to the river to catch fish and were pleased to see their foreign guests trying to fish the Tupi way. Creppin and Anthony were successful, catching two fish each but none of the others managed. The Irish lads spent most of the time laughing at each other's lame attempts to spear fish that moved at lightning speed with the strong current. When the tribesmen were satisfied with a decent catch they all returned to the village.

At nightfall everyone went inside the longhouses where women prepared food for their own family. The communal atmosphere was comfortable and pleasant with each clan occupying one of many compartments. The chief and his first wife lived in the first section on the right of the entrance. As his honoured guests, Moses and Anthony enjoyed a meal of cornbread and fish soup before joining their women. The others ate with individual families who had offered their hospitality. During mealtime a group of Cimarrones were escorted into the longhouse. The African men had requested to speak with the chief. Anthony soon learned from Shrimp that they had received word from Grace O'Malley and wanted to fight alongside Patrick. The chief introduced them to the blacksmith and his men and they were invited to eat. Anthony was starting to feel a little more confident with such skilled and loyal warriors on his side. He looked forward to returning to the plantation with the new volunteers to hear Patrick's plans.

Moses lay on a hammock enjoying the warmth of the fire. He watched the flames flicker in the cool darkness. The woman he was with had fallen asleep. She moved her tiny hand to rest on his large chest. He felt satisfied after over an hour of sex. It felt good to be lying with a woman again but the pyrate could not stop wondering how Patrick was coping. Many candles made from sweet-smelling gum lit the crowded interior. Their heady aroma helped to mask any unpleasant odours and repel insects. Creppin smelt unusually pleasant. He had been taken down to the river earlier where his 'borrowed' woman had scrubbed him clean. The candlelight illuminated his face softening misshapen features. He was grinning broadly. Ironically, he did not look that ugly. It was plain for all to see that the hunchback was over the moon. The Tupi woman lifted her head and smiled at her temporary lover. He still could not believe his luck! Consensual sex! The hunchback was overwhelmed with all kinds of emotions. As they lay together, he gently stroked and caressed her small breasts. 'Th'art soooo bootiful my love', he told her secretly wishing that she could be his. Not understanding a word that he was saying, the young woman giggled and began to stroke his hardened shaft.

The poor wretch had never felt a woman's touch before. His own mother had been disgusted by her disfigured baby and cut the umbilical cord herself, leaving him in a back alley to die. A passing vagabond had heard a strange gurgling sound and gone to investigate. In his drunken state, he had found the hideous baby and decided to keep it. He had the bright idea that it could make him some money when he went out begging. If he chose the right wealthy area it was surprising how many young women would take pity on a man with a child, especially a deformed one. They would make so much fuss over 'the poor little darling!' that their beaus would feel obligated to give a donation to make a good impression. Creppin had always been a survivor. Now he was very happy that his and Anthony's paths had crossed. Feeling fantastic, he lay back and enjoyed the touch of his sexually experienced companion.

Danny had been granted his wish and was still pumping away at a tiny Tupi woman whose husband had kindly offered to gratify the randy Irishman. His fellow countrymen had been spent hours earlier. Every few minutes, they offered a humorous jibe at the rampant pyrate. Cathal egged his virile friend on, 'Yer farder'd be proyd of yers me lad!' Lifting a clenched fist in triumph the lust-driven pyrate continued to slam his hard shaft into the girl's shaven silky cunnie. Danny responded, breathless, 'Ahhhh... feels soooo good... ter pummel... a smooth... toyt... juicy... cunnie!' The Tupi woman was aroused beyond belief. Her pretty young face flushed bright pink as she took every inch of the stranger's ample penis. Colm felt his own begin to harden again at the sight of his shipmate swiving the petite wench. Now she was on all fours, being taken from behind. She kept looking over at the other man. Her small, neat lips formed a natural pout as she gazed at the voyeur whose appearance was so different to the men she knew.

Finding it an incredible turn-on to watch the inhibited young woman indulging in carnal pleasure, Colm grasped his cock. As he massaged his erection, he imagined gently teasing her sweet, swollen clitoris with the tip of his tongue. Still openly watching Danny with the woman he craved to enter, he pulled his own sexual companion closer. Although she was very young, probably no more than sixteen years old, his girl was overweight. Her conical breasts were plump with puffy nipples. Luckily, her large labia were still lubricated as Colm had ejaculated inside her earlier. Focusing completely on his fantasy, the horny Irishman lay flat on his back so she could straddle him. He licked his dry lips and looked at the prettier girl only a few yards away. His heart pumped so fast that his breathing was erratic. He could see the profile of her round breasts swaying as her perfect body undulated to the rhythm of Danny's powerful thrusts. Danny knew that Colm desired his prize match and that fact aroused him even more. He fucked her deeper and even harder. The beautiful woman's lips parted and her eyes closed as she gave way to the most intense orgasm that either man had witnessed. Her whole body thrashed with unashamed ecstasy. Small but strong muscular thighs trembled as she threw back her head and let go completely. That did it. Danny yelled aloud as he arched his back and erupted inside her. With an urgent need to urinate, he grabbed his trews and pulled them on quickly. He farted loudly as he did so and ran outside to relieve himself. Cathal laughed, 'Yers an eejut!' he shouted after his friend.

The exotic-looking beauty rolled onto her back and smiled warmly at Colm. She said something to her friend who was riding him gently. The two women giggled.

Colm's stiff penis slid in and out of his girl with ease. She emitted a prolonged moan as she lowered herself down slowly, inch by inch, onto his rigid shaft. His ideal beauty eyed him sleepily as she watched her friend giving him pleasure. Still in a high state of arousal she rolled her erect nipples between fingers and thumbs. Running her hands up and down the inside of her thighs, she allowed her delicate fingers to brush against the inner lips of her cunnie. She put wetted fingertips to her mouth to taste the dew-like juice. Her effortless, primal sensuality stirred a deep, emotional longing inside Colm. He felt the need to hold her tightly and never let go. At the age of twenty eight, the worldly man had led a life of debauchery yet nothing had even come close to the erotic pleasure that he felt right now... and that was only whilst looking at this temptress. It was as though his entire body was tingling with static electricity. A surge of warmth spread over the crown of his head. It continued to flow downwards over his body, ending in the tips of his toes. His heart was beating faster than it ever had before as Colm felt the internal muscles of his plump lover pulsate in a series of contractions whilst he imagined making love to his princess. Suddenly feeling the need to touch his soul mate, he lifted the other woman off him to reach out. As if sensing his desire, she responded by touching his fingertips with hers.

The married Tupi tribeswoman swooned inside. How she wished that she could allow the foreigner to touch her. Biting her lower lip, she raised her eyebrows and closed her eyes. Danny came running back and got into his hammock. Ignoring the gorgeous woman who he had cum inside only moments earlier, he settled down, 'Noyt lads. Jesus, Mary 'n Joseph, it doesna get any better dan dis does it?' For the first time in his life, Colm felt insanely jealous. He harboured an absolute repulsion towards the heartless libertine. This rude awakening had seriously affected him. Feeling ashamed to be associated with the disrespectful Irishman, he clenched his fists in anger. Subconsciously, he reached for his gutting knife. With a sudden sick realisation, he stood up and pulled on his clothes. This behaviour was so unlike him! Rushing outside, he felt relieved to breathe in the fresh air. He was going to have to harden up and forget the enchanting temptress before he did something that he would regret. It had been made clear that an adulterous Tupi woman would be killed for her crime. Colm had too good a heart to allow that to happen. Crouching down to pet one of the tribal dogs, he decided to stay outside.

The sounds of the forest fascinated the foreigner. He had never expected it to be so noisy and doubted whether he would manage to sleep out in the open air. A myriad of insects provided a humming, clicking and hissing background sound, cicadas the loudest of all with their constant high-pitched chirping. Thousands of frogs screeching mating calls soon joined in the wonderful night chorus. Snapping twigs and rustling leaves could be heard as nocturnal creatures foraged in the undergrowth. The falling temperature prompted the Tupi warriors who were on guard to add more logs to the fire. It was bitterly cold that night. The haunting call of owls could be heard as they hooted from the trees. The nearby riverbanks provided perfect hunting grounds. Just before he pulled a heavy blanket around him, Colm saw a group of bats flitting around in circles as they caught insect prey. As if he had been hypnotised by the strange and mysterious sounds of the rainforest, the frustrated Irishman soon fell asleep.

Patrick needed to be alone. Relieved that his two friends had realised that he needed some space and offered to take the visitors off his hands, he had packed early and left them all sleeping back at the plantation. Moses had given him a subtle nod of approval when he had sneaked past him. The vigilant pyrate never missed a thing and Patrick was yet to catch him out whilst on guard. Before he could take on the responsibility of involving anyone else in this extremely dangerous mission, he had to come to terms with his mother's death. Try as he might, he could not bring himself to accept that she had really gone. This time, she was never coming back. He smelled the acrid scent of bats' urine as he approached the dark gaping entrance to a cave. Stealthily, he climbed up the slippery rocks and disappeared inside. Patrick knew that this was one place where he could stay for a few days without fear of discovery.

An ancient Tupi legend told of two young warriors from rival tribes. They were so well matched with their fighting skills that their duel had lasted for a whole day until they came to the mouth of this very cave. As the fighters had invaded their roost, the bats became agitated and began to fly around the warriors' heads. The sound of their leathery, membranous wings flapping above him unnerved one of the men. That split second's distraction lost him his life. As he slipped on the thick layer of bat guano on the smooth lava stone floor of the cave, his opponent delivered a fatal blow to his head. Finding it difficult to breathe with the acrid stench of ammonia, the victor stumbled out of the cave, desperate for fresh air.

Later that night, the victorious warrior returned to his tribe without his enemy's body and explained what had happened. Two others volunteered to go back with him to the cave to collect the body. Unfortunately, they found that the corpse had sunk into the rotting mass of bat shit and had been covered with even more of the putrid droppings. On closer inspection, the warriors learned that flesh eating beetles that lived in the excrement had started to eat the corpse. Deciding that the rancid flesh was no longer fit for human consumption, the tribesmen returned to their village empty handed. All Tupi people, including Patrick's friendly local tribe, still believed that the angry spirit of the dead warrior still haunted the cave. It had been a terrible dishonour when his enemies had failed to eat his body to absorb his brave spirit. The corpse had been left to be devoured by mere insects so the angry life-force remained in the cave. Trapped for eternity in the stifling, ammonia-filled atmosphere, the spirit thrived on its own bitterness. It was time for Patrick to fight his demons and conquer his fear of spirits.

Carrying a lantern and a bag full of extra candles, the young man ventured deeper into the cave. The candlelight caught the shimmering wet surface of the beautiful stalactites and stalagmites that had formed a perfect natural barricade over millions of years. They deterred most from risking passage but Patrick squeezed between phallic columns and ducked under spikey overhead obstacles. It was very cold. The moist atmosphere was oppressive… suffocating. At last he reached a small hole that appeared hardly big enough for him to pass through. Patrick lay down on his belly, took out his rapier and pushed his bag of supplies, then the lantern into the darkness. He only just managed to shimmy through the shaft, grazing his upper back on the serrated rock surface.

The struggle was all worthwhile when he reached the womb-like inner sanctuary. He stood upright, picking up the lantern to illuminate a wondrous grotto. The enchanting interior before him took Patrick's breath away. He stood perfectly still, taking in the calm stillness of the pale green pool. Milky-white reflections of natural rock formations could be seen on the water's glassy surface. 'Hauntingly beautiful', Patrick whispered. Climbing down a slippery slope to the edge of the pool, he took out his tinderbox and lit a small fire. Tucked beneath an outcrop of rock there was a small chest. He opened it, taking out a scroll, quill and inkpot. Solitude would be the only way for Patrick to be able to release his despair. He began to draw, concentrating only on the fine lines that he marked on the paper. Looking above him, he admired the ancient cave paintings and absorbed the tranquillity of isolation. Closing his eyes, Patrick began to weep. If only he could banish the intense pain that filled his broken heart.

CHAPTER 12

A Merciless Crew Sign in the Round

It was mid-September when a remarkable vessel docked in the deep water harbour of Mindelo. Grace O'Malley had sent a vastly improved carrack with a crew made up of some of her best sailors over to São Vicente. Since the vessel's purpose was to carry Patrick, Anthony and their supporters safely back to Ireland she had been aptly named 'the Deliverance'. The pyrate queen had ensured that the sturdy ship had undergone a full overhaul. Considerable alterations had been carried out before leaving Eire. She was square-rigged on the foremast and mainmast and lateen-rigged on the mizzenmast. Her forecastle had been removed to make navigation easier and quarterdecks lowered to create an obstacle-free fighting platform. Her hull had been pierced to carry more cannons. Blistered with forty six in total, twenty six culverins on the lower deck and twenty demi-culverins on the upper, timbers had been strengthened to carry the extra weight. All unnecessary partitions had been torn out to allow more space for the gunners to work. On the outbound voyage the experienced sailors had been impressed by the re-vamped ship's speed and improved manoeuvrability. She had already proven to be a formidable class of craft. A good job too, as the crew sailed into Mindelo on a stormy tide. Grace had nominated a pyrate called Finn Keniry to captain the outbound voyage. A fair but strict leader, he managed the crew well and kept every command simple, short and clear. Upon docking, he ensured that adjacent vessels were given a wide birth as the ship swung precariously. Relieved to have finally docked in the busy harbour, the crew knew that they would not be sailing the Deliverance again for a while.

The Irish pyrates had arrived with even more plunder to add to Patrick's cause. A few days earlier, they had sighted a merchant ship. Taking advantage of an opportune moment, they sped up alongside the bulkier craft. A rally of cannon fire prompted the captain of the slower vessel to order his gunners to retaliate. Grabbing their boarding axes, the pyrates boarded the ship. Showing no allegiance to their leader, the sailors waved a white sheet, shouting their wish to surrender. Sensibly, they wanted no trouble with pyrates. After calling his men, 'filthy cowards', the inexperienced young officer grabbed their makeshift white flag and threw it overboard. Drawing his flintlock pistol, he aimed it at one of the invaders. The bumptious fool then had the audacity to shout a warning that pyracy was a hanging offence. When the Irish crew heard harrowing cries coming from below deck it became clear that they had boarded a slave ship. As the hatch was lifted they were met with a terrible reek of death and disease.

Countless African men, women and children lay in their own filth, shackled together in heavy irons. Appalled at the state of the helpless captives the Irish freedom fighters demanded the keys to release them. When the cowardly captain made a sudden bolt for this cabin he was tackled by one of Grace's hefty men. He yelled obscenities at his own crew who responded by jeering and spitting at him. Not one of them showed compassion for their callous officer. He had been known as a 'tight packer' who would brag about how many slaves he could force into his ship. Complaining to the pyrates that the captain was a tyrant, his crew were keen to see him punished for his sadistic ways. Stripped naked, the terrified bully was thrown into the lice and maggot-infested pit 'tween decks' where his human cargo had been forced to live. The keys were tossed down after him. It did not take long for the emaciated men and women to turn on their abuser. Not a single weapon was used. Piss trickled down his leg as the desperate officer begged for mercy. His pleas were ignored. Still shrieking and yelling as he received his just deserts he was kicked, clawed and bitten until he lay lifeless. Even then, the violence did not stop. Dismembered by bare hands, his bones were ripped out and thrown to the rats that had gnawed away at weak and diseased slaves as they lay dying in the bowels of the slave ship. The captain's avengers did not stop their vicious assault until nothing but a thin layer of bloody pulp remained on the filthy boards. Undoubtedly the ship's vermin would lap them clean. No-one emerged from below deck until each of their foreheads had been daubed with a smear of their abductor's blood. Even the children bore the ghastly mark of retribution. When they had been given decent food and water, most of the freed slaves volunteered to join the Irish pyrates. Finn selected a few of his men to sail the captured vessel to São Vicente. The port was fast becoming infamous for its expanding slave warehouses so they were bound to be offered a fair price for a carrier. The proceeds from the sale would be split fairly amongst the African people, crew and pyrates.

Whilst looting the slave ship, Grace's men had found a cabin boy cowering in a dark corner of the captain's quarters. After some gentle coaxing, he told the liberators that his name was Joe. It was clear that the unkempt child had suffered abuse at the hands of the cruel captain. Eventually, the pyrates managed to reassure the lad that they meant him no harm. Before long he felt comfortable and began chatting away to them. Joe eagerly accepted the pyrates' invitation to join them. Before he left, he crawled under the late captain's table and pulled up a loose floorboard. He emerged with a triumphant grin and handed the pyrates a large bag of fine gold jewellery. The new recruit explained that his abuser had been married to a wealthy woman. Every time he returned home, he would steal from her. Apparently, the addicted gambler had never been able to keep anything of value for long.

Back on board Grace's ship Joe was keen to join one of the pyrates up in the crow's nest. He was shown how to turn the sand-glass and ring the ship's bell every half-hour during the four hour watch system. This new responsibility gave the boy a tremendous boost of self-confidence. He soon earned respect from the crew, taking every duty he was given seriously. The youngster never put a foot wrong and always paid attention, staying alert at all times. Joe felt more at home on the Deliverance than he had ever felt anywhere before. Ever since he had climbed aloft with the friendly Irishman, the crow's nest had become his favourite place to be. Well-used to his own company, Joe rarely suffered from boredom and was more than happy to entertain himself. People-watching and guessing games had long been his favourite pastimes. Mindelo Harbour fascinated him. Despite heavy rain, brightly dressed locals bartered for seafood or traded local produce for goods brought from overseas. Menacingly dark clouds loomed above as Joe soon became engrossed in a world of make-believe. Captivated by the tiny figures below, the child imagined that he was a powerful dragon. Stretching huge, green, leathery wings out wide, he shielded his pyrate friends from the rain. Lifting his head skyward, he drew in a deep breath and blasted out a blazing arc of flame. Many of the clouds turned to steam which quickly dissolved into fine drizzle.

A long way below the enchanted boy, empty casks were being taken apart so that their shakes could be stowed. Finn had predicted that a severe storm was on its way so the men were working fast. Everything had to be secured to prevent damage to the vessel. As Joe watched his friends load containers into the cockboat, he tried to predict the contents of each. He yawned and giggled as he envisaged a puff of smoke escape from his large, charred nostrils. His imagination was so vivid that he had actually felt it tickle! He narrowed keen, amber reptilian eyes and focused on the cook who was now standing ashore. Surrounded by a group of animated women, the agitated pyrate scratched his head, cursing loudly. He was undoubtedly bartering for the best price to make up a decent sized slush fund. At the end of every voyage, he would prepare a tasty slurry by adding boiling water to empty storage barrels that had contained salted meat. Many locals loved the unusual taste of the meaty concoction. They would often pay a decent price to take home a large barrelful. The rain bounced off opalescent scales that formed striking armour to protect the giant reptile's body. Without any warning, the Deliverance made a sudden, severe tip. The dragon grabbed the main mast digging lethal razor-sharp claws into the hard wood.

A brisk wind had slammed the ship against harbour side rocks. Once again the beast opened his large jaw wide. This time, he let out a deafening roar as he sprayed the moody skies with a jet of scorching flames. A halo of mist surrounded his great head. As timbers creaked beneath his grip, he felt no fear. After all... dragons are invincible!

Great curtains of rain fell from depressing gunmetal skies and Joe stayed in his fantasy world as he watched the two ship's cats flit back and forth pondering whether to venture ashore. Finally they decided to stow away in one of the rowboats when no-one was looking. Instinctive curiosity had won over their fear of the unknown. Predators openly prowled the docks yet the felines had decided to take a risk. The boy enjoyed a dragon's eye view of the crafty animals as they bolted past the pyrates on reaching the port. They both lay low for a while. Before long, one of the crafty pair caught a local stall-holder's attention whilst the other stole a large fish from her basket. Scampering back onto the boat, prey still wriggling between its jaws, the cat screamed a jubilant 'mieeaaooww' to summon its partner-in-crime. Smiling at the cheek of the cat-burglars, Joe checked on his pyrates' progress on the deck below. He noticed one of his friends looking up at him. The pyrate gave a shrill whistle and shouted a friendly greeting. Casually, the dragon flapped his impressive wings in response. Human acceptance was alien to him but it felt really good to be liked, appreciated... wanted. With a contented sigh he leant his great body against the mast and tucked into the marchpane that Finn had given him before he had gone ashore. His mouth began to water and his taste-buds exploded when he sampled the deliciously sweet treat. 'Mmmmm', Joe exclaimed, his cheeky face breaking into a huge smile, dimples appearing in plump, rosy cheeks. In blissful contentment, he closed his eyes and savoured the moment. He noticed that the raindrops were getting warmer as they fell steadily onto his face. Waiting patiently for his friends to finish their tasks, the rumble of distant thunder could be heard. The dragon was not concerned about the gradually encroaching storm that would eventually hit the small island.

Joe's short life had been harsh but he had never allowed his misfortune to dampen his spirit. Orphaned as a baby, the lad had been a street urchin in the city of Bristol until he was invited to join a gang of cutpurses. Their leader was a one-legged man who suffered with terrible flatulence and stank of stale sweat, tooth decay and rancid ale. He owned a small room at the dockside where he encouraged sailors to buy alcohol and play cards. An addicted gambler, it never took him long to lose his boys' ill-gotten gains. When all loot had been lost, the oaf would get drunk and send them back out to steal more for him to gamble away. It had not been so bad for the boys during the first couple of years when their boss had been on a winning streak. Unfortunately, his luck had soon run out. As the drunken lout became more desperate he grew careless and frequently lost his concentration during an intense card game. Ever confident that he would make up for his losses with his next deal, he constantly promised his lads that they were going to be fine. After all, he was not the one risking his neck! Although the young thieves looked out for each other, there was nothing they could do when one of them was caught. Their callous boss would always take his gang to watch their friends swing. He saw it as a way to make them more vigilant. The thug even expected them to work the crowds at the execution and relieve as many spectators as possible of their heavy purses. It was not long until the man became desperate, building debts up with money-lenders who charged high interest on loans.

It was late one night when a naval officer dropped by to collect his dues. He became livid when his punter was unable to pay. When one of the lads arrived home, the officer took an immediate fancy to him. Taking advantage of a bad situation, the cunning man took his debtor to one side. When told that he would accept the young cutpurse as a payment the despicable man was delighted. From that fateful night onwards, everything changed. The loser continued to borrow from the wealthy captain and simply used more boys to pay off his ever-mounting debts. That was how poor Joe had ended up as a cabin boy. One day he was running around with his knife, cutting purse strings from wealthy folks' belts, the next, he was out at sea being sexually abused by a sadistic brute.

Joe liked the pyrates who had rescued him. Someday, he hoped that he would be just like them. Breathing in the fresh sea breeze the lad looked down at the busy harbour. He watched a small native boy steal from an old woman and frowned. Wondering whether the two were related, his mind wandered. Despite his dubious background, he lived by the motto 'Honour amongst thieves'. Joe would never steal from his kin. Spitting out a stone from a delicious fruit that he had never tasted before, he continued to take in his new surround. Having volunteered to stay aboard the Deliverance until danger threatened, the lad was keen to enjoy his newfound freedom. When he had joined the Irish crew, they had even allowed him a space below deck to sleep. He could not remember sleeping so soundly in years. This life suited him well and he was determined to please the pyrates who had taken him in. Having never experienced such kindness and trust before, Joe was finding the situation far too good to be true. He had even befriended the two ship's cats who snuggled up next to him every night. Joe watched some of his new friends leave. A few hours later, he was still up in the crow's nest and saw them return with Patrick, Anthony and some others.

Patrick was over the moon with the vessel that Grace had sent for him. It had been modified especially for the pyrates' needs. Her men had been given strict instructions to prepare the Deliverance for departure as soon as possible. Although he and the crew were keen to get on their way, Patrick knew that the impending storm would delay them considerably. Finn was ready to hand over captaincy to Patrick and gave him a warm welcome. Although his men respected their stand-in captain, they found him very odd. A wiry, muscular man of average height, he was always smoothly shaven with pale skin and greying mousey-coloured hair. Quite a good-looking man, the Irish pyrate had a temper to match his quick wit. His dry sense of humour never failed to amuse but his social skills were almost non-existent. Preferring his own company, he was self-centred and selfish to the core. Finn lived purely for his own pleasure and gain. The creepy man harboured a dark and well-guarded secret; although he occasionally indulged in sexual activity with women, he felt deep resentment towards them. The sole reason for his bitterness was envy. Ever since he could remember, Finn had always wanted to be female. The smug man enjoyed being adored, especially by homosexual crewmembers. He had a limited circle of friends who had been carefully selected for their affluence, standing or connections. Finn only ever associated with people who could help him some way or another. Pleased when young Joe had come aboard, he had instantly taken him under his wing. The light-fingered nipper would come in handy and Finn wanted to keep him close.

Patrick and his group boarded the Deliverance to the therapeutic sound of heavy rain beating steadily upon soaked wooden boards. Two crewmembers were proud to give them a guided tour. Anthony was moved when he discovered that Grace had allotted a small section of the ship to him. A workshop had been set up just above the gun deck. He was pleased to see a brazier that had been firmly fixed to the floor. All tools required to make weapons and ammunition were neatly displayed in racks. Different sized moulds were ready for the blacksmith to cast his first shots and cannonballs. Anthony beamed with satisfaction; he was in his element. Grace knew him all too well. He could not wait to start working metal again. On closer inspection inside the brazier he found a piece of folded parchment that had been pushed right to the back. Still smiling, Anthony pulled it out and read Grace's words. As expected, the proud pyrate had kept her message short and sweet, 'Cast shots to blast a queen! I await thy return.' As he read between the lines, Anthony felt happy that such an amazing woman was missing him. Totally out of character, the handsome young man blushed. His heart swelled as a familiar, wonderfully warm rush spread through his body. Every time he thought of the Irish pyrate queen he would become instantly horny. The blacksmith tucked the letter inside his belt pouch, lit a fire in the brazier and set to work in his fine, new workshop.

It had taken Patrick, Anthony and Moses a few days to collect the booty they needed to take back to Ireland. Sushana Culley's ample hoard had been hidden in numerous locations beneath tons of volcanic rock. Each treasure cove had been carefully marked on maps and given to trusted members of her crew. The select caves that held priceless plunder could only be reached by navigating through some of the countless narrow tunnels that snaked in an underground maze. Anthony had enjoyed every minute of his treasure hunting adventure. Despite the freak storms that had hit São Vicente Patrick still hoped to reach Ireland by mid-November. That would allow them time to sail to Lundy Island to seek out his legacy then onwards to Plymouth to collect his new ship. Taking advantage of the extra time, Patrick showed Anthony and the others as much of the tropical island as possible. Despite torrential rainfall and thunderous lightning storms, he made sure that his visitors sampled all kinds of different seafood. The Tupi hunters brought tuna, mackerel, lobster, crab and mussels for Patrick to cook, always adding tasty spices to the dishes.

It was now late September and storms still circled the Cape Verde Islands. Although the slave ship limped lamely into Mindelo harbour, she was quickly sold for a decent amount considering the repairs that needed to be done. As promised, the funds raised were split and the African people who had chosen not to join the pyrates were taken straight to the Culley plantation. There, they were given a warm welcome. Delighted to be offered a home and employment, they settled in to a new life in the friendly community. Patrick decided that he would have to make a move soon if they were to reach Ireland in time. He had heard word from Hawkins who had been pleased to announce that he had settled back in Plymouth and had arranged for them to pick up a brand new vessel from his shipyards. Deciding to take advantage of a lull in the storm, Patrick ordered everyone to board the Deliverance. He could not wait any longer.

When plenty of supplies had been loaded, the captain called the whole crew to the main officers' quarters. There, a large oak table had been covered with his mother's flag. The Culley pyrate emblem was a profile of a hideous skull, its jaw wide open in a silent scream. Below it swung a set of broken shackles and a pair of Sushana's decorated trophy bollock pouches. The black background had a splattering of red to represent the blood of the enemies of the Culley clan. Patrick had placed Fazenda's skull upright in the flag's centre. His two crossed ulna bones had been set below its sorry death-grin. A large piece of parchment, numerous quills and several inkpots had been prepared for the pyrates to pledge allegiance to Patrick's and Grace's cause. Everyone was invited to sign in the round, at exactly the same moment. Following a short speech from their elected captain they each took a quill. Every man and woman present vowed their steadfast loyalty to Captain Culley. Patrick promised that everyone who signed would be well rewarded. Even Creppin and Joe managed to pen their mark. Patiently, the hunchback helped the urchin copy his own signature and two feeble x's were added to the document; side by side. Moses brought out two kegs of ale and drilled a bunghole in each. Everyone filled their tankards and drank to fellow pyrates. Spirits were high and Patrick and Anthony felt a sincerity and determination amongst their militia. Moses took the signed document to display on the wall of the captain's cabin. For the first time in a while, Patrick felt optimistic. The pyrate captain addressed his eager crew, 'Let's be on our way lest we lose more time.' Then he gave his first order, 'All hands on deck!' Immediately, the sailors took to their stations.

Cathal led the shanty whilst the anchor was weighed. The others shouted back the chorus. Patrick took his bodhrán and beat a soft, steady rhythm. The bosun had always been chantyman and had the sweetest singing voice. He knew a different nautical ballad for each arduous task that his men had to perform. Singing always seemed to make the workload lighter, especially whilst doing unpleasant jobs like pumping out bilge. As the men heaved the bars up and down to work the windlass, the anchor was slowly raised. Cathal sang, 'Stormie's gone, dat good ol' man…' The men responded, 'To my way hay, storm along, John!' Cathal jumped up onto a barrel and sang louder and a tad faster as he encouraged the men to pump harder; 'Stormie's gone, dat good ol' man…' The huge anchor chain clanked noisily as the pyrates worked harder to lift the heavy weight quicker. 'To my aye, aye, aye, Mister Storm-along!' came the response. Cathal really did have a stunning voice. Those who were hearing it for the first time could not help but stare in awe at the talented singer. It was a pleasure to listen as he continued; 'They dug his grave with a silver spade…' Standing portside Patrick paused briefly when he heard a warrior's chant coming from below. Looking down towards the source of the unmistakable war cry, Anthony saw that a large group of young African men had gathered at the harbour front. Their leader shouted in his foreign tongue. Instantly recognising the deep powerful voice, Patrick's eyes lit up with optimism. Hailing a welcome reply in the warriors' dialect, he ordered the gang plank to be let out. The men began to hum as they stood, tall and proud, waiting to board.

Obi was the Cimarrones leader's eldest son. He had brought forty men along to join Patrick in his war of vengeance. Having received word from Grace O'Malley of recent tragic events, many amongst the community of liberated African slaves had been keen to volunteer. Obi had been elected to lead them. He and his men boarded the Deliverance. They added their signatures to form an inner circle on the document, witnessed by the whole crew. Obi joined Patrick and Anthony in the captain's cabin. The chief's son looked uneasy. Patrick assured his concerned guest that it was safe to speak openly in front of Anthony. With genuine concern, Obi explained how his ancestors had visited him in several dreams. The man's face appeared unusually drawn. Apparently his spirit guide, who in life had been a prominent tribal chief, would not stop plaguing him with warnings. Patrick felt a familiar dread as he listened to the spiritual man's account. Obi's news reinforced his belief that Sushana's soul was restless. Ever since the first day when he had sensed that his mother faced terrible danger, he had felt that her spirit would never rest until retribution had been served. The only way that Sushana Culley's clan could ever gain peace of mind and move on would be by the death of the English Queen. Obi swore that he and his men would give their lives to help Patrick fulfil his dangerous mission. The three men embraced and re-joined the crew.

Dark, menacing skies hovered above the distant horizon but a hazy rainbow offered hope. As Cathal continued his interrupted shanty, the huge anchor finally came into sight. As the Deliverance creaked back to life, her crew felt a tremendous buzz as they set her sails. The superstitious pyrates were pleased to pass under nature's colourful, lucky arc that looked as though it had been woven between wispy fingers of cloud. Joe was warned not to look back once the craft had left port. A wise seadog had told him that if ever he did, then bad luck was sure to follow him and the Deliverance. The young lad had listened intently to a long list of superstitions and omens that he would be sure never to forget. He hoped that he would recognise an albatross if he saw one. The albatross and the seagull are believed to host dead souls of sailors and if a sailor ever killed one, he would seal his own doom. If a cormorant or curlew was sighted at sea, that would also bring bad luck. Swallows, on the other hand, were lucky birds and an anchor tattoo was believed to guarantee that if a sailor went overboard, he would never drift far from his ship.

Anthony had been pleased that the Tupi chief had allowed Creppin to keep Skips. The Tupi women had been grateful to the hunchback for looking after their children so well. Since he and the wee dog had shared an immediate bond, the chief had decided that the pet would be the perfect thank you gift. The odd little man was over the moon and Skips appeared to be just as happy with his new owner. Patrick hoped that Creppin's new pet might keep him occupied rather than constantly bugging Anthony. A ship was definitely not the place for a nuisance and, so far, that is how the captain regarded Creppin. The pyrates believed in certain rules that were steeped in myth and superstition. One of these was that it was unlucky to have a deformed person or a dog aboard. Unfortunately the Deliverance now had both! Patrick was amazed to find out that the hunchback had actually volunteered to be swabby. Swabbing the decks and manning the bilge pump were unpopular chores that most tried to avoid like the plague! At least this gesture had brought the weird little man some favour. Also keen to start scrubbing the crap off the boat, the hunchback later admitted to the captain that he enjoyed looking after, 'Crrreppin's shite seatsies'. Since he had lowered his rear on the first seat of easement he had ever encountered, back at Rockfleet, he had been able to think of little else. The stinky man enjoyed his new job and did it very well. He did not even mind washing out the arse-wiping sponges! The foul stench never bothered him and very soon, Creppin became his filthy, stinking and unkempt ol' self again. Despite the dreadful odour, Anthony was pleased to see his unconventional companion settled and content.

As bosun's mate, it was Moses' job to second-check the rigging and the ship's condition. He would then report to the bosun. Observing his efficient deck crew, he watched Shanny climb the rigging with such ease and confidence it was as if she had been raised at sea. Moses' badly scarred lips stretched uncomfortably over stained teeth to form a rare smile. The Moorish pyrate recalled how he had taught her mother, Abi, how to manage the miles of cordage in an equally complex rigging system. The only way of keeping track of all the lines was to learn the location and function of each. This was always a daunting task for any inexperienced sailor. Moses remembered, as if it was only yesterday, when Abi had begun her training on the ropes. Not a thing had fazed his student. She had shown the same determination and drive that her daughter now demonstrated. Moses noticed Cathal scanning the busy deck. He was sure that the experienced seaman would have noticed Shanny. He too must have been impressed by her skill and nerve. Catching Moses' eye, the bosun nodded his acknowledgement of the young woman's seemingly ingrained sailing abilities. The big black man's heart swelled with pride. He only wished that her mother could see Shanny aloft right that moment. She would have been so proud. Abi was sorely missed. Shanny reminded him so much of her. Like her mother, she was an attractive young woman with short, auburn hair. Grace had cut it into a neat style that suited her pretty face and elfin features perfectly. Slightly built, Shanny could easily pass as a young man with her boy-like figure, small breasts and narrow hips.

When the sails were secured, the pyrates began to brag amongst themselves. Danny held the record for fastest man to reach the crow's nest. No-one had ever managed to beat him aloft. The handsome Irishman stopped his banter when he heard a jibe from an unseen heckler. 'I lay a wager on't wench yonder ter beat Danny boy hands down!' Moses' ears pricked up. He scanned the deck for Saul who he believed to be goading his rival. Secretly amused by the English lad's crafty bait, Moses decided to stay and watch how the cheeky Irish pyrate chose to deal with this unexpected challenge. Believing that Danny would fall for it, hook, line and sinker, the bosun's mate's was proved right within minutes. The predictable man's man had already stripped off his shirt. Spitting on the palms of his calloused hands he challenged Shanny. 'Me darlin' Shanny-shoin! Ye can keep yer shirt arn and oi'll gi' ye tree seconds head start!' Danny teased further, 'Come hither, moy pretty... let's see yers chase an Oirishman ter der top o' de world!'

A ripple of excitement spread through the gathering crowd as everyone began to lay wagers. Keen to witness the outcome of Shanny's unofficial initiation ceremony, Patrick stood back and waited. Stakes were high, with not many backing the new girl. Moses found Saul and nodded silently, pressing some gold coins firmly into the palm of his sweaty hand. Josh and Gift added a decent amount to back their friend and urged her to accept the challenge. To Moses' surprise, Shanny agreed without a second thought. She stretched her arms and legs ready for the strenuous climb. Cheers and shouts erupted and Joe giggled with excitement as he rang the bell from the crow's nest. The group of spectators grew and everyone was eager for the competitors to start the race. The captain walked forward and added three doubloons to the mounting pile of coinage, 'My wager's on the wench!' A roar from the men startled Micken who started screeching loudly from the captain's cabin. More cheers erupted at the welcome sound of clinking coins as they were tossed into the growing pile. Remando fetched a hemp sack and filled it with money. The good-humoured pyrate always enjoyed a healthy wager and promoted the event loudly, boasting that, 'This tough maiden is akins to my dear Abi.' 'C'mon m' laddies! Take a chance and choose your rope monkey!' Shanny cast a mock look of disapproval Remando's way and Danny jumped up and down on the spot like an over-excited chimpanzee. The crew cheered loudly, wild with enthusiasm. This was just the thing to lift morale and Patrick hoped that the event would encourage his new crew to bond. A loud bark startled Anthony. Skips had jumped up onto the gunnel so his long nose was level with his. Feeling a familiar prod in the ribs, the blacksmith felt rather pleased that Creppin had joined in the fun. 'Marrrster, wherefore shall I place me' gamblins pennies?' No matter how annoying the hunchback could be, he still managed to retain an appealing childlike naivety. Creppin pushed forward through the mass of sticky, sweaty bodies until he reached the quarterdeck. There he could see Danny and Shanny getting ready to climb the ratlines. The smelly man made it but only just managed to throw his meagre offerings into the sack before it was tied securely.

When Joe shouted down, 'May the best pyrate win!' Anthony was pleased that the boy had paid attention and not uttered a 'good luck' call which seadogs believed to be unlucky. The captain fired his flintlock pistol and the race began. As promised, Shanny was given a head start but soon proved that her challenger had made a mistake. Every time she went aloft a rush of adrenalin would give her such a high. The nimble, energetic woman literally flew up the rigging and gave her audience an impressive finale when she grabbed hold of the side of the crow's nest. Flipping her light body over with ease, she landed next to an astonished Joe. Ringing the bell in victory, she leapt back over the side and shimmied down the lines to pass her opponent. Danny whooped as she sped past him, admiring her nerve as she yelled sarcastically, 'Who's chasin' who m' laddy?!' Shanny felt good as she heard her friends and supporters screaming her name in triumphant glee. The winnings would be split amongst the lucky few who had put their money on her.

Shanny's feet had scarcely touched the boards when Anthony grabbed her around the waist and lifted her effortlessly onto his broad shoulders. Laughing heartily, she was paraded around the decks so that everyone could congratulate her. It was doubtful that anyone would ever dare underestimate the tough little wench again. As she felt the warm breeze caress her tanned skin she totally understood why her mother had fallen in love with a life at sea. Showing good sportsmanship, Danny winked at his victor flirtingly. Shanny nodded back with a friendly grin. He started to make up a ditty about their wager but his muse disappeared below decks before he had the chance to finish the vulgar song.

Despite Danny's mischievous nature, Anthony and Patrick both liked him. Although he often played the fool and could infuriate those who did not really know him, he was an excellent sailor and helmsman. The Irish pyrate had managed to steer many a ship through troubled waters and was valued and respected amongst his peers. Josh tried to divert Saul's attention away from the crazy Irishman. With fists clenched in anger, he glared at his rival as he pranced around happily singing the filthy song. Moses thrust a jug of ale into the angry lad's chest and gave him a stern look. Sensibly, Saul took heed and gulped back the tepid draft.

To avoid further friction between the two men who had clashed in a ridiculous bid for Shanny's attention, Saul was assigned to join Anthony, Josh and Gift as a gunner's mate. Colm was master gunner and was keen to begin training his new men. Serijipe and Jaeci were also happy to man the guns so Patrick agreed to accompany them for their first lesson. He was able to translate Colm's basic instruction. The captain was confident that the two bright warriors would learn quickly. After all, they both possessed a perfect eye for a target. Still wearing their tribal clothes, Serijipe and Jaeci carried bows and arrows wherever they went. Joe was asked to help as an extra powder monkey and was soon organising the younger Irish lads and teaching them how to help load the cannons safely. It seemed that Joe was a natural-born leader who was able to get along with everyone.

Colm became particularly fond of the hard-working powder monkey who shared his love of animals. Everywhere the pair went they would be sure to have some type of critter in tow. Every morning before duty, and each evening after pipe down, Colm and Joe would help Creppin tend to the animals. Although the hunchback was always first to rise, he would wait for the boy so that he could collect the hens eggs. Skips was banned from going anywhere near the livestock but was never far away from his master. When everyone was busy, he would find a way to gain access to steal the animal feed. It amused Colm how, every morning, the hunchback's first words to Joe were always the same, 'Make haste m' laddie! There are cacklefrrruits a-plenty for thee ter gather an' we pyrrratical folks hunger!' Creppin gained great pleasure watching Joe collecting the daily hatch. When their duties were done, the three would enjoy boiled eggs before joining the deck crew. Colm was insistent that they break up the shells into tiny pieces to make sure that 'no witch could sail in them.' The hunchback quickly realised that he actually loved Joe. Love was a whole new emotion for Creppin. He could not do enough to ensure the gentle child's happiness.

The crippled man had been feeling somewhat dejected of late since Anthony no longer seemed to have time for him. When Joe had shown him nothing but kindness, he believed that he had found a true friend. The boy really did care. Whenever Creppin had work to do, he would always ask the lad to keep an eye on Skips. All of the crew enjoyed Joe's company and he soon built up a healthy stash of money and an interesting collection of keepsakes. Of all the pyrates, he looked up to Anthony the most. In absolute awe of the handsome blacksmith, he hoped to grow up to be just like him. Whenever he had a spare minute he would drop by his workshop to watch him work. When Anthony gave him a small pouch with some coins and an iron shot inside, it was as if he had been given the world. 'Tis a lucky shot.' the blacksmith told him, smiling, as he ruffled the boy's hair. Crouching so he could be eye-to-eye with the delighted child, Anthony told him sincerely, 'If I had a lad like thee, I'd be proud.' Joe was surprised by his peer's words. Fatherly love was something he had never known. Feeling emotional but very happy, Joe's heart leapt with pure joy. Never in his life had he felt so good. Skipping off with treasured pouch in hand, he thanked God for pyrates.

Anthony easily applied his metalworking skills to the production of ammunition. Meticulous in his work, he took special care when making cannonballs and shots. After the casting process, he would remove any surface projections with hammer, chisel and file. Each shot would be checked with a gauge and had to pass through the metal hoop to ensure that it was the correct size. Poorly cast ammunition would most likely jam a bore or burst a barrel causing irreversible damage. The ship's carpenter had constructed units made up of planks with circular holes cut into them to store different sized cannonballs. Before long, Anthony had a well-organised production line running. He had trained Creppin and Joe to carry out quality checks on all products. They also learned how to assemble a variety of ammunition. Each would achieve a different result when fired. A well-aimed chain shot would bring down an enemy ship's rigging causing damage to her sails. Scatter projectiles like grapeshot and canister shot flew apart when fired to hit several men, clearing enemy decks for the pyrates to board. Creppin and Joe would chat away happily as they filled cans or canvas bags with iron shots to make the lethal missiles. It was crucial for Patrick's militia to have a constant supply of ammunition and Grace had ensured that the Deliverance would arrive in Eire with plenty. She had also been certain that the crew would return better skilled and ready to start a revolution that would never be forgotten.

It did not take long for the blacksmith to become a popular and well-respected member of the crew. Nothing was ever too much trouble for Anthony. Everyone went to him for blades to be sharpened or firearms to be repaired. He gained great satisfaction from modifying older weapons and was always up to the challenge of rectifying design faults. He often helped carry out repairs on the ship by replacing or fixing metal fixtures and apparatus. He had even started to make a false arm for Moses. The talented engineer planned to make a selection of attachments that would enable him to carry out tasks as well as any able-bodied sailor. Pleased with the prototype, Anthony had managed to produce the claw-like mechanism that he had envisaged back in São Vicente. He would never forget the day he gave the silent, gentle giant his new prosthetic arm. Moses could not believe that Anthony had made such an effort to replace the crude false limb that he had been used to. The replacement allowed the wearer a much wider range of movement and gave him control over its strength of grip. The bosun's mate was absolutely delighted. With a head full of ideas for different attachments that would turn the pyrate's whole appendage into a lethal weapon, Anthony returned to his workshop. Completely trusting the able metal smith, Moses grabbed onto the rigging that he had not been able to climb for way too long and decided to put his new arm to the test.

Patrick was pleased how the blacksmith's enthusiasm and dedication had affected the rest of the crew. Everyone had been amazed when they saw the bosun's mate working confidently, high in the rigging. The Moorish pyrate had become a completely different man now he was whole again. It was clear that the crew had grown keener and more willing to help one another. Their comradeship had definitely helped ease their captain's apprehension. The Deliverance was running like clockwork under Patrick's captaincy. Feeling much more self-assured and relaxed, he was able to enjoy the ideal sea life once again. He had dreaded taking his mother's place. Sushana Culley had been a tough woman who had possessed a zeal and charisma so rare that any of her followers would have laid down their lives at her slightest whim. Although Patrick knew that he had the ability to command an army he also recognised his weaknesses. Lack of self-confidence was his greatest. Ever thankful for his new friend who was proving to be a strong right-arm man, Patrick decided to include Anthony in all future decision-making. It felt good to sense his group of loyal partisans' bond growing stronger each day. The proud captain recognised that this was mostly down to the blacksmith. Everything seemed to be falling into place on this voyage. The young captain smiled to himself when he thought of Grace. As always, the canny warrior woman had devised clever plans to empower the crew. She had simply provided a basis to allow the right people to develop and strengthen. Even her most subtle deed was sure to spark new and better things.

As bosun, Cathal was in charge of the upper deck and assigned his crew to their tasks. Always alert and attentive, he made sure that everyone did their job safely and efficiently. He managed all ship maintenance and the supply stores. He inspected all sails and rigging every morning, reporting their state to the captain. The bosun would also supervise handling of sails and weighing and dropping of anchor. Unfortunately, many thought the handsome, blue-eyed, black-haired Irishman to be aloof. This was not the case. Walking upright with a natural swagger, the elegant pyrate had a habit of pushing out his chest and holding his head high. Immaculately dressed in the most flamboyant and extravagant attire, Cathal wore his dark, wavy shoulder-length hair tied back with several colourful silken ribbons. He kept his beard and moustache neatly trimmed. Often misjudged and misunderstood, Cathal was actually a humble man who openly admitted that he preferred animals to most people.

Despite his imposing appearance, the Irish pyrate viewed himself as an ordinary man and never acted above his station. Fluent in Irish Gaelic, Latin and English, Cathal was an ardent reader who always had a book at hand. As the fifteenth child in a poor Roman

Catholic family, the bosun had not had it easy until he was taken under the wing by his parish priest. The kindly cleric had given him a fine education and Cathal had never forgotten the teachings of the bible. Ironically, his Catholic faith had remained strong despite his choice of career. Living by a strict set of personal moral codes, Cathal tried to suppress lustful desires and would only kill in self-defence or to protect another. Occasionally he would lapse and give way to sexual indulgence but then he would repent and devote himself to prayer, penance and fasting.

Cathal was pleased with his crew's efforts since they had set sail. As the superstitious bosun stood on deck, facing a brisk southerly wind, he looked up uneasily at grey-blue skies mottled with stray clouds. Recognising the call of a pair of storm petrels he shivered. Subconsciously, he crossed himself and shouted a warning, 'Hark! Mudder Carey's chickens' call! Take heed, storms-a-brewin'!' Sighting the smallest of seabirds was a bad omen for sailors. They had gained their nickname from the Spanish 'Mater Cara' meaning 'dear Mother' referring to Mary, Mother of God. Sailors had corrupted the words to 'mother Carey's chickens' but also referred to them as 'water witches' or 'satanites'. Cathal was not alone in his belief that this breed of bird, along with the albatross and gull, hosted the souls of dead seamen. As the Holy Mother was the sailors' protector, she would send a storm petrel to forewarn them of bad weather. Feeling the need to empty his bladder, the bosun walked leeward where he could relieve himself. As he counted his steps, he untied a pouch that he always kept on his person. Taking out his lucky turtle bones, he began to roll them between thumb and fingers. As he asked Mary to intercede for him, one of the storm petrels began to flutter like a bat then swooped down to the sea to catch a tiny fish.

The bosun was in two minds whether to be too concerned about the deformed man who had been allowed on board. It was bad enough to have a disfigured person on board but Creppin had also tempted fate by breaking an age-old seafarer's rule. The haphazard fool had already gained enemies amongst the superstitious Irish crew when they had heard him being scalded by an angry Finn. When Creppin had bounded clumsily off the gang plank, he had set his right foot first on boarding the Deliverance. Any sailor knows to step on and off a vessel with their left foot first to avoid disaster. Anthony could not believe what Creppin had done when they had first set foot on Grace's ship. Evidently, he had failed miserably in his efforts to drum the strict codes and rules of ancient mariners into the hunchback's thick skull! Creppin had been so excited about his new pet that superstitions had completely slipped his mind. Even considering his poor memory there was one rule that Anthony could guarantee that his unsanitary friend would never break. As human hair and nails had once been popular as an offering to the Roman goddess, Proserpina, it was believed that Neptune would become jealous if either were cut whilst sailing in his realm… No chance of Creppin breaking that rule!

Before Cathal had the chance to untie his trews, a dreadful commotion stopped him in his tracks. Fangs and Claw burst from an open hatch and tore passed him with an insane-looking mutt on their tail. 'Ah! Tinkin' o' the devil!' the bosun cursed as he saw Creppin hobbling clumsily after the wild creatures. His little mongrel's jaw snapped shut on the ginger moggy's tail tearing a healthy chunk of meat and hair from bone. With a loud screech, the injured cat turned to swipe extended needle-sharp claws at her attacker. Living up to her name, Claw gave Skips five neat slashes across his nose. Yelping in dismay, the dog did not give in but continued the chase. With lightning speed, the cat shot up the ratlines to join her mate. Skippy circled the base of the main mast. His determined tawny coloured eyes were fixed on his escaped quarry. Barking loudly, his hackles rose in fury. With an expression of utter distain, the cats looked down on the beast that they considered far inferior to their species. The black tom yawned widely displaying a sharp set of teeth. Snuggling closer to his mate he noticed, for the first time, that blood was dripping from her wounded tail. He had the audacity to start licking it clean. Fangs jumped back in surprise when he received a swift but heavy dab from the disillusioned feline. She gave him a disapproving look. Slowly blinking her beautiful almond-shaped eyes, the female cat took time to ponder over recent events. As if chastising him for leaving her in tow when she was being chased by the ferocious animal, she lifted her ruined tail to display her pretty pinkness. She would not be allowing him access to that delight for a while. Suddenly remembering the tasty morsel that he had stripped from the cocky creature's tailbone, Skips scampered off to retrieve the treat. Grabbing his trophy in his mouth, he wagged his tail in eager anticipation. The mischievous hound jumped up onto a coil of rope to guarantee his spectators a good view. The little dog gained great pleasure eating the end of Claws' tail. He gave a triumphant bark before disappearing through the hatch. The smell of fresh meat had diverted his mind away from the cats... for the meantime, at least.

Patrick sat with Anthony inside the captain's small cabin as the ship heaved, pitched and rolled in a moderate swell. They had left the new crew with good news; Hawkins had already arranged for them to pick up the best galleon from his shipyard. John had sent word with a messenger who Patrick had paid well to deliver a letter listing the gangs' false names so he could prepare necessary papers. The Naval Commander would ensure that every rule was followed to the letter to avoid any suspicion of foul play. Patrick and Anthony felt their bond strengthening as they sat together, totally relaxed, whilst discussing the progress of the newest members of the crew. As a capable sailing master, Patrick was in charge of navigation and piloting the Deliverance. Part of his job was to direct course and mark maps during the voyage. Grace had ensured that he had the most up-to-date navigation equipment. Keen to pass on his navigational skills, Patrick showed the blacksmith the route that he had charted. He planned to sail to Lundy first, then on to Plymouth and finally, Ireland. Anthony's spirit soared at the thought of being re-united with Grace. Patrick explained his reason for the copious amounts of citrus fruits that had been stored. He wanted his men to stay as fit as possible to avoid further delays. To combat the problem of lack of vitamin C in the crews' diet, Captain Culley insisted that every man drink a cup of a mixture of lime and orange juice daily. His mother had told him that a deficiency of the essential vitamin caused a terrible disease that was common amongst sailors with poor diets. 'I've seen too many a good man riddled wi' 'scorby', Patrick told Anthony with a grave look on his face. 'After ten or more weeks at sea, they'd begin to experience mis'rable aches 'n pains, 'oft complainin' o' stiff bones. Whoppin' purple spots'd cover their nether regions. 'Twas then when their gums'd swell like rotten peaches and grow o'er any teeth they 'ad left. They'd soon drop out.' The blacksmith looked concerned as he listened to his captain speak of the dreaded disease, 'Twas a blessin' when 'twas o'er for the poor blighters. I recall watchin' one mate drop, dead as a doornail, in front of me. Didna' even finish his sentence!' By complete coincidence, there was a knock at the captain's small door and the cook entered carrying a large leather pitcher of the medicinal beverage.

Anthony noticed that one of the cook's arms was twisted and had shrivelled to half its original size. He guessed that he had suffered from rickets at some point in his life. The lame pyrate had an extreme bow in one leg but it did not seem to affect his walking. Like many a hardened seadog who had become disabled, he had taken on the role of cook. When no longer able to climb the rigging or man the cannons, most seamen would take any job on board to avoid a miserable life as a land-lubber. The cook stepped carefully down the few steps that led into the small cabin. All of a sudden he was taken by complete surprise. He only just managed to hop aside to avoid being knocked off his feet. Fortunately, his balancing skills were excellent having spent many years at sea. Wild-eyed and full of excess energy, Creppin's naughty hound bolted past the alarmed cook into the cramped quarters. Luckily for Skips, not a single drop of the valued liquid had been spilled. Totally ignoring any commands, the crazed dog sped around the table, clearing any obstacles with ease. Reacting at exactly the same moment Patrick and Anthony both leapt up to try and grab him. Head-butting each other painfully in the confusion, they tried in vain to trap the pesky mutt.

Totally oblivious of the havoc that he was causing, Skips continued sprinting his frenzied tight laps. Without any warning, he suddenly stopped in his tracks and began to wag his tail rapidly. The canny tribal dog stood, stiff and alert, sniffing the air with his long nose; it was about time for him to check this place out. Panting enthusiastically, he quickly scanned the area for anything edible. A sudden racket from the open doorway alerted Micken who squawked his signature call, 'Mickeeen, yeeeaaahhh! Mamaaa!' That did it! As the hunchback appeared in the doorway, he lost his footing and tumbled down the steps to land head-first at the foot of the table. Once again, the cook expertly dodged the intruder. Skips hurled his little body at the parrot's cage knocking it over. Micken gave out a piercing squeal and green, white and yellow feathers flew above the upturned cage. Stunned and confused, the little bird struggled to his feet.

Skips thrashed about as he tried to free one of his front legs that had become trapped between the cage's metal bars. It took a few minutes for the wee bird to recover from the shock but, when he had shaken himself out of the daze, he saw red. With an evil, piercing squawk Micken puffed out his chest and lifted his wings in a menacing manner. Hopping over to perch on the trapped dog's paw, he opened his strong, sharp beak and bit hard onto his leg. Yelping wildly, Skips jumped up and managed to free himself. Skidding on slippery boards he pelted out of the door and out of sight.

Creppin lay flat on his face in a pool of blood that was expanding on the boards around his head. No-one said a word. Instruments were strewn everywhere and upturned furniture lay around the jumbled cabin. Before Patrick had time to think, the cook piped up, without a care in the world. His jolly Irish lilt never failed to charm even the most miserable of souls, 'Will yers be needin' me t'add more from der 'wee pot' Cap'n... or shall yers trust an Oirishman ter gi' yers arl a healty mix?' Patrick looked at Anthony who raised his eyebrows and smiled. They both burst out laughing at the rosy-cheeked pyrate's casual remark following such a calamity. Not surprisingly, it had been Remando's suggestion to add alcohol to the sour medicinal juice mixture. Patrick had to admit that it had been a good idea and had certainly improved the taste. The addition definitely made it easier on the pallet and would also help to preserve the juice for longer. Little did Remando know that Patrick had brought several barrels of his home-brewed poitín aboard and he wanted the alcoholic to remain ignorant of that fact too. Creppin's muffled words could just about be made out, 'Pardy, pardy me marster! Yon Skipster slipped frrrom me grrrasp when I trrried ter snips his toesy nailses.' With eyes streaming, the captain and his friend fell about with renewed laughter at the irony of Creppin's remark! The hunchback had certainly received pay-back three-fold from his new pet for the hard work that Creppin's groomers had had to put in only a few weeks earlier. Thanks to Skippy for escaping a manicure, Neptune would not be on the warpath!

After a few days, Shanny had showed boundless courage whilst manning the rigging. She appeared to have no fear so was often assigned to work aloft in bad weather. So far undaunted by any task thrown her way, she had already proved herself an able sailor. When the wind was fierce the energetic woman would be the first to volunteer to go aloft. Confidently, she would step out onto the yards, untie the gaskets and let the sails down for stowing away. At first, Shanny had found it difficult working the rigging on dark nights. It had been frightening when there was no moonlight to help her see. Undeterred, she soon memorised the various routines when climbing the lines. From then onwards, even in the pitch black of night, she managed as well as any other. When strong winds thrust the Deliverance through breaking seas, the confident woman would work nimbly and swiftly high in the rigging, moving with the motion of the rolling vessel. The woman was amazing to watch. As wild winds roared, her slight form was often tossed around like a ragdoll but her grip was firm as she stayed calm and in control. Shanny tackled the ropes like a trapeze artist, swinging and balancing so skilfully, however violently the ship dipped and bucked. She would gain an unbeatable high when manning the sails during hazardous weather conditions.

The Deliverance continued to battle on through breaking seas until she reached a stretch of seemingly less troubled waters. A menacing arch of darkness emerged from beyond the sweep of the sea. An abrupt change in the wind caught the helmsman unawares. Danny's warning call alerted everyone to prepare for a hard ride; 'We're taken aback!' Several orders followed, barely audible over the crash of tumbling waves, 'Batten down the hatches!', 'Strike th' royals!', 'reef th' mainsail', 'Hold her steady!' Danger loomed as the helmsman battled to keep the wind behind the sails as the sailors fought to obey orders. It was all he could do to stay upright, desperately trying to grip slippery wet boards with his bare feet. Despite Danny's efforts, the Deliverance was flipped around as unforgiving gusts pressed her sails back against her masts forcing the ship astern. In their efforts to reef the sails, sailors lost their grip and fell shrieking, one by one, into the tempestuous depths. Like ants, others immediately replaced their mates and eventually, the job was done. There was little more they could do now but try to stay on the ship and ride out the storm. The Deliverance bounced around on tumultuous waters as men rigged ropes fore and aft along the deck. This precaution gave them something to grab onto as the ship swayed violently in heavy winds. A few pyrates had grabbed a line and wrapped it around their waists to prevent them from being flung overboard. As the gale blasted its destructive force, huge white-capped waves were thrust against the ship. Countless more lined up behind pushing forward on an unavoidable course of destruction. Kegs packed full of precious food supplies were tossed around as if weightless, smashing against men who fought to save what they could. Sheets of rain teemed down as a hazy glow of moonlight occasionally appeared between heavy banks of charcoal cloud.

Patrick managed to keep his wits about him as the terrible squall caused his head to thump in agony. His head burned and he felt as though his skull was about to explode. The captain's tension was clear to see. Squinting sore, bloodshot eyes he felt his pulse rapidly pounding his temples. The extreme penetrating pressure was becoming harder to bear. Still high up in the crow's nest, Joe hugged the thick girth of the solid wooden mast. Mesmerised by the beautiful white forks of light that danced above in blackening skies, he threw his head back in glee. Feeling woozy as he watched grey clouds speeding above him, he heard the pyrates' cries as they battled below in their efforts to keep control of the ship. The spellbound boy looked down, giddy with excitement and nervous anticipation. The lad's imagination ran away with him as he envisaged himself amongst the pyrates trying his best to ride out the storm. A strange sensation made every one of his nerve endings tingle. Joe felt the hairs on the back of his neck stand on end. A nauseous feeling overtook him. Lightning flirted with the mizzen mast then suddenly leapt over to flash a fork of static electricity right above the crow's nest.

It was a direct strike. Thunder roared as the lightning bolt hit the boy dead centre in his forehead. He took the full impact of the electrical discharge which coursed through his small body. Joe had seen a bright white flash that instantly blinded him. Seething heat sped through his body and a loud 'pop' startled him as his eardrums burst. Violently flung from the crow's nest, he was propelled several feet into the air. The crew watched in helpless horror as the boy's body hurtled above them. The storm raged on. Thunderous booms echoed as if the skies were performing a disturbing final death-roll. The Deliverance was tossed helplessly over tumbling waves of a dark, foam-lashed sea but her crew managed to keep her afloat during the angry torrent. Gale-force winds continued to thrash the wooden vessel that had made no progress in hours. It was all the men could do to keep her above the seething waters. Now, pelted by hailstones, they fought to keep the Deliverance afloat. She was tossed in the waves as though she was a small barrel. The ship's carpenter continued to work repairing her surface wounds. Holes were temporarily plugged and oakum was placed in seams between damaged boards. Masts and yards were bound to strengthen splintered wood. Ruthless waves lapped greedily at the sides of the reinforced ship trying to pull her down into the deadly depths. At least three men had been washed overboard. There was little anyone could do but watch in despair as their battered bodies were tossed around like delicate driftwood.

Patrick was devastated. All colour had drained from his face. Anthony was concerned about his friend and tried to keep him focused, 'Cap'n, we need more hands te' man the pumps an'...' Still in shock, Patrick's mind was locked in a whirl of confusion. He felt nothing but guilt and terror. The boy... Although the blacksmith's words were barely audible over the sound of crashing waves, they suddenly registered as he continued to urge the captain to take action. Patrick managed to pull himself together, 'Shrimp, Saul...' he reeled off several other names and those still present obeyed, rushing down to help empty the bowels that were constantly taking on water. As Anthony and Patrick stood astern, they watched in despair as the dead became small specks in the vast ocean. Angry waves heaved beneath the hull. Patrick guessed that the freak storm must have claimed at least ten of his men's lives now. He saw Danny standing steady at the helm, his bare feet gripping the boards as the ship bucked on thrashing waves. One minute he was below the captain, almost obscured by waves as he fought to steer the Deliverance, the next, he was high above him as she bucked defiantly on raging seas. The determined helmsman had tied a rope around his waist to secure him as he steered. Each time he was thrown high into the air he yelled a rebellious defiance into the spray, 'Is dat all ye can muster?!' he goaded. The sound of the wind was deafening as it ripped through the rigging. After what seemed a lifetime, Anthony felt relieved to see Danny looking triumphant. Once again, the expert helmsman had managed to hold the craft steady whilst the crew had kept her afloat. Anthony was breathless. Barely able to take in what he had just experienced, he was pleased to see that Patrick had taken charge again.

Despite their exhaustion from the trauma of riding out the maelstrom, the experienced crewmembers immediately returned to their original duties. It almost seemed as though nothing had happened. Drained of energy, everyone was running on adrenalin and an innate will to survive, no matter what. The blacksmith joined the skilled veteran pyrates and began to carry out repairs under their instruction. Their perseverance was infectious. From the bridge, Patrick commanded, 'Ready about!' The crew yelled, 'Ready!' The helmsman shouted 'Lee-ho!' as he steered the ship leeward. As the gunnels dipped into a sea dimpled with heavy rain that teamed down diagonally, the Deliverance was back on route. Although the worst of the storm had passed, prowling grey clouds looked ominous as they rolled slowly on overhead. A blinding flash of golden sun appeared momentarily then disappeared behind another murky dark veil.

When the Deliverance had picked up speed, Patrick summoned the entire company to the main deck for a headcount. Everyone had stayed alert in hope of spotting any survivors but no-one had surfaced during the dying storm. As the mighty, triumphant ship ploughed her way through the ocean, the sun finally won over. Warm rays cast their brightness on billowing sails as a school of flying fish skimmed the waters alongside the vessel. They looked so pretty as they leapt together in arches like silver darts. Witness accounts confirmed Patrick's fears as his crew began to relay their news; 'E was knocked clean out...' 'Split 'is head on the deck...' 'ripped away from the riggin' an trown into de' depths...' Remando began to panic when he could not see Shanny. Moses patted him on the back and nodded calmly to reassure him that she had survived. A sea of weather-beaten faces showed hopelessness and regret for lost shipmates as they stood amongst the debris. Dismissed by their frustrated and forlorn captain, the crew returned to their stations. The bell sounded eight times but no-one took any notice. Adrenalin kept their brains alert and everyone pushed their weary bodies on to work on auto-pilot. They were still not home and dry.

Utterly traumatised, Shanny had been the first to reach little Joe's lifeless body only minutes after the terrible incident. A sharp intake of breath caught painfully in her throat as she pulled his scalding hot corpse close to her breast. Intense radiating heat caused her to wince with pain as she burnt her sore fingers. Trying her hardest not to gag from the smell of burning hair and sulphur, she embraced the dead child tightly. Letting out a mournful wail Shanny began to rock the boy back and forth. 'Breathe!' she commanded in desperation whilst staring intensely at Joe, desperately willing him to open his eyes. As if convinced that her movements would bring him back to life, the young woman rocked more vigorously. During his short life, it was doubtful that Joe had ever been held in a nurturing embrace. His clothing had been torn off when the lightning bolt had struck. Shredded pieces of cheap, singed cloth had landed a good distance away from the corpse. Internal haemorrhaging had caused bleeding from his ears and nostrils. Unable to understand the reason why God would take such a precious life, Shanny felt utter hatred towards the deity that she had come to despise. Ironically Joe looked peaceful as he lay with his head resting on the bitter woman's breast. A small burn mark showed a deep entry point where the fatal blow had struck. Only a small piece of cloth from the lad's hat had remained in place, melted into his flesh. Vapours rose as the rain dropped onto Joe's skin, yet it looked just as though the distressed woman was holding a sleeping child. Danny had witnessed the hit and approached the dreadful scene. Flinging his arms around Shanny, he tried to calm her. Saul ran over to offer his help. Under the terrible circumstance he was unconcerned by the Irishman's closeness to his grieving friend. The few who had witnessed the dreadful incident stood in silent disbelief. They found it hard to accept that such a loveable child with an infectious lust for life lay lifeless before them.

As the raindrops turned to a fine drizzle, the fragile body eventually cooled. Red, blistered skin gradually faded to a pinkish-grey. Shanny watched fern-like patterns appear on Joe's trunk, left arm and shoulder. As Anthony approached, his pace slowed to a halt. All he could do was stand and stare. A feeling of deep despair filled his heart. Amidst the commotion, the blacksmith had not realised that Joe had suffered a fatal wound. Placing a hand on Shanny's shoulder, he stared down at the boy who he had thought so much of. Hearing Patrick's voice but not registering his words, the blacksmith's stomach flipped when he noticed that Joe still clutched the small pouch that he had given him. The metal coins and shot had fused fast into the palm of his small hand. Anthony needed to scream, to punch someone, to smash his head against the broken mast. Frozen to the spot he looked like a startled hare. Suddenly, Patrick's words registered. It was the captain's turn to be strong for him now. Patrick shouted, 'Anthony! Tend to the injured!' Unable to cry, the blacksmith turned and fled on his officer's firm command. Confusion reigned as Patrick scanned the deck. Acting on pure impulse and trusting his instincts, he made a mental list of casualties, position of the crew, who needed most help and yelled out clear and precise commands. His natural leadership abilities surfaced and the crew of the Deliverance was pulled together again. Ten had gone overboard, drowned. Thankfully, no-one had suffered any serious injuries. The longest three hours that Patrick had ever had to endure passed by before the wind finally dropped. At last the sea had quelled its foul temper... for the meantime, at least. As turbulent waves calmed to a steady roll, the crew finally regained control of their sturdy vessel.

It was Moses who had silently persuaded Shanny to take Joe's body below deck to be washed and laid out respectfully. Creppin insisted on staying with the corpse and held his little hand as everyone walked solemnly by. As they paid their last respects the crew half expected the lad to get up, grinning widely and ask what they wanted him to do next. Shanny had washed and dressed Joe in clean clothing that was too big but she had folded it under him to look as though it fitted. Only the small burn mark in the centre of his forehead gave away the terrible truth. In sheer despair, Shanny sat with her head in her hands. Having witnessed Joe's little body hurtling towards the stern before it smashed onto broken boards, she felt sickened with grief. Why the hell could it not have been her? Finally giving in, the young woman sobbed her heart out. Creppin joined in, bawling loudly as Danny and Josh came to collect the body.

Gathering around the scuttlebutt, Moses, Anthony, Shanny and Josh stood together quietly. Not usually one to spend time with those amongst the crew who met in the same spot to exchange mindless ship's gossip, Moses had made an exception that day. When he had noticed Shanny about to dip her wooden cup into the large, insect-infested water barrel he stopped her before the putrid, musty-smelling water reached her lips. A drink from the old scuttlebutt would only be consumed as a last resort when all ale and spirits had gone and survival was the pyrates' sole concern. That morning, most of the crew would have done anything to help take their mind off the tragic loss of their little pal. Deeply wounded by Joe's death, the small group of friends stayed silent.

Moses wished that some of his men could feel comfortable enough to stop wittering on in a poor attempt at false bravado. Talk about contemporary medical skills and midwifery having barely advanced since medieval times went way over the Moorish pyrate's head. The Irish pyrates went on to ridicule the English Queen with her army of medical professionals who still held the firm belief that illnesses were caused by the influence of the stars, hence the term 'influenza'. In the lands of Eire, herbalists and natural healers were still highly respected and always the first to be consulted with illness. Their cures were often more effective than expensive English professionals. In Britain, epidemics were rife and medical knowledge insufficient to the extreme. Many people died as a result of infected wounds. Typhoid, dysentery, the sweating sickness, scrofula known as the 'the King's Evil', smallpox and the Black Death had claimed so many lives with around twenty five percent of children dying before they reached their first year. Fifty percent perished before turning ten years old. As the pyrates became more animated and passionate in their discussion, many gave personal accounts of how they had lost an infant relative.

Joe's sudden death hit everyone hard. They were angry as well as sad. The harrowing truth was that they had been blessed with an extremely loveable, innocent child who had suddenly been torn from them. Joe had displayed such a zeal for life despite having been through such perilous, traumatic times. The hardened criminals had respected him greatly for that. He had simply won their hearts. A fighter and survivor, Joe had shown true passion for Patrick's cause in such a short space of time. Everyone was sure that his spirit would always linger. The Irish crew, in particular, had taken him under their wing. He had been eager to learn everything about their illicit, daring and adventurous trade. Somehow Joe had given everyone hope. Many of Grace's men were staunch Catholics. As the breeze gently teased the sea's surface, voices became hushed and a group began to say the Rosary. Tears flowed freely. Covered with the Culley pyrate flag, the infant's body was laid on a piece of sailcloth with two cannonballs placed at his feet. Someone had pierced the dead boy's ears to insert a large pair of gold earrings. Superstitious sailors believed that the ferryman would take the jewellery as fare to carry the dead over the River Styx. Colm had sewn the body and weights into the hemp shroud with thirteen stitches. He made sure to pass the large needle through the child's nose on his final stitch. Sailors always did this to make sure that the person was dead.

Looking solemn and forlorn, Patrick and Anthony emerged from the captain's quarters. Every face was cast downward and held a grave expression. The atmosphere was stifling with a heavy air of despair. Waves slapped lazily against the resting ship. Watery-grey skies added a miserable backdrop to the heart-wrenching scene. Even the wind seemed to hold its breath for a short while. The men did the same and took off their hats. It was going to be difficult to lift spirits. Creppin sat on a large coil of thick rope stroking Skips who was unusually calm. Sensing the sorrow, the sensitive dog sat bolt upright and cocked his pretty head. With ears pricked up, his tail could be heard thumping on the timber as he looked up at his master with perplexed concern. His occasional whining added to the melancholy ceremony.

Cathal's beautifully soft voice made Shanny sob deeply as he began to sing. Remando took her in his arms and pulled her close, comforting her as a father would his daughter. Moses' eyes were sore from too many tears. A few men cleared their throats but Creppin suddenly broke down, his tears leaving clean tracks after they had streamed down grubby cheeks. Skippy finished the job by licking the whole of his master's face. Patrick gave a short speech that touched everyone deeply. His voice quavered as he spoke very highly of a boy who had made an amazing impression in the very short time spent amongst them. Danny stepped forward to lead a prayer 'Remember nat our wee brother's sins as we are moindful of Thy loving mercy from all eternity. We beg Thee noy ter cleanse Joe's soul of his sins and fulfil his ardent desoirs that he may be made worthy to behold Thee face to face in Thy glory. May eternal rest grant unto him, O God an' let perpetual loit shoin upon him.

Amen.' Anthony added the final words, 'We will ne'er forget thee, Joe' before the tiny corpse slid from the plank into the grey sea. There was scarcely a splash as his tiny form broke through the smooth water's surface.

The night following the burial at sea seemed never-ending. When his shift was over, Shrimp reported to the bosun that all was well aboard the Deliverance. Cathal took the logbook and carefully copied the speed, distance travelled, headings and tacks that he had recorded during his watch. When the pyrate returned to the upper deck, Josh was waiting near the helm ready to take over for the next eight hour watch. "Tis good ter wipe the slate clean, mate.' he said as he wiped the chalk from the tablet. 'Ay 'tis that', came Josh's reply taking the chalk to add the time. He had nothing else to say as he rang the bell once. With a sigh, he turned over the sandglass for the 4am watch. Josh dropped the log off the stern and turned over a thirty second sandglass. When the grains had run through, he hauled in the logline to count the knots. For once the two pyrates were glad of a laborious task.

Chapter 13

Return to Lundy Island

On the thirteenth of November 1578 Patrick Culley turned eighteen. He felt pleased with himself having successfully captained the Deliverance on the voyage to the northern coast of Devon. The crew sailed past Hartland Point until Lundy Island was sighted. Ordering the anchor to be dropped a safe distance from the isle's lethal shores, Patrick felt apprehensive. He had expected it to feel strange to be back. Fond memories flooded his mind. Many happy times had been spent in Lundy with his mother and a good many others who had served under her command. Now he felt lucky to have his own reliable crew. The pyrates' bonds had grown stronger every day. Even Creppin had managed to make himself more useful as he became less dependent on Anthony. Patrick was very pleased with everyone and would reward them well.

A slim crescent moon glowed pearlescent white against a midnight blue sky. The captain gazed up at a magnificent canopy of brilliant stars. It was a chilly night. The wind gusted and the sea was as dark and dangerous as ever. Lundy was the perfect pyrates' lair. Having a natural deadly coastline, the isle's vast honeycomb caves provided a hiding place for countless hoards of precious booty. With only a vast stretch of sea separating it from the colonies of the New World, the sharp granite outcrop was only half a mile wide and a little over three in length. For many years, the welcoming golden glow of a lantern-lit shoreline had lured countless ships to their doom. Unsuspecting crews often fell for the pyrates' trap. Their vessels soon joined others in the ships' necropolis only to be looted as their crew were mercilessly slaughtered. No life was spared unless the murderous thieves found a woman amidst the wreckage. Heaven help her poor soul if she was unlucky enough to be captured. She would have been better off dead. Women had been known to endure unimaginable atrocities at the hands of such sadistic brutes.

Patrick, Anthony, Moses, Shanny, Remando and Shrimp boarded a longboat. They headed towards the rugged shore. As they rowed through the eerie ships' graveyard Shanny felt an unnerving sadness. Although the boat was relatively light, she found it hard work manoeuvring between an obstacle course of bleached, broken spars of wood that jutted awkwardly from unsettled waters. It was devastating to see the meagre remains of magnificent ships that had met their doom, smashed to pieces against treacherous rocks. A brisk wind agitated the tattered, faded cloth that had once been a fine regal flag. As the pyrates pushed on, Shanny shuddered. The wind whistled ominously as she imagined the crew who had once raised their colours high on the main mast of a majestic vessel. Their skeletons now lay on the seabed trapped in a watery grave. Trying to focus on the coastline, the unsettled woman continued to work her oar as hard as she could. Heavy waves crashed on coarse rocks as the crew fought to steady the boat. Without a doubt, there was something sinister about the island that the ancient Celts had referred to as the Isle of the Dead. The first settlers had held the firm belief that Lundy was one of the holy gateways to the Otherworld, where their bodies would be taken by ferry after death.

Patrick felt a shiver of anticipation as he rowed towards the flickering flames. Despite immense danger, the island still felt like another home from home to the captain. He had nothing to fear here. This was his territory. Although Patrick wished that he could have instilled a little more optimism into Shanny and Anthony, he knew how pointless it would have been to try. Lundy was a foreboding place where many atrocities had occurred. He could not lie. They would simply have to put their trust in him and the others. Seagulls' plaintive cries mingled with a harsh whistling wind. Waves mercilessly pummelled the cliff base.

Patrick had described Lundy's menacing approach perfectly. For the first time since leaving his hometown, Anthony felt genuinely scared. Glancing at Shanny, he noticed how tightly she gripped her oar handle. It was clear to see she was terrified too. The blacksmith was determined to protect her. Having heard many horrific accounts of the brutal rape and torture of women by pyrates, he was not going to let Shanny out of his sight. Although he understood why Patrick had allowed her to accompany them, he hoped to God that no-one discovered her true sex. He prayed that everyone would remember that her name was Séan when disguised as a boy. At least he could be thankful that Creppin was not with them. If anyone was stupid enough to let the cat out of the bag, then it would definitely be him. As if he had read the blacksmith's mind, Moses looked over and gave him a reassuring nod. A split second later, Patrick turned to check on Shanny. It was as if they had both heard his thoughts. 'Hold her steady!' the captain commanded.

A large wave covered them with bitterly cold water. Gagging on a mouthful of salty wash, Shanny started to choke. Reaching out, Patrick grabbed her oar. Remando smacked her firmly on the back. When she had recovered, she grasped her paddle and continued to pull against the swirling current. Patrick encouraged her to stay strong, urging her on with every stroke she made, 'Tha'v rowed well! Tha'll be first on shore after Shrimp!'

The rapport between the band was incredible. This was the first time that Anthony had experienced such solidarity. He felt safe. Despite his anxiety, he was certain that everyone present would defend each other to the death. Rolling on roaring breakers, the crew of six struggled to manoeuvre their boat to the safest landing point. Expertly, Shrimp cast the mooring line. The loop dropped over a natural stone pillar and the short, stocky pyrate made sure that it held fast by applying his body weight to the rope. Satisfied, he cast another line onto an adjacent rock. Ensuring that the boat was as secure as possible, Shrimp steadied himself. The others watched as he made a brave leap towards a slippery narrow ledge. A huge, white-foamed wave hit the rocks obscuring their view. For a few seconds everyone stayed put. A loud whistle soon confirmed the pyrate's safe landing. The captain ordered Shanny to disembark. Heavy, sodden clothes stuck to her body and her legs felt shaky and weak. She crouched low, ready to jump. Patrick's voice became muted as a deafening blast of cannon fire took away her hearing. Her ears hurt as she heard another, then another. Feeling suddenly dizzy, Shanny took an unsteady step forward. Gripping the side of the boat with her toes, she lunged herself blindly towards the cliff base.

By some miracle, she made it. Shrimp grabbed her arm, pushing her into a tight crevice. She was wedged in and could barely move. At last she felt stable. A leather flask was thrust into her icy cold hands. Glad to taste the warming spicy fluid, she gained an instant kick. Before she had the chance to regain her wits, Shanny saw Patrick's serious face in front of hers. She still could not hear anything but a muffled, 'ssssshhhhhhh'. The flask was whisked away to be replaced by a pair of leather gloves. Unable to make her stiffened fingers work she looked at Patrick in despair. Pulling the gloves roughly onto her sore, wet hands, her captain clapped his together, miming for her to do the same. She complied. He yelled aloud, 'Climb!' Her hearing returned. The noise of the waves was deafening! As if suddenly awoken from a bad dream, Shanny inhaled deeply. Her ears hurt like hell. Wrenching herself free from her temporary safety nook, she grabbed onto an outcrop of rock. She was grateful for a leg-up from an unknown aid.

The determined woman began the treacherous climb to the top of the cliff. Each time her bleeding bare feet found a steady foothold, Shanny thought of her mother making the same climb. Crippling fear filled her body but the woman had grit. She could do this! She pushed herself on. Anthony and Patrick had held back just in case she lost her grip. Patrick had been climbing steep rocks for years and Anthony was managing the challenging ascent well. Sea spray hit the granite rocks with some force stinging Shanny's flesh before it fell back into the seething foam-lashed waters. The slippery rock face made the ascent even more difficult for the climbers. At last they reached the cliff top. Shivering and exhausted, Patrick was relieved to recognise a pyrate who he knew well. Cut-throat Bill had spotted their ship and recognised her three shots that signalled a pyrate crew's homecoming. Patrick's choice and method of landing had also confirmed that the strangers were returning inhabitants. Signalling for them to follow, Bill led them towards the nearest shelter limping along as fast as his injured leg would allow.

Grateful for Bill's welcome hospitality, the captain and his band enjoyed a meal of smoked fish and ale whilst warming themselves by a welcome fire. As Patrick had anticipated, he soon learned that many more pyrate crews had laid claim to much of the island since Shana's departure. Territories had been invaded and occupied. Sadly, far too much blood had been spilt. Bill spoke with a thick Cornish accent, 'Brother, Oi'm forrrlorn ter reporrrt o' murrrder an' mayhem 'ere arn Lundy.' A look of grave concern showed on his tanned, weathered face. Dragging deeply on his long clay tobacco pipe, ornamented with silver, he was soon surrounded by a cloud of thick smoke. Dressed entirely in black, Bill had long, wild, white hair and a full beard to match. Having lost his left eye during a raid, he wore a black patch. Unsightly scars surrounded a sunken socket where a healthy eye had once been. He wore an expensive ankle-length cloak and a black hat that Patrick had never seen him take off. Bill's only clear blue eye watered as he was overcome by a sudden coughing fit. Taking a good, long swig from his flask, he cleared his throat.

An African grey parrot sat on a perch behind the heavyset man. The intelligent bird cocked his head. Shanny and Remando laughed when he mimicked his master's cough. Bill introduced his parrot to the visitors, 'Forrrgi' moy mannerrrs. That there's Cap'n Bones.'

The parrot echoed, 'Cap'n Bones, Cap'n Bones!' Bill gave out a raspy chuckle. The picturesque character opened an ornately decorated ivory box and took out a generous pinch of moist tobacco and a set of silver tongs. When he had packed his pipe he used the tongs to pick up a small glowing ember from the fire and lit the baccy. Taking a series of quick puffs, Cut-throat shifted his bulk on the primitive wooden bench. He looked pensive as he spoke, 'There aint nay loyalty 'ere nay morrr. T'aint loik yesterrryearrr afore thy mother left.' Bill signalled for the others to help themselves to more ale and the group listened to the aging man's news. Cut-throat had been amongst the first pyrates to make regular retreats to Lundy. Having known Patrick's mother when she had been in her prime, he admired her son greatly for his desire to avenge her death. Bill had heard of Shana's downfall and had not been surprised to see Patrick turn up. Even though her lands remained unchallenged, Shana Culley would have been disappointed by her fellow pyrates' barbaric behaviour of late. She had always lived by the adage, 'honour amongst thieves'.

Ever since Lundy had been a pyrate haunt, inhabitants had used the Old Castle on Castle Hill as a meeting place. Everyone was free to come and go as they pleased and there was rarely trouble within its walls. Patrick recalled making many trips south to visit the fort where pyrates would go to trade. In his youth he had been well-known for driving a hard bargain. A gutsy lad, he would never return home until he had struck a fair deal. Having obtained many an admirable weapon from his dealings at the fort, Patrick was disappointed to hear that everything had changed up there. Hailed as neutral ground where regular auctions took place, the Old Castle was one of the few places on Lundy where Patrick had felt uneasy. His reasons were not due to the villainous company. Although drunken, foul-tempered, barbaric murderers would frequent the haunt, the child had never felt threatened in their midst. They may have been murderous marauders but they would never have allowed him to come to any harm. Only one thing had ever frightened Patrick Culley; the supernatural. The thought of the unknown had always disturbed him. Although he had never told anyone but his mother about his ghostly experiences, everyone was aware of his phobia.

Patrick was appalled to learn that Captain John Ward's' crew had claimed Castle Hill. They currently occupied the fortress. When Bill told him the bad news, Patrick lost his temper. Infuriated that Ward had claimed a position of power on Lundy, Patrick knew that this was to be his final visit to the once anarchic isle. His mother would never have allowed a single ship of the blaggard, Ward's to even land, let alone tolerate his possession of the castle! Shana had despised the sadistic pyrate almost as much as she had Queen Elizabeth! Born and bred in Faversham, Kent, Ward was from a long line of seafarers. When capturing a vessel he would steal all she carried then convert her into a warship to add to his expanding fleet. Not only did he rob her precious cargo but every person aboard too. All skilled sailors were forced to join his pyrate crew. Any other unfortunate souls were captured to be sold as slaves. The devious villain had been denounced by England for forcing 'poor Christian people' into slavery yet English privateers were unashamedly running a profitable slave trade from West Africa. If only he had enough time, Patrick would run the bastard from the hill! There was nothing that he could do but leave the others to deal with their own plight. He had far more urgent matters to settle.

A child happiest in his own company, Patrick had spent much of his time on Lundy taming and riding wild ponies bareback. A natural-born horseman, he had always possessed an uncanny affinity with horses. On his many treks around the isle he had come to know and document every cave, trail and landmark; even the lie of the land. Anyone would have believed that he had been born there. The earthquake cracks had always intrigued the young explorer and he would often disappear on a new venture to learn more about his habitat. Patrick remembered many happy times spent on Quarry Beach not far from Quarter Wall cottages where Shana's crew lived. As he sat in the smoky cabin, he told his friends how his mother and Abi would sit together, talking and laughing, for hours. They would slowly roast lobster, fish and crab on a spit over a fire. Enjoying his reminiscing Patrick promised Shanny that he would share his mother's secret spice mixes that never failed to turn the blandest of meals into a tasty delight.

As Shanny sat huddled close to Remando, she became mesmerised by her captain's tales. In an effort to reassure her, Patrick continued to share exciting adventures that he had enjoyed with both of their mothers. Despite her sadness over Abi's choice to leave home when she had been very young, Shanny had never found it hard to understand her mother's reasons. Deeply traumatised, Abi had been unable to accept her husband's tragic death. She had also known that her daughter would be far better off staying with her aunt, uncle and grandmother. It was a weight off Shanny's mind when Patrick told her how happy her mother had been in her new life as a pyrate.

She was glad that she had also dared to venture into the same dangerous world. Every minute that she spent with Patrick made her feel even more at ease. The two were bonding well and the captain felt very protective towards the first female recruit to join his gang. Where the gutsy young woman was concerned, he had already taken on a brotherly role. In fact, the more time the crew spent with Shanny, the more of them began to feel the same way towards the spirited, likeable wench.

Lundy not only provided an ideal sanctuary for pyrates but also for thousands of migrating birds. Razorbills, puffins, kittiwake gulls and oyster catchers were amongst the many species that flocked there every spring and autumn. The marine life was spectacular too. Colonies of grey seals thrived in reefs rich with cup coral, pink sea fans and dead man's fingers. They loved to frolic in the waters along the island's east coast. Lundy boasted stunning bays, sheltered coves and fringes of rugged cliffs that had been worn down and hollowed by relentless waves. Since Patrick had been born during winter he never had a problem with the bleak, harsh climate. Like many others, Cut-throat Bill loathed the winter months on Lundy. He warned of violent westerly winds so strong that he had actually seen cattle blown over the cliffs. The wise pyrate stoked the fire well whilst keeping watch throughout the night. The visitors slept soundly. The following morning, Patrick and his gang said their farewells. Anthony and Shanny would now be able to see the unique island in a new light.

Goats and sheep grazed the stark, windswept heathland. Although the landscape was wild, there was a peaceful serenity about the place. Patrick led his team over rolling grasslands and through fragrant moors mottled with cream and purple heather. When they came across a band of hardy native ponies Anthony approached them with care. Showing no concern by the stranger's presence, a stallion nuzzled his hand to reassure his mares that the blacksmith meant them no harm. Once again, Patrick surprised his friend by displaying a natural affinity with the notoriously wary animals. Remando and Shanny fed the ponies some apples before leaving them to graze. Luckily the winds were not as strong as the previous night and the sea had calmed. After traipsing through thick gorse bushes, brambles and bracken, the gang eventually reached Coemgen Shercliff's tattoo place.

Coemgen ran a successful tattoo business in the middle of Lundy. His place had become the hub of the lawless isle. The tattooist had been an old friend of the late Shana Culley. The talented artist had spent years tattooing sailors, pyrates and prostitutes. He had travelled all over the known world, doing much of his work aboard. Having the gift of the gab, he was a born leader. Even the most hardened criminals held him in high esteem. Whenever Sushana had needed help, Coemgen would have been there for her. Now, the same could be said for her son. The extraordinary man's contacts were innumerable and invaluable. Busy as usual, his place was packed with a selection of dodgy but colourful characters. Coemgen was happy to see Patrick again. The captain was also surprised to find Jock Mackenzie amongst the customers. The Scottish pyrate was thrilled to be reunited with some good past shipmates. He greeted Patrick with a firm embrace. 'Devastated ferrr yers, mah laddie.' he declared in a strong Gaelic burr, rolling his 'r's attractively. Moses sensed his emotional pal's sombre demeanour and hugged him quickly in an attempt to divert his attention. Shrimp and Remando followed suit, both knowing how close the Scot had been to Shana Culley. Introducing Shanny, as Séan, and Anthony to everyone Patrick felt relaxed in good company. He soon caught up with island news and activity that had yet to reach Cut-throat. Pleased to hear that Abadeyo and Babatu had stayed at the base with Jock, he looked forward to seeing them again. He had always been fond of the good-natured African pyrates who he had grown up around.

It was essential that a select few of Sushana's crew were always present to guard the base during her absence. Respected and feared amongst pyrate circles, Captain Culley's crew were well organised and armed. Regularly patrolling their terrain, they would lay mantraps around the numerous treasure coves. Anyone who dared try to steal their treasure would be strung up and skinned alive. The remains of their sorry carcass would be left out in the elements. Recently, the pyrates' haven had become over-populated but Jock and his gang had managed to protect the land that the extended Culley clan had staked as their claim. 'I didnae derrream that our Shana'd meet herrr end by a hangman's noose, tha' ken?' Tears filled the handsome Scotsman's eyes as he showed genuine grief and concern for his grieving friend. It was a rarity for the tough pyrate to show any emotion. Patrick felt his heartbeat quicken and eyes well up with fresh tears. A sudden feeling of self-consciousness prompted Jock to invite Patrick and Anthony to swim with him. Shrimp and Remando were busy trying to persuade 'Séan' to have either an anchor or a swallow tattoo whilst Coemgen was staring at her chest. Patrick had let his friend into their secret about

Shanny's true sex. As the three pyrates discussed her first piece of ink work, the tattooist was trying to guess how big her breasts were under the bulky clothing. Moses stood over his ward, arms crossed in front of his impressive torso, scowling menacingly. Coemgen was one of the few men who did not feel threatened by the Moorish pyrate. Although Patrick had insisted that Shanny's true identity would go no further, he was sure that the secret would be out before the Deliverance had left for Ireland.

Patrick remembered the tall Scotsman telling him the story of his initial encounter with Lundy Isle. Jock had been amongst the first people to rediscover the natural fortress. He had been aboard a ship that ran aground during a terrific storm. Jock was one of the lucky few who had made it safely to the fatal shores. As a young lad, Patrick had been fascinated by the pyrate's story. Jock's graphic description had almost made him believe that he had been there with him as he gasped for air. The boy had known that someday he, too, would have to conquer the icy waters that had numbed the desperate man's exhausted body. He had been right. Many times he had felt that same dread that Jock had described so well. He would always remember his tale when he thought his lungs could no longer inhale the freezing cold air. Jock had grabbed onto broken pieces of sunken vessels. Yelling aloud he had refused to yield to the violent waves. Harrowing cries from dying shipmates made him even more determined to reach dry land. When he made it ashore, he and the other survivors lived off anything they could catch and any berries or roots they could find. The seashore teamed with life and crabs and shellfish inhabited the many rock pools. The men had little else to do but explore the place where they had been lured to their misfortune.

The water was very cold when the three men dived in. It was not long until Jock, Patrick and Anthony were joined by a pod of ever-inquisitive seals. It could be guaranteed that the friendly creatures would be waiting every day for their human friends' return. The group often split up to glide through different passages within the fantastic underwater terrain. Anthony watched miniature turtles munching on endless fields of multi-coloured soft coral that swayed gently with the motion of a placid underwater current. Countless schools of fish darted past the swimmers in perfect synchronisation. Now and then, their jewel-like scales glinted as they changed direction, still in unison, to confuse predators. Rocks were swathed in sea fans sheltering pretty seahorses that bobbed and ducked gracefully within the delicate folds. Re-grouping, the divers decided to swim out to a wreck about half a mile from the shore. It was a challenging swim as the surf was up. Patrick was thrilled to spot some baby sharks sheltering in the murky shadows at the base of the sunken hull. The three men enjoyed the long swim. When they arrived back at their starting point, they climbed onto some rocks where they sat silently to drink in the fresh sea breeze.

Pulling their rough woollen clothes back onto cold, damp bodies the pyrates talked about future plans. Patrick told Jock that he intended to shift all Culley treasure to Ireland. He had decided to let Cut-throat move his depleting crew onto his mother's land. He knew that the veteran seadog would keep the Culley memory alive and defend the territory for as long as possible. Bill was no fool. The brave pyrate had a reputation for holding out until the bitter end. Jock agreed that it was time to move on and assured his captain that he and the remaining few would be honoured to join his fight. The strapping Scotsman surprised Anthony with a firm hug before he left to pick up the others from the tattoo centre. It was about time for Shanny to visit the Culley's pyrate base and meet the last few survivors of Sushana's original gang. The two men who looked like identical twins found themselves alone again. Comfortable and relaxed in each other's company they chatted and laughed as if they had no cares in the world. The pair felt as though they had known each other for years as they enjoyed the occasional comfortable silence. Both men realised that they were good for each other. Patrick also knew that they were in for very rough times ahead. He only hoped that Anthony realised that too.

Patrick followed his tiny map which led him and the blacksmith to Dead Cow's Point where Sushana and Abi had buried the treasure. Patrick's mother had hidden the two most valuable yellow diamonds ever discovered inside a monkey's skull. The precious stones had been the prize find amongst spoils taken from an Indian trade ship bound for the Persian Gulf. Her wooden bowels had been laden with precious cargo for a wealthy prince until the craft had been attacked and looted by the pyrate queen. She and Abi had placed the skull, concealing the rare diamonds, inside a tiny metal-lined wooden casket. They knew that no-one would touch, let alone open, a child's coffin; even the most hardened grave-robbers were known to leave an infant's final resting place undisturbed. Sushana had claimed a substantial area of land in the middle of Lundy Island where she and her crew had built sturdy shelters using local granite.

Two dry stone walls still stood marking and isolating Culley territory. They were aptly known as Quarter and Three Quarter Wall. Each of Shana's pyrates had named a key landmark on their territory. Names included Devil's Slide, the Pyramid, Dead Cow's Point, Devil's Chimney and the Battery. Patrick ran the blade of his cutlass between the hinges of the casket and forced open the tight-fitting lid. Anthony gasped at the sight of the gleaming contents.

Resealing the chest, the captain placed it in his pack and took out a scroll of parchments. Pointing out several caves with a choice of numbered underground routes, in case a rock fall had blocked access, Patrick warned Anthony, 'We have toil a-plenty ahead, my brother.' His term of endearment touched the other man. Studying the immaculately detailed maps, the captain spoke seriously, 'I'm a-loathed to leave a single spoil that may o' been the cause of any o' our kin to a' lost a life in the takin'. Patrick's honour and respect for fallen shipmates knew no bounds. He would make sure that the Deliverance left for Ireland with her sizeable belly packed full of treasure. Lundy's days as a pyrate sanctuary were limited. Patrick predicted that it would not be long before Ward slaughtered and robbed every sea rover on the isle. Unlike Lundy's original pyrate pioneers, Ward had no morals. He would have slain his own mother for a cob!

Moses, Shrimp and Remando were pleased to be reunited with everyone back at base. Babatu and Abadeyo beamed all over their faces when they saw the surprize callers. They whooped loudly and jumped up and down in a tribal celebration dance, making Shanny giggle happily. Jock fetched a couple more barrels of ale to celebrate. Whoo was a Spanish pyrate whose name had conveniently been shortened from Juan-Pedro Primondramendos. As was customary, the friendly character gave his welcome speech. Small in stature, he was as rotund as ever. To Remando's horror, he brought out his vihuela and began to play excruciatingly badly. His singing was no better and the confident pyrate spoke quite poor English with a strong Spanish accent. Even so, his speaking voice was far more attractive than his singing. Shanny sensed rivalry between her late mother's lover and Whoo. Remando put his arm around her shoulder rather possessively but the patient young woman allowed him the privilege. She would not pull away, at least whilst her pyrate 'protector' was re-establishing his position as alpha male. It was not too long before Patrick and Anthony returned. Jock laughed when Whoo made a huge fuss of the captain stretching up his chubby form to plant wet kisses on each of his cheeks. 'Ccchhhow fair thee, my darlinks?' he asked dramatically, shaking Patrick's hand vigorously, with tears welling in his dark eyes. Throughout the evening the annoying pyrate kept looking at the captain and shouting, 'Wouldst thoust alooka dis a'maaan!' or, 'Chhhwhooo would'a drrreamda… el capitain!' The more he drank the louder he became. Remando's eyes bored into his rival's and he stayed right by Shanny until Whoo finally passed out, inebriated.

It was almost dusk when Smith, the cook, appeared. He entered the building dragging a large, bloody torso behind him. On seeing his old friends, he dropped the carcass and yelled a greeting. Jock went to fetch another barrel of ale. Smith was a wiry pyrate who wore a primitive hook on a leather cap tied to his wrist in place of a missing right hand. He wore an apron covered with spatters of dried blood of various shades of reds and browns. This concealed most of his lean body. Looking like a crazed butcher, Smith went to embrace Shanny. At first she flinched. The pyrate still wielded the bloody chopper. Suddenly realising the reason for her caution, he let out a burst of maniacal laughter. With an expert twist of the wrist, he twirled the heavy weapon then threw it hard, sending it spinning above his friends' heads. No-one raised an eyebrow as they were all used to Smith's skilful demonstrations. He was yet to miss a target. The chopper landed smack in the middle of a crude wooden table. Great chunks had already been hacked out of the few pieces of furniture in the small building, undoubtedly caused by the crazy cook's target practise. Smith had never been able to resist an opportunity to show off. Whoo woke up momentarily and tutted at his friend's flash display, then addressed Shanny, who he still thought to be a young man. He 'hacked' his 'h's dramatically, 'Hcchhhe willnay hccchhhurt thee, my darlinks boy!' His head dropped back onto his arms and he was soon snoring loudly.

Whoo's face had been terribly scarred when he had defended a fellow pyrate. He had punched a man who had unfairly attacked his drunken, ailing friend. The villain's razor blade had sliced through the brave pyrate's face, almost swiping off his whole nose. Abi and Moses had held him down whilst Shana had sown his face back in place. The psychotic looking man had no teeth and wore false, soggy wooden ones. The dentures did not fit his gums properly, made him lisp comically and were always falling out but Smith was so mean that no one dared to ridicule him. A few hours passed whilst old shipmates caught up and Shanny learned a little more about her late mother and Sushana Culley. When Patrick and Anthony returned, everyone was told that they were vacating the isle. They split into groups and each were given treasure maps. A leaving celebration was soon in full swing and the pyrates drank well into the early hours. A gruelling few days lay ahead. It would be hard graft collecting and transporting the substantial haul back to the Deliverance. The Scotsman made sure that everyone partied hard.

As the fates had decreed, Patrick and his crew sailed away from Lundy Island for the last time. Not having a terribly superstitious nature, Anthony stole a quick glance back at the wildlife haven. The seas were surprisingly calm for the time of year and he felt glad to leave the daunting pyrate retreat. Creppin's chatter could be heard coming from the bow so he decided to take advantage of the decent weather and catch up with his loyal friend. Sighing to himself, the blacksmith felt quite guilty for not having made time for the hunchback of late.

Patrick was grateful that Jock had joined the crew. As an experienced master gunner he had always assumed that position during his years spent roving the seas with Patrick's late mother. His reputation was famous in the pyrate ring and he was soon elected as quartermaster. Jock now had the added responsibility of representing the crew and speaking on their behalf. Seen as the captain's equal, unless they were engaged in battle, it was the quartermaster's job to keep ships records and account books up to date. If Patrick decided to take possession of another vessel, then Jock would take over her captaincy. As a fair but strict man, Quartermaster

McKenzie maintained order and was very good at settling disputes. Despite his new responsibilities the tall Scotsman kept on his role as master gunner so was also responsible for all guns and ammunition. A disciplinarian, he made each of his men maintain and service their firearms regularly and inspected them daily to make sure that they had done so. He would also check that all cannons were in full working order, ordering them to be fired every morning and noon. Since they had a competent metal smith aboard there was always an ample supply of ammunition. The master gunner insisted that powder in the barrels was sifted regularly to keep it dry. As quartermaster, Jock always ensured that everyone received a fair share of food and other rations. When serious crimes were committed the accused would face trial by the crew but the quartermaster had the authority to punish any of his men for minor matters. Flogging was administered by the Bosun's Mate. Moses used a rope for whipping. It was kept in a leather bag and, so far, he had rarely had to put it to use.

The captain stood on the bridge and watched the deck crew at work. He was worried about Shrimp. Unable to see the small pyrate, who had not been himself for a while, Patrick called Jock over to ask his advice. He explained his concerns. Something was not right and he had to be sure that their friend was fully committed. Jock agreed that if something was bothering Shrimp then he would have to face his demons before he did something that he would regret. Lives were at risk. This mission was going to be dangerous enough. If a single person was not completely focused, things could go terribly wrong. Jock found a forlorn and weary Shrimp sitting alone on the freshly scrubbed poop deck. He soon learned that, since Joe's death, he had been unable to stop fretting about his children back in São Vicente. His voice wavered when he told his old friend that he had frozen on the spot, watching in hopeless despair, when the boy's body had hit the deck. What if that had been his son? The seasoned pyrate did not have to mention that he was tormented by guilt for leaving his wife and children. As he listened to Jock's reasoning Shrimp's mind was bombarded with thoughts. Had he made the right decision? Shana would have been angry with him for joining her son to avenge her death, especially now he had the responsibility of a family. His concerned superior told him to get some rest. The anguished man nodded a gesture of thanks and shook Jock's hand. He appreciated the big man's consideration but his mind was too pre-occupied for sleep.

Shrimp headed towards the bow where he stopped to go to the privy. He sat over one of the holes in the plank mounted on the beak head. Saul sat at the opposite end patiently whittling a good luck talisman out of a piece of wood. 'Good eve' mate' he said without looking up, respecting the other man's privacy. Sticking out the tip of his tongue in concentration he continued to carve. Shrimp was quicker to defecate and pulled up a thick long rope. He wiped his arse with its cold, wet end then dropped it straight back down to dangle in the sea. The sea would soon wash it clean again for Saul to use. Retying his trews, the small pyrate decided that a smoke might help him to relax. Still feeling lost, he climbed down the narrow, steep wooden ladder that led down to the berth deck.

Several lanterns offered a dim but essential light. Knowing that Smith always had a good stash of tobacco Shrimp headed for the cook's quarters. He would no doubt have hidden it well. Baccy was worth its weight in silver these days. Disappointed to find his friend was not in, he continued along until he reached the carpenter's cabin. No-one was around. Nervously, the small man opened the door and stepped inside the tiny room. He wasted no time in scanning the area. Spotting a chest with its lid propped open, he went to investigate. A bloody saw lay on top of several small wooden boxes, each neatly labelled. Finding the box that contained 'laudanum' he breathed a sigh of relief. Hearing the padding of footsteps, he hurriedly grabbed two small bottles and replaced the lid. He shoved the tincture of opium into his tight belt. No-one saw him leave.

Shrimp quickened his pace, continuing sternward until he came to a large area where many of the pyrates slept. Some occupied hammocks that had been suspended wherever they had found enough space. Others were smoking but he did not know any of them well enough to ask to trade. Besides, baccy could wait now. Shrimp had what he needed. A few men were playing cards and two evil-looking characters were arguing over a book of pornographic sonnets by an Italian poet. One was accusing the other of stealing the best picture. Aretino's explicit volumes contained graphic illustrations of sexual positions. During long voyages, this type of coveted wanking material had been known to cause many fights, some actually ending in fatality. Shrimp scurried on past an Irish lad who was singing a sad folk song. His friends accompanied him on a fiddle, pipe and bodhrán. Not wanting to get involved in any chitchat or recreational activities, Shrimp put his head down and continued on his way. He descended more steps. Despite the cool, damp climate, he began to sweat. He licked his dry lips. Arriving on the gun deck where the heaviest cannons were housed, he spotted Abadeyo and Babatu, together as usual, servicing their cannon. They saw their friend and smiled. He waved a hand. Only a few of the other gunners were gathered here and no-one took any notice of the visitor as he walked along, pretending to check the cannons.

The Deliverance rolled steadily onward and Shrimp held onto the ropes to climb down another steep ladder that led to the orlop, the lowest deck. This was where the wild stock was kept in separate pens for pigs, sheep and chickens. Creppin and Colm were throwing down fresh straw. Greeted by a self-satisfied 'mieeaaaoooww', Shrimp saw Claw biting into the head of a dead rat. It still twitched as she held it firmly between her paws. 'Zounds!' he cursed loudly when Fangs leapt out, making him jump. The irate pyrate kicked the surprized animal hard sending it skidding across the floor. Scrabbling up the ladder to freedom, the moggy sat down on reaching the safety of the upper step. Shrimp heard Whoo's sing-song voice. The comical Spaniard was talking to Smith who responded every now and again with a loud curse. As always, the cook had a pipe wedged firmly between his teeth even when he had run out of tobacco. Deciding not to interrupt the two men's heated conversation, he passed quietly by. A brick structure in the form of a firebox supported two large cauldrons. Whoo was fuelling the fire with logs which were stored nearby. Smith was adding large pieces of thick bacon and beans to the boiling pots. Pease pottage was the usual staple diet during winter months at sea. Neither man was concerned about Shrimp. He quickened his pace. Below the orlop lay the hold. Climbing down an almost vertical ladder, he could go no further. Now, he stood totally alone, right above the ship's bottom planking, below the waterline.

Pre-occupied with his woes the small pyrate checked the storage rooms that were separated by partitions. Here, rats and mice were rife and weevils infested the hardtack. With a lack of ventilation, the bowels of the ship reeked of rancid bilge but Shrimp did not care. He was alone and that was all that mattered. To increase the stability of the ship, ballast was placed in the hold where most of the supplies were stored. Now, it had been replaced by wooden chests of all different shapes and sizes. The hoard of treasure had added a substantial weight to the Deliverance. Deciding to miss Anthony's exciting nightly story, Shrimp climbed up onto a chest that had been balanced on top of another. Taking the two bottles that he had stolen, he pulled out the small cork of one and drank the whole bottle. Scowling deeply, his face crumpled in disgust as he tasted the revolting medicine. Taking a comfit from one of his many pouches, Shrimp lay on his side as he felt an immediate calming effect. Popping the sweet treat in his mouth, he swigged back the remaining laudanum. Allowing the small bottle to drop to the floor, the tired pyrate lay listening to the sound of it rolling gentle across the damp wooden boards. Soon he was in a trance-like state of bliss. Nothing mattered to him now.

Creppin yelled like a small child as he sat on the floor of Smith's temporary surgery. The cook had left the stew to simmer to carry out a particularly unpleasant, but necessary, duty. Two young lads giggled as they waited their turn to be de-loused. 'Be still tha' swi-vin' daff-y-ish cod's head!' Delivering the insulting words in his usual quick tongue, the callous cook rapped the hunchback's skull hard with a nit comb each time he yelled a syllable. 'Owwwwa!' cried the complainant as the fine toothed comb was yanked through his unkempt, shoulder length hair. It had not seen a comb since Creppin's first ever grooming session back at Mary Maggy's. His matted hair was interspersed with dead lice, their shed skins, milky eggs and faeces. It absolutely stunk, adding yet another unpleasant note to the abhorrent little fellow's reek. 'Gotcha!' snarled the cook as he caught and crushed a well-gorged head louse between his fingernails. The powder monkey sitting next to the infested man giggled, then panicked when one of the parasites was knocked onto his leg. The horrified boy received a swift kick from Smith who never missed a trick. He continued the challenging task. ''I daresn't imagine 'ow tha hasn't scraped tha whole scalp off wi' scratchin', tha'v so many o' these little bleeders livin' in there!' Screwing his face up hideously, Creppin' grunted. Even the hunchback's few pathetic tufts of chin hair had not been rejected by the infestation. 'How dost tha' do it, tha' cruddy-crusted shitester!' yelled Smith, swiftly clipping his patient's ear. 'Creppin's all'ays had yon itchy grrrublets. They tastsies good if tha can catch the big'uns! Speedy li'l cri...' Instantly regretting his cheeky retort, the hunchback received a hard blow to the back of the head. Blood started to pour down the side of his face from a nasty gash caused by one of the cook's large, heavy, gold rings.

''Nuff now I tells tha!' ordered Smith. One of the young lads started to cry. Creppin calmed him, 'Dunnay crrry, child. 'Tis'nae as bad as it looks.' he said as he wiped away the blood with the back of his hand. Smith scooped some ointment of mercury mixed with pork grease out of a large bowl and smeared it over Creppin's hair. 'Be gone, smeg smuggler!' he roared, chortling at his own witty insult. 'Come on urchin! I's needin' a skinful o' the cap'n's strongest liquor!' It was almost time for Anthony's tales so Smith hurried the lads along.

Anthony's storytelling had become a popular nightly event. Entertaining the crew for an hour before pipe down, he would narrate whilst Creppin added extra hilarity by acting out little scenarios to each tale. The pyrates enjoyed the blacksmith's comical stories of his past life as a landlubber, back in Plymouth. Popular with local women of all ages, shapes and sizes he was seen as a really 'good catch'. Anthony shared a few of the hairy escapes that he had just managed to make following some daring trysts and forbidden romps. The hunchback played brilliant comedy roles as the scorned lover or naughty wench. Shanny had lent him a skirt and bonnet and made him a wig out of untwined rope. Creppin went to great lengths to look the part by applying animal blood to his lips as make up! The pair ended the night with a hearty song and Creppin danced drunkenly. Neither of them had a tuneful voice which made the ditty even funnier:

'A lusty young smith at his vise stood a filin',
his hammer laid by but his forge still aglow.
When to him a buxom young damsel came smiling,
an' asked if to work at her forge he would go.'

Creppin and the rest of the crew sang the chorus whist making filthy gestures,

> 'With a jingle, bang jingle, bang jingle, hi ho!
> 'I will', said the smith and they went off together,
> along to the young damsel's forge they did go.
> They stripped to go to it, 'twas hot work and hot weather;
> She kindled a fire and she soon made him blow.'

Creppin bared his smelly arse to roars of laughter and everyone sang the chorus again. Anthony could barely sing through fits of laughter but managed to carry on;

> 'Her husband, she said, no good work could afford her;
> His strength and his tools were worn out long ago.
> The smith said, 'Well mine are in very good order,
> And now I am ready my skill for to show'

Micken screeched loudly, annoyed that he was missing out on some fun. The captain had heard the men's roars of hilarity and was intrigued to hear his friend's song. He went out onto the weather deck to join in the chorus, 'With a jingle, bang jingle, bang jingle, hi ho!'

> 'Red hot grew his iron as both did desire,
> And he was too wise not to strike while 'twas so.
> Quoth she, 'What I get, I get out of the fire, then pri'thee,
> Strike hard then redouble the blow!'

As they mimed to the risqué rhyme the pyrates' actions became more obscene with every verse. Creppin was lapping up attention; with uncharacteristic confidence he continued the next verse solo;

'Six times did his iron, by vigorrrous heating,
Grrrow soft in the forge in a minute or so.
An oft' was it hardened, still beating and beating,
But each time it softened it hardened more slow.'

As the lame little man was now sporting an erection of his own caused by all the excitement, the men started to swipe the bulge with the backs of their hands. Creppin hopped and darted around just managing to dodge the hits. Skips went wild, trying to protect his master, wagging his tail and barking at his pursuers. When Anthony felt a hard tap on the shoulder from Cathal he knew it was time to wrap up for the night. Necking back his last tankard of mead, he finished the song on a high;

'The smith then would go, quoth the dame, full of sorrow,
'Oh, what I would give, could my husband do so!
Good lad, with your hammer, come hither tomorrow,
But, pray, can'st tha' use it once more, 'fore tha' go?"

Hearing the bosun's whistle that signalled pipe down everyone but the watch went to their sleeping quarters. Ship's rules meant that all lanterns and candles had to be put out at eight. If anyone wanted any alcohol after that hour they would have to drink it on the open deck without a light. The Deliverance was soon in darkness save for a single lantern swaying high in the crow's nest.

No-one had noticed that Shrimp had not been at the get-together. The pyrate lay amidst a slurry of stinking slime in the bottom of the ship. He roused briefly when a rat bit into his lower lip but quickly fell back into a stupor. Bristling its dark, stiff fur, the vermin scurried away to find food. Feeling no more anguish, Shrimp slept soundly as the Deliverance pressed on through a bleak, moonless night.

Whoo was one of the few men who Micken trusted. Running the infirmary, the portly Spanish pyrate was also ship's surgeon. Carpentry tools were ideal for teeth extraction, amputation and various other surgical procedures so ship's carpenters took on this role. Whoo had a few specialist instruments that he used solely for surgery. There was one in particular that Creppin was keen to try out. Ever since he had spotted the nasty looking crescent-shaped amputation knife he had not stopped harping on about it; 'Crrreppin wouldst make a fine surgeon's apprrrentice' he insisted, spraying spittle as he pronounced his p's. 'He'd be swift wi' yon knife whilst marster couldst saw.' He begged, 'Pri'thee have a heart and allow it, kind sir! Tha' wouldst ne'er rrregret it. Creppin would nay need pennies fer me trrrouble neither.' Similar to a small scythe, Creppin's favourite implement was used to make the first cut around a useless limb. The carpenter liked to get as close to the bone using the fewest incisions, hence the reason for the curved blade. A competent surgeon could slice the entire circumference of a limb with a single sweep of the nifty tool. Then he would saw through the bone and, hopefully, cauterize the stump in the nick of time.

In Whoo's small workspace every board had been painted red to hide the copious amount of blood that would often spray everywhere during some surgical procedures. The floorboards were always covered with a thick layer of sawdust. This prevented the surgeon from slipping in the blood. Tooth extraction was Whoo's most common practice. A combination of a poor diet at sea, an excessive consumption of alcohol and sugar and tobacco smoking often caused teeth to rot. When Creppin started to spend a lot of time hanging around Whoo he decided to trust him by allowing him to prepare the surgery. After a week of doing a decent job, he let him yank out a few loose teeth when patients were too drunk to care who did the job. Surprisingly, Creppin was very efficient but the ship's surgeon was reluctant to allow him to perform any part of an amputation. The little humpbacked fiend had become obsessed with the idea of cutting off a limb! So much so that if anyone on board had any kind of leg injury he would be there, 'Dost yon limb need 'armpitatin'?' he would ask his superior, rubbing his hands together in eager anticipation. 'Bing a waste, tha' devilish freak!' was often the patient's reaction. Amputation became an obsession and, after slaughtering livestock, Creppin began to amputate legs whilst imagining that he was performing the operation on a live person. The procedure had to be carried out as quickly as possible to avoid excessive blood loss. Despite his concerns, after constant pestering from the morbid nuisance, Whoo agreed to let the unhygienic deck-hand assist him in any future surgery. He could not see the harm in allowing the pest to apply a tourniquet. Crazy with glee and triumph, Creppin hurried off to find Anthony to relay the wonderful news of his promotion. When left alone, the carpenter could not believe what he had allowed the crippled fool to talk him into. Already, he knew that someday he would be made to regret his decision.

On sighting a windward vessel that was approaching at some speed, Shanny alerted the rest of the crew. Ringing the bell from the crow's nest, her instinct told her that there was something untoward about the caravel. Shanny yelled aloud a warning and the position of the sighted vessel, 'Enemy ship! Starboard, dead on end!' She was heading straight for them. There were hardly any crew on her main deck; a sure sign that pyrates were aboard the quick, light vessel. 'Prepare ter change tack!' came the captain's order. 'Helm! Hard a-port!' Patrick ordered Danny to steer the ship sharply portside. Repeating the command to acknowledge that he had heard correctly, the helmsman yelled loudly, 'Helm! Hard a-port, Cap'n!' The thrill-seeking Irish pyrate grinned as he forced the ship around. There was little more to beat a challenging sea scrap. The heavily laden vessel creaked as the spritsail was brought in line with the ship so she could be pivoted as quickly as possible. 'Gently does it!' the captain warned as the relevant lines were hauled and secured to make a safe manoeuvre. ''Tis a fight that thee want, then tha picked the wrong ship!' Patrick growled between gritted teeth, feeling an instinctual pre-conflict rush as the adrenalin kicked in. Ready to play devil's advocate, the cunning pyrate had ordered a change of course. In a bold plan of action, he planned to head straight for the rival craft. If they moved now, the Deliverance would have turned full circle before the other rig had the chance to come close enough to steal wind from her sails. 'Make haste! Gi 'em chase.' 'We ha' the wind o' 'em! She tacks about', Patrick yelled as his team worked hard to follow commands. It was time to show the 'sea robbers' who they were threatening. When fighting under the pyrate flag, pyrates were showing that they would give quarter whereas under a 'bloody flag' there would be no mercy. 'Hoist the bloody black!' Patrick referred to the flag that displayed the same menacing Culley pyrate emblem but its background was solid red.

As Patrick had hoped, the hostile presence had attempted to retreat when her captain had realised who they were up against. As he had rightly predicted, they had left it too late. The Deliverance had swung around fast enough to catch up with the fleeing vessel mid-turn. 'Run a good berth ahead of her!' came Patrick's next command. He ordered a sharp turn back, 'Tack about and keep your luff! Be yare at the helm! Edge in on her! Gently does it!' High from the thrill of the chase, the captain readied his crew for a quick, deadly battle. 'Bear down 'pon her!' he yelled. The enemy had been given enough chances and their defiance was beginning to infuriate the angry captain. 'Deal 'em a volley of small shot! Prow and broadside and keep tha' luff!' Patrick ordered. The top of the range cannons blasted causing damage to the enemy's remaining rigging and foremast. There was a strong stench of smoke and saltpetre as another volley of cannonballs slammed through the caravel's hull, sending splinters of wood flying into the eyes and flesh of crew. Men were blown to pieces and fell through damaged decks. Others abandoned ship.

Patrick had taken a chance and managed to pull off an aggressive counter-attack. Thankfully, the risk had paid off. Many of the other ship's large, cumbersome shots fell way short of their target. When warned to cease fire, the enemy captain responded with an order to attack. In retaliation Jock led his gunners to fire a damaging broadside. When each cannon had been fired gunners wasted no time and immediately reloaded. This carried right on down the line. The Deliverance managed to keep up a constant barrage as Danny manoeuvred her around the elegant vessel. To Jock's delight, his predecessor had trained his team of competent gunners well. They continued to bombard the caravel with lighter cannonballs. Now in charge of another deck of gunners, Colm delivered another broadside straight into the hull of the battered caravel. Jock's team would have finished the assault with a final round of chain shot but there was no need. The rival vessel pulled back when a stray cannonball from one of her own cannons blasted through the ceiling of the gun deck, ricocheting around the interior. The projectile had smashed through boards into a cabin below the quarterdeck, sending shrapnel flying everywhere. Cruel shards of metal flew straight into an enemy pyrate's throat. He fell to his knees clutching the gaping wound which would soon cause his death. More men lay dead and wounded from the blast. Still with plenty of kinetic energy, the cannonball shot diagonally up through another deck. Crashing into the mizzenmast, large shards were sent flying at the few survivors left on the ruined ship. The heavy missile's course had been altered by the hefty obstacle, so it continued to travel through the air. Finally, the stray shot demolished the fancy wooden railings surrounding the poop deck and dropped into the sea. The enemy had suffered irreparable damage. Her crew had ceased baling water.

Aiming his flintlock musket at the captain of the other vessel, Patrick fired a single shot. Hitting his target straight in the eye, he watched as the shot smashed through his skull, penetrating his brain. Buckling at the knees, the victim fell forward, his brains spilling onto the deck. The mizzenmast toppled onto the collapsing waist of the vessel, its extra weight tipping her leeward. Carpenters aboard the Deliverance were busy carrying out temporary repair work. Her only damage had been to the hull of the orlop deck aft the mainmast. Whoo worked quickly patching up the hole whist Anthony reinforced damaged beams with new pieces of wood. Creppin had been terrified by his first taste of a sea skirmish and had hidden in Patrick's cabin with a squawking Micken and a mad tribal dog. Skips had been a nightmare to tether. The hunchback was exhausted following a difficult struggle with an enraged dog. With hackles raised and barking loudly in his bid to escape and defend his crew, Skips had scratched Creppin all over.

In the heat of the attack, one of the mounted swivel guns had blasted loose from the deck after Gift had loaded. Another gunner had fired the cannon which had, luckily, blown the cannonball clear. However, the gun had been jolted so violently by the blast that her bolts had been ripped from the boards. Unable to get out of the way in time, Gift had been knocked over by the heavy weapon. Having heard about the accident, Creppin was there like a shot. The morbid hunchback stood gawping at the mangled mess that had once been the gunner's healthy lower limb. Shanny smelt his presence and promptly dismissed him with a look of disgust. The hunchback bounded clumsily off to find Whoo to beg him to allow him to assist. It took three men to lift the cannon long enough for Remando and Colm to release Gift's crushed leg. The injury was severe. His limb looked like a limp, bloody piece of steak hanging from the hysterical man's hip. Thankfully, Smith had soon arrived armed with poitín. The wise pyrate forced the terrified man to gag back a whole mugful, telling him, 'Drink, matey, 'twill numb the pain!' He poured the rest of the jug over his entire thigh. Whoo was notified quickly. He prepared the makeshift operating theatre. Gift lay, in shock, against the hull. In sheer agony, he screamed in his native tongue. Smith pressed a flask to his lips and forced him to drink. The poor man was instantly sick. With a dreadful look of panic, he begged Patrick to forbid anyone from chopping off his leg. He became hysterical, thrashing his skinny body around in fear. Patrick yelled at Smith, 'Tha' canst nay control tha'sel!' Cupping a bloody fist with his other hand, Smith retorted heatedly, ''E would a died o' terror ba now hadst I nay knocked him senseless, poor bleeder!' Anthony and Shanny threw a despairing look at each other as the wiry little cook punched a solid oak beam in anger. He stormed off, red-faced and cursing aloud. The unconscious man was placed on a large wooden board and carried to the infirmary.

The temporary operating theatre had been prepared and Whoo's temper erupted when the hunchback skidded in, panting. Before the carpenter had a chance to speak, Creppin began to hound him, 'Tha' gid'st tha' word that Crrreppin canst give aid! We must make haste! Yon Gift needs 'is leg cuts orf, marster!' Eventually, the angry man slapped the hunchback hard around the face. Enough was enough. He chased him out of the room with a sharpened axe. Back in his room, Whoo had the cauterizing iron heated at the ready. The nervous barber surgeon said a silent prayer to ask God for strength. Sweating profusely, he remembered the last leg amputation he had performed. The patient had died on the table. He had just not stopped bleeding. Summoning one of the lads to tell the captain that he was ready for the patient, Whoo grabbed his flask and guzzled back the burning liquor.

Creppin was upset. He skulked around, kicking anything that was not fastened down. The Deliverance was back on course and he had missed the sinking of the other pyrate ship when he had heard about Gift. He could have watched that instead of wasting his time talking to Whoo. He might have known that the oaf would break his word. 'Bah! I 'dish-pies-es' the lots of 'em!' he muttered bitterly. Skips came bounding over to his resentful master and began to bark. 'Shove off!' the hunchback shouted. By now, the tribe dog had become used to not being wanted. Still wagging his tail, he blew out from his long nose and pranced off to see where the cats were. He could pester them whilst everyone was busy. Creppin grumbled aloud to himself as he grabbed the handle of a heated loggerhead. Cathal had assigned him to deck duty. His job was to seal the pitch that had been poured into a gap between the boards. Wielding the heavy tool, he continued to moan as he ran its heavy spherical head over the sticky black substance. 'Meaaaghhh! Miff!' he grumbled.

The angry young pyrate came out of nowhere. Saul snatched the hot loggerhead right out of Creppin's hand. He swung the long handled weapon with all his might. The hunchback cringed as he saw it crash into the startled Irishman's forehead. He was knocked backwards by the tremendous blow. The back of his head hit the deck, instantaneously knocking him unconscious. Fighting amongst the crew carried a heavy punishment. Whilst Whoo battled to saw off Gift's leg amid ship, Danny had chosen the worst time to tease Saul. This voyage was turning out to be a nightmare, thought Anthony as he rushed to the Irishman's aid. Luckily, he was still alive. Patrick announced that Gift's surgery had been successful and was angry to hear that there had been trouble amongst his crew. Saul was dismissed whilst a group of neutral pyrates were selected to form a jury. A trial was to be held immediately and a fitting punishment given before they reached Ireland.

Saul had a fair trial. Everyone but Creppin, Anthony and Shanny wanted to see the young hothead punished. Creppin was called as a witness. He spoke up for his English friend, addressing Jock and the captain, 'Pardy my 'umbly soul. As God's me wetness, yon laddy meant nay 'arm t' Irish rrrrogue! E' was a-tauntin' 'im, sire. Saul swiped 'is nut wi' logger's 'ed ter quits 'is jabber! By my shite-swabber, I swears that Saul is an insolent man.' 'Boos came from portside where the Irish pyrates stood around the seated injured party. Danny and a few of the brighter lads sniggered at Creppin's mistaken word but his humorous faux pas was wasted on most of others who were unable to read or write. Before Jock had a chance to thank Creppin for giving his statement, the hunchback screwed up his ugly face. Gurning at the cheeky Irish victim, he clapped his cupped left hand firmly into his inner right elbow and raised his lower arm to flick an overly exaggerated 'V' at his mockers. 'B' Jasus, Mary n' Joseph, ye're ugly.' Danny yelled. Shouting as loud as he could as the laughs and jeers grew to a crescendo, Creppin struggled as Moses and Jock dragged him away, 'Yon Irish fiend causes trrrouble agin!' Despite Creppin's attempts to save Saul from harsh punishment, Jock decided to deal him ten lashes. The entire ship's company was required to witness flogging at close hand. Everyone crowded around. Jock was a stickler for discipline and order. Saul was tied over a deck cannon and Moses dealt him ten hard lashes with the cat o' nine tails. From that day onward, the young man held a grudge against Jock who he believed to have sided with the Irish lout. Although Danny would have happily forgiven and forgotten the incident as he often did, Saul held a grudge. As far as he was concerned, the two were enemies and that was that.

One morning, following her graveyard shift, Shanny had asked Patrick if she could use his cabin to bathe. The captain often let her as it would allow her some privacy. Everyone knew never to disturb him when he bathed. No-one entered his cabin without prior permission. Although a few were aware that Séan was actually a woman, Shanny always dressed as a man and the truth had not been revealed to the newcomers. It had completely slipped Patrick's mind that Jock had always had free-run aboard every ship that his mother had captained. Naturally, he had assumed that it would be the same on her son's vessels. When the vigilant quartermaster had seen steam coming from the great cabin he had gone inside. Expecting to find Patrick boiling a small cauldron of coffee, he had not been prepared for the sight before his eyes. He had stood absolutely speechless when he had opened the small wooden doors. A beautiful woman sat in front of a sandbox of smouldering embers that were keeping her warm. She was completely naked.

A divine aroma filled the cabin. When Shanny bathed, she would hang sweet smelling sandalwood pomanders around the room. She had brought many with her from Mary Maggy's. The potpourri freshened the stale, mouldy atmosphere and reminded her of her absent kin. The woman before him was totally naked. Jock was mesmerised. He saw that she had been washing herself with a large sponge. He smiled and kept staring. A cauldron of steaming water was suspended over the hearth. For once, the Scotsman was speechless... His hardening cock gave away his lustful thoughts. Without trying to conceal his erection, Jock approached the naked woman confidently. 'Jings! I had'nae guessed, bonnie lassie…' his deep, soothing voice made Shanny's whole body quiver. He knelt down beside her. Taking her chin in his large hand, he placed his other between her wet thighs. 'Oh y'arrr a wondrrrous sight tee behold…' Brazenly, he kissed her.

Shanny responded wildly, her body shuddering with desire. Jock's seduction was powerful. Resistance would have been futile but no woman could refuse Jock Mckenzie's advances. He was a fine looking man; tall and muscular with the air of an ancient Viking. His Scandinavian ancestry was clear to see. Unkempt, straw-coloured hair hung loose, way past his broad shoulders. Lustful, grey-green eyes took in every curve, protrusion and nook of Shanny's firm, young body. Stripping off his clothing the Scotsman craved her body, drinking in every inch that he planned to kiss, to caress, to taste… and, finally, to enter. With equally brazen desire, the young woman stared at the horny man. She wanted him to fuck her so badly! Her small hand was already between her legs. Gently, she teased herself, tracing her fingertips over the silky skin of her outer lips. She moved her fingers to touch the hard bud of her clit as she watched the pyrate undress.

Jock untied his breeches to release a hard, thick shaft. Aching with arousal, Shanny pushed two fingers inside her tight wetness. Slick and smooth, she wanted nothing more than to be entered… right… that… second. Dropping to his knees, Jock threaded his arms between the eager woman's legs, engaging his inner elbows with the damp flesh behind her bent knees.

She grabbed him firmly around the neck and their mouths came together in a passionate kiss. Jock broke away first and lifted Shanny's legs to lay her on her back. Pushing her knees, still bent, wide apart he lowered his head to taste her natural lubrication. 'Mmmmm', they groaned in harmonic pleasure. It felt incredible when his full lips kissed her inner lips firmly. Jock took time to look at her pinkness as he sucked every part of her, then pushed his tongue against her tiny hard bud. Shanny's face flushed pink as she watched him give her the most wonderful oral pleasure. Before long, she let out a satisfied sigh, 'Aaaahhhh... oh!' Jock pushed a large finger inside as she came, feeling her blissful internal muscular contractions. Shanny's back was now arched and she had thrown her head to one side.

With eyes closed in absolute content, Shanny did not expect to feel Jock enter her so soon. Pushing his way inside her whist she was still in the throes of orgasm, he felt a slight resistance as his cock tore her delicate hymen. Shanny cried aloud in ecstasy and wrapped her lower legs around the man who had taken her virginity. As he ejaculated inside his lover, she came again and again. Jock continued thrusting until she had cum three more times. Never had he experienced such a sexual bond, such passion. Their combined juices were overflowing, pouring from her. Withdrawing, Jock was breathless. 'Wo, Séan! 'That was surely akin to a wet derrream... only I wasnae derrreamin!' Shanny let out a coy giggle. The big Scotsman embraced Shanny roughly. The couple snuggled together in total contentment. A loud knock startled them. ''Tis th' cap'n', Shanny alerted. Giving him permission to enter, she covered her nakedness with Jock's large shirt. On entering his room Patrick was met with a heart-warming scene. Surprised to see the pair together the tired pyrate just laughed and dropped into his bunk. Feeling good that at least something was going well aboard his ship, he wished them both well. He advised them to find another place for privacy as Creppin would be staying there again that night. Having reminded himself of yet another inconvenience, Patrick groaned and covered his head with his arm. Micken squawked loudly as if he had understood. The parrot had been so quiet since the quartermaster had first entered the cabin. 'Aw, my wittle bootiful! Th'art verily a gooooood boy!' Shanny cooed taking the parrot out of his cage. She gave him some love before she and her new lover left the captain in peace.

Patrick woke abruptly. He saw the foul face of a middle-aged woman hovering above him. She stared down menacingly. Cocking her bony face to one side, she stretched her jaw hideously wide to deliver a blood-curdling scream. Wild white hair swirled around her head framing a sallow, bony face. The spectre held a human heart in her skeletal hand. Scowling as her piercing grey eyes stared out from sunken sockets, she slowly squeezed the muscle. Patrick saw that the heart was still beating… then the woman's long, sharp, yellowed nails pierced its tough outer skin. Thick, dark blood burst from the organ, splattering over Patrick's face. He had recoiled at the strong metallic taste. On waking, he could still imagine its foul bitterness. Somehow, it lingered at the back of his throat. Utterly confused and soaked wet through with sweat, the captain jumped up from his bed, dagger in hand. Breathing so fast that it made him giddy, he realised that he had been having a horrific nightmare. It had all felt so real. Anthony was fast asleep on an adjacent bunk but Patrick's anxious groans had woken Creppin. Ever loyal and ready to protect his few friends, the hunchback held his knife at the ready. He grabbed his bludgeon and leapt up from the floor where he had been sleeping with his dog. Skips raised his eyebrows and stood up to stretch. Paying no heed to the perplexed men, the sleepy hound circled the warm blanket and plumped himself back down. He let out a long, weary sigh and went straight back to sleep.

'O' what art th' afeared, marster Cullsey?' the grubby little man asked. His face was contorted with a look of genuine concern. Micken swapped legs to stretch the one he had been perching on all night. He extended a wing and yawned. Sneezing the cutest little sneeze, the parrot made a few gentle trills before fluffing his wings and settling back to sleep. Micken was renowned for being grumpy as hell if he did not have a good night's sleep. Patrick lit a lantern. He shivered uncomfortably as a cold draught swept over his damp flesh. Rubbing his sore eyes, he sat back on his bunk. He flexed his stiff muscles and held his face in his hands. What the hell was that all about? Having been raised with the full knowledge of his Irish Gaelic ancestry and culture Patrick was all too aware of the dire consequences of a visit from a banshee. Creppin's presence had completely slipped his mind until he was rudely reminded by a foetid stench of bad breath. The hunchback was hovering around, waiting for an answer to his question. 'Tis' nay tha' concern!' Patrick snapped. The harmless cripple shied away from the angry man. He had not expected such a nasty retort. Huffing in response to such ingratitude, Creppin scratched his arse and shuffled back to his floor space. He settled back down next to his adored pet's warm little body.

The hunchback's recent feelings of rejection had been concerning the blacksmith who had asked Patrick to allow him to sleep in their quarters for a couple of nights. When he had agreed, the captain had already known that he would regret his leniency. He had been persuaded to put up with the snivelling oaf's wreaking carcass for the last two nights! 'That bloody blacksmith needs to toughen up like I was forced to!' the captain thought to himself. Making a decision to throw the aggravating runt out the following day, Patrick noticed a small piece of fine grey silk that had caught on a protruding nail. A wave of fear crawled over his skin. The hairs on the back of his neck stood proud. He knelt to pick up the swatch. It disintegrated like a moth at his touch. He watched the dust-like wisps dance above the draught that blew them gently across well-scrubbed boards. 'Fuck!' he whispered, unnerved. He banged the outer sides of his clenched fists hard on rough wooden boards until they started to bleed. Anthony sat bolt upright in his bed. When he saw his friend's turmoil he thought it best to leave him be. It was the right decision. Patrick needed space. Death had already tainted the mission with the loss of Joe and the others. Curse the thought of losing another member of his fine, honourable crew. A tear escaped the corner of Patrick's eye. 'Why the feck did tha' leave me, Mama!!' his enraged mind yelled. The pyrate captain felt desperate, alone and very scared.

As a child, Patrick's mother had told him that the spirit of the Banshee would appear to foretell a death in the Culley clan. He remembered how frightened she had been when the disembodied soul had appeared to her one night, wailing her lament. Patrick recalled Sushana saying that the forlorn and bitter spirit's screams resembled the melancholy wail of a dangerously wild wind or the thin screeching cry of an owl. Apparently, the Banshee who followed the Culley clan had been murdered by a chieftain hundreds of years before. Confused as to why he would suddenly have his first visit out of the blue, Patrick tried to calm himself. He only wished that Grace was there. He had to consult someone who understood. A myriad of thoughts rushed through his tortured mind. Dread filled his heart… maybe this had not been the wild spectre's first visit after all! That would explain his innate fear of ghosts! He had heard that it was possible to erase fearful memories. Maybe his abrupt launch into manhood had spurred him to start to accept the terrible truth. Until her death, his strong mother had softened every blow for her precious child. Her absence had left a horrible void. He thought of his crew, his extended clan. Patrick shuddered openly at the sudden dreadful thought that the Banshee might have been warning that another of them was soon to die. Acting on impulse, the captain pulled on his boots and long, heavy coat. Taking the lantern, he felt compelled to check that all was well aboard the Deliverance.

Thankfully, there had been no fatalities during the night so the captain had shed his fearful thoughts for the meantime. He woke to the sound of birdcall. Jock had a caged crow called MacCaw. He was a tame bird with a lovely temperament. The quartermaster had raised him as an abandoned chick when visiting a Polynesian island. MacCaw loved his master who he had always been able to recognise, even when amongst a large crowd. It was common for sailors to take a crow to sea. Whenever they were unsure of their position in coastal waters, they would release the bird. It would fly straight towards the nearest land, giving the pilot a rough navigational fix to work from. As the Deliverance sailed towards the prosperous town of Plymouth MacCaw cawed pleasantly at Micken who gave a perfect imitation in reply. Happy to be in avian company, the parrot seemed to have beaten his depression during the mourning process.

The Deliverance passed through the channel on a morning tide amidst a swirling mist. There was a fresh bite in the air but it was a cheerfully bright day. As they docked in the large, natural deep water harbour of Plymouth Anthony felt apprehensive to be back at the delightful old port. The town's intimate connection with the sea had brought great fortune to her shores. Patrick, Anthony and Jock chose a group of the most benign-looking characters from the crew of pyrates. It was crucial that no-one caused any suspicion on collecting the new vessel. A skeleton crew stayed with the Deliverance and carried out maintenance and repair work. In Patrick's absence, her thin, worn sails were to be dressed down and treated with wax. All standing rigging was to be given a new coat of tar. This extra layer would add strength and protection from the harsh elements. A few of the crew went ashore to drink at the nearby Journey's End Inn but most stayed aboard. There was plenty of ale and food left to keep the pyrates happy while they worked.

Shanny and Remando had found Shrimp in a drug-induced stupor. They had fed him warm broth and given him plenty of sweet coffee. On coming round, he apologised for his inappropriate behaviour. The friends vowed never to speak of the incident. They decided that a short time ashore would do them all good, so planned to book room and board for the night. When Shanny attended to Saul's wounds from his recent lashing, he asked if he could join them. 'I've a mind ter head back home.' he confided in his closest friend. Totally understanding why he felt that way, Remando gave him his share from the last raid. 'Take it', the paternal pyrate insisted. 'Th'art a fine pyrate. Alas, methinks tha'd make an even finer Papa.' Shanny agreed and gave the orphan a big hug. 'Besides', she added, 'Th'a'll surely av' been missed at Mary Maggy's.' Remando went off to find Josh who also agreed that their friend had made a sensible decision. It was a touching farewell. Gathering his few belongings, Saul did not look back when he left the ship. The rest of the crew were not aware that he had left for good. Shanny and Remando thought it best for them to explain to the captain and Anthony when they had reached Ireland.

The Journey's End was a comfortable newly-built inn. Oak-panelled throughout, the beamed ceilings were low and walls freshly white-washed. Each room had a fireplace and well-stuffed goosedown mattresses were covered with crisp, clean sheets and patchwork quilted bedspreads. It was a luxury for the visitors to stay in such a cosy modern, dwelling. Following long, gruelling weeks spent at sea Shanny, especially, had been looking forward to some home comforts. She looked forward to simple luxuries like being able to sleep alone, wash without fear of being disturbed and take her clothes to be washed at the laundry. 'Sheer bliss!' she thought when she walked to her upper storey room. The sloped floors had creaking wooden floorboards and she could not help imagine how much noise she and Jock would have made if he could have joined her. Feeling aroused, she reached between her thighs to feel the wet patch that had appeared on her tight modern trews. What a surprise it had been to lose her virginity to a pyrate, of all people! Shanny would feel a rush of sexual energy every time she thought of her handsome lover. She could not wait for the next time they were together.

Patrick, Anthony, Jock and their selected crew disembarked. Those acting as ordinary sailors were wearing a uniform of loose, calf-length breeches, jerkin and a standard doublet with a knitted hat. The captain and bogus officers each wore Venetian knee breeches, padded doublet, cloak and hat. They looked very smart. Patrick had carefully considered what they should wear. It was crucial for them all to look the part and convince the shipyard officer on duty that they were a reliable professional crew hired by Hawkins. They trudged about a mile along the main cobbled street until they came to a line of brick warehouses.

Set back from the dockside, Hawkins' shipyard was a hive of industry. It was fascinating to see ships in various stages of construction. Unlike most shipwrights, Royal Appointed Master Shipwrights were very well paid and often took on private commissions as well as working for the Crown. Ironically, many of them were illiterate therefore unable to even sign their own name. On arrival at the Royal Shipyard, Patrick introduced himself as Captain Peter Croft and produced his forged papers. Satisfied by these, the officer briefly scanned the rest of the crew's documents. 'So far, so good' thought Patrick. He had expected more security measures to have been set in place, especially since Hawkins' innovative new design of warship was top secret. The whole project had been kept under wraps until that day.

Apparently Hawkins had explained to the officer in charge to expect a Captain Croft and his crew who had been hired to test the vessel. He had given strict instructions that one of the new warships was to be handed over to the captain after his paperwork had been approved. As John had promised, an impressive new ship was ready and waiting. After their documents had been inspected they were authorised to board the craft. An efficient and surprisingly patient engineer took them on a detailed tour and explained all her mechanisms. He went into great detail with the complex rigging system. The ropes were more intricate than Patrick was used to but he was confident that his able crew would soon master the new system. The engineer told the sailors that Hawkins' nimble new 'race ship', as he liked to call it, was a sleek ship that had been designed to sit low in the water. She had a long prow and her foresails were thinly cut to make it easier to maintain point and not be blown off course. The new design would enable the ship to sail closer to the wind, with increased speed and vastly improved manoeuvrability. It was explained that an outer sheathing had been added by coating the hull with a mixture of soap, tallow and brimstone that had been boiled together. This would preserve the caulking and make the vessel even more streamline.

At the end of the tour, Patrick could not wait for the launch of his new ship. Extremely grateful to Hawkins, he was pleased that they had parted on good terms. Had it not been for the Naval Commander's inestimable help, there would have been no way on earth that Patrick could ever have gained such a marvellous model. The craft that towered before him was a rare beauty. The pyrate captain stood speechless, in absolute awe.

Patrick planned to name her 'Queen Culley's Revenge' as the ultimate insult to Queen Elizabeth. Imagine, one of the English monarch's pioneering modern vessels being named in honour of the very woman who had spent much of her life plotting to overthrow her. Now her equally strong-willed and bloody-minded son, Patrick, was ready to continue the battle and avenge her death. The determined captain had word sent to the Deliverance that they had picked up the new ship and would soon be setting sail for Ireland. Giving orders for them to depart the following evening, the captain told his hungry crew that it was time to find somewhere to eat. They had some recruiting to do so Patrick suggested a local sailors' haunt. As he left the shipyard he took a final look at the majestic vessel. He could not wait to take Grace out in this one!

In the meantime, after the four friends had located their rooms in the Journey's End, they all met in the bar. The place was full of sailors. The pyrates joined in the conversation and were soon sharing their adventures of faraway lands. Everyone had crowded around a pair of seadogs who had been born and bred in a place called Woden's Feld in Middle England. The obscure little town was not far from Bramwich ham and apparently famous for its lock makers. Bernard and Jack made it quite clear that they loathed the thought of anyone mistakenly thinking that they were from 'Brummajum' as they called the large city. There was fierce rivalry between the two vastly different neighbouring territories. 'Wi b'ay Brummies', insisted the comical duo, both wearing very serious expressions on their tanned, weathered faces. Bernard and his friend would gain attention wherever they went because they still used an old dialect that most people could not understand. Almost stone deaf, Jack always shouted in his native tongue which was now only used in the west of the Midlands. Sounding exactly like Middle English, theirs was a language that had been spoken way back in the 11th century. It had not changed since medieval times and had died out a hundred years earlier in most areas of England.

Bernard had learned to translate Jack's 'spake' for people by using more common words without the strong accent. Whenever Jack spoke people would gawp at him in utter bemusement. 'Ow b'ist?' he would ask and, more often than not, would be met with a vacant stare. ''E means 'Ow am ya?' Bernard would helpfully translate but people would still be confused. 'How art tha?' Shanny guessed and was proud of herself when Bernard beamed and raised his glass to show his respect. 'Arr! Yower roight, ow-a wench!' he exclaimed in delight. The others were impressed that she had managed to decipher the strange lingo that they were struggling to grasp. Shanny thought it was wonderful that an old way of speaking had survived in a small area of her country. Intrigued by the friendly men's broad regional accent, Shanny was keen to learn more. Ordering two large pitchers of ale, she invited them to join her and her friends. Shrimp and Saul were fascinated by their brogue too but Remando had no idea what all the fuss was about. He already had trouble understanding most British accents, especially Scottish. For the Spanish pyrate, the experience was nothing new. He sat quietly, for a change, drinking ale whilst the rest of his party became acquainted with the new guests.

Bernard was a really sociable person who was renowned for telling jokes whilst Jack kept himself to himself. An avid people-watcher, the timid man felt uncomfortable when communicating with strangers. Almost deaf, poor Jack was also painfully shy around women. The pyrates soon learned that he adored birds and would often have a variety of lame rescues on his person. Shanny knew that he would get along with Patrick who was also a bird lover. Despite his hefty size, Jack had such a gentle way with the creatures that even the tiniest, most fragile species always trusted him. He often went around with chicks that had been abandoned by their mothers and left to die or older birds that had survived a predatory attack. That evening, one of his feathered friends was tucked under his large, salt and pepper beard. Shanny was delighted each time the tiny hatchling popped its beak out to be fed a grub or insect that Jack always had handy in a leather pouch. Bernard kept everyone entertained with his colloquial gags that he often had to explain to his baffled audience. 'Mar missiz' Mom fell dowen a well lost wikkend. Arr cor believe i'! Arr day now them wishin' wells werked!' It took a good while for Shanny to explain this one to Remando. When he finally understood that Jack's mother-in-law had fallen into a wishing well because her son-in-law's wish had come true, he could not stop laughing. Time passed by too quickly as the new friends enjoyed a brilliant night. They chatted away long after the landlord had locked up and gone to bed. He told the boarders to make sure that all lanterns were extinguished before they went upstairs. By the time they all said good night, Shrimp had insisted that Bernard and Jack join Patrick's crew. The compassionate men decided to give it a try.

Very drunk but happy, the guests parted company and went to find their rooms. Shrimp's was on the ground floor so he tottered off with a large key. Remando insisted on walking Shanny back to hers. Saul's was nearby so the three staggered unsteadily up the narrow, rickety stairs. Shanny led the way and Remando held the lantern. He stopped unexpectedly. Saul bumped into him, giggling childishly. 'Sssssshhhhh!' he hissed, swaying on his feet. Dropping the lantern, the older pyrate clutched his left arm. Luckily, the younger man retrieved the lantern before it could do any damage. Remando tried to speak but could only manage a moan. Ahead of him, Shanny was still tittering when she turned round to see her dear guardian's horror-stricken face. His lips turned blue as he gasped for breath. Falling forward onto the wooden stairs, Remando began to panic, 'My rosary' he pleaded softly. Immediately sober, the young woman shouted for Shrimp's help.

The small pyrate came rushing up the stairs. He helped Saul pull the suffering man up onto the landing. Shanny tried to make him more comfortable. She found the prayer beads that he had requested. Clutching his grandmother's rosary beads tightly in his sweaty hand, Remando began to pray to Our Lady. The pain in his chest was almost too extreme to bear but he tried to stay calm. The last thing he wanted to do was worry the woman who was like a daughter to him. 'My beautiful angel,' he addressed Shanny. 'I larve thee with all o' my heart. Methinks I shall be with tha' precious Mama, anon.' Shanny wept openly. She dreaded the thought of losing the man who she had become so close to. She had loved her own papa dearly but Remando had been such a kind, loving ward since they had met. Now, she felt completely akin to him. Having lost both parents in tragic circumstances she refused to believe that God would tear another away from her. Holding her loved one close, Shanny joined in with his prayers.

The landlord came to see what was going on. When he saw Remando's eyes suddenly widen in fear he rushed to his side. He saw the heart attack victim suddenly keel over. 'Take heed! Lay him on his back!' the landlord ordered. Remando had stopped breathing. Shanny let out a desperate wail. Some other guests came out to see what was wrong. A woman screamed, 'Heaven forbid!' and recoiled at the sight of the dead man. The pyrate wench bawled at her. 'Be gone lest I smack tha' cursed mouth!' The woman hurried back into her room. Saul held his head in his hands. He had no idea what to do to help. Shanny felt sick with worry. 'This can'nay be!' Stroking the dead man's face, she urged him to breathe again. 'Papa! I love thee! In God's name, breathe!' Saul punched Remando's chest hard in his desperation to regain a heartbeat. He stopped and looked at the deceased's pale, waxy face. Nothing. Shanny pushed her young friend out of the way and straddled the lifeless man. Lifting her small fists above her head she brought them down hard, together, hitting the lower half of Remando's breastbone. She kept the momentum going in her desperation. 'Breathe tha' thievin' sea mutt!' she screamed at the top of her voice. Her final blow to the middle-aged pyrate's chest made him jolt violently.

A forced surge of expelled air caused Remando to cough painfully. Although his chest felt like it had stopped a cannonball, at least he was breathing. Shanny felt his heartbeat under her hand. It was weak but the blood was pumping once more. The colour gradually returned to his lips and face. Sobbing with relief and exhaustion Shanny kissed her treasured companion's forehead. Bernard and Jack appeared. They helped Saul to lift Remando and took him to his room. Jack spoke too loud, "E's proper poo'ly, ay 'e, cock?' No-one but Bernard understood him. 'Arrr, 'e ay 'arf, mare't.' came Bernard's reply. Everyone else was bemused by their comments. Remando was beside himself with gratitude. Emotions ran high. One of the happiest drunken nights that they had enjoyed in a long time had turned into a horrible nightmare. They all left the patient in Shanny's care. Thankful that Remando had survived, everyone returned to their rooms where they slept until the morning sounds of the busy port could be heard.

Shrimp, Saul, Remando and Shanny would never forget their night at the Journey's End. They actually felt relieved to return to the Deliverance where the surgeon took a weak and shell-shocked Remando into his care. Saul decided to continue on with the adventure. No-one ever learnt of his plans to leave. The young man had been taught a stark lesson. In future he was determined to let his old enemy's harmless cracks go over his head. Life was too short. The maturing lad was surprized to be met by an apologetic Danny who had been ashore to buy him a decent blackjack. The helmsman had felt bad that he had goaded him into attacking him. He had noticed that Saul had been drinking out of a small wooden vessel that often leaked. 'Let's let boygone's be boygone's, m' friend,' the Irishman told him, holding out his hand in a gesture of reconciliation. They both laughed and embraced each other. Christening his new tankard, Saul proposed a toast to the Irish pyrates. Wincing as Danny thoughtlessly slapped his back he rolled his eyes and knocked back his ale. The lacerations caused by the whip would take time to heal but he had to be honest, his reprimand had done him some good. Now, he felt like a real man!

Grace's crew were pleased to welcome the new recruits aboard the Deliverance. Danny had a field day when the deaf sailor and his mate came aboard. Fascinated by their unusual accents, the Irish rogue soon had their 'spake' down to a 't' which delighted the new-comers. Very proud of their roots, like all other indigenous folk of England's Midlands, Bernard and Jack soon settled in. The distinctive characters mixed well with the jovial, laid back Irish lads and were keen to learn about their culture too. The cocky helmsman quickly learned that the Midlanders were really good sports who could take his harmless jibes. They could give as good as they got too and often scolded the bold pyrate, 'Yow moind yower tongue else ar'll gi' yo a roight lampin'!' Jack told the younger man one day. ''E sez 'e'll gi'thee a good 'oydin'.' Bernard warned. Whistling happily as she climbed the rigging, Shanny shouted her translation, 'He'll strike thee hard if tha' du'nay stop tha' insolent speak!' 'Ah! Tanyers koindly moy pretty.' Danny replied adding a heavy hint of his custom sarcasm; 'Oy'd a ne'er a guessed!' All the Irish pyrates were amused by their friend's cheek but rolled around in stitches at Jack's reaction. He marched over to Danny and smacked him straight on the jaw, 'Ar warned yow, yow bloody big lommock!' the deaf man shouted then went back to work. The helmsman took it on the chin. Accepting the older man's discipline, he skulked off sheepishly. Everyone was glad of the peace. Finally someone had managed to put Danny in his place. He was a funny fella but his foolish antics could be too much for anyone after a while.

The new recruits were sound, hardworking sailors who were definitely going to get along well with Patrick's crew. After a few hours of heavy toil, the Irish pyrates cracked open another few barrels of strong ale and began to celebrate. On the following day they would be heading home! Everyone began to sing folk songs from the Emerald isle and the musicians joined in. Jack took out a simple whistle and Bernard played the bones. A rowdy party was soon in full swing and some prostitutes were welcomed aboard. Lanterns were lit on the Deliverance and the cook produced a special sea food dish that everyone enjoyed. Bernard and Jack were pleased that they had joined a decent gang. They were in for another long night of boozing so Jack fed his little friends and refilled his tankard with ale. He always had a lame bird somewhere on his person, often settled snugly in one of many leather pouches tied to his belts. Each had been stuffed with feathers or rags to keep the little ones warm. 'Gentle Jack', as Bernard called him, had been allotted a section of the ship between decks near the chicken pen. There, the larger injured birds that he had brought aboard could recover inside wooden boxes on a bed of reeds or straw. The lovable character always had plenty of worms, seed or grain to feed his foundlings. He was often seen feeding chicks from his mouth as their mothers would have done. Colm was pleased to have another helper in the animal pen. The two characters were similar so got along well. He wondered how Creppin was going to react to the new hand. Having shown signs of jealousy already, the hunchback would probably take a while to get used to Jack. Only time would tell.

Gift had begun to show symptoms of malaria. His usually healthy brown skin was now an unpleasant deep grey and very dry. He had not had any teeth in his lower jaw since Patrick had known him but now his gums were so badly swollen that he could hardly close his mouth. His wiry build was now skeletal. The sweating sickness had overtaken him and he had been delirious for the last twelve hours. Gift's pleasant, milky-eyed gaze had become a vacant stare. His body was fatigued from the symptoms of the flu-like illness which had begun with shaking chills and a terrible headache. Usually robust and healthy, no-one had ever known him to be ill. The African man had convinced himself that he had been cursed. Speaking in his native tongue, he kept insisting that he had seen a shark following the ship when they sailed from São Vicente. Sailors believed this to be a sign of inevitable death. Jaeci recognised his friend's genuine terror and knew that could be fatal if the pyrate would not calm down. The Tupi tribesman had insisted on staying with him in the infirmary. He always carried a variety of healing balms and salves along with his poisons. He prepared an infusion from medicinal fever bark that he had taken from the cinchona tree. All being well, the natural remedy would bring Gift's raging temperature down.

Having only been gone for two days Patrick and the others were surprised to see him fever-free on their return. Jaeci was pleased by his patient's progress. Although Gift's condition was now relatively stable, his wound had not heeled well since the primitive amputation. He still suffered from awful phantom pains in the absent leg. The simple man could not believe how that was possible. Once again, his fear was causing him further distress. Other amputees tried to reassure him by confirming that they had felt the same at first. Smith was stern with his lecture, trying to convince the frightened man that his pain would eventually stop. Jaeci was concerned. He did not want to lose his patient. His loyal best friend, Serijipe, sat with Gift whilst he took regular breaks. Whoo kept checking on Gift's progress but he appeared to be giving up. Everyone feared the worst for the passive man.

Creppin had kept out of the surgeon's way since the day he had chased him off with a hatchet. Whoo decided to make amends and went off to find his would-be apprentice. Finding the hunchback on the gun deck, he tried to act as if nothing had happened, 'What ho, mate!' Creppin grinned like a child when he heard the pleasant greeting. Hobbling stiffly over to embrace the carpenter, he said nothing but felt relieved that someone still cared. When Whoo noticed that Creppin was becoming lamer, he decided to make something to help him get around more easily. A wheeled wooden contraption, similar to a truckle-bed, would be ideal. Returning to his workshop he began to sketch out a design. Over the next couple of days, the carpenter built the device. He made it so that the cripple could sit inside and still have room to carry objects. By using his long arms to push himself along in the primitive method of transport the hunchback should be able to save his arthritic body from more damage. Not allowing anyone in on his secret, Whoo finally called Creppin to his quarters.

On seeing something quite large covered with a large piece of sail, the inquisitive hunchback wondered what it was. 'Tis a gift fer thee, my friend' he was told. A well of emotion built up inside the sad little man. He stood, stooped over badly, with knuckles stuffed into his drooling mouth, eyes pouring with tears and giggling hysterically. 'No-one nay ne'er givest Crrreppin a gift afore, marrrster. He's 'nay clued o' the manner ter rrreact', he confessed, not knowing what to do with himself. Whoo cleared his throat in embarrassment and pulled off the sheet revealing a newly painted wheeled crate. 'Ha! Ha… Oh my!' Creppin jumped on the spot, slapping his hands on his thighs in excitement and sheer glee. 'Try it out, siree!' the carpenter joked, bowing his head as if presenting an order to a dignified customer. 'Oh my… Crrreppin's crrrate! Oh my! I needs a piss, marster!' he said clutching himself. The carpenter laughed as he watched the hunchback hobble off to relieve himself.

Pleased by Creppin's reaction, Whoo re-checked the small vehicle. Rushing back with pee dribbling down the inside of his thighs, Creppin slumped his crooked carcass down into his new truckle-bed. He manoeuvred it perfectly around the small area, the swivel wheels worked even better than the carpenter had expected them to when carrying a load. From then on, Creppin spent most of his time in his crate. He even slept in it. Everyone would hear him going mad whenever the ship's cats dared to jump inside. He allowed Skips to sleep in there with him and occasionally took the crazy little dog on a short ride. Everyone could tell when the hunchback approached due to the distinctive sound of 'Crrreppin's crate' rolling along uneven boards. Whoo would have to ask the blacksmith to make some hardy metal wheels if the hunchback expected to take his truckle-bed on land.

When Queen Culley's Revenge was launched from the shipyard Creppin was over the moon to finally be able to take Skips away from the two mangy ship's cats aboard the Deliverance. They had held a grudge against the lively dog ever since he had eaten Claw's tail. The cripple was glad to see the back of the Irish crew too; especially

Danny, who was the worst tease he had ever met. More sailors had been hired to make up numbers and Jock had given everyone a pep talk before they embarked on Hawkins' warship's maiden voyage. During a short ceremony to name the striking vessel, Patrick stood on the bow and asked for blessings. After pouring red wine on the deck, everyone drank a toast to their ship and asked that she be protected on her maiden voyage. The captain then poured a fine red wine into a silver bowl and passed it to Shanny. 'I name thee 'Queen Culley's Revenge", she hailed emptying the bowl into the water to appease King Neptune. Now the warship's bow had been splashed with red wine that represented the blood from a human sacrifice that would have given life to the ship in days of old. Had the pyrates not had to remain incognito, they would have spilled the blood of an enemy, for sure. Patrick delighted in the knowledge that the fine vessel would gain nourishment from the blood of his enemies that would soon soak her decks. Shanny threw the empty silver bowl into the sea as a gift to the ocean king. It is believed that the younger the woman who performs the ship's baptism the better, as they would both share the same life-span. Anthony nailed a horseshoe to the main mast to repel storms at sea. Abadeyo and Babatu chanted an incantation asking for protection from the curse of 'Duffy Jonah'. Every pyrate on the deck kissed their lucky talismans, charms or holy items at the mention of the cursed demon of the deep's name whose locker held drowned mariners for eternity. Everyone cheered as Queen Culley's Revenge had her first real taste of the sea. She creaked and swayed therapeutically on her way.

Back on the Deliverance, a triumphant scream came from her belly. Fangs sank his teeth into the throat of a large brown rat that had managed to avoid capture since scurrying aboard back in Mindelo Harbour. He dropped the limp body of the rodent in front of Colm who made a big fuss of the self-satisfied feline. The ship's cat lapped up the attention from his favourite human, purring contentedly as he rubbed his face against the pyrate's legs. Claw joined her mate rubbing her soft body against his and tilting her pretty face seductively in hope of receiving a generous share of the reward. Colm already missed his smelly companion. The hunchback had been a great help caring for the livestock. It had made a big difference. Before he went below deck to feed the new stock that Patrick had ordered to take to Rockfleet, the Irishman looked out to see if the new vessel was in sight.

Only a short distance along the shore the new captain of the Revenge stood confidently on her bridge. He wished that his mother was standing next to him. What she would have given to have owned such a craft! Thankfully, the warship sailed out of Plymouth Docks on a favourable wind on the cool, dry November day. She sped steadily onwards over tumbling waves. A contented deck team climbed her immaculate shrouds. They soon mastered the rope system thanks to excellent instructions from the efficient Naval Officer back at the shipyard. Having had enough of Creppin's nuisance pet, Whoo insisted that Skips was penned down with the livestock. Lately, Patrick had heard too many complaints about the dog. The most heated had been from Smith. Skips had noticed that the cook would occasionally take out his false teeth to clean. A couple of times, when the angry little man was not looking, the crafty dog had grabbed the wooden gnashers and run off with them. Having found somewhere safe to hide, he had chewed them and caused a lot of damage.

When Whoo discovered the naughty animal, he had scampered off with teeth clamped firmly between his own. It was a comical sight to see Skips wearing a ridiculous toothy grin with the fat carpenter in hot pursuit cursing, 'Madre de Dios!' as he tried, in vain, to catch him.

Reluctantly, Creppin handed over the culprit, who had run to him for protection. The little dog did not go willingly. He put up a hard struggle. Whoo and Smith took great pleasure when they kicked Skips into a lockable pen where he would be confined during the voyage. Distressed yelps and howls could be heard coming from below deck. Having enjoyed freedom all his life, the tribal hound did not take kindly to being confined in a cage. He made sure to let everyone know that too with his persistent loud protests. The hunchback released him every night so they could snuggle up together in his crate. He petted the disgruntled animal, 'Yon shellfish crrrew dun'nay gi' a flyin' swive forrr us nay more, my little frrriend', he complained as his dog licked his face enthusiastically, ''tis thou n' me frrrom now on. Mark my turds, by my 'blunderrry-bust', they shalt, someday, verrrily rrreceive their cum-uppance!' Trilling his 'r's in rather a hysterical manner, Creppin's mismatched eyes looked evil. The angry man's appearance even made the alpha male canine drop his gaze. The hunchback could not wait to see Rockfleet Castle again. With a bit of luck, Queen Culley's Revenge would reach Eire's green shores before the month was out.

Chapter 14

Plotting Shana's Revenge

John Hawkins' new warship was exquisite. The robust craft was trimmed with rigging far superior to any other that the sailors had manned. A sophisticated rope and pulley system ran so smoothly causing little friction when raising and dropping the flatter sails. Much longer than her breadth, the warship's mainsail had been positioned further forward to allow more manoeuvrability. The craft out-performed every single one of her predecessors by leaps and bounds. Patrick and the crew were delighted with the new vessel. They had been assured that her construction had been carried out with the utmost respect of maritime superstitions. Viewed as a living creature by its builders and engineers, the assembly of the fish-shaped hull had involved important ancient nautical rituals and superstitions. The building of the keel was exceptionally important as it was believed to be the heart of the vessel. A westerly wind had been blowing the day that the momentous laying of the keel took place and the tide had been high. These were both good omens. The bell, the ship's soul, was made of the finest brass. Gold and silver coins had been added in the casting process to ensure that it would produce a soft ring. For good luck, the carpenter had hammered the first nail into the heart of the warship through a horseshoe. The nail had been made from pure gold and its head enamelled blood-red to symbolise life and good health. A piece of stolen wood had been worked into the keel so that the ship would sail faster, in her effort to flee from capture. A silver coin had been placed under the masthead to ensure many a prosperous voyage. On the day she left Plymouth Port, Queen Culley's Revenge flew the Royal Standard. Patrick had brought along other flags and, once it was safe to do so, he would hoist another in place of the bitch Queen's. Until then he had no choice but to fly her colours.

Before Patrick had the chance to try out new navigational equipment that had been supplied with the ship he heard Jock's urgent call. Rushing out to see what had alerted his friend his heart pumped fast when he saw a brigantine ploughing through the waves towards their stern. Pyrates! This attack could not have been timed any better if the bloody fools had tried! Already aware of his new warship's swiftness Patrick was sure that they would have no problem outrunning the advancing vessel. However, he was keen to test the efficiency of his new cannons. If Hawkins' engineers had been right, the Dutch pyrate ship that was bearing down on them would soon be in for a nasty surprise. Before long, they would surely be 'kissing the barrrnacles on Neptune's arrrse!' as Jock would say. As the excitement mounted Patrick took a second take. He could not believe his eyes. This was turning out to be even better than he had first realised. As luck would have it, the oncoming vessel was sailing under a pyrate flag that he recognised. Wearing a shrewd smile, Patrick warned his crew, 'Prepare for an onslaught!'

'Time for some fun', the young captain thought to himself. From his childhood years, Patrick had remembered this evil pyrate's tactics well. He decided to call his bluff. Instead of steering away from the brigantine's fast approaching bow, he ordered the helmsman to speed ahead. The first bout of enemy cannon fire was heard. Unconcerned by the threat Patrick ordered a speedy retaliation. Crouched in the small, dark space between cannons, Jock's gunners listened for the order, 'Take the strrrain…' The master gunner waited until cannons had been aimed. The success of the hit all depended on Jock's timing. It took great skill and experience to choose the best time to order a missile launch. So much had to be considered, including enemy position, wind direction and force, rise and fall of waves, speed of the current… One minor miscalculation could bring disaster. When satisfied, Jock shouted, 'steady…' The men lit the touch powder when they heard the command 'Fire!' There followed a tremendous din as the murderous missiles were launched, one after another. Hoisting the Culley pyrate flag Patrick felt a rush of pride and anger. He felt more concerned about the Deliverance since it was packed full of Culley treasures. She would be making this voyage the following day. Not having expected such a confident counterattack a giant of a man, armed to the hilt, yelled from the weather deck of the enemy ship. Patrick only just managed to make out his words over the sound of the waves, 'Avast thee! I gi' thee nay quarter!' The aggressor had no other choice but turn his brigantine. As she sheered from her course, the red flag was hoisted. A fight between two pyrate crews meant that their honour was now at stake. Neither captain was prepared to show mercy.

Rolling heavily windward, the enemy vessel pitched hard just managing to avoid a collision. Still surging ahead at an impressive speed Patrick's ship scraped alongside the other craft's hull. The Dutchman screamed loudly at his baffled crew who struggled to veer away from the destructive path of the larger ship. The enemy pyrate's bullying tactic had always been to terrify the prey into submission. Most captains' instincts would tell them to avoid impact by swerving out of the predator's path. The retreating vessel would then be easy to board. Patrick had done exactly the opposite. With a false sense of superiority, the attacker had misjudged his quarry's reaction and ordered his cannons to be discharged too soon. The damage to the Revenge was minimal as the missiles thudded against her tough hull. Anthony watched as the light cannonballs dropped harmlessly into the sea. As it was nudged, the brigantine toppled unsteadily. Anthony watched as she was helplessly thrown around in the wash.

Giving the order to slow speed, Patrick felt the addictive thrill of battle. Blood raced to his head as adrenalin stimulated his mind and body. When he yelled his next order, 'Hard to port!' the helmsman began to turn the sleek ship about. As she came alongside the brigantine, Jock ordered broadside after broadside. Heavy metal missiles bombarded the wooden carcass of the floundering vessel. New improved cannons placed low on the waterline enabled the Revenge to sweep alongside the other vessel, deliver high velocity volleys and be away before the enemy had even had chance to load their cumbersome cannons. The brigantine's mainmast took a hit. Her thick oak post snapped in half like a dry twig. Crashing down, it crushed a man, killing him instantly. Several men were now trapped under the tangled mass of rope and heavy canvas sails. Screams of agony could be heard over barked orders, cannon and gunfire. The brigantine was in a bad way. Her damaged hull began to take on water fast. The disturbing sound of terrified animals trapped within could be heard as they struggled to escape from fallen debris.

The Dutch captain growled loudly when he lost his balance but continued to fire his loaded pistols. Seething with anger, the menacing brute aimed his musket at Patrick. He pulled the trigger. He missed. The man was colossal, thought the blacksmith. He must have been at least a head taller than Anthony and he was six foot tall! On firing his musket, he had hardly moved from his weapon's powerful kick. As the blacksmith went aloft he aimed his pistol at a hostile and fired. A perfect shot. Pulling another loaded gun from his belt he fired again blowing an arm off a pyrate who was mounting the rigging. Managing to hold on for a few seconds, he suddenly lost his grip and fell backwards. As he plummeted to his death he stared up at his killer flailing his limbs hopelessly before smashing through the broken deck. All of a sudden, Anthony began to see everything move in slow motion. Having reached a yardarm, he held tightly onto the ratlines. The heartless Dutch captain yelled his commands and continued to fire his guns, one by one, in a desperate attempt to kill or maim his enemy. Anthony had never witnessed such nerve. The assailant's rage had been clear from the start when he had realised Patrick's intentions. He was going to fight to the death. For him, retreat was not an option.

Whilst the deck crew of the Revenge manned the rigging Jock gave his orders and her first-rate guns fired another barrage of cannonballs into the other craft. Gunners on the Revenge had been trying out a new rope and pulley system that pulled the cannons to gun port and held them steady. Having been used to violent recoil on old cannons which would throw them back across the deck, they were impressed by the lack of jolt in these new models. 'Hove to windward!' Patrick roared. His voice was hoarse from screaming. 'Ease the main sail!' As her hull had such a long keel Hawkins' warship was able to reduce speed gently. The pyrates worked quickly and the ship heeled, drifting very slightly leeward. Realising that he finally faced undeniable defeat the Dutch captain was livid. In desperation, he shouted last-minute orders at his perplexed crew. Patrick's warship swept full circle to deliver another round of cannon shot. Patrick ordered Anthony, Jaeci, Josh, Serijipe and Jock to follow him. They all boarded the ruined vessel and fought hard to finish off her remaining crew. The Tupi warriors held back, shooting many of the enemies with poison-tipped arrows. Serijipe was pounced on by a hatchet wielding attacker. Jaeci reacted quickly drawing back his bowline. He aimed. The skilled archer shot the fatal arrow. At that exact moment Josh leapt forward to tackle Serijipe's assailant. Grabbing him around the neck, he drove his cutlass up under his ribs piercing his lungs.

Serijipe had known that his Tupi brother had him covered. He had managed to separate himself from his attacker. Neither of the warriors had expected Josh to come to his defence. With a feeling of sickened dread Jaeci watched in hopeless anguish as his swift arrow flew towards its target. As Serijipe realised that Josh had put himself in the firing line to save his life he made a split-second decision to push his defender to safety. The final thought to pass through his mind, before the deadly tip pierced his body, was of respect for the 'Tapuya' who had leapt to his defence. Josh had been willing to give his life for him. The Tupi were a shy people who mostly avoided any contact with strangers. Since joining

Patrick's crew Serijipe and his friend had kept themselves to themselves. As Jaeci watched the tip of his poisoned arrow graze the neck of his closest friend he thought of the man's family. Rushing over to his dying warrior brother, he cradled Serijipe's head in his arms. He felt like he had torn out his own heart. Trying hard to hold back angry tears, Jaeci looked into his victim's eyes and said that he was sorry. The seemingly feeble words were carried away by the wind. Filled with self-loathing he knew that he had to get his friend back over to their ship.

The poisoned man's eyelids flickered slightly as the potent muscle-relaxant began to take effect. Serijipe felt the venom that he had used for many years to kill prey high up in the forest canopy travelling through his own bloodstream. Despite the cold wind, he felt warm but so very dizzy. He felt his jaw become weak. Next, his neck and whole head relaxed. Deep sounds became clearer as the small muscles in the middle ear slackened. Literally petrified, the poor man's upper, then lower, limbs became heavy as he struggled to move. In a final agonising attempt to signal to his friend that he was still alive, the brave Tupi warrior managed to move the tip of a finger slightly. He squeezed a tear from his left eye. His breath became short and desperate. No longer able to swallow, the dying man felt as though he was choking on saliva that had collected in the back of his throat. Unable to clear the mounting spittle Serijipe's eyes bolted wide as he emitted a disturbing gurgling sound. Still fully aware of the chaos surrounding him, he could not prevent his bowels from opening. Piss poured from his slackened bladder. Within a few minutes total paralysis had struck.

Josh was injured. He had killed two pyrates but the second had stabbed him in the shoulder. He was unable to move his right arm. The huge Dutch captain loomed above him. Unsheathing his cutlass, he swept the weapon in a wide arc slicing into Josh's side. As the shocked pyrate slumped forward to land at his attacker's feet Patrick aimed his flintlock pistol and fired a shot into the ear of the enemy captain. It penetrated his brain causing an instant kill. The only enemy survivor was a young lad who threw down his weapon. Terrified, he explained that his captain had believed that the fine new vessel was a prize not to be missed. Patrick had thought as much. Word must already be out of his movements. The Dutch captain had been badly mistaken. Luckily, he had picked on the wrong vessel. It would now be widely known within the pyrate world that Patrick was transporting immense hoards of Culley treasure to Ireland. 'God speed the Deliverance' he prayed silently for his Irish crew.

Jaeci shouted for help with Serijipe. Patrick and Anthony were with Josh and Jock rushed to Jaeci's aid. Moses' heart sank. He grabbed his boarding axe and leapt over onto the sinking ship to help Jaeci. Pulling off a dead man's shirt, he quickly tore it into strips. He and Jaeci managed to bind his best friend's semi-naked body so they could lift him easier. Water was rushing into the ship's aft section and the broken craft made a sudden severe list starboard. Serijipe was dragged roughly over the side of the sinking ship. There was only a matter of minutes now to get to safety. In sheer agony, the poisoned Tupi warrior fought for breath as his diaphragm and lungs gradually closed down. Shocked by the fear and intense pain that his own poisonous mixture had caused, the pyrate was helpless as unseen hands hauled his limp body back onto Patrick's ship. Jock accepted the sole survivor's surrender and helped to drag Josh's corpse away from the wreck. With tack altered and a decent wind behind her sheets, the Revenge was carried smoothly away from the sinking vessel.

The annihilation had taken a mere forty minutes. It had been absolute, one-sided carnage. Charlie, a new cabin boy, had timed the whole conflict using a minute glass. The lad watched as the enemy ship was pulled under. She rolled over on her starboard side. She dipped her head slightly then took a plunge. Her stern reared high into the air and, with a final roar, she disappeared into the swirling depths. The sound of her huge body being crushed under immense pressure made the sailors shudder. Patrick and his crew cheered loudly in jubilation. Hawkins' engineer had been right; the cannons had proven to be merciless mechanical beasts! 'Astounding' was all that the breathless captain could muster the strength to say.

Patrick knew that the enemy pyrate captain had been a hard core trouble-maker from the Netherlands and a well-known multiple mutineer. He was definitely not going to be missed. Paying immediate attention to the state of his own crew, the captain rushed over to Jaeci to find out what had happened to Serijipe. Seeing Creppin running around like a maniac chasing Skips, who had managed to escape onto the main deck, Patrick suddenly lost it. 'Below deck tha' swivin' clapperdudgeon!' he ordered. The hunchback scurried off with Skippy in tow. The animal was no fool when he sensed danger. The two fugitives headed for the bowels of the ship where Creppin stayed, sulking for hours. When Anthony urged him to fetch himself some food, the hunchback refused to go above deck. The blacksmith's patience was wearing thin, 'Tha' snivellin' dungbie!' he shouted, leaving him to brood. 'Bing a waste!' came a furious reply. 'Crrreppin needs some time by his selllvies!' he griped as he was left alone in the dank darkness.

Patrick explained to the crew about the Tupi ceremonial tradition of cannibalism. Jaeci was going to honour his dead warrior friends by consuming their flesh. Whoo suggested to the captain, albeit reluctantly, 'Perhaps we should allow Creppin ter aid me in preparin' Serijipe's and Josh's bodies fer th'eating? Perchance the deed may entice him above deck.' Patrick consulted Jaeci who was happy for the hunchback to do that. The crew that gathered on the weather deck showed mixed emotions. Some puked on the spot at the thought of the cannibalistic ritual but others accepted the custom. Not many expressed the wish to eat cooked human flesh. Creppin was delighted to be asked to help Whoo wash and cut up the bodies. The hunchback thoroughly enjoyed the experience although he did have to be chastised when he became too eager, 'I've bin' a-wantin' ter rrremove a limb frrrom an injured matey. This shalt surely aid me ter make a fine surgeon's apprrrentice.' Whoo was disgusted by the hunchback's lack of respect. 'Show our fallen mates some dignity!' he ordered. Creppin was rudely reminded that he had actually cut up his friends. He became very depressed and skulked off to find Skips. The little tribal dog had sensed Jaeci's sadness and was lying at his feet. Creppin curled up next to them and fell asleep. When the sacrificial meat had been cooked, the captain took those who wished to participate in the ancient ceremony to his quarters. Jaeci blessed the area and he, Shrimp, Patrick, Anthony, Moses, Jock and Whoo ate the sacred warrior's flesh. According to Tupi tradition each took on the consumed warrior's names whose strength they had all absorbed. The captain mourned all of the fallen. He only hoped that their sacrifice had not been in vain.

Patrick's crew managed the challenging approach into O'Malley territorial waters well considering the terrible weather conditions. Thick fog hung heavy in the damp air as the warship sailed cautiously on. The dense vapours would not allow even the faintest view of the green shores of Eire. It was as if the swirling clouds had been drawn down by the dark grey surface of the miserable sea. As the wind speed gradually increased the crew became wary and reefed the sails. Spotting a faint glow ahead of them, Anthony yelled aloud. The watch had obviously seen the hazy light too as the alarm bell sounded loud and clear. A familiar voice came out of the fog, 'Name d' vessel dat enters moy warters!' Patrick yelled in reply, 'Ahoy yer Majesty! 'Tis 'Queen Culley's Revenge'!' A familiar, guttural laugh gave him an immense feeling of relief and joy. 'Feck! Lord, Gard 'a morcy!' came Grace's delayed reply. The waves lapped at the unseen vessel that was not far ahead. 'Trow 'em a loin!' came the elated pyrate queen's order and a large metal ring landed on the poop deck with a thick rope tied fast to it. 'Tha reached us first attempt!' an unidentified pyrate shouted in surprise. Anthony grinned broadly when he heard the pyrate queen's response, 'Fer feck sake, oy should tink so too, me lad! Yers in O'Malley territory noy so yer'll oft' be witnessing perfection amidst us Celtic folk, so yers shall!' As the Revenge was towed to a safe place to lay anchor Patrick bantered with his friends on the other vessel.

Patrick was so happy to be back in his beloved Eire. Nervously, the hunchback waited by the boat that would take some of them safely to shore. He wanted to be certain that he was one of the first to land at Rockfleet. Following the captain's command to make ready the landing vessels, a whimpering voice emerged from the fog, 'O'er yonder!' Creppin directed. 'Launch the penis!' he added. Shanny sniggered at the hunchback's error and stepped into the pinnace to sit opposite him. The small boat was lowered and twelve men rowed to the shore. Although Anthony could not wait to see Grace again he returned to collect another boatful of men. Grace and Patrick were both very emotional when they reunited. She was pleased to hear that the Deliverance had served them well and was due to arrive the following day. Merlin and Mistlytoes bounded out to meet Creppin and welcomed Skippy who barked loudly to warn them not to presume that his size matched his ferocity. The hunchback giggled hysterically and he and his canine companions disappeared, en masse, inside the fortress. Eventually, the whole crew were settled in Rockfleet, appreciating the warmth of a homely peat fire, a good Irish pottage and a tankard full of ale.

As expected the Deliverance was sighted early evening on the last day of November, 1578. A substantial haul of treasure was taken inside Rockfleet that night. Over the next few months Patrick and Grace plotted the assassination of the Queen. Some of the Grace's spies had already stolen vital maps and were also in possession of forged documents. Captain Culley had devised a plan to use Hawkins' inside information on the Queen's movements. He was glad to learn that his late mother's lover had already sent vital information to Grace. This proved that the English Queen's Naval Commander was still willing to be involved in the treacherous scheme. Knowing how fickle the admiral could be, Patrick wanted to gain as much from Hawkins as he possibly could while he was still mourning his lover's death. Patrick, Anthony, Grace and Jock met, every day and night, to discuss their plans of action. When the final plot had been decided, everyone was put to work. So much had to be done and time was against them. Various back-up plans also had to be set in place in case anything went wrong. Everyone involved had to be totally trusted and scrutinised before allowing them access to Grace's quarters. Messengers rallied back and forth to London carrying vital news to and from Hawkins. All letters were written in a complex secret code that would take the cleverest scholar months to decipher. Whilst all of this was going on, the pyrate militia was expanding in numbers as word spread around Ireland of Patrick Culley's return. Every new recruit was given the best combat training. Each did a stint on one of Grace's border patrol ships. So many Irish people wanted the English Queen dead. Before long, Patrick was hailed as Eire's new hero.

The time came to select the final thirteen who would make up the assassination team. Grace, Patrick, Anthony and Jock considered every volunteer carefully. Each was vetted and shadowed for weeks before they were interviewed by the four headstrong leaders. Many brave volunteers were willing to die for the cause and it took a long time to choose the right team. The time and place of the assassination attempt had been set. They were to strike at the hugely popular annual festival of St. John the Baptist. Spies in London had already made contacts who were willing to help in the conspiracy. Spain and France were keen to attack following a successful assassination attempt and liaisons were happening on a regular basis. Grace had facilitated

Patrick's original plans and everything had been set up ready for the plot to go ahead.

When the time came to sail for England Grace held a huge farewell party for Patrick and his gang. A massive figure-head exquisitely carved with a perfect likeness to the late Sushana Culley was presented to her son. The late pyrate heroine was naked, in the maritime tradition, as it was believed that a woman's bare breasts would shame the stormiest of seas into calm. Two large pale blue aqua marine stones had been set in each of the immaculately painted pyrate queen's eyes. It was believed that they would enable her to see the way if the ship became lost at sea. 'I've a-counted Crrreppin's bitsies' the hunchback told Anthony. 'I's savin' ferrr sevrrral pokesies when we lands in Londinium towwwn' he spluttered eagerly. No matter how often Anthony tried to convince the little cripple that England's capital was a city called 'London', Creppin still insisted on calling it by the original Roman name. 'Sunday sail, ne'er fail' shouted Grace as the most skilled sailors and warriors she had ever known boarded the Revenge.

Pushing Creppin out of the way, Jack shouted, 'Y'am as gain as a glass oy!' Still blocking the gangway as he waited for Anthony to board, the hunchback grumbled as he picked up Skips. Having no clue what had been said, he was sure that the Midlander had insulted him in some way. Reluctantly he limped aboard, left foot first, dragging his treasured crate behind him. Bernard and Jack stood waving at the massive crowd that had gathered to bid Patrick and the crew farewell. The men could not believe how many had turned up. 'Them Oyrish ay arf a bostin' lot ay they Jack?' Bernard had to shout louder so the deaf man was able to hear, 'Ar, I ay a-used t' fond terrars. Wi' mi lost ship ne'er a wun cum a n'ee" Shanny joined the two men and translated for the bewildered pyrates who stood, puzzled by their strange jargon. 'Meet my two good friends', she told the crew. 'They sayeth that the Irish are fine people. They've scarce seen so many come to wave 'em off.' ''E ay arf a canny by, ay 'e, Jack?' Bernard said, beaming with pride at the young man's ability to understand their dialect. The majority of pyrates believed that Shanny was Séan, a tough lad in his late teens. It was safer for them to think that. Only a few knew her closely guarded secret. Anthony was the last to board. He had to kiss Grace one more time before he left. As their lips met he tasted her tears. 'Be safe!' she called as he jogged along the gangplank to join his crew.

The morning of the 27th January 1579 was cold, frosty but dry when Queen Culley's Revenge sailed away from the Emerald Isle. Thirteen pyrates who had committed their lives to Patrick's cause gathered in the captain's cabin. Their leader addressed the other twelve. 'Teignmouth be our first port o' call. A few days there, then we'll head back t' Plymouth. Tha'll all be aware of our final destination; the River Thames is where we'll dock our beauty for a good while.' Everyone was given forged papers that stated they were journeymen. Only Anthony's and Creppin's valued documents were authentic and had been signed by the Guildhall bailiff back in their hometown. As visitors to London, the gang would have to produce their crucial documents for inspection to gain entry into the walled city. Queen Elizabeth had passed a law to make all travellers carry a license which made it more difficult for people to move around the country. Many were concerned about strangers carrying the bubonic plaque and citizens feared that their city would be the next to experience an outbreak of the killer epidemic. The captain continued, handing out maps, code deciphering instructions and a list of the gang with the names that they would all be using from then on. As Creppin, Moses and Shrimp could not read they were given simple symbols to guide them. Everyone was given a leather bag to keep their information safe. Anthony had dismantled and adapted various tools or utensils that could conceal the secret articles. Shanny unrolled her scroll and read the list;

Patrick - Peter Croft - Artist - Painter of Miniatures and Moses, slave of the aforementioned

Anthony Brown - blacksmith and Saul Rees, apprentice of the aforementioned

Danny - Daniel Dale - Fletcher

Remando Fromond – Apothecary and Shanny - Sean Chamberlain, apprentice of the aforementioned

Shrimp - Friar Sheraton Franklin - Herbalist

Colm - Dr. Colin Rochforth - Physician and Abadeyo and Babatu, slaves of the aforementioned

Jock - Dr. Joseph Byfield - Astrologist and Creppin Leech, servant to the aforementioned

So, thought Shanny, her alter-ego's name had been anglicised to 'Sean Chamberlain' who was a trainee apothecary under Remando. Glancing discreetly over to her self-appointed ward, she felt happy to see him smiling as he read the list. She was so relieved that the pyrate had regained his strength and proved to Patrick and Grace that he had fully recovered from his dreadful scare. Silently, the observant woman studied everyone in the room. From now on, she would have to remember to use their false names. Patrick was to be Peter Croft, the artist, whose slave was Moses. As an accomplished artist the captain would make a wonderful painter. The popularity of miniature paintings was flourishing with even the Queen herself owning 'diverse little pictures wrapt within paper' as treasured keepsakes. Anthony felt no need to change his name or trade and, as his new apprentice, Saul felt the same. The helmsman, Danny was a weaponry expert so a fletcher's trade would suit Master Dale perfectly well. As Shrimp had an unusually extensive knowledge of herbalism which had expanded since he had become a Tupi tribesman, he had been blessed with an honorary monastic title. 'Friar Sheritan' suited the homely-looking character who already sported a permanently tonsured hairstyle. Self-educated intellectual, Colm, had been promoted in the medical profession under the guise of Dr. Colin Rochforth. Shanny pondered... Yes, she could get used to that title. Of course, the good doctor had two African slaves, Abadeyo and Babatu who were also skilled homeopathic healers using natural remedies from their native lands. Jock, a skilled sailor, who knew the stars like the back of his own hand, had become Dr. Joseph Byfield who was unfortunate enough to have been paired with Creppin. As the best mentor for the hunchback, Jock would be able to discipline his servant whilst being allowed the space that Creppin would never have given the blacksmith had he been allocated to him.

'Yes', Shanny thought, 'A fine team.' She was sure that the other twelve could be trusted but Danny still made her feel a little uncomfortable. Shaking off any doubtful feelings, she smiled sweetly at her captain. Creppin eyed

Danny. He did not trust the lout but the feeling was mutual. Saul had become close to Danny since they had reconciled but still felt some resentment towards Jock. The captain could not understand why Grace and Anthony had insisted that the hunchback went along. Although their idea was good to use the foul-stinking freak as a decoy, so people would remember only him in their desperation to flee from his presence, he did not like the useless cripple. As Anthony observed the others psychoanalysing one another, he could not help a faint smile. He was sure that he could trust every person present and hoped that, in time, they would all feel the same. Looking over at the captain, he did not envy the responsibility that he had undertaken. Since getting to know him well, the blacksmith recognised the same caring, loyal nature that he too possessed.

The impending visit to Teignmouth was going to be a difficult one. Patrick, Danny and Saul had all decided that it was best to deliver the tragic news of Josh's death in person. Their extended clan at Mary Maggy's were bound to be devastated. Anthony had asked to return to his hometown in the hope of finding his father alive and well. A visit to Plymouth would also give him the chance to take Patrick to the place where he had buried his mother's severed head. Although the captain needed to pay his last respects, he was dreading the moment. A dull pain pounded his temples as his mind seethed with unquenchable rage. For the meantime, Sushana Culley's head would have to remain in Isaac Bromley's coffin. One day her son would make sure that she was honoured with a tomb fit for the brave and dearly beloved Queen of the Seas.

Chapter 15

Finally: Fianna Fail's Hour

Grace O'Malley was determined to launch a heavy attack on Elizabeth's navy following Patrick's assassination attempt. Hawkins had already helped by sending vessels to add to her growing fleet. If the plan to foil the Protestant Queen into believing that the Spanish had attacked the vessels that patrolled the Thames, Grace would move her army in to invade London. The King of Spain was eager to play a part in Elizabeth's downfall and awaited news from Connaught to begin the assault. When the time came, Irish ships would lie in wait, ready to attack and destroy the skeleton naval presence left to defend England's capital. Once they had landed, the well-trained Fianna Fail would wreak havoc through the capital city, storm the Palace of Westminster and overthrow parliament. The citizens would be defenceless and scared following their Queen's assassination. Grace would have to wait with enough ships to protect her own land in case English vessels attacked Ireland. Knowing the hatred that festered within the paranoid English monarch's soul, Grace firmly believed that she would already have plans in place for an attack on Ireland in the event of an attempted, or successful, assassination. There was much to accomplish while Patrick and his gang primed the trap for the witch Queen.

Feeling a much needed boost of positivity Grace took to her seas on a midnight patrol. She stood on the upper deck, steering the vessel by means of a whip staff, an extension of the tiller. This gave the helmsman a clearer view ahead rather than having to peer through a small opening when steering from the lower deck. A deathly cold wind stimulated her senses. As the therapeutic sound of waves hushed the night seas the tall woman guided her galleon towards the shimmering reflection of a lilac moon. As it danced upon the waters beneath its mystical source the flame in the lantern above the compass box flickered. Grace's plaited copper locks were whipped in the wind as the sails billowed above her. Sailing had always been the best way for the Irish noblewoman to get things straight in her mind.

There was something about vast stretches of water that seemed to balance Grace O'Malley. The magnetism of the sea had drawn her from the very first time she had sensed its essence on a gentle breeze. Akin to her beloved ocean, the Irish pyrate queen possessed immense power. Her mind knew unfathomable depths. Her emotions would change as often as the tides. With the full moon in her sights Grace felt an edgy shiver of doubt about Hawkins' loyalty. Her tanned face seemed aglow with the lustrous moonlight. Her brow furrowed as she reflected back on her original notion. After all, she had never felt entirely comfortable with Hawkins' interest in Sushana Culley. He had once been the English monarch's favourite before he had fallen in love with her friend. His cousin, Drake, had taken his place at court to distract the jealous Queen's attention from his prolonged absence but now he was back in the viper's next. She could not shake the feeling that a trap would be awaiting them.

Following an uneventful four hour patrol, Grace returned to Rockfleet. Grabbing onto the thick rope used to winch booty up into her fortified home she gave an order for her men to haul. As she was raised swiftly up towards the small arched doorway, the female chieftain ran her fingers over the cold grey stone of the bleak-looking structure. On reaching the narrow entrance, Grace swung herself through to feel the welcome warmth of a well-stoked peat fire. It was comforting to hear the sound of her dogs' tails thumping the richly decorated rug that covered the coloured flagstones. Heavy snoring reverberated through the castle. She heard her night crew enter via the main door and their footsteps padding up the spiral staircase. Picking up a scroll that had a shamrock neatly drawn under the seal, the she-king unrolled the thick parchment. Pondering over the notion of Hawkins betraying Patrick, she traced her fingers over his hand-written proposal. Maybe she felt wary because the admiral planned to be miles away, at sea, when the assassins were to make the hit. After all, they had gone along with his suggestion of striking during a huge celebratory event.

Why would Hawkins decide to be absent? Stroking Mistlytoes and Merlin as they lay warming their great bodies by the hearth, Grace tried to shake her doubts and begin to think more positively about the lover of her late friend who she missed so dearly. She would have to do some more background work on the dashing courtier before the St. John's Eve plot was set in stone. Having put together two separate, carefully planned strategy's, she and Patrick would select the most appropriate when all of the circumstances were clear. This offered protection in case of leakage of any part of their scheme not forgetting the chance of discovery by the many agents that Queen Elizabeth had spread throughout her kingdom. Patrick's team were going to prepare and train rigorously for both plans of action. Location could be changed right up until the very last minute. There was a possibility that this would be their only chance to attack. Grace O'Malley and Patrick Culley were pleased with the growth and progress of their Fianna Fail. If everything went to plan the first ever organised pyrate militia would be remembered for the destruction of a mighty empire that their royal foe was expanding day by day. Enemies were now prowling England's coasts, awaiting the time to strike.

Chapter 16

Wrath of a Dead Witch's Heiress

On a frosty February morning in 1579 Queen Elizabeth's carriage pulled up outside Norwich Cathedral. The royal party had been taken on a planned route which had brought them to their destination via Elm Hill where prosperous merchants, craftsmen and civic dignitaries lived. Augustine Steward had watched the impressive pageant pass by from the first floor window of his house before his party joined the bishop to greet the Queen. Augustine was a wealthy well-known local merchant whose family were accommodating her Majesty for the duration of her visit. Security measures were tight for fear of an assassination attempt. Many local Catholics harboured hatred for the Protestant monarch. Four magnificent horses pulled the Queen's carriage along the important commercial thoroughfare. Many weavers, dyers, tanners, goldsmiths and other expert craftsmen had made their fortune and built houses along Elm Hill.

Shortly after lunch, the mayor of Norwich had left the city to meet the Queen. A great pageant had taken place. Sixty bachelors led the procession followed by an actor who represented the legendary founder of Norwich, King Gurgunt, riding a great horse. The King was accompanied by three henchmen. Important gentry and wealthy citizens were next in line, riding fine stallions. Officers of the city were followed by the Master Sword Bearer then the mayor surrounded by twenty four aldermen. Twenty four sheriffs followed with whifflers 'to keep the people from disturbing the array'. Elizabeth and her royal entourage were waiting at Hertford Bridge where the mayor handed her a silver cup, addressing her in Latin, 'Sunt hic Centum libri puri auri' which meant, 'there is a hundred pounds in gold here.' On accepting the gift, Elizabeth stated that, 'Princes have no need of money', but added that 'they place great value on the love of their subjects.' She handed the prize to a footman and told him, 'Look to it, there is a hundreth pound'. Everyone laughed at the humorous way the Queen had warned her servant not to steal any of the money. The royal party continued in coaches to Market Street where a second spectacle awaited. A wall had been painted on a structure of wood and canvas and positioned across the street. An elaborate main gate, flanked by two smaller ones and each adorned with insignia had been added. Musicians played a fantasia from arches and the grand construction that had been topped with a stage. Five actors sat on thrones, each impersonating an ancient heroine. When the Queen drew near, the music stopped and a male actor, dressed as Dame Norwich, gave the English Queen a hearty welcome to her city. The Queen's jester had dressed as a fair lady and was invited to join Elizabeth in the leading carriage.

Many citizens of Norwich and the surrounding area had lined the streets to see the spectacular Royal Procession. All of the stocks were full that day. Elizabeth noticed the large amount of eggshells that lay broken around the criminals. Healthy looking children pelted the unfortunate captives with rotten food. To the Queen, these were both good signs that the citizens of Norwich were well fed. A local dignitary took great pride in joining the Queen and her party to give them a guided tour.

He spoke with an annoyingly monotonous voice and harsh local accent. Elizabeth had to hold her perfumed silk handkerchief to her face to conceal the odd yawn. Laughing Dick responded by faking a sneeze followed by a high-pitched squeak. He knew that his pranks would keep the Queen alert and amused. 'O'er yonder, Ma'am, thou hast a fair view of our famous George Coaching Hotel…' The elderly man's voice droned on and on. 'Ahhhh…choo! ee!' Dick added another tiny feminine squeal to the end of his sneeze. Elizabeth smirked and winked playfully at her friend whilst their tour guide was concentrating on reeling off drabs of over-rehearsed information. The Queen feigned occasional interest as expected from a member of royalty. With an air of forced politeness that scarcely hid her monotony, she addressed the boring guide, 'Ah, delightful! From hither one may take the stage to London.' she observed. 'True, Ma'am!' came an over-enthusiastic reply. She had fooled the chaperon who was flattered by her faked interest. His voice mingled in with the clopping hooves of the gorgeous bay horses that drew the carriage. Pulling the fur covers higher, Elizabeth wished that she had the freedom to be able to yank open the door, unhitch a horse and gallop off into the distance. 'The Holt to Thetford coach also taketh passengers on board from o'er yonder.' 'Hell's bells' thought Dick as he realised that the fellow was still wittering on about the coaching house! Local inns of no importance to her Majesty or Dick, for that matter, became a haze as the carriage passed by.

Elizabeth thought of nothing but her Robin as she peered through the small draughty window. Although many had turned out to catch a glimpse of the Protestant Queen, they would soon be demeaning her once her coach was out of sight. For the meantime, though, each waved a grubby, work-ruined palm with enthusiasm. At least they were showing their gratitude for the day off work that the Royal Visit had allowed them. '... The Angel... the Swann, the Griffin and the Bull...' A loud fart suddenly erupted beneath Laughing Dick. Elizabeth managed to hide her delight. She stifled a laugh and addressed him in French, as if chastising him, 'Nouveau temps de merde!' 'Oui, Merrrde!' came his cheeky high-pitched reply as he over-exaggerated the rolling French tongue. The prettily clad, clever jester bowed his head in mock shame. The Queen smiled inwardly at the dignitary's ignorance when he continued on with his oration, having believed that she had used French to save his embarrassment. Quite the opposite, she had merely expressed to her amusing friend that 'the weather was shit!' Cheekily, Dick had repeated the word meaning 'shit' in the pretty language.

By the end of the tour, the sleepy jester doubted that either he or Elizabeth had learned anything of importance about Norwich. They were already well aware that crafts, trades and businesses were flourishing in the prosperous area. As Dick watched Elizabeth subconsciously twisting a beautiful ring around her finger, he could tell that her mind was on other matters. She would, no doubt, need to talk to him later that night. He never minded her unburdening her soul. She treated him well and he appreciated her trust and genuine friendship. Dick often felt sorry for the woman who had no other choice but reign. The jester had watched his queen become increasingly bitter every day. His mind drifted back to happy days during his marriage. If he had not met his late wife then, he too, would probably have become hostile towards others. 'S'truth!' he mumbled quietly. Now the dignitary was reeling off lists again... butchers, bakers, brewers, cobblers, blacksmiths, tanners, wheelwrights, saddlers and coopers were all doing well. Overall, the most important industry was the manufacture of woollen cloth. By official mass invitation Flemish weavers had been flocking over to the area to avoid religious persecution. Many of these skilled immigrants or 'strangers', as locals called them, had been encouraged to help expand the wool and cloth trade. Naturally, the most influential men were now the mercers who dealt in the flourishing business. 'I bid thee most welcome, ma'am, to the second city of thy kingdom.' Ending with a perfect finale that was accompanied by a peel of welcoming bells, the most boring man that Elizabeth and Dick had ever come across exited the gilded coach. Sweeping his arm, he made an extremely low bow which was impressive for his age. He walked slowly backwards until the Queen alighted the carriage to stand before the glorious Cathedral of Norwich.

The majestic Norman structure loomed above them as Elizabeth walked along a red carpet towards the entrance of the presbytery. An imposing tower stretched skyward. Dick gazed up to view a cornflower blue autumn sky with delicate wisps of cloud hovering way above its seemingly sharp pinnacle. The afternoon was pleasant but as cold as the Cathedral's French limestone walls. The Queen's personal entertainer found it incredible to think that the foundations of the structure before them had been laid way back in the Middle Ages, almost five hundred years earlier. Elizabeth ascended the steps that had been cut into the north side of the building solely for her use. A fanfare of cornets welcomed the monarch and people shouted from the crowds that had gathered beyond the cathedral boundaries. Pausing briefly to look up at the beautiful stonemasonry Elizabeth thought of her mother, Anne Boleyn. Beginning to panic, she looked anxiously around her. Feeling quite faint, she took a deep breath and asked one of her ladies-in-waiting to arrange for a glass of mead to be brought to her. A concerned bishop awaited the Head of the Church of England's presence.

On entering the dramatic building, a feeling of tranquillity overcame Elizabeth. She was led to a splendid throne where she sat and waited for her drink. Having tested the mead, the lady-in-waiting brought the glass that had been placed upon a richly embroidered cloth on a fine silver tray. Without saying a word, the Queen sipped the welcome fluid and replaced the empty glass. Her throne had been placed opposite the tomb of her great-grandfather, Sir William Boleyn. The Saxon stone on which she sat felt cold despite its cushion of rich, red velvet. Elizabeth sat perfectly still as she studied the Boleyn arms. Ironically, Dick noted that his friend appeared to be a marble statue that had been elaborately dressed to represent the Queen. The thought unnerved him. He tried to concentrate on singing the psalms.

The music was exquisite but solemn. Elizabeth was in no mood for worship. Although she went through the paces, her heart was not in it. Unable to rid her mind of the memory of her own father ordering her mother's death, she felt a bad pain behind her eyes. Subconsciously she fingered the delicate ring she always wore. Inside were tiny likenesses of herself and her mother. They had both known the dangers of being powerful women in a man's world. Elizabeth's mind raced forward as she imagined her own tomb. She had already predicted her epitaph in a speech not long after her coronation, 'a marble stone shall declare that a Queen, having reigned such a time, lived and died a virgin.' 'Curse the thought' she whispered to herself. To think, the sacrifice that she had made for her true love! The service dragged on until Elizabeth had to perform once more. Following the knighting ceremony of Nicholas Bacon and the mayor the Queen was relieved to leave the heady smells of frankincense behind. The unhealthy atmosphere in holy places had always clogged her spirit. She detested hypocrisy and knew full well that the sanctimonious clergymen fucked whores or choirboys at every given opportunity. How she longed for the following day when she would go on a hunt in Cossie Park.

On their return, the royal apartments were ready for Elizabeth and her entourage. Elizabeth was as hungry as a horse and glad to see that a fine feast awaited them. The meal was delicious but her thoughts were still preoccupied. She could not wait to consult Laughing Dick later that night. When she had been attended to, Elizabeth dismissed her ladies-in-waiting. Never having been one to enjoy the company of most women, she did not feel in the mood to humour a bunch of over-grown, giggling girls. Henry VIII's daughter did not suffer fools gladly. Once she was alone, she took her silver looking glass and arranged her coif so that small curls of her red hair could be seen. Her hair was sparse as she had suffered severe hair-loss over the last few years. Checking her timepiece she sighed. Dick was always on time so she would have to wait another five long minutes. Smoothing her embroidered smock with the back of her hand, Elizabeth opened the box that she kept on her bedside table. She took out Robert's latest letter but on hearing a jolly song, she replaced it and locked the lid.

'Oy bid thee good eve' moy pretty queen!' Dick shouted, 'Pri'thee, may oy enter thy chamberrr?' His west country accent cheered the Queen up instantly. 'Enter, my faithful friend!' said the Queen, urgently. Entering the large room the jester bowed low. He danced on tiptoes, waving his arms in the air whilst humming a lively tune. 'Be seated, my dear Dick', Elizabeth told the spirited man. A silver tray had been set with pieces of candied orange and lemon peel, stems of angelica and gingerbread. Pouring a generous glass of imported wine, the Queen was desperate to confide in her friend, 'Alas, I have more news of my Robin's deceit.' Dick felt bad for her. She looked so tired and forlorn. 'Forsooth, I trust in no soul more than I trust in thee, Richard.' It was unusual for Elizabeth to use the actor's full name. Taking a handful of delicious treats, Dick nodded a gesture of thanks. 'Moy dear queen, oy be honoured, as thy 'umble servant an' devoted friend.' Skilfully juggling three squares of gingerbread, he opened his mouth to catch one after the other. Clapping her hands together with sheer delight the aging monarch appeared to be much younger in the soft, flickering firelight. She always looked so much better when she smiled. Speaking in hushed tones, Elizabeth leaned towards her confidant. 'Hark my words. I speak softly for fear of eavesdroppers.' Dick had to strain to hear her hushed words. She confessed that lately she had been brooding over her unfaithful lover far too much. When Elizabeth admitted to her concerned companion that she sought retribution, Dick feared for Lettice Knollys. Feeling that she had shown her niece far too much compassion, she told the concerned man that she had finally made a decision. Robert Dudley's lover was going to be punished for her audacious deceit.

As Dick watched the animated Queen's lips draw into a cruel, narrow slit and her face twist into a spiteful sneer, he prayed silently for her resentful soul. In her unhealthy state of mind she had allowed bitter jealousy to ensnare her. Lately, Dudley's ridiculous obsession with Lettice, as Elizabeth liked to call it, had been torturing her. The jester was beginning to wonder whether she ever thought of anything else these days. It was useless for him to comment so he listened patiently. He tried to separate the twisted, venomous woman who sat opposite him from the intelligent, noble leader that Elizabeth had once been. As the candles burned lower he provided a much needed ear. When the Queen had finished her rant he could not resist offering a warning. ''Tis'nay wise ter seek revenge, moy fair queen.' Sucking her cheeks in, Elizabeth rose from her chair and began to pace around the room. Dick continued calmly despite his hostess' obvious annoyance, 'Take heed o' my warning. Thou knowest, full well, how thy dear mother met her demise. 'Twas jealousy that ruined good Queen Anne. 'Tis'nay a shrewd path ter follow.' The wise jester said no more. He waited patiently for his friend's anger to subside.

Elizabeth was not angry with Dick for his honesty. She was already aware that her popularity would diminish towards the end of her reign. Her astrological charts had told her this and her tarot cards too. The Queen had been feeling unwell lately. Having confided in Lady Blanche, she had asked Dee to produce a more in-depth horoscope for the year. A griping pain in the base of her stomach made Elizabeth wince, 'Dick!' she cried, 'I'm afeared!' After taking a sip of tonic that her apothecary had mixed for her earlier, she continued, 'Dost thou recall, a fair few years since, I begot with child?' The jester's heart sank. Heaven help her if she was carrying her second child, Dick thought to himself. Elizabeth began to weep. Taking her hand, he tried to offer comfort, although he knew that only one man on earth would succeed at that. He understood how difficult it was for the Queen not having Robert by her side. Dick missed his deceased wife terribly. No one would ever be able to take her place.

Over the next two hours, the distraught noblewoman shared her turmoil with the empathic older man. The jester learned that it had been over two months since she had last bled. Having been through nine weeks of hell, Elizabeth knew that she could not bear the thought of another baby being taken from her. She dreaded having to tell Robert that, once again, she carried his child. Shortly after her coronation Robert had been upset when she had forced him to take her on an unplanned Royal Progress so she could go into hiding for the last three months of her confinement. He was devastated that she had to keep the pregnancy, and their mutual love, a secret.

Plans had already been made for a wealthy childless couple to take care of the bastard child. Over the years, many ladies-in-waiting had become pregnant whilst at court. They had needed help to hide their condition, until delivery, to protect their name. Decent couples who were unable to conceive would be called in the early hours to collect an unwanted infant. No questions were ever asked. Both parties were happy with the arrangement. A substantial sum of money accompanied each tiny bundle; the amount made it obvious whether the offspring was that of a noblewoman or servant. In the case of the Queen and Dudley's lovechild, the parents had been carefully chosen and made to promise that the boy was schooled well and brought up to speak Latin.

The couple had both been crushed when Elizabeth gave birth to a fine, healthy baby boy. After her mother had been unable to provide her father with a son and heir, the Queen felt that she was being punished by God for her sinful ways. In a cruel twist of fate, a birth that would have been a blessing for Anne Boleyn had turned out to be a curse for her daughter. Elizabeth and her lover had produced a perfect, healthy heir yet it was impossible for them to marry and keep their son. Dudley was loathed by many. Despite numerous proposals of marriage and Parliament's constant nagging for her to take a husband, Elizabeth had remained true to her lover. To add further insult to injury, together, they had produced a child who was 'English through and through' which would have even placated Parliament had the father not been Robert Dudley!

Elizabeth's and Robert's fated deal had been sheer irony at its best! The Queen remembered flinging her windows wide open to scream the ultimate blasphemy, in the eyes of the male dominated Church, over the rooftops; 'Hell, God She hath a fine sense of humour!' Caring not whether she lived or died, the wretched woman had fallen into a severe state of depression. Her melancholy lasted for weeks after she had literally been forced to give up their precious baby. Made to take prescribed medicines by her surgeons, the broken-hearted Queen endured a full month of daily blood-letting. She was then put on a new diet that she did not want to follow. Robert became hostile towards her for refusing his visits but, even during those stressful times, neither could deny their mutual undying love. Dick felt drained as he recalled the terrible postnatal devastation that Elizabeth endured. She had never seen her beautiful son again. As her tears flowed freely, Queen Elizabeth whispered, 'My Robin is my soul mate.' Dick sat still and silent.

The fire had burned down to glowing amber embers. The Queen's pale face was stained with tears. She had told her trusted friend her woeful tale. Not wanting Dick to respond, the exhausted woman dismissed him without another word. He understood. Lifting cold, slender fingers in a weary gesture of thanks, Elizabeth stayed slumped in her chair. Dick had done exactly what she had required. She loved her jester as she should have been able to love her father. How on earth could a daughter have ever trusted a father who had ordered the beheading of her mother? Elizabeth stood. As she stretched her stiff body she recalled the words that had come to mind back in Norwich cathedral. She had to write them down before going to sleep. Taking out the parchment on which she had written the first part of the poem, she dipped a fresh quill into an ink pot;

> I seem stark mute, but inwardly do prate.
> I am, and not; I freeze and yet am burned,
> Since from myself another self I turned.

When the ink was dry, Elizabeth rolled up the parchment and crawled into her bed. The following morning, she woke to the sound of a baby crying. Leaping up from her comfortable mattress, she panicked. Her dream had seemed so real. The Queen's pace slowed as she reached the window. Pulling the heavy curtain to one side, she felt tremendous disappointment when she saw two beautiful peacocks displaying their shimmering turquoise, purple, blue and gold feathers. Their call had sounded so similar to that of a human baby! Elizabeth's head pounded. Sleep had not eased her anxiety. Her stomach pains had worsened. Calling her close friend and lady-in-waiting, Lady Blanche, she complained to be suffering from a bout of costiveness. 'Codso!' cursed the Queen who had been snapping at her servants since they had first appeared to help her prepare for the day. Blanche offered to massage Elizabeth's lower back and she gratefully accepted. She had been known to suffer from this ailment since childhood so Lady Blanche had become well-used to the common gripe. As the Queen sat forward on her seat of easement, she was relieved to feel a hard stool begin to emerge. 'For pity's sake, woman, draw it out!' Elizabeth commanded, her patience wearing thin. Her heart sank when her lady-in-waiting fetched some strips of soft white linen. She had started her period. No baby was developing within her wilting womb.

After a few days of discomfort and plenty of fruit the Queen felt well enough to cope with the long journey home. The Royal Progress set out and made its way back to London. Each stately manor that welcomed Elizabeth managed to outdo her previous hosts. Lately, the Queen's temper had been foul. She had literally reached boiling point. Everyone in her party feared her mounting wrath. When seeking counsel from Dick, Elizabeth revealed that her aggravation was largely due to a meeting that had been arranged in her absence. She was dreading the upcoming event. On arrival in London, in only a few months' time, the Queen would be expected to meet with the French ambassador. He was due to land at Greenwich on the 17th June. Without a doubt, his motive was to try, once again, to persuade her to marry the Duke of Anjou. She had planned to turn him down, of course. That notion did not change the fact that she was sick to the stomach of being forced into such awkward situations. From the beginning of her reign Elizabeth had made herself quite clear. She had also reinforced her original decision to stay unwed numerous times since. Why would these impertinent men not listen?!

On the day that Elizabeth returned to her beloved loyal residence, Windsor Castle, she demanded to be left alone. The stunning Norman fort had always been an ideal retreat for the Queen who saw it as a safe haven built to withstand a siege. Stripping herself of her jewellery, she ordered her maids to derobe her and pulled on her riding gear herself. Having spent a couple of hours inspecting her lavish apartments she called for her favourite stallion, Red. Although the State Rooms had been prepared for an imminent meeting with some privy councillors, Elizabeth told her Gentleman Usher that 'they canst bloody wait!' After all, the sessions were always dominated by questions about marriage and succession! She had also heard that it was to be put to her to bring about reform in the Church of England. As head of the Church, Elizabeth was not going to have any of that nonsense.

The only time that Queen Elizabeth felt free was when she was riding. Keen to see the progress of the projects that she had commissioned on her last visit, Elizabeth rode her stallion around the estate. Lately she had spent a considerable amount of money on conversions and repairs to the royal property. Ten new brass cannons had been ordered for its defence. Satisfied with the work so far, the Queen reluctantly returned to carry out her duty. As Elizabeth had invited Dick over for a fencing duel later that evening, she wanted to warm up beforehand. Impeccable self-control, a balanced psychological state and excellent concentration were all essential when she fenced. Since her jester was a fencing master and extremely good swordsman Elizabeth always liked time to prepare herself for a fight. To her Majesty, defeat was not an option.

When Laughing Dick arrived, Elizabeth was invigorated and ready for a challenging fight. The friends' fencing skills were dazzling, the speed of their swords faster than the eye could follow. Both passionate swordsmen, they were so well-matched that it was a while before Dick managed a hit but the Queen scored against him soon after. Finally, Elizabeth out-smarted her opponent and the two freshened up before enjoying a light tea. The announcement came as a pleasant surprise. Instantly cheerful, the Queen called for her ladies to apply fresh make-up. She had an important visitor. Sir John Hawkins had requested to see the Queen.

'My dear John!' Elizabeth cried. 'Thou art, verily, a breath of fresh air!' She welcomed one of her most favoured privateers warmly. Kissing her gloved hand, he complimented her immortal beauty, telling her that he had missed her terribly. The Queen received her Naval Commander in her drawing room where he presented her with the most extravagant gifts. Ten of John's servants entered, one by one, to present each to the cosseted Queen. The offerings included a small chest full of half sovereigns, a gold tooth pick with its head set with a ruby and seed pearls and several pieces of exquisite jewellery. Her favourite, by far, was a small cheetah in an ornate cage. The male cat wore a golden collar set with yellow and white diamonds to match its eyes. Her ladies-in-waiting gasped when they saw the beautiful creature. All dressed in black so that Elizabeth glowed in contrast, the women were dismissed to leave her alone to flirt with her returning knight. Hawkins' charming performance belied the fact that he had been absent from court. For over three hours he doted over her. Praising her brilliant mind, her political skills, charisma and magnificence, the devious admiral played to the sovereign's immense vanity. It worked. She was enamoured.

The Queen was captivated by Hawkins' detailed description of his new warship. When explaining his new method of sheathing, Elizabeth and Dick were keen to learn more. Hawkins explained how the whole keel would be smothered with a layer of pitch mixed with human hair then another layer of nailed elm planks were added. He bragged that his new invention would prevent destructive teredo worms from eating their way through to the internal layer of ship's boards. Instead, they would become tangled in the hair and die. His idea of introducing detachable top masts was invaluable as they could be hoisted in fair weather and stowed away in heavy storms. The shrewd man who had been the late Shana Culley's lover had managed to convince the Queen that he was still her loyal, loving and devoted servant. His plan had worked. He was back in her favour. After sharing a nightcap with the Queen and Dick, Hawkins retired to his room. Elizabeth was pleased to have Lord Admiral Hawkins back at her side. She had missed him. Maybe she should make her sweet Robin jealous when he next came to court. Laying her head down on a soft down-filled pillow, Elizabeth breathed in the soporific smell of lavender. She thanked God that her head had stopped aching. The Queen soon fell into a deep, peaceful asleep.

CHAPTER 17

Brotherly Love and a Pretty Wench's Charms

Patrick and his crew moored Queen Culley's Revenge in Teignmouth harbour on the 3rd February, 1579. Having suffered another loss on the voyage over, they all felt disheartened. Creppin and Whoo had prepared Gift's body ready to take back to the only family he had known since being forced from his African homeland. With no expense spared, Patrick and Anthony hired a large carriage from the city undertaker. Painted entirely in black with gold trim and large ebony ostrich plumes on either corner, it rattled along the narrow cobbled passageway pulled by two black horses. Whoo had made a coffin for his deceased shipmate who, sadly, had weighed very little when Anthony and Patrick had placed him inside. Travelling ahead of the body, Patrick, Anthony, Creppin, Shanny, Jock and Saul took a stagecoach to Mary Maggy's. Creppin was the only excited passenger who kept his ugly face pressed against the dirty window for the duration of the journey. Children threw stones at the carriage and the coachman lashed his whip at them, 'Garrr! Git!' he shouted as they ran away screaming.

Patrick comforted Shanny. The poor girl was dreading having to tell her family the sad news. She was most concerned about their reaction on hearing that some of the crew had eaten Josh. It began to rain and the dry, dusty tracks soon became muddy. The coachman struggled on until he could go no further. 'Oy've brung thee s'far as she'll go, maties.' Handing over payment, together with a generous tip to cover the cost of room and board for the night and stabling for his horses, the captain thanked the pleasant driver. Grabbing their own bags, the gang trudged through the mud along winding lanes past charmingly picturesque thatched cottages. They climbed over stiles and took short-cuts through fields owned by farmers who Patrick knew would never lay mantraps. Finally, the weary travellers sighted the large gates of Mary Maggy's Orphanage.

It came as a great relief when Patrick saw Fr. McGillacuddy standing under the shelter of the stable roof in the large field. He was talking to Robert who looked as if he was tending the horses. Shanny could hardly contain herself, 'Uncle Rob!' she shouted running ahead of the others. Patrick felt bad for her. The poor wench had known so much loss. As heavy rain hissed down, he felt a strong sense of déjà vu. Something was terribly wrong. Oh my God! No! Shanny was screaming, bent over double in traumatic pain. Taking off again at lightning speed, Patrick could just about make out the retreating figure. He ran hard and fast against the stinging wind and rain. Surely there could be no more tragic news! Tears streamed down his face as he ran past the stables in pursuit of his distraught friend. She ran so fast! As he reached the flagstone terrace he noticed that all the curtains were closed. His fears had been confirmed. Feeling sick to the stomach, he entered the open door and heard Shanny's troubled wails. The scene before him would be etched in his mind forever. Shanny's cousin, Louisa, sat slouched on the floor, cradling her in her arms. Saul skidded into the gloomy room. He stopped dead with a look of disbelief. Joining the women on the rush-covered floor the sorrowful young man held them close.

Princess and Kia were wailing and wringing their hands. They pulled at their hair as they rocked together in a wretched display of sorrow. Several of the older children stood around a fine walnut coffin that had been placed on a table in the main hall. Clutching strings of sandalwood rosary beads, the orphan girls wept whilst the boys stood speechless. Occasionally, their eyes darted back and forth to each of the grieving women. Once he had taken in the distressing scene Patrick noticed a small boy crouched alone in a dark corner. The poor little thing was exhausted from crying. Sweeping Kia's son up into his arms, the captain left the room. As he walked through the long corridor of the orphanage he saw few of the children. Those who felt comfortable enough to venture out of their rooms had dressed from head to toe in black. The usual happy, buzzing atmosphere of Mary Maggy's was absent. Rain poured down reflecting the mood within the walls of the orphanage. The echo of Fr. McGillacuddy's deep calming voice could be heard, 'In nomine Patris, et Filii, et Spiritus Sancti. Amen.' The Catholic priest began to pray for the dear departed soul of Flo Turnbull. Trying to console Taru, the captain headed for the playroom where he remembered playing as a child.

Taru had become so distressed over the past few days that he would not stop clinging on to Patrick. The child would cry whenever he tried to put him down. Louisa finally managed to persuade the boy to go with some of the older girls. At last the captain was able to relax a little. He joined the others and learned that Flo had choked on her own tongue a few days before their arrival. Apparently, Robert had kissed his paralysed wife before leaving her in their marital bed whilst he tended to the horses. On his return he had found her dead. Somehow, Flo had rolled onto her back and was unable to turn. Robert was wracked with guilt. It was doubtful that he would ever be able to forgive himself. Shanny would now have to relay the terrible news to Remando back on the ship that Abi's twin sister had also suffered an unpleasant end. Without a doubt, he would blame himself for not accompanying her to the orphanage. Plagued by misery and death, the young pyrate wench gripped her broken-hearted cousin tightly as they both wept.

As everyone had expected, Princess and Kia took the news of Gift's death badly. Due to terrible road conditions, the hearse carrying his body did not arrive until the following day. When the two African women saw the coffin they became hysterical. According to their tribal custom, a corpse should not be confined in a wooden box. Respecting their beliefs, Anthony and Jock removed the wrapped body from the coffin. The women insisted that Gift's corpse was unwrapped. They freaked out when they saw that his lip had been sewn to the tough hemp cloth. Princess and Kia appeared to be terrified of the cadaver. Patrick spoke to them in their native tongue and apologised for the unintentional disrespect. He felt awful when Kia explained that her tribe always followed funerary laws vigorously to avoid bad karma. It took a while for her to calm down enough to give instructions on how to dispose of the body.

The Zulu funeral ritual began with the burning of every last one of Gift's belongings. The women were petrified that malevolent spirits might linger, as anything that had been touched by the dead man was now deemed impure. The African sisters collected everything that Gift had left behind in his room. Anthony took responsibility and stripped the decomposing body naked. He was glad of Jock's help to carry it outside. Saul had already lit a fire a safe distance from the building. All of Gift's possessions were burned. Princess and Kia led Anthony and Jock into a small copse behind Mary Maggy's where they told them to lay the cadaver down on the ground. When the men looked up, they realised that the women had already run away. The sinister sound of hungry crows' came from the treetops as they called one another to feast upon the dead. The captain called the men back inside to explain that the corpse had to be left to be eaten by scavengers.

According to Zulu belief, anyone who had touched the corpse was already defiled, so Princess insisted that the pyrates ate a horrendously bitter herb. This was believed to banish any bad spirits that may already have invaded their body. She was most concerned about the people who had prepared the body, especially those who were absent. The captain reassured her that he would ensure that the others cleansed themselves on his return to the ship. A very damp, dirty Creppin, who had been hovering nervously ever since his arrival, snatched a large clump of the herb from Princess' hand. Ramming it all in his mouth at once, he chewed nervously as he stared, bolt-eyed, through the open door towards the copse where Gift's rotting body lay. It was as if the hunchback had seen the devil himself! Kia and her sister gave everyone a talisman for further protection. Finally satisfied that they had done all they could, considering the harmful mistakes that had already been made, the unnerved women went off to find Taru. The child would need to be cleansed too.

When everyone had gone to bed, Shanny was unable to sleep. Jock lay next to her, snoring gently. Lighting a lantern she pulled on her boots and cloak and stepped out into the corridor. It was so cold and still teeming with rain. Fr. McGillacuddy and Robert's prayers were hushed and she could just about make out six dark figures standing around the coffin in the hall. Noticing a thin line of light at the base of the studded oak door she knocked before she entered the kitchen. After her sexual encounter with Jock, Shanny had become more cautious when entering an occupied room. 'May I enter?' she asked politely. No reply. On hearing the sound of wood scraping against stone she decided to enter. Nothing could have prepared the pyrate wench for the scene that she walked in on. A heavy, musty smell of boiling herbs hung in the air. Kia sat at the table with her sleeping child lying across her lap. Princess sat beside her holding a large meat cleaver. She had rested the heavy blade just above the joint of the little finger of her left hand.

Before Shanny could get to grips with what was going on, the beautiful woman had lifted the chopper and whacked the blade through the delicate digit. Without delay, Kia took a heated knife and pressed it against the bleeding stump. Hearing the sickening sizzle, Shanny approached the table. Although she found the act of self-mutilation repulsive, she had learned to respect other cultures. As Kia patiently applied thick healing paste to her sisters wound, Taru stirred. Rubbing his eyelids with a dimpled fist, he turned his head to one side. Thankfully the boy stayed asleep. Princess stroked her child's forehead with her unharmed hand then beckoned for

Shanny to take a seat next to her. In broken English she explained that she had cut off her finger as a sign of grief. She held up her hand to show the pyrate that the ring finger was also missing. She spoke in a monotone, 'Precious, Kia husband... dead.' Kia began to weep again. She took the amputated finger outside where a small fire had been lit. She threw the body part into the flames and watched it burn. Returning to the kitchen, Kia held out one of her fingers for her sister to bind. Tying a piece of cord tightly around the extended finger, Princess began to hum a strange tune. Anticipating what was about to happen, Shanny started to cry. She stood up and kissed the two women on the top of their heads before leaving them to their personal ceremony. If she did not go back to bed she would be awake all night. Flo's funeral was the following day. Shanny had to get some rest or she would not be able to cope with the early morning hoard of visitors that were expected. Money would be distributed to the poor and a fine feast of mourning would be put on at the orphanage after the funeral. Everyone in the community was welcome to attend. Shanny seriously doubted that anyone would want to miss the banquet, especially the single women of the parish. Now the tall, handsome widower was available and viewed as a fine catch. As a joint owner of Mary Maggy's, he was a wealthy man.

It was not until the early hours when Patrick finally managed to have a private conversation with Fr. McGillacuddy. He told him about Josh's death and was surprised at the priest's response. He hardly reacted at all on hearing that the dead man's body had been consumed by his close friends. Having the strong conviction that, during the sacrament of Holy Communion, all Catholics actually consume the body and blood of Jesus he had no problem accepting their actions. Since the African folk had joined the extended clan at Mary Maggy's, the elderly priest had become more accepting of mysterious cultural rituals. Josh had been a well-loved man who would be sorely missed. Fr. McGillacuddy told Patrick that he would explain everything to the others after the pyrates had left. There had been so much sadness within the orphanage walls that he wanted to wait a while before delivering any more distressing news. Promising that he would include Josh in his prayers, the kindly priest blessed the pyrate captain before re-joining Robert who had stayed with his dead wife. They began another all-night vigil and waited for the sin-eater to arrive. As Flo had not made her confession before her death, she had died still bearing her sins.

When the beggar arrived she was invited in. Fr. McGillacuddy blessed the bread and communion wine. Placing the 'body of Jesus' on the dead woman's chest, the priest began the Catholic ritual and the sin-eater took the bread and ate it. Passing the holy chalice over the deceased, Fr. McGillacuddy invited her to drink the blood of Jesus. The homeless widow prayed and recited her words with care and conviction, 'I give easement and rest now to thee, Florence, dear lady. Come not down the lanes or in our meadows. For thy peace I pawn my own soul. Amen.' Before the poor, desolate woman left, Robert paid her fee. She disappeared into the dark night. Closing the heavy door and bolting it safely behind her, the widower returned to take his place by the priest. Their prayers were soft and comforting as the rest of the orphanage was still and quiet. Only the clicking sound of a death-watch beetle, in search of a mate, could be heard high in the rafters above the sleeping pyrate captain.

All of the orphans were early to rise and sat at the long table in the main hall eating a hearty breakfast. Determined that the children all ate well before they faced the traumatic day ahead, Louisa and the resident cook made sure that every plate had been cleared. As was customary, everyone had dressed in black. The girls wore black dresses and gloves and the boys, black doublets, hose and hats. Shanny put sprigs of rosemary in each girl's hatband and pinned one to every boy's doublet. Mourning rings had been made for the adults. Cast in gold, the men's were shaped like skulls and the women's crosses. Each held a tiny compartment which contained a small lock of Flo's hair. Anthony had visited the tailor the previous day and bought black cloaks and hats for himself and the other pyrates.

The funeral procession was almost regal, the carriages all finely decked out. They arrived at St. Michael the Archangel, the oldest church in East Teignmouth. Moses was a treasure. He stood patiently at the lych-gate with a basketful of rosemary and lavender handing sprigs to the congregation as they arrived. Flo was buried inside the church next to her mother, Ma Turnbull. A heavy black marble slab had been removed and a new plaque included Flo's epitaph along with her mother's. Sadly, Flo's twin sister Abi's body had never been brought home so the inscription now included the dates of both twins' births and deaths. All of the children placed their bunch of herbs on the coffin before it was pushed into the gaping vault.

Shanny was very worried about Robert. He stood tall and sombre, comforting his grieving daughter but his face looked as grey as his hair. Unable to shed a tear, the steadfast man felt cold, angry and distraught. Unable to understand why his wife had been made to suffer such degradation during the last few years of her life, Robert was a broken man. After the funeral, the stream of guests who visited the orphanage were all served fine claret or ale. Everyone remarked on the excellent food and Robert and Louisa had ensured that there was plenty for everyone. Shanny and her cousin were disgusted by the amount of young, single women who had the guile to kiss Robert on the cheek on offering their condolences. One girl was only twelve years old, for heaven's sake! Despite being of legal age to marry, the overconfident little brat should never have even thought of approaching a Godly man in such a brazen manner. Louisa insisted that her parents must have encouraged her. At one point, Shanny became so angry that she shouted at one of the hopeful suitors and drew her large gutting knife. Josh intervened and led her away from the horrified girl whose face was flushed with shame and embarrassment for her inappropriate behaviour. Robert paid no attention to his unwanted admirers but stood solemnly with his arms around his daughter and niece. Glad to see the back of the last guest, he shut the great oak doors of Mary Maggy's and pulled the large bolt into place. The other adults took the children to their dormitories and headed for their own bedchambers soon after they had settled. Robert extinguished all lanterns but one which he took to his room. It was going to be difficult for him to get used to sleeping alone.

The following morning began when the cock crowed at dawn. Everyone pulled on their outer garments and met in the main hall for breakfast. Robert had already ridden into town to hire a coach to pick up the guests from Mary Maggy's. Princess and Kia had made Shanny a large parcel of food to share on the journey to Plymouth. Since her return, the three women had become much closer. They were all reluctant to part. Patrick, Anthony, Creppin, Jock and Moses waited for Saul and Shanny to say their emotional goodbyes. All luggage and large weapons were put into a netted basket and secured with ropes that were tightened by an iron windlass. When the pyrates boarded the horse-drawn carriage, Saul and Creppin climbed up into the rearward facing seats behind the coachman. The pleasant old man had already invited Moses to sit next to him. 'Ye be a monster of a man! Ye canst sit wi' me an' ye'll scare any highway filchers 'alf ter death afore ye've even drawn yer pistol, says oy!' Saul had drawn the short straw and was stuck out in the elements with Creppin who was happy to ride on the roof. Saul did not mind either as the weather was moderately windy and dry that morning. Patrick and Anthony climbed inside the leather-lined compartment. Jock lifted Shanny up to kiss her gently before setting her down on the passenger step. She ducked inside the small door and he followed pulling the catch shut behind him. Shanny found it hard to leave Louisa and Robert now her aunt was gone. Despite her offer to stay and help run the orphanage, father and daughter had insisted she continue her adventure. They had both given her and Josh their blessing and wished them well. Laying her head on her lover's chest Shanny waved to her family through the small window.

As the horse-drawn coach rocked and jolted its passengers along the narrow muddy lanes that led to the main thoroughfare, the pyrate captain revealed his next plan of action. Although Anthony dreaded the thought of returning to Saint Xaviers Church he looked forward to taking Patrick to the place where he had buried Shana Culley's head. Had the blacksmith not taken a risk, the infamous pyrate queen's remains would have been buried in a mass unmarked grave together with countless other victims of capital punishment. He hoped that his friend would be pleased when he saw the peaceful, well maintained little graveyard. Patrick had sent word to the crew who had stayed aboard the Revenge to sail on ahead to Plymouth docks. Jock was to take Shanny, Saul and Creppin to the ship. She would be moored outside a memorable and relatively trouble-free inn. Anthony felt as though he had been away from Plymouth town for years rather than mere months. When he banged his head on the roof as the coach was pulled over a large hole in the road, the others began to laugh. They all felt a little easier now they were away from the stiflingly depressive atmosphere of the orphanage. Making a silent wish that the sound of children's laughter would be bouncing off the walls of Mary Maggy's again soon, Shanny cuddled up to her man and closed her elfin eyes.

Snorting a pinch of snuff whilst he worked the reins, the old driver pulled a flask from his belt and took a long swig. He offered it to Moses who accepted eagerly. Taking a gulp of cider, he grinned before handing it back. Nodding his appreciation, the lofty pyrate was glad to quench his thirst and soothe his dry throat. The outside packers were already filthy. Creppin had eaten more mud than the piece of dry bread that Princess had given him. 'Mi!' the ugly man kept complaining as muck splatted up from the wheels onto his food and face. 'Serves tha roight fer wantin' ter eat tha snap afore we reach next stage!' laughed Saul. Inside the cabin the four friends were quiet. It was noisy and uncomfortable but at least they only had to get out once to rock the coach free of mud when it became bogged down. Creppin had rolled around with laughter as he watched the men struggle. Jock and Anthony got back into the carriage absolutely covered in thick, brown and very smelly 'mud'. Patrick had been on the front corner so remained pretty clean but Saul had fallen arse over tip in the sticky, squelching sludge. Getting his own back on Creppin, he grabbed some freshly expelled horse manure and threw it at him. Then he climbed back up to a sulking hunchback who had crossed his arms and legs and turned his back on his companion. This suited Saul as it kept him quiet for the rest of the journey. Aching, bruised and tired, the pyrates were relieved to reach a main staging inn where they had their tankards refilled a few times. It felt good to stretch their legs and lighten their load by knocking some of the dried mud off their clothes before boarding a larger carriage. Hopefully the next journey would only take a few more hours. If the fresh horses could average around seven miles an hour they should just about cover the sixty mile journey before nightfall.

It was late February when Anthony returned to his birthplace in Rotten Row, Plymouth town. He had decided to visit his old home alone. As he navigated through the cobbled rows that he had trod since he was a small boy he felt a sudden urgency. At first he began to jog, zigzagging with agility through the throng of market-goers but soon he was darting along. Bumping into people, he apologised aloud but continued to press on running faster until his old house came into view. Instinct told him to slow down. He already knew in his heart that he was too late. Looking up at the picturesque half-timbered building where he had spent many happy years, the blacksmith felt a lump in his throat. The shutters of his father's bedroom window were closed.

Walking up to the front door, Anthony paused. He ran his fingers over the simple brass door knocker that he remembered making as a child. Despite having helped with most of the casting process, his patient father had been so proud of his boy's efforts that he had invited everyone in the row round to celebrate. After he had screwed the knocker securely onto their door he waited patiently for the first knock and insisted that Anthony welcome each guest inside.

Anthony caught his breathe and left the door knocker in place. 'Nay need ter knock no more.' he whispered softly. Just at that second he felt a heavy hand on his shoulder. Turning slowly, he saw the solemn expression that he did not want to see. His father's loyal friend, the butcher, stood wringing his hat with large, fat fingers. His red face glowed with perspiration. Wiping sweat from his brow, he looked into his young neighbour's eyes and swallowed slowly. The blacksmith knew that it could not have been easy for the man to convey the bad news. The butcher spoke tenderly, unusual for him, 'Anthony, moy lad…Oy'm afeared th'art too late…Alas, I loathe ter quothe…' Swallowing again to hide his sorrow, the butcher looked down at the ground. Anthony just stood and stared, waiting for the inevitable. It came with a horrible feeling of alarm. 'Oh my God! Noooo!' his conscience screamed. His mind flooded with horrific thoughts of his father dying alone. Why the hell had he left…? To go on some half-hearted mission half way across the world?! For what?! The butcher's words were registering in the blacksmith's mind much slower than they were being delivered, '...tha father passed from this world a mere three days hence.' The red-faced man paused briefly. He swallowed, then continued, 'E left this fer thee...asked me ter keep it safe 'til tha' return. 'Twas loik 'e knew tha was 'omeward bound.' Anthony could not silence his cursed conscience. He felt like smashing his head against that pathetic effort of a door knocker! How could he have left the most wonderful parent ever? With bottom lip trembling and tears brimming on the tiny ledge of his lower eyelids, the blacksmith held out his hand. 'Yay! BLACKSMITH!' he reminded himself, 'NOT bloody pyrate!'

Anthony scolded himself inwardly. His behaviour had been so selfish and stupid. His father had known all along that he was dying! All he could think of was unlocking the door to burst through, leg it up the rickety stairs and tear through his late father's room...and hurl his useless, great hulk of a body out of... 'Dost th' ave need o' anythin' m' lad?' the butcher interrupted the young man's suicidal thoughts. His late father's friend was becoming nervous now. He had placed both fat pink hands on Anthony's shoulders and was looking into his eyes, concerned. Managing a 'Nay, thank ye fer tha' koindness', the bereaved young man must have looked dreadful. Realising his rigid stance and 'hare caught in the lamplight' stare, Anthony tried to act as naturally as he could. Accepting the parchment just as the tears spilled from his eyelids, Anthony watched them fall. The two men stood together for a minute as they splashed onto the shakily written words;

For my dear son, Anthony Brown, Blacksmith

As the black ink letters merged together to form a cloudy pattern on the mottled parchment Anthony shook the butcher's hand and said goodbye. Turning to push his key into the keyhole he was thankful to feel the locking mechanism click to release the latch. Pushing his way in quickly, the blacksmith shut the heavy door behind him. He leant up against it, his forehead pressed against the hard oak. Idly, he fingered the deeds to house and his father's business. His mind began to clear. There was no way that his father would have wanted him to stop his adventure! He had to hurry. He did not have much time if he was going to sell a house, farrier's business and arrange a fitting funeral for his father; a fond farewell that would be the most talked about event in Teignmouth town for centuries to come… and the wake would soon begin with a group of pyrates gathered around Arthur Brown's coffin, right there in Rotten Row. Forcing a small smile, Anthony decided to begin with a visit to the undertakers where his father's body would presumably have been taken. He needed to see him once again before he left Plymouth. It was almost time to introduce his Da' to his new friends.

Anthony's spirits were low. After he had visited the stonemason and ordered a headstone with an endearing inscription, he decided to investigate the area where Sushana Culley's last ship, the Emaleeza, had gone down. Before he had left Plymouth, Anthony had heard many a drunken confession of secret late night dives in the well-known vicinity where the wreck lay untouched. Many were convinced that hordes of treasure had gone down with the doomed ship, so were willing to risk breeching strict rules of curfew to probe the wreckage. Regardless of their convictions, Anthony knew the truth.

Nothing of any great value lay on the seabed where some of Patrick's mother's crew had perished. Even though the blacksmith knew this, he was willing to take his chances of retrieving some precious items that he knew his friend valued more than any amount of gold. By a sheer stroke of luck the local watchmen on duty that night happened to be Anthony's childhood friend. Claiming a return favour, the blacksmith asked him to turn a blind eye to his presence. It was the night-watchman's job to stop anyone who was caught out after curfew. The duty constable had the power to arrest anyone who disobeyed and detain them until the following morning. The Queen's law stated that 'if any 'night-walkers' or 'lodge-strangers' should resist arrest, then a hue and cry would be raised.

Under the brilliant light of a low-hanging full moon Anthony was able to see his way without the need of a lamp. He was glad of the guiding glow but the frenzied screams from insane and demented townsfolk unnerved him. Whilst families struggled to keep their crazed ones safely at home, Anthony's friend told him that he despised working when the moon was full. According to the night-watchman a grisly incident had already occurred that night. A young mother who was known for her outrageous behaviour had cut her own throat. She had been found by her mother who had to prise her blood-saturated baby out of her dying daughter's unyielding grasp. Repulsed by the sight of the self-murderer who had been such a pretty girl in life, the young man had suffered a nauseous attack. When the coroner had arrived he had confirmed that her death had been suicide. Angry that he had been called out so late at night, the hateful magistrate posthumously tried and convicted the woman for her blasphemous crime. In the eyes of the Church her abhorrent sin was against God, king and Nature. Tragically, the dead woman's tiny, helpless heir had also been savagely punished for his insane mother's crime. Everything that she had owned had to be surrendered to the Crown. The sickened magistrate left the gory scene with a curse and huff, spitting on the dead woman's blood-covered face before storming past her mother and baby. He had known full-well that the poor seventeen year old girl had been stricken with madness since her father had been savaged by a bear. The story of the attack had shocked the community and a riot had ensued. A foreign man had been careless with his maltreated animal and had not chained it securely to the large iron ring in the bear-baiting pit. When the unfortunate animal managed to break loose from the chain that tethered him it attacked the nearest human. The spectator had not a chance in hell and was ravaged by the huge beast that had been scarred from head to toe from years of horrific abuse. The man had been half-eaten before the animal died of multiple shot wounds. It had taken over thirty shots to finally kill the mad bear. The suicide victim had not been able to function normally following the attack. Unfortunately, she had been present and saw her father being torn to pieces as he screamed in agony.

The dead girl would be denied a Christian burial. Her naked body was to be carried by churchwardens and parish officials to a crossroads. There, her corpse would be thrown into a ditch and a wooden stake driven through her chest to hold it in place in the shallow grave. Not a single prayer would be uttered and no priest would be present. A few shovels of earth would be thrown onto the body and the family would never know where their loved one had been buried. Anthony said a prayer for the unfortunate girl and her family. He had given his childhood friend a large payment to allow him safe passage and added extra for the afflicted family. As the blacksmith stripped off his outer garments, he pondered over his own final resting place. Hoping to God that it would be more appealing than that of the wretched girl's, Anthony took a rope from his bag. Taking a deep breath, he dived into the icy sea. Soft beams of moonlight streamed through the water to illuminate the recent shipwreck. It took the strong swimmer no time at all to locate and retrieve Shana's heavy chest. Exactly as Patrick had described, the richly carved coffer would have been difficult to miss. He would be glad to see it reach its rightful owner.

Patrick had spent a few hours alone in Plymouth town. He had sorted out some personal business but had also needed some solitary time. Not yet used to the responsibility that came with a pyrate captain's role, he understood how pressured his mother must have felt at times. He had truly lost his best friend. Patrick was hurting again. He still could not believe that she had really gone.

Whilst Anthony was sorting his father's funeral arrangements and dealing with his inheritance Patrick went to meet Jock, Shanny, Moses and Creppin. They had found a friendly tavern near the dock. Remando and Shrimp were there too and Whoo, Smith, Colm and Danny joined the party shortly after the captain had arrived. Keen to make the most of their time practising being newly acquainted travellers, the gang began to relax and enjoy a rare and valued break. They were already managing, quite well, to conceal their pyrate mannerisms and barbaric behaviour. The captain/artist, Peter Croft, was even impressed by Creppin's performance as Jock's (Dr. Joseph Byfield's) obedient servant. His behaviour was impeccable and Patrick even found himself slowly warming to the weird little man. As long as the hunchback stayed well beyond arm's length and kept wearing the small pomander that Princess had made, the captain believed that he might actually make decent company after all. Even in her deep grief, the thoughtful woman had made the wooden container and filled it with lavender, mint and rosemary. Since she had tied it onto a leather thong and placed it over Creppin's head, he had clutched onto it as if it was a precious jewel. Everyone was impressed when, even after consuming a few tankards of strong ale, the hunchback/servant managed to remember everyone's bogus name. He even stayed in character whilst doing so. During conversation he would occasionally fall back into his eccentric habit of referring to himself in the third party. No matter, Creppin had managed to impress the captain so felt elated to finally feel accepted as an important member of the assassination team.

Creppin felt happier than ever. As an enjoyable social afternoon faded into a drunken evening for the contented gang, they were pleased to see Anthony enter the crowded tavern. Patrick decided to go outside to get some fresh air. The blacksmith joined him. Beneath a dark blood-red moon the two men walked together, side by side, along the busy main street of Plymouth port. As they strolled, Anthony told the captain about his father. No words needed to be said, Patrick just listened. Finding a private place away from beckoning prostitutes and drunken pyrates and sailors, the friends sat together on the cold cobbled street. The captain took out his knife and made a deep cut in his left thumb. His friend did the same. They pressed their bleeding thumbs together and embraced. Now, they had blood-bonded. Vowing to look out for one another until one of them died, the two men sat in silence, taking in the sights and sounds and hustle and bustle of dockside life. After a short while Anthony passed the big sack over to his astonished blood brother.

Patrick untied the top and saw the carved chest. He ran his fingers over the carving of his mother standing proudly in front of her ship. Shaking his head in amazement and disbelief, he untied a leather thong from his wrist and took off a small key. Unlocking the chest, he took out each precious artefact to study with respect and care. A surge of mixed emotions overcame him. He remembered the silver rabbit foot brooch that Sushana's lover, Richie, had had made for her. The rabbit's foot had been given to her for luck by old Albert, her guardian. When she had become orphaned as a baby, he and his sister, Bess, had taken parental responsibility. Unwrapping one of Albert's kerchiefs that Bess had embroidered with his initials, Patrick found a lucky silver penny. Bess had placed the coin inside the cot that Shana's Granddad had made before her birth. The compass that Albert had given to the late pyrate queen's mother on her wedding day had been wrapped neatly inside the kerchief with Bess's penny. Wherever she roamed Shana had always kept her chest of treasures close. It had been lined with copper so the seal was water-tight when closed to ensure that the contents would be preserved. Next to the invaluable pieces lay Bess, the peg doll that Shana had named after its maker. A leather map case contained some of Patrick's childhood drawings and treasured pictures from a loyal soul who had lost his life whilst serving with the female pyrate captain. When Patrick found these, he took a sharp intake of breath. Not having regained enough emotional strength to see Irish's drawings, the captain put them back in the map case and retied the sack.

The pair sat in silence for a while, both in deep thought. Patrick would be eternally grateful to his blood brother. Next to Irish, Anthony was the most compassionate man he had ever met. The captain was pleased that Irish's drawings had remained undamaged. Shana's coffer had done its job. Although none of its contents held any monetary value, every last sentimental piece had been priceless to Patrick's mother. Now, they had become as precious to him. Irish's drawings were priceless, a perfect 'recording' of the pyrate queen and her crew's adventures. Patrick hoped to have them published someday. The shy and handsome Irishman had been the only man who Shana Culley had ever truly loved. Killed by another pyrate Irish died without knowing that she had always longed to be with him. He had felt the same about her and adored Patrick bringing him up as his own son. Neither the boy nor his mother had ever been the same after Irish's death. They harboured an ever-present mutual bitterness within their hearts. Now, the captain had inherited his mother's resentment which burned his soul with an almost inhuman vengeful craving.

Without a mention of the retrieved artefacts, Anthony told Patrick the funeral arrangements. The old farrier's imminent burial had given them the perfect opportunity to return to St. Xavier's graveyard without causing suspicion. His dear old Da' had done it again, the blacksmith thought with a hint of a smile. Astonishingly, he had even managed to help his son from beyond the grave! Anthony had organised Arthur Brown's funeral and had been allotted a plot for his late father. Luckily, the undertaker offered him a decent price for his inherited property. They shook hands to strike a deal. Patrick was comforted to learn that Anthony's father was to be buried near to Isaac Bromley's grave. The blacksmith had put Shana's head inside Isaac's coffin on that fated Saturday the previous July. In a pleasant, albeit melancholic, twist of fate their parents would share the same graveyard.

The two men took an easy stroll to the tavern to rejoin their friends. By the time they reached the lively drinking den, more of the crew had arrived. They had taken over the entire pub and were all blind drunk. A few, who were still able, were making out with the local 'cunnie pedlars'. Patrick was so moved by Anthony's kind deed that he announced that he was going to wear his late mother's rabbit's foot brooch on the night of the assassination. Hoping that the talisman would bring him luck and success, the captain proposed a toast to dead loved ones. He ordered four barrels of the strongest ale. After a long night of debauchery and self-indulgence, everyone staggered off to their sleeping quarters. Creppin and Shrimp slept where they had collapsed. Danny fell asleep with his face wedged firmly between a huge pair of breasts. The innkeeper had locked himself in his room after Jock had paid him well for 'the rrrent of yerrr 'stablishment' before he had become too inebriated to pronounce the words. It had been a night to remember and the wake would begin when everyone arose.

Arthur Brown's wake was well attended. The pyrates sent the old man off with great respect and cheer. The funeral went well and Anthony was glad that his new friends could be there. Many fellow craftsmen and traders crammed into the church to pay their last respects to a good man. It was a harrowing experience for Patrick when he stood near to Isaac Bromley's grave. All he could envisage was his mother's beautiful face after her head had been torn from her neck. Full of hatred and anger, he clenched his fists, grinding his teeth as he recounted the events that had led to her death. When the mourning party returned to Rotten Row he and the blacksmith were the first to get drunk. The pyrates all spent the night in the blacksmith's birthplace.

Up in Anthony's room Creppin was the first to fall asleep leaving the two friends to talk in confidence. Patrick gave Anthony the brooch to wear on the day of the assassination attempt. 'Tha'll need all the luck tha can muster, I tell thee.' He wrapped the peg doll and compass in Albert's kerchief, which he tucked safely inside his belt. Anthony felt proud to be involved in the conspiracy. He was glad that fate had led him to meet Patrick. The captain ensured the blacksmith that his mother would have been very proud of them both. When Anthony asked him what he would want if he could have anything in the world Patrick's answer surprised him. He confessed that his dearest wish was to live in Ireland and fight for Grace's cause as a nameless soldier. Although proud to be a Culley, Patrick could feel an inherent resentment and the need for vengeance gradually destroying him. The heavy burden that he was fated to bear gnawed painfully away at his soul. He desired nothing more than to be able to return to Connaught. There, he hoped to marry, settle down and raise a family. He promised the humble farrier that he would name his first son Anthony after his brave, new friend who had risked everything to ensure that he received his mother's necklace. The blacksmith was very moved by Patrick's words. He felt glad to be alive. The two men fell asleep and the morning came too quickly.

Anthony told the others to carry on ahead to the docks. It felt strange to know that he was turning the key in the lock of his old home for the final time. As the butcher returned from a long day's work, he did not notice the lone figure walking away from Rotten Row. Taking the deeds and the key to the wealthy business man's home, the blacksmith exchanged them for a heavy bag of gold. He had decided to keep his father's spare key which he threaded onto a leather thong to wear around his neck. Neither man had been fond of jewellery or ornaments so this was the only thing that Anthony had as a keepsake. The hourly toll of the church bells rang. The streets swarmed with people rushing to reach home before the night-watchman rang his bell to signal the beginning of night curfew. It was time for Anthony to return to the Revenge. He was ready to embark on an intrepid escapade.

It was mid-March when the crew sailed into the Thames estuary where they found a good place to lay anchor. Although many had stayed aboard the Revenge, the landing party erected a large sign on the shingle beach. Patrick had painted 'Property of Her Majesty, Queen Elizabeth's Royal Navy. KEEP AWAY!' on a large board. For the benefit of the many illiterate citizens he had painted a hangman's noose next to the Royal insignia. It was doubtful that anyone would be brave, or stupid, enough to chance going anywhere near the mighty vessel after seeing such a stark warning. The sight of the well-gunned warship was enough to deter even the bravest of pyrates.

It was a dark night with a pale moon that resembled the wooden puppet Mr. Punch's profile complete with long chin and pointy hat. Patrick and the chosen twelve rowed their longboat down the Thames towards Shoreditch. After mooring at a pre-planned destination, the captain hired a linkboy with a lamp to guide them to the local boarding houses. The disreputable, poverty-stricken area was outside the boundary of the city walls; a shantytown of cottages and two-storey timber-framed homes surrounded by gardens and fields. The main streets were cobbled with round stones with a gutter running along the middle of each. Road conditions were terrible. Deep ruts had formed where destructive iron wheels of noisy shod carts had broken stones. This made it difficult for coachmen who frequently needed help to heave their carriages out of potholes or thick muddy ruts. Many a horse had to be shot having broken a foreleg when stumbling in uneven tracks.

A pair of kites swept down to search for the best pickings that were buried under the build-up of filth and slime. As the pyrates were led through the darkened streets scavenging pigs and dogs made their presence known. Skippy's hackles rose. The brave little dog went wild. Thrashing himself around he tried to escape from the tether that tied him to his master's crate. Barking, squealing and baring filthy, sharp teeth, the stray animals warned the intruders away from their territory. Babatu and Abadeyo were wary of the swine and drew their knives in case of a vicious attack. Had they realised Creppin's background, they need not have bothered. With cudgel at the ready, the hunchback had them all covered. Micken squealed loudly. Shouts of warning were heard as residents threatened to wring the bird's neck. Many of the residents had already extinguished their lamplights so the single lantern bobbed brightly as the boy carried it along. Now and then the odd shutter would open for an inhabitant to hurl out the contents of a full chamber pot. Thoughtful tenants would shout a warning, 'gardy loo!' before emptying their jordans but the occasional occupant would gain perverse pleasure at the thought of a potful of their piss and turds landing on an unsuspecting passer-by!

Patrick had chosen Shoreditch to seek lodgings for several reasons. The most important being its location well beyond the jurisdiction of the Civil Authorities of London City. This made it an ideal place for strangers to become acquainted and mix with members of a transient community. Here, the assassination team would be able to remain relatively incognito. In Shoreditch questions were seldom asked. It was not unusual for visitors to wear masks or disguises to protect their identity. Many people who operated in the seedy suburbs of sin had a past life that they wanted to bury or a present occupation that they would rather not disclose to all and sundry. Underhand dealings were common in the immoral area which suited Patrick's gang perfectly.

On reaching Holywell Street, the tower of St. Leonard's Church could be seen in the near distance. Her bells had been made famous by the nursery rhyme, 'Oranges and Lemons'. Danny began to sing with his quaint Irish lilt '...when oy grow rich, quothe the bell's o' Shar-ditch!' The hunchback wailed the next line, 'When wilt thou 'pain' me quothe the bells of 'Obey Lea'!' Everyone laughed at his misconstrued words. Creppin had not yet cottoned on to his shipmates' mockery. Laughing along with them, he was blissfully unaware of his habitual malapropisms. Patrick planned to rent lodgings close to the church. By joining the congregation of St. Leonard's the pyrates would avoid arrest for non-attendance at church. Sunday service would also give them an opportunity to befriend local players. The Saxon house of worship had been fondly named 'the actor's church' since many of the parishioners were thespians. As the gang approached a lively tavern Patrick stopped to check everyone's travelling licenses. Once again, he made it clear that it was essential to carry their documents at all times.

The Red Lion Inn had been the first public playhouse in England. This was where Patrick hoped to stay. Nearby, 'The Theatre' was an octagonal wooden building that had been built the previous year. All performances were now put on at the new venue, so the Red Lion had become the most popular boarding-house in the area for actors and tourists. In nearby Curtain Close, another theatre was currently under construction. Only a couple of hundred yards from 'The Theatre' its location was already causing a controversy. A gentleman by the name of Henry Lanman had funded the project. James Burbage, the proprietor of 'The Theatre', was not impressed that a rival playhouse was being built. The two managers met regularly to discuss how they could operate both businesses and maintain a fair balance of audience. This burning dramatic issue was the talk of London; another good reason for Patrick's choice of location. As Shana's old ward, Bess, used to tell her, 'If folk are talkin' bout thee, my lovely, they'll leave everyone else be!'

Shoreditch was a rough area to live in and self-preservation was a must to survive. It helped to be a certain type or, in short; 'tough as old boots'. Most of the local prostitutes lived at the Red Lion where cheap rooms were available for punters to rent for an hour with the girl of their choice. The landlady of the establishment was Mabel Brayne. Mabel was a podgy, jolly woman who enjoyed the company of bohemians, thespians and harlots alike. She found them far more fascinating than the shallow gentlefolk who hid behind a façade. Many upper class citizens would frequent areas of disrepute wearing masks, for fear of being discovered. The spineless visitors would never dare to live the free and exciting life that the lively lot under the roof of the Red Lion had embraced.

Mabel provided her working girls with board and lodging at a fair price. The kind-hearted innkeeper was renowned for her hospitality and non-judgemental attitude which was unusual in this day and age. As a daughter of a gong farmer and woad dyer, Mabel had been brought up to empathise with those who had little choice but work in an unpleasant trade. Her parents' jobs made them outcasts of society yet they had both been determined not to raise their children to suffer the same degrading fate. The conditions that they had to endure were deplorable but there had been no other option. Mabel would never forget the last time her father had gone out late to empty the privies and cesspits of 'night soil', as the more refined citizens called their waste. His job was to take it to a designated tip outside city boundaries or spread it over fields as manure. On the fateful night, the unfortunate soul never returned home. Mabel's mother had spared her daughters the vile truth that her father had been overcome by obnoxious fumes, choking to death whilst up to his neck in human shit.

Two young lads, who he employed to heave up the buckets that he filled, had tried to pull him out of the stinking sewage pit. Sadly, their efforts had been to no avail. They had run to fetch another gong farmer but it had been too late.

After her husband's death Mabel's mother had been unable to provide for her family on a single wage. She had always worked hard from dawn until dusk producing foul smelling dye for meagre pay. To make ends meet, she had remarried soon after becoming widowed. Mabel's new step-father was another gong farmer from their small, exiled community. Since her mother's job made her reek as badly as her new husband, they were forced to live away from everyone else. Mabel recalled watching her scrub her hands until they were raw and bloody as she tried to get rid of the unsightly blue dye. Her efforts were futile as her skin had become permanently stained. Queen Elizabeth detested the disgusting odours that came from the woad-dyeing workshops. She passed a decree ordering that they should be no less than five miles away from wherever she was staying.

Mabel and her sister were encouraged to sew until they became experts at embroidery. Their grandmother had taught them from an early age and they quickly learned how to embroider with delicate, expensive silk threads. Every penny that their family could spare went to buy materials. The girls would take their fine work into the city to sell. Taking pity on the woman who worked hard and never complained despite terrible conditions in his workshops, the owner of the dye company prepared papers that permitted her daughters to sell their craftwork within the city walls. The thought of them having to marry within the insular group made their mother worry herself silly. Since those born into the lifestyle mixed only with their own kind, inbreeding was rife. Tragically, Mabel's poor mother died of consumption before her daughters married decent tradesmen. Mabel was devastated that she never had the chance to care for the poor soul in her old age. Having known poverty, first hand, the landlady would never turn a desperate pauper away. The woman had a heart of gold.

Mabel's big, beefy husband, Johnny, was a gentle giant who loved and appreciated his wife. He provided the muscle in their joint business and heaven help any man who dared lay a hand on any of their 'girls'. The majority of prostitutes who worked for the couple had come from poverty-stricken homes. Sadly, many were opium addicts and could often be found in a Chinese family's small shack where they would rush to spend their earnings. The Lings had twelve children, both sets of parents, three brothers and their wives all living in the cramped, filthy hovel. Everyone was unkempt. They depended totally on their oldest son's regular opium trafficking. The majority of prostitutes had been forced into the sex trade during early childhood. As young orphans, some had been lured into the sordid profession by bawds who had been kind at first then forced them to have sex with strangers. There always were and always will be plenty of predators on the lookout for vulnerable, desperate young women to exploit. When good-hearted Johnny Brayne was not looking out for the wenches, he fought in bare-knuckle fights. Romany-raised, Johnny was a hard man who had fallen for his wife and grabbed her as his claim. Mabel had been swept off her feet by the muscular young gypsy who had run away from an abusive, drunken father. The youngsters were quickly married and had been happy ever since.

Johnny and Mabel had decided to make their first home into an inn house. Sadly, the couple remained childless. To ease the pain, they decided to make a family of their own. The friendly couple's tavern quickly became the heart of the roughest area in London's South. Always packed, the entertainment at the Brayne's establishment took place in a large courtyard where cock fights, bear baiting and bare-knuckles fights were organised regularly. The Red Lion was renowned as a heathen's lair; the perfect place for Patrick and his men to lay low. Over the years, the property had been extended so Mable and Johnny were able to offer block-renting. This enabled actors and travellers to rent rooms to share for a discounted, upfront payment. Many past lodgers had died in their rooms. Mabel had nursed actors, writers, artists, prostitutes and all sorts of different characters through life-threatening or terminal illness. Ague, cholera, smallpox, syphilis, typhus and tuberculosis were all rife in the area. Typhus-ridden faeces of body lice would infect their host's cuts or sores then enter the bloodstream. When high fever, delirium and gangrenous lesions soon developed the sufferer had little chance of survival. Ague was carried by infected mosquitos that swarmed in the bogs surrounding the theatre district. The current theory was that, in warm weather, the disease-ridden marshes emitted vapours which would be inhaled by many thus spreading the life-threatening malady. Mabel had tended to boarders who had contracted typhus and seen them suffer the most horrific symptoms. The fever, vomiting and seizures plagued the poor souls until they would eventually lapse into a comatose state before dying.

As always, Mable welcomed her new lodgers warmly. All thirteen liked the maternal woman. She was happy for Skippy to stay in Creppin's room and Micken melted her heart. The landlady grabbed the parrot's cage and hung it on a hook near the hearth in the kitchen where she spent much of her time. Her initial impression of the gang was good despite them having all arrived at the same time. Mabel had even taken a shine to the smelly hunchback! Creppin instantly warmed to the kindly innkeeper and was glad of the rare attention. Trying hard to please her, he would be up at the crack of dawn to take his longbow out into the fields to hunt. Every day he made it his duty to bring her 'rrrabbits culled by me own handsies'. Skippy always retrieved the dead animals, dropping them at his master's feet undamaged. The grateful innkeeper returned the kindness by giving the hunchback a discount to swive his favourite girl.

Twills was a skinny, plain looking wench with saggy breasts but an appealingly sassy air. On the downside, she always emitted a particularly pungent body odour and had to wear a merkin to cover unsightly sores that covered her vagina. The other girls had nicknamed her 'Twills be the death of thee!' as the prostitute was riddled with syphilis. Most could not bear her ridiculously annoying masculine, guttural laugh. Mama Mabel, as she was known, felt sorry for the suffering girl and made sure that she always had plenty of mercury salts. Since Twills had been diagnosed, the physician had recommended regular inhalation of the healing vapours. This was the only way the poor wretch could gain relief from the horrible symptoms. The raging fevers and torturous body aches had lessoned since Mabel had been giving her the treatment. Twills had insisted that she would continue her trade until she was no longer able. Now, she could only gain pleasure during sex. Luckily she had few body pustules which were easily concealed by thick make-up. Although Twills knew that the foul disease might cause blindness, meningitis and, eventually, insanity she still tried to stay positive. She was happy to ride Creppin as he enjoyed giving her 'Lunny Kingus' as he called clitoral oral pleasure. Neither of them was bothered about the other's bad smell and both understood how it felt to be rejected. They got along famously. The hunchback was proud to report, 'Crrreppin's bagged 'im selvies a prrretty 'strrride-wide brrride!'.

With four decent sized rabbits strung together by their hind legs and thrown over his large hump, Creppin stood at the door of Mabel's private quarters. Licking the palm of a grubby hand he tried to smooth down his matted nest of hair. He knocked three times. The landlady and her husband were amused to hear the hunchback's polite call, 'Mama Brrraynes? 'Tis thine frrriend, Crrreppin here at tha' dwelling. I's a-come fer me 'fanny-jiggly' pleasure. Prrri'thee, does me Twillies 'ave a few minutes ter ssspare forthwith?' Not wanting to hurt the poor soul's feelings, Mabel and Johnny took a while before they could answer so they could stop giggling. When the landlady opened the door, Creppin thrust the dead rabbits into her hand. He stood back, grinning proudly. Thanking him, Mabel called Twills. No reply. 'S'a lil' early for our Twills lavvy, so's I'll gi' thee tha' own key.' Taking a key tied with a red ribbon from a large box, the innkeeper gave it to her caller. The hunchback could not believe that she had trusted him with a key to Twills' room. 'Art tha' alright me darlin'? Mabel asked, concerned by the shocked look on her tenant's face. Tears streamed down Creppin's cheeks and he bowed low as if thanking the Queen. 'Giddaway wiv yers!' Mabel chuckled, throwing Skippy a bone before shutting the door. Unable to reach around to scratch a recent fleabite, the hunchback pressed his hump against the wall and wriggled left and right until the itching ceased. With a triumphant skip, he headed down the corridor towards Twills' room. Skippy sat outside Mabel's door chewing happily on his bone.

Creppin had been allowed a free half-hour with his favourite girl in exchange for the rabbits, so Mabel became concerned when she heard the pair still going at it. Carrying a jugful of blood, she was worried that it might congeal. Twills' next client had arrived so she could not allow the couple anymore time. Knocking loudly on the door, she yelled, 'Hie thee, eanlings!' Creppin replied between short, strained gasps, 'Fain, we'll...ah ...be... a...a...done in a...a...tick, Ma...ama...Brrr...ayne...' The horny pair were still bonking on Twill's thin mattress. Their vigorous movements caused the rickety bedframe to jolt in a steady rhythm across the wooden floorboards. As Creppin rushed to finish, their bouncing became faster and faster. Twills yelped as loose bed strings strained at Creppin's every thrust until he was finally done. Some of the other girls had gathered outside the door to listen to the comical cavorting. They all found it hilarious when the hunchback carried on talking to Mabel as he climaxed; 'Ooo...oh...oh... aft I's...oh...ooooo...Jack-elated! Agggghhhh!'

Within a matter of seconds a frantic scuffle could be heard from inside Twills' room. The eavesdroppers still stood outside sniggering at the thought of the odd couple having sex. Concerned that he had upset the mistress of the bawdy house, Creppin burst through the door with his trews half-mast. Flabbergasted by the speed of his exit, one of the girls almost lost her balance as the hunchback hopped by. He shouted back to a giggling, satisfied Twills as he stumbled past, 'Tho hast the finest, most scrrrumpshlicious nibbles, Crrreppin's e'er set eyes 'pon, me love!' Suddenly remembering his manners, he turned to Mabel and the girls to add a sincere apology, 'Pardy me mistrrresss, ladies… I was besides meselvies wi' me organism! 'Twill'nay happen again, tha' hast me word!' Leaving his audience with tears streaming down their painted faces, he disappeared down the stairs and was gone. Skippy tore after him.

The landlady fell about laughing at her strangest ever lodger. She had to sit down before she could pull herself together. Entering Twills' room, she took an empty pig's bladder and poured the fresh rabbit's blood inside. Making sure that it was tied securely she helped the smelly girl insert it into her vagina. When it was far enough in not to be discovered by Mabel's highest paying punter, a wealthy surgeon, she reminded Twills, 'Be sure to push 'ard as tha canst when e' first shoves his pillicock in, sweetie. Twill'nay burst' lest tha squeeze tha quiver tight. E' ne'er lasts more'n a few seconds 'n the blighter always checks for a fresh blood mark on the sheets afore 'e coughs up 'is spondulicks' The landlady pulled a couple of pouches containing fresh lavender from her belt. Hanging them on the bedposts, she gave the room a quick scan before rushing off to leave the flushed girl to entertain her next client who always insisted on swiving virgins.

It was time for the pyrates to pay a visit to the inner city. The pets were left with the prostitutes who always spoiled them rotten. London Bridge linked the city to Southwark on the south side of the River Thames. Westminster City was a mile to the west and miles of open fields and marshlands lay to the north of London. On approaching the bridge from Bridge Street Creppin became nervous. 'Yi!' he yelped. Next thing, he was seen wheeling his wooden contraption quickly off the road and out of sight. Loud farts were heard as he defecated behind a bush. Abadeyo and Babatu stood watching creatures scavenging amongst the rubbish. Anthony pressed a handkerchief to his nose in an effort to stifle the horrible smells wafting from the river and surrounding bog land where all the waste was dumped. Creppin re-emerged from behind the bush. As he pushed himself along in his wooden transporter Shanny noticed that he looked weak and ill. His face had an unusually grey pallor. The hunchback was unable to stay quiet for long, 'Phew! One minute more an' Crrreppin's trrrewsies would ssstink akin ter London shitty'. Patrick scowled. ''Tis London 'City!' tha clenchpoop!' he corrected. Biting her lip as she tried not to laugh, Shanny took a small jar of salve from her pouch and passed it to the suffering man. She could not understand why some of the men were so impatient with the harmless cripple. Burying the jar under his filthy blanket, Creppin exposed rotting, blackened gums in an unsuccessful attempt to produce a thankful smile. 'Grrratified muchly, Sean, m' laddy' the hunchback whined in a rather pathetic voice. Shanny gave him a boyish wink and caught up with the others.

At Bridge-foot, as the Southwark end of the bridge was locally known, the gang passed the Bear, one of the most popular taverns in London. 'We may, perrrchance, derrrop by the Bearrr on our rrreturrrn.' Jock suggested winking at Anthony and whispering, 'Southwark brrrewers arrr rrrenowned fer theirrr nappy ale.' Shanny quivered when she heard her man's Scottish brogue. His accent always affected her. Her sexual appetite was increasing now he had introduced her to a wonderful world of multiple orgasms. She could not wait to get back to the inn where Jock would sneak into her room every night. Traipsing on through the first fortified gate onto London Bridge, Patrick recognised the names displayed on painted wooden signs above two tall buildings; 'The Angel' and 'The Looking-Glass'. He remembered reading books with the names of these famous publishing houses printed on their title page. Imagining someday that a book would be written about his mother's life, he took out a tin and offered the others a comfit.

Creppin heard a passer-by mention a privy so he asked where it was. Wheeling on ahead of the others, the hunchback disappeared through one of two entrances. He gained plenty of attention from those inside and outside by voicing his approval loudly, 'Oh my! Crrreppin's delighted ter see such luxurrries atops Londinium's Brrrridge!' As he marvelled at the multi-seated public convenience that overhung the parapets, he was oblivious to peoples' scoffs and sneers. Slowly, he rolled himself along in the queue until a seat of easement became free. Parking up close, he hurled his stiff body out of his crate and pulled down his trews. Skippy cocked a leg and pissed on the floor, jumping into Creppin's crate for a ride. Peering down the hole to see the rushing river below, the hunchback yelled excitedly, 'Yi! Come see, Marster Anthony! Our crrrapsies drrrop frrrom hither to splash down thither, into the rrrriver!' The plank vibrated as everyone using the toilet chuckled. The weird man giggled unrestrainedly hardly able to contain his glee. Anthony and a very serious Moses took a seat a couple of holes down from the over-excited fetishist who had now perched himself over to one side to watch his turds tumble down into the river. 'Pshhhhh!' Creppin made a splashing sound as they hit the water. Moses was not a bit impressed by the childish behaviour. Some children copied the hunchback. One of their parents clipped her son around the ear, 'Enaff! Cam 'ither! Freaks like 'im shouldst'nay be allowed ter ran loose!' Anthony felt empathy for his friend but Creppin took no notice of the ignorant woman's disdain. He was far too engrossed with his invaluable find.

Shanny and Jock stood together waiting for the others. They both found it difficult to keep their hands off each other. Jock kept winking at 'the lad' who would respond with a handsome grin. London Bridge was remarkable. Jock guessed that there must have been two hundred buildings along its span some as high as seven storeys, each overhanging the one beneath. Many were owned by wealthy merchants who had added levels above expensive shops. A few were connected by stabilizing beams and walkways to form a tunnel below. It was easy to think that they were walking down a normal road rather than over a bridge. Some constructions appeared to be about to topple and fall into the river, their upper storeys overhanging the rushing waterway. There was even a drawbridge to allow the passage of tall ships that sailed up-river. When the others returned, the gang continued along the narrow road.

Heavy traffic crawled by on their journey to and from the busy city. It was utter mayhem. Pedestrians, horses and riders, carts, coaches and wagons crammed into the left lane of the twelve-foot wide road. Foreigners added further confusion by trying to walk on the wrong side! Back in their homelands they were used to travelling on the right hand side whilst the English travelled on the left. It took the pyrates two hours to walk across the ludicrously congested bridge. Patrick had opted to cross this way rather than hire separate wherries to row everyone across the equally overcrowded river. Cries of wherrymen could be heard yelling, 'Eastward-Ho!' or 'Westward-Ho!' to announce which side of the Thames they were heading for. The fixed fair to cross, either way, was a penny. Other vessels carried passengers up and down the river. A trip along London's main highway, between London and Greenwich, would cost 8d per passenger with the tide and 12d against. Wherrymen were renowned for their bad manners, quick temper and rude retorts. You would have to be quick to get one over on a werryman. Life was tough trying to earn a living this way. Competition was harsh. They owned their own boats and made them as comfortable as possible to attract customers. All wherries had covers for shelter and most had upholstered benches made to seat four or five. Some would have embroidered cushions for extra comfort and blankets to cover passengers in cold weather. Depending on the tide, the trip across river could be extremely dangerous. Although wherrymen were skilled oarsmen the Thames had claimed many lives.

London Bridge had been built on great pillars with irregularly spaced arches along its length. The foundations had been set into the riverbed. As more buildings were added, these had to be been widened to support the extra weight. These extensions slowed the flow of the river. During wintertime the Thames would occasionally ice over and Londoners would enjoy skating on its surface. The river could be a beautiful or horrific sight to behold. Many fishermen lined the banks in the hope of catching plenty of fish. As swans glided gracefully by on a glittering silver surface two men could be seen dragging a bloated, blackened corpse out onto the muddy banks. They placed it in a filthy shell which they hauled over their shoulders and another man helped to carry the body away. A crowd had gathered to watch and many covered their noses as the stinking cadaver was carried by. The men had a good mile to walk to the dead-house where they had taken four bodies the previous day. An old man stood next to Shrimp to observe the sorry scene. 'Poor soul o'er yonder 'elped ter feed the fish, eh', he mumbled before shuffling away.

Eventually the pyrate gang reached the city walls. As they passed the medieval Church of St. Giles, sounds of busy inner-city life roused the strangers. They joined the end of a long queue to gain entrance via Bridge gate. Jock looked up in absolute disgust when he counted over twenty decapitated heads that had been shoved onto pike-ends. They had been dipped in tar for preservation. The gruesomely topped weapons had been fixed to the turrets for all to see. The Scotsman cursed under his breath, not wanting to draw attention to himself. The head of his fellow countryman, the noble William Wallace, who had led the Scottish rebellion against Edward I, had been the first to be displayed. Shanny noticed his dismay and, with subtlety, pressed her body close to his. As they neared the huge gated tower, the gang chatted amongst themselves to pass time. Patrick explained some of the history of the three walls and fortified gates that guarded the entrances to the city.

It was believed that the body of St. Edmond had been carried through Cripplegate on its way to London from Bury St. Edmonds. In the year 1010, a group of holymen were relocating the martyr's corpse. They had escaped from the pillaging Danes raiding East Anglia. Patrick looked at Creppin as he spoke, 'Folk spake of miraculous healings that occurred when the holy body passed through Cripplegate.' Whooping loudly, the hunchback was convinced that he would be healed if he entered London via 'yon healing 'Creppinsgate' as he renamed it. From then on, he constantly pestered Anthony to take him through someday.

As they queued outside, the pyrates could hear the inner-city bedlam. The sound of many hooves and unrefined metal cartwheels clattering and grating along cobblestone streets failed to stifle the din of traders competing for the best pitch. Drunken brawls were common. It was quite normal to hear spluttering and coughing amidst the clamour. Citizens drank ale, mead or wine, all day every day, because the contaminated water was unsafe to consume. A clash of swords could be heard. Babies cried, children laughed or whined, dogs barked, chickens clucked and pigs squealed and grunted. The visitors found it difficult to make themselves heard over the rumpus. Soon, they all became weary of shouting and longed to return to a life at sea. A town crier's bell tolled. A deep, bellowing voice followed promoting bearbaiting at noon. At last, the gang stood in front of the entrance to the city.

Patrick knocked at the large, heavy oak doors. The group waited in silence looking up at the building that towered above them. A small hatch door, a little higher than the captain's head, creaked open. A rough-looking, unshaven guard with a booming voice peered suspiciously at the gang. Each pyrate shuffled closer to show him individual papers that would, hopefully, gain them entry. Since this was Patrick's first visit to the capital he was completely surprised to find that Abadeyo and Babatu were the only two who were not subjugated to a thorough questioning from the pedantic security guard. 'Thou art players?' he asked Shanny/Sean and Patrick/Peter suspiciously. Rolling his eyes impatiently, Anthony dared to tut at the official. The blacksmith's rudeness seriously irked him. Shooting a warning look at his friend, Patrick answered the gatekeeper's pointless question. As if any actor would admit his trade! 'Nay, I'm an artist.' he said holding up his travelling documents together with a scroll of parchment which he unrolled to show an immaculate drawing of a bird. Anthony stepped forward, 'I'm a smith, sir. We've bin on the road since dawn. My companion is fatigued.' He took Shanny by the shoulders and led her protectively, before the small hatch. 'I'm Sean, apothecary's apprentice, sir.' Shanny declared her stance like a young man's. 'Step closer!' the bad tempered guard ordered. When Anthony heard the memorable sound of metal wheels that he had made for the cripple's mobile crate, rolling on hard pebbles, he thanked God. The blacksmith allowed himself a quick smirk. He could have kissed his grotesque companion's slobbering lips when Creppin produced a filthy sponge from under his blankets. Anthony continued as if nothing had happened; 'We have a spice trader, two slaves and a crip...' Without realising, the hunchback had done it again! Not even trying to hide his disgust, the guard panicked. He had visibly recoiled at the sight of the utensil that Creppin used to wipe his arse. Shanny was mortified when she noticed that diarrhoea was dripping from its end. Heaving back a surge of bile, she was glad to hear the guard unlocking the great gate. It creaked open on rusty hinges to allow the gang entry into London city. Not wanting to risk another vagrant soiling the area in front of his gate the sentinel gave in all too easily. Important people entered the prosperous city and he had been previously disciplined for allowing filth to accumulate at its entrance. He was not going to allow that to happen again!

It was unbelievable how packed it was inside the city walls. People and animals swarmed everywhere. For once, Anthony was glad to feel the hunchback's urgent tug on his woollen tunic. He allowed himself a subtle smirk. Since Creppin had succeeded in gaining entrance for everyone, the blacksmith tolerated his distressed whines, 'Marster, verrrily, I's in urgent need to crrrap once mo'er! Wherefore shalt Crrreppin drrrop 'is load? Methinks 'twerrr rrrrottten apples on hill back yonder that caused us to sssquit so oft!' The hunchback's face was a picture. Expressive eyebrows and doleful eyes showed his anxiety. Moses found the cripple's desperate pleas amusing. Chewing on his knuckles and plaiting twisted legs, Creppin rocked violently back and forth in his small wooden carriage. Shanny saved the day and pointed to an empty alleyway that she had spotted nearby. The hunchback pushed off enthusiastically and his crate carried him over uneven cobblestones to the alley. 'Make way ferrr an 'umble crrripple!' his fake feeble voice could be heard repeating his appeal until he had made it to the private spot.

Not wanting to spend too much time in London, the captain gave everyone tasks to carry out. Danny and

Colm were to spend all day at a specific inn where they had to persuade an important man to hire them. Remando and Shanny had a list of drugs to obtain and Jock agreed to take Creppin, Moses and Shrimp to a tailor. Due to their unusual shape and size, each needed to be measured for some special clothing. The Scotsman already had everyone else's measurements together with garment designs. A trustworthy craftsman had been recommended by a reliable source. The captain had been assured that the tailor kept his clients and their orders confidential. Everyone split up after arranging to meet back at their lodgings later that night. Saul, Abadeyo and Babatu were left with Patrick and Anthony. It was time for them to visit the Tower of London. As tourists, they would be fools not to check out the famous palace and fortress. The entrance fee was three and a half pence but it was rumoured that if a cat or dog was taken, their owners would not be charged. For the visitor's amusement, the unfortunate animals would be thrown to the lions in the Queen's Royal Menagerie.

After a successful, but tiring, day the pyrates returned to the Red Lion. Danny and Colm's mission had been successful. They were meeting their new boss the following afternoon. All outfits were being made and would be ready for pick-up the following week. The gang were enjoying a few tankards of ale when their landlord, Johnny, introduced them to some fellow tenants. The group of friendly thespians invited them to join them for a night out on the town. The captain accepted and they all headed for the Bear. It came as a pleasant surprise to learn that the leader of the dramatic bunch was none other than James Burbage, one of Robert Dudley's men. Their troupe was famously known as 'Leicester's Men'. Having financed and built 'The Theatre' in Finsbury Fields, Shoreditch, Burbage had become the first English theatrical impressario. As one of the Queen's lover's troupe of actors, James had gained her support. She had helped fund the project. Welcoming the new arrivals, James ordered strong ale and claret for his new guests. For the first hour, the gang felt quite tense. On discovering that Shrimp's character, Friar Sheraton, had an extensive knowledge of herbalism the actors were fascinated to hear his recommended treatments and remedies. Colm played the role of Colin, the physician, and was also consulted by sufferers with common medical conditions. He gave excellent advice to his gullible new friends. As Dr. Joseph Byfield Jock was able to give astronomical advice which fascinated the entire inn. Shanny was enjoying being Sean and had caught the eye of some young prostitutes battling for his attention. After a few drinks Sean was comfortable enough to allow one of the girls to kiss him. Shanny was glad of the false phallus that Jock had given her to wear to save any embarrassment should she experience a steamy encounter as Sean. She felt a flush of sexual arousal when one of the young women pressed her soft, full lips against hers. When invited to join her and her buxom friend in a dark corner Sean was eager to please. Suddenly remembering Jock's presence, Shanny had second thoughts and decided to decline. Looking over to the bar, she noticed that he was happy as Dr. Joseph being entertained by two over-painted but very attractive young actresses. Feeling suddenly naughty, Shanny decided to use her disguise as an excuse to satisfy her bi-sexual curiosity.

As the affected wenches ran their hands all over Jock's upper body, he felt his erection swell at the idea of his lover being with other women. Her mother, Abi, had been Sushana Culley's lover so it made sense that bi-sexuality ran in the family. As the two actresses teased the Scotsman by kissing and caressing each other's breasts, Jock felt a pleasant ache in his groin. One of his brazen admirers pressed herself against his hardness. He knew that he would not be able to help himself. Watching Shanny sneak craftily into a dark corner with two provocatively dressed women he bent to kiss an actress' neck. She giggled when her friend took his face in her hands and kissed him passionately. Sitting with her back to the room, Shanny slid her fingers beneath her belt and into her trews to move the horn against her hard little button. She knew how wet she had become as she watched one of the prostitutes untie the other's corset to loosen it. The shameless wench lowered her lips to her companion's exposed nipple. She flicked her tongue over its tip. Her plump red lips kissed it firmly then she took the whole thing into her mouth and sucked steadily. Shanny could not resist. Leaning forward she pulled up the layers of skirts and reached her hand beneath. Running her fingers slowly up the inside of the aroused prostitute's thigh, she eventually felt the warm, silky wet opening and slid three of her dainty fingers inside. The feeling was incredible. Now, Shanny had no doubt: She was definitely bi-sexual.

James Burbage and Anthony were deep in conversation and the blacksmith felt proud that he had gained his trust so easily. Although he felt relaxed and happy his conscience was making him feel a little uneasy. James seemed like a good person. Whilst the proud player became overly-animated as he described Queen Elizabeth's passion for theatre Anthony felt a strong pang of guilt. Having made a connection with someone who he could have become close to had he not been a pyrate/would-be assassin, he grew increasingly uncomfortable. James spoke with a pleasing accent in perfect, clear English, 'Her Majesty granted her Royal permission to build…' As the blacksmith listened to the words they became meaningless. Swigging back his warm beer, Anthony slammed his empty tankard on the table top and slapped his new companion on the back. 'God bless good Queen Bess! Let us toast our monarch!' he proposed. James accepted his offer of another chalice of fine claret and the blacksmith was glad to join Jock at the bar. Anthony hated deceit.

Patrick had heard his friend's words and excused himself to check on him. A proposal to toast the Queen was the signal that the gang had been told to use should they feel uncomfortable or in need of help. Having guessed that the blacksmith was fighting a battle with his conscience, the captain took his place on the bench beside James Burbage and urged him to continue his story. The sociable character told how the Queen had advised him to choose a plot well away from the complaining nobles and stuffy dignitaries who she secretly despised. Naturally, the actor was fond of the monarch and felt angry with the snivelling creeps at court. 'The conniving cut-throats betrayed our queen's mother, accusing her of the most degrading, obscene misconduct!' James banged his fist hard on the table. The man really cared about the spoilt royal bitch, thought Patrick incredulously. Allowing him to vent his anger on those in power who had encouraged Anne Boleyn's execution, Patrick listened to his every word. He needed as much information as possible. The more the irate man became, the more likely he would be to reveal Elizabeth's weaknesses and secrets. Burbage's hatred of the hierarchy within the Church became clear as he cursed them for their objections that had led to the banning of players and theatres within the city walls. The excuse for the ban had been the protection of London's citizens from travelling players who were likely carriers of the dreaded plague. Patrick managed to calm the actor's anger just as Anthony brought over more booze. The tavern erupted. Everyone cheered aloud, flocking towards the entrance. The pyrates looked at each other quizzically. 'What now!?' thought Anthony.

Laughing Dick, the Queen's personal jester, had been the source of the excitement. After chatting to the proprietor he scuttled comically over to his troupe. 'Oy bid one an' all a very merry eve!' he shouted. He was funny. It could not be argued otherwise. The man was a natural comedian. On introduction, the friendly jester shook everyone's hand. Patrick was delighted that his plans were beginning to fall into place sooner than expected. Tarleton's presence was a bonus this early on. When the wine was flowing, tongues soon loosened. Dick was renowned for being in constant debt. An addicted gambler, he could never keep his winnings for long. Buying drinks for everyone in the house, the fool was too generous by far. His favourite prostitute, Em Ball, accompanied him that night. A very young, attractive woman with long auburn hair, Em did not have the air or manner of a harlot. Although the comic actor had taken many prostitutes to his bed, he had never managed to get over the death of his wife. Em Ball, had been offering a reasonably priced 'intimate service' to local men, and women should they desire, since her childhood years. As her most frequent punter, Dick had recently asked her to move in with him. They thoroughly enjoyed each other's company and sex was great between the unlikely couple so the arrangement suited them both. As the night went on, the pyrates learned much about the company of actors and their associates who heard nothing but lies in return. The team of criminals had been accepted into their thespian circle.

Laughing Dick lived in Holywell Street. His mistress was a sensitive soul who loved him dearly. She complained when he joked too often about being buried in the grounds of St. Leonard's alongside his idol, the late Will Somers, who had been Henry VIII's Court Jester. The thought of losing her lover genuinely upset Em. A very camp, effeminate homosexual actor called Valentine developed a big crush on both Anthony and Patrick. 'I wouldssst taketh both of thee big boys if thoud'ssst permit me to pucker up and disssplay my blushing blosssom.' He cooed, cheekily, toying with the heterosexual men. Despite their embarrassment, the two hunky pyrates were not homophobic. Having been brought up at sea with plenty of pyrates who were openly gay, Patrick respected every crewmember as a trustworthy shipmate. He paid no attention to anyone's sexuality which he viewed as entirely their own business. The over-amorous Valentine's best friend was a young woman called Violet. During the course of the night, she and Patrick had the chance to get to know each other better. Their instant mutual attraction had been clear from the start. The longer they chatted, the more comfortable Violet felt with her handsome companion. As the mead flowed, she opened up more and more.

Patrick felt guilty that he could not be himself in front of the woman he fancied. Feeling totally at ease with the man who she believed was Peter Stempton, she decided to confide in him. The captain's heart sunk.

As Peter, Patrick listened as the beautiful woman shared her secret. He could not believe her confession. The dainty, slightly build angel confessed that she was also 'Victor', a young 'boy' actor who regularly played a female role. Ironically, since actresses had been banned from the stage during Henry VIII's reign, many young actors who appeared as women really were female! As it was still unlawful in England for a woman to appear on stage Violet had revealed a very dangerous secret. Patrick admired her nerve for confiding in him but dared not return the favour. He would not risk anything that could impede his plot to kill the Queen. Besides, there were other lives at risk, not only his own. Violet poured her heart out to Patrick. She told him that she worked at the inn most of the time cooking and serving ale but her true passion was acting. Only Burbage and his troupe knew the true identity of the young boy who took on the main female role. As Violet told Patrick her story, he took in every part of her; her boyish figure, wide waist, narrow hips and small breasts. Her nipples were large and erect. The captain could see them through her white linen shirt. The actress was a really pretty girl.

A few amongst the gang were becoming concerned that Patrick was falling for the actress. Everyone but Moses, Shanny and Anthony shared a strong suspicion that Violet was a prostitute. Danny could not stand the woman who he swore to be a common bawd. He feared that Patrick would allow her to get too close. If she found out about their plot, the Irishman was sure she would betray them to claim a reward. Saul began to watch Danny like a hawk… he was beginning to mistrust him again. Regardless of the woman's suspect profession, Saul had confidence in Patrick who he believed to be bright and caring enough not to involve any outsiders in their dangerous dealings. Having been brought up with a complete respect for women, the orphan did not like the derogatory way that Danny looked at Violet.

Henry VIII's law to ban actresses suited his vain daughter well. There would be hell to pay should any pretty young thing dare to grace the stage in her Majesty's presence and take attention away from her! All female characters based themselves on the Queen as the ideal beauty. The pathetic reason for their façade was sheer adulation. Acting companies dared not become unpopular with the self-obsessed monarch who had ruled that each required a license. Troupes also had to be sponsored by one of her courtiers. No wonder actors began to impersonate their Queen! After all, imitation is the best form of flattery. Players would apply thick make-up to emulate her pale complexion, neat rosy mouth and cheeks and narrow nose. Her wide-set bright eyes would be neatly framed by carefully painted narrow arched eyebrows.

Violet took pity on Creppin who started to follow the pretty woman wherever she went. 'I cannay helps puttin' 'Violent' on a 'petting stool', stated the starry-eyed hunchback as he sat with Shanny drinking mead. Tipping back her tankard to drink, she just about managed to stifle unavoidable laughter until she snorted some ale in the process. With pretty eyes watering Shanny spluttered and coughed, having to cover her nose and mouth with a cupped hand. Feeling suddenly self-conscious, Creppin blushed deeply. The hunchback was mortified by her unintended ridicule. In his humiliation, he pushed his crate away from the table. His pointed chin jutted forward and forced his lips into an ugly grimace. He sat with arms folded tightly and fists clenched waiting impatiently for everyone to finish their drinks. When the gang went outside to relieve themselves in the alley before they headed off Creppin continued on ahead. Trundling along in his crate, he mumbled curses that were purposefully inaudible to the others. As he rolled too quickly over uneven cobblestones he caused more discomfort as his wooden contraption jolted his damaged body, 'Ouch! Yi!' he yelled. 'Crrreppin knows nay whyforrre the pretties all'ays mocks us!'

The large group reached the docks where they had been told of a visiting 'Freak Ship' attraction. Patrick looked forward to meeting his late mother's jovial friend, John Clarke, again. He asked the others to wait on the dockside so he could check whether John would allow the large party to board together. Leaving everyone chatting away happily, the captain boarded the vessel. John was delighted to see him. Patrick took him aside to ask him not to reveal his true identity. 'Ne'er fret, Peter!' John winked, remembering to use his character name. Calling the party to board, Patrick hugged John out of sight, 'Good ter see thee, matey.' he told him and handed him a heavy pouch of coins.

Many of the visitors were scared to board the 'the Devil's ship', as one of them called it. Patrick and Jock found it amusing to see Babatu and Abadeyo smiling and pointing at the attraction. They recalled the two African pyrates' terror when they had first visited a freak show. In Pidgin English, the two were busy trying to convince the wary actors that 'Dem freaks cheer dee well well! Nay wahala!' Society deemed anyone who was disfigured or disabled as the devil incarnate. Many believed that physical or mental impairment was the result of divine judgement for sinful acts. Even Protestant reformer, Martin Luther, had been convinced that he had seen Satan in an innocent, severely deformed child. He had recommended killing all deformed babies at birth. The children were often thought to be changelings; evil spawn that malicious faeries had substituted for human infants. Parents of the inflicted would frequently be accused of witchery. A book called 'The Malleus Maleficarum', written in 1487, declared that 'abnormal offspring' were the product of Satan's impregnation. Their mothers could face being tried for witchcraft. Heaven help them if they had a third nipple like poor Anne Boleyn!

The pyrates led the others onto the floating entertainment venue. When Creppin boarded the ship he began to feel unusually at ease. Even the ship's cat was abnormal, having massive double paws with multiple claws. John began with a dramatic introduction to the tour then led everyone below deck. The atmosphere was perfect. To spook visitors the captain made sure that all guests were given an unnerving encounter to remember. 'Pri'thee, my dear ladies and gentlemen! Th'art at the beginning of a voyage into the unknown where tha'll be thrilled and astounded by the monstrosities th'art about to witness. Come hither, folks! Let us venture into a world o' terror!' With a particularly unsettling cackle, the ex pyrate pulled back a black curtain and invited the hunchback to lead the way.

The passageway was very dark, lit only by one or two lanterns with feeble, flickering flames. Long, shivering shadows crept over deck boards ahead of them. Cautiously creeping into the narrow alley women and men held tightly onto each other, terrified of the consequences that might occur. Nervous giggles and sudden squeals added to the tension. To everyone's surprise, they all enjoyed meeting the show's stars who turned out to be friendly and pleasant despite their unfortunate appearance. Anthony and Patrick were fascinated by the mutant animals that included a double-headed python that fed on rats and mice and an albino chimp called Booboo. Booboo was a favourite with the women as he mimicked the men, making them blush with embarrassment.

As the party snaked through the immense ship's interior along dank, gloomy passageways they were treated to an eye-opening encounter with each exhibit. The human collection included 'Pinhead' twins, a girl and boy, who had the tiniest heads with conical crowns. There was a grossly obese tattooed woman, who John had urged to gain weight to make room for more tattoos, and a bearded lady. A tribeswoman with an elongated neck wore sixteen rings in a long brass coil that she never removed. Since the age of five, the coil had been replaced with progressively longer ones with more turns. 'Ghi', the longneck tribeswoman was Jolly John's lover and such a cheerful soul. The women all wanted to touch the metal rings supporting her neck. She allowed them the privilege, explaining how her tribe would punish adulterous women by removing their metal coil. Since their neck muscles had weakened severely, they faced a life either lying down all the time or supporting their head with their hands. Shanny stayed in the role of Sean to look after the two painted wenches who enjoyed being revolted by the human monstrosities. James' lover, Em, and Violet felt deep sympathy for the entertainers, especially Leo, the 'lion man'. Leo had a large head and a grotesque facial disfigurement that gave him lion-like features. He also had a full, golden mane. The poor soul had hideous scars on his back from being beaten. The 'Master of Freaks', as John had become known, had helped him escape from a miserable existence in his hometown in Ceylon. Unfortunately, Leo was timid and nervous around strangers but very loyal to John. When the two young women went to kiss him on the cheek he flinched, imagining the worst. When Violet reassured him that they meant him no harm he was still wary, as if he was waiting to be the butt of a cruel joke.

The interior of the freak ship was like a multi-layered maze with narrow passageways leading past each attraction. Sometimes, a freak's stall was at the end of the deck where it seemed there was no way on. Then John would appear and draw back a false floor to reveal the hatch for the bravest to take the stairs down to the next level. A woman from the Hottentot tribe of Africa attracted the most attention. Patrick remembered seeing a woman just like her when he was a young boy. A wolf boy who was covered from head to toe with black hair howled as he heard the tour approach his den. Two dogs lived with the boy who behaved exactly like them. A rubber man with stretchy skin had been discovered by John living in the New World and Cathayan Siamese twins, Kim and Min, were contortionists who were skilled in acrobatics. The petite girls were joined at the hip. Both had such pretty faces and smiled sweetly as if they had no troubles in the world. Creppin had a thing for Bonnie Bridie, an unusually self-confident Scottish woman with massive breasts. 'Me 'carnival designs' 'ave taken o'er Crrreppin, sire!' he admitted to Anthony. He hung back to get to know the four-legged woman whose most popular performance was a seated dance. She had blown the hunchback's mind. He stood and stared as he wondered what it would feel like to have sex with her. Bonnie wore matching stockings and slippers on her good legs as well as the tiny malformed pair that jutted awkwardly from under her shortened skirts.

A shrill scream came from below. Anthony, Patrick and Dick went down to investigate. The women huddled close to the man, only just managing to squeeze down the narrow gap at the same time. The discomfort was worth it when they were met by a skinny man with a huge mouth. He had a tiny snake that he was encouraging to slither up into one of his nostrils. After a minute or so, the reptile's little head peaked out of his other nostril. When the snake emerged, he put it in a box. Next he astounded everyone by placing a large cannonball inside his mouth. John had a wonderful collection of mindboggling oddities and the crowded aisle of visitors was treated to one after another. A painted plaque was displayed in every cubicle with the name of the curious creature on show. 'Sea boy' had webbed fingers and toes. He shared a stand with a girl who had a hole in the middle of her face where her nose should have been. It was incredible to think she could eat with only two tiny teeth sticking out of her lower gums. The final attraction was a friendly dwarf couple with a normal size baby son. Everyone, especially the men, delighted in seeing the large baby suckling from his mother's miniature milk-filled breasts. Laughing Dick led his friends with a cheer and a round of applause. The freaks all lined up to say farewell.

John Clark's 'Floating Carnival of Freaks' had been a spectacular experience for all. A tired and happy bunch disembarked in small groups and headed back to their lodgings. Patrick and Violet walked back to the Red Lion together. When he walked her to her room, the captain dared to ask her on a date. The actress's face lit up and she flung her arms around his neck and kissed him. She was over the moon. Violet was a delightful young woman who still had the innocent charm of a girl. Patrick smiled at her enthusiasm when she invited him to watch one of her plays, 'Throbbing Hood and his Meddling Men'. He could not wait to see her performance. Holding her firmly in his arms, the pyrate captain kissed her rosebud lips. Violet pressed her body into his and felt the heat of passion engulf her entire body. Breaking away before the handsome man had a chance to take advantage of her, the actress blew him a kiss, 'I bid thee good night, Peter… and the sweetest of dreams.' As she left him alone, Patrick felt his stomach turn. He had been having such a happy time that he had not even thought of his hypocrisy. How on earth was he going to explain? The pyrate captain could not deny his selfish behaviour. He was falling for the actress and knew that he had found the woman that he wanted to be with forever. As usual, for his luck, the timing could not have been worse.

Chapter 18

A Snitch in Time

Time had flown by and Patrick had been receiving regular reports from Hawkins of plans for the celebratory event that they had chosen to strike. Surprisingly, the admiral had not yet backed out. The captain trusted him despite some of the gang's concerns that he might still deceive them. The courtier had too much to lose. He would be doomed if ever the Queen discovered his betrayal. Grace was ready. Spain and France were on their side. Laughing Dick had been so helpful and informative and the naïve man still had no idea how much he had given away. If ever, God forbid, their first attempt failed then there was a second plan in place.

Continuing to keep the company of thespians, artists and prostitutes, the gang had become well-loved and trusted members of the community. They all enjoyed being amongst the players and spent many hours either helping at 'The Theatre' or partying with the troupe. Once again, the pyrates' knowledge of rigging was invaluable. One night when watching a play, Jock had a great idea. He got to work designing a system that would make it easier to change backdrops between scenes. The result of his efforts was brilliant. Anthony, Shrimp, Moses and Colm built a wooden framework high in the rafters to support a rigging system. They set up pulleys, blocks and ropes and attached huge painted canvas scenery, created by Patrick, to batons. These backdrops could be hauled or lowered during performances.

The system could be hand-operated in a similar way to a ship's rigging and sandbags were used to counterbalance heavy scenery. The pyrates also built a loft high above the stage to store scenery when not in use. They enjoyed manning the rigging and James and his troupe were delighted with their success.

Playhouses in taverns had long been viewed as a social nuisance. 'The Theatre' was a permanent auditorium that had been built on the grounds of a dissolved priory in Holywell. It had three galleries and a large, open cobbled yard. Commoners dropped a penny in a box at the entrance to stand in the large courtyard in front of the stage known as 'the pit'. This area was always crammed full with poor punters who the actors referred to as 'groundlings' or 'stinkards'. Tuppence would buy a theatre-goer standing room in one of the galleries. For a penny more a stool could be hired. Wealthy spectators often paid to be seated at the side of the stage, well away from the rabble. Regulars of 'the pit' were rough, uncouth individuals who would frequent the stew houses when not gambling, thieving or causing drunken mayhem. Plays were often as blood-thirsty and brutal as the bear-baiting and cock-fighting that were presented on nights when there was no theatrical performance.

The theatre company stayed busy and put on five different plays every week, two performances of each. The weary actors only ever had time to practice twice which included the dress rehearsal. Food and drink was sold during performances and the audience was encouraged to comment and interact with the players. It was also common for the crowd to talk throughout the play. Playwrights often used obscenities in their scripts and the filthy-minded audience lapped up plentiful use of puns. Playgoers loved to heckle and encouraged actors, like Laughing Dick, to ad lib with lewd phrases and sexual references. Fights often broke amongst the 'groundlings'.

Cut-purses, harlots, gamblers, poets and pyrates blended perfectly into the massive crowds that gathered to watch the risqué plays. Many a purse was cut from the belts of the three thousand punters who crowded together to watch every performance. By the time the victims had noticed their valuables were missing, the thieves had moved on or hidden amidst the crush. Occasionally, a cutpurse would be caught in the act using their cuttlebung to slice the purse strings of an unsuspecting target. The hoodlum would literally have the living daylights beaten out of them. Many amongst the crowd would join in with their fists to teach the thief a lesson, or even worse, stomp them to death there and then.

The actors continued on with the play, regardless of the commotion and would often add-lib, making a joke of a bloody pit brawl. Playwrights and actors were in a class of their own. Patrick and the gang had integrated well with the free-spirited individuals of Southwark who had chosen to lead an alternative lifestyle. The pyrates loved the relative freedom, which was unusual in a landlubber's world. Even so, every one of them longed to return to sea. Over the past couple of months Patrick's alter-ego, Peter, had gained a name for his exquisitely detailed pen and ink drawings of nudes. He had an uncanny ability to capture his model's character, just like his childhood hero, Irish, had done. With fresh quill and ink-horn in his button-hole, he would walk the streets and draw. Actors and 'ladies of the night' lapped up the attention from the handsome man so he was never short of volunteers to pose. Commissions kept him busy and people paid well but, most of all, he wanted to draw his lover. To his frustration, every time he asked Violet to pose, she had refused. After much contemplation she agreed to model semi-nude, wrapped in the finest delicate silk. Feeling a little apprehensive, she had asked Mabel's advice. Mabel oozed encouragement, 'Aw, my petal. Peter's trustworthy, I tells thee. E's a good'un, mark my words'. Mabel and Johnny loved Violet like a daughter and wanted the best for her. The couple had been pleased that she had met the good-looking artist and, over time, had both agreed that he seemed a decent type. During his stay, he had proved trustworthy, loyal and kind. Most importantly, it was obvious that he loved the actress. That was all the Braynes needed to know.

Since he had been hanging around actors, Creppin had picked up their fondness of using elaborate words that he frequently pronounced incorrectly. His spoonerisms and malapropisms were completely uncontrived which made his natural errors even more amusing. Creppin's 'mistooks' simply rolled off his tongue to delight the troubadours, especially Laughing Dick. The jester would grab a quill and scroll to record each comical blunder. He even put the hilarious 'Creppinisms' to good use. In an ironic twist of fate, the Queen of England was being entertained, albeit indirectly, by puns that had come straight from the mouth of one of her potential assassins. When Dick told the hunchback this, he became more confident in himself and began making the most of his natural talent. One night, when he needed to rest between parts, Dick allowed Creppin on stage. He was a blast! The crowd loved him. It was a welcome relief to have a deformed comic at hand who only had to act naturally to have the crowd in fits of laughter.

On the night when Patrick and Anthony took their seats in a box they were pleased to see their hideous friend appear on stage. Violet had arranged for them to watch 'Throbbing Hood and his Meddling Men'. It was a special night for the captain as she had invited him to the launch of the play three months earlier when her male alter-ego had performed a wonderful rendition of 'Made' Merrymen'. Due to popular demand, the troupe's most successful play of the season was now on its second circuit. When the curtain lifted the captain and the blacksmith had been surprised to see Creppin standing centre stage wearing a grubby jester's costume and his usual huge hideous grimace. Valentine could be heard throwing a hissy fit when he saw the hunchback wearing what he had thought to be a false beard. In fact, he had glued the popular cross-dresser's best blonde merkin to his filthy chin. 'The Theatre's' resident diva had a few of these to match every colour of his head wigs. Made with real human hair, merkins were expensive but essential for male actors when they played a female role. The pubic wigs would conceal their genitals during nude scenes. Valentine thought that the cripple had intended to ridicule him but the opposite was true. Creppin admired the conceited actor, always raving about his performances. Whilst the cripple was entertaining the audience, the stroppy diva minced out from behind the curtain. 'How darest thou steal one of my best merkins!' he accused before tearing it from the flabbergasted hunchback's chin. Lifting his nose in the air Valentine stomped off backstage holding his merkin at arm's length. Creppin further agitated the star by complaining to his audience, 'Tis 'loo-dick-rust' ter e'er of imagined I'd a' swiped 'is pillicock tufty! I 'ad the thought they was chinny whiskers!' The crowd erupted with laughter thinking that the whole scene was part of the show.

In a mardy, Valentine protested vehemently and refused to perform until the hunchback had publicly announced that he would never touch anything that belonged to him again. 'By my crrrate, I'd daresn't touch another o' 'is prrrettiness's cock wigsies. Thou canst pulls out me' tongue an' I'd says it agin!' Bowing low, Creppin waited for the laughter to die down before he yelled his introduction, 'Prrri'thee, ladies and gentlymen, Crrreppin the Comedic Crrripplet inviteth thee ter Nuttingham. Throbbin' Hood awaits us! Let us show our apprrreciation with a rrrround of 'a claws fooooor… 'Leicester's Men!' The captain and the blacksmith were impressed and joined in with the ovation. Creppin backed off stage, bowing low and sweeping his arm in such wide circles that he almost lost his balance. This only made the crowd laugh even more.

It was a full house that night. Patrick felt so proud of his talented girl when she delivered every line perfectly. Throughout the performance the actress, who the audience believed was a young man, played the role of 'Made Merrymen' who bragged that she was still chaste. 'Oy 'as other 'oles that can satisfy a man!' she said behind her shielded hand. With a cheeky wink, she then confided in the audience that 'e'en 'is 'oliness, 'Try-a-Fuck' is partial to the odd rear entry.' Players ridiculed the Catholic Church throughout the play with double-entendres that were always popular. The audience erupted when the monk, 'Try-a-Fuck', asked 'Made Merrymen', 'Wouldst thou beatst me off if I gave thee a blessing, my dear?' Laughing Dick played the most creepily perverse Friar whose sexual innuendos were so degrading that even the pyrates would not have been able to come up with such perversity. It was a particularly rowdy night and Patrick and Anthony were not only entertained by the play by also by watching the dirty deeds going on in the pit. When the curtain was lowered everyone exited the building and the pyrates waited for Patrick's lover.

To protect her true identity, Violet always disguised herself as her alter-ego before leaving 'The Theatre'. Somehow two drunks had managed to sneak back into the building and were waiting for the popular young actor. When they saw Violet, they homed in. The tallest of the rough-looking pair stood in front of her, way too close for comfort. His dodgy associate grabbed 'Victor' by the arm, pouted his dry, scab-encrusted lips then made a sarcastic kissing sound. Feeling instantly threatened, Violet looked around the dimly lit pit, hoping that her lover and Anthony were nearby. 'Ello pretty boy! Fayncy bendin' o'er fer me n' me mate 'ere?' The hooligan's breath was foul. Violet began to gag. It was easy for the men to bend her over double and she struggled, managing to yell before the smaller man shoved a rag into her mouth. Luckily, Patrick and Anthony were not far away and heard the cry. The captain felt sick. They reached her just in time as the men were about to rape the actor. One held the terrified woman in a firm headlock and her trews had been pulled down to reveal her backside.

Drawing his sabre and cutlass before he had reached the attackers, Patrick nodded to Anthony who was already taking the opposite approach from the side of the stage. Before the blacksmith could reach the men who held Violet, the pyrate captain had struck. Anthony saw the glint of Patrick's shorter blade as it was plunged up under the smaller man's ribs. He instantly lost his grip of Violet as Patrick used his cutlass to slice through his neck in one clean sweep, almost taking his head off. An arc of scarlet blood sprayed over the other assailant's face. His eyes widened with shock as he saw his friend's head drop back onto his spine. Violet coughed and spluttered, automatically feeling her neck to check for damage. Anthony leapt forward with his double-edged sword and slashed the impeccable weapon through his victim's side, severing his spine. Dropping helplessly onto the compacted earthen pit, the paralysed casualty begged for mercy.

Violet collapsed on the ground in pain as she continued to struggle to breathe. Anthony retrieved Patrick's knife and dragged the victim out of sight. This was not good. Now he would have to go to James' house and explain. There was no way he and Patrick would be able to dispose of the bodies without being seen. After hiding the first body, the blacksmith threw a drinking horn over for Violet. Patrick held it to her lips. She had stopped choking and sipped the burning fluid. 'Seek out Burbage! He'll deal with this' the captain told Anthony. With a sudden surge of hatred, Patrick growled between gritted teeth smashing his foot down into the paralysed man's face. Kneeling over the powerless man, he took his knife and slit his belly wide open. Violet looked away and was violently sick. 'Peter! No!' she managed to splutter. Her words were unheeded. The captain was in an uncontrollable rage. His fists delivered blow after blow into his victim's face and head, 'How…darest…thou…attack…an…innocent!' With each word, he delivered a powerful punch. Even after the skull had caved in and the face was an unrecognisable mass of pulp, the savagery continued until Patrick's hands and wrists were covered with sticky brain matter.

Anthony intervened only to save the poor witness from anymore of the sickening display. Had it not been for Violet, he would have let his friend deal out the filthy would-be rapist's just dessert. After the blacksmith had shifted the second body, he wiped his blade on the dead man's clothes and sheathed his sword. Still feeling the intense adrenalin rush another fleeting sense of guilt stirred his conscience. Over the past few months Anthony had felt himself changing. His senses were suddenly awakened by the sound of the dead-cart's wheels on cobblestone. 'Bring out tha' dead!' the bleak call invaded Anthony's thoughts, then echoed eerily into the dark still of the night. Having no time for self-analysis he grabbed his lantern. He left quickly and quietly following his shifting shadows. Burbage would be home by now and he wanted to catch him before he turned in for the night. The blacksmith quickened his pace.

Patrick washed his hands and wrists in a barrel of filthy water, one of several that had been placed around the building in case of fire. As the ripples settled he caught a glimpse of his dark reflection in the dim lamplight. The pyrate shuddered outwardly as he saw black holes of shadow in place of his eyes. The Banshee's baleful stare stirred his memory. Wiping his hands on his black cloak, he dared not allow himself to dwell on the thought. Patrick took Violet's face so gently in the hands that had just beaten a man to death. Lifting her carefully, he cradled the actress in his arms. Curling her slight form into his embrace, she stammered, 'I... I... I'm af… feared, Pe… Peter' Her beautiful green eyes sought comfort and reassurance. The captain dared not look into them for fear of exposing his vindictive hatred. 'Nay need ter be afeared now we're one, my princess' he assured. Kissing her lightly on the forehead, he told her that he loved her. Bravely stifling her tears, Violet focused on becoming Victor until they had reached the safety of the Red Lion.

The night-watchman led his English bulldog towards 'The Theatre'. The fierce dog's hackles rose. He began to growl viciously. Lowering his pike in warning, the street guard's gruff voice was menacing as he spoke, 'Steadyyy, Spike, ma boy!' He saw a tall, muscular man carrying someone holding a small lantern low. Muttering to himself suspiciously, ''oo'd we 'ave 'ere, eh?' his deep, gravelly voice was intimidating. Sensing the guard's uneasy manner, Patrick stopped in his tracks. Turning to face the advancing man and his dangerous animal, he waited for the street guard to approach. Spike bared his teeth, growling and barking intermittently. His strong, muscular body tugged against his master's rope. With confident aggression the watchman delivered his warning lines, 'Halt! 'Oo goes there? Stand and be identified!' When Violet lifted the lamp higher to illuminate 'Victor's' and 'Peter's' faces, the guard instantly recognised them. Spike caught the couple's scent on a night breeze and felt the street warden's tension lessen. Both dog and master relaxed. Wagging his tail excitedly the guard dog whined in anticipation. Spike's master pulled him back on the tether forcing his front paws off the ground, so he paddled the air comically whilst using all the strength he could muster in his strong hind legs. Violet had always made a fuss of Spike ever since he was a pup small enough to fit in the night watchman's hand. Of course, the dog had always detected the actor's true identity when his master had accepted what his eyes had seen. The three chatted for a few minutes whilst Patrick explained the earlier incident, conveniently omitting the fact that he had beaten the living daylights out of one attacker while his trusted pyrate blood-brother had almost sliced the other in two! Concerned for young Victor, the guard told Peter to take him back to the Red Lion and have Mama Mabel mix a good strong posset for them both. He promised to watch out for the rogues. Patrick had no doubt that the tough, streetwise character would 'stick 'the barstards roight frew shouldst they be anlacky enough ter cam face t' face wi' me!' Patrick thanked the wrathful man before carrying his lover back to the inn house.

Mama Mabel made a big fuss of Violet so the captain was happy to leave her in safe hands. When he reached Burbage's home, Anthony was coming out. Patrick was thankful to hear that the actor had already taken care of the problem. Burbage had been outraged that someone had dared attack a member of his theatrical clan. Having given the blacksmith Violet's share of that night's takings, that included a generous bonus to treat herself, he had arranged for the bodies to be picked up straight away. Burbage knew local surgeons who were keen to get their hands on fresh specimens to dissect. The medical men always offered a good price for a fresh corpse. On their way back to the Red Lion, the two pyrates found Nobby the night-watchman and gave him a pouch of coins for his vigilance. His was a dangerous job, no matter how well paid. It was good of him to watch out for the culprits and the friends were grateful to the tough character. Embarrassed by yet secretly pleased with, the unexpected windfall, Nobby docked his cap and disappeared into the darkness. The two men walked back along the deserted streets. Arriving at their lodgings, Anthony went straight to his room. Patrick joined Mama Mabel, Johnny and Violet who was looking much brighter. The innkeepers had cheered her spirits and her cheeks were now rosy from the effects of a warm alcoholic drink. When he took her hand and led her to his room, Patrick knew how precious Violet had become to him. He hoped someday to have a chance to explain the error of his ways and also that she would find it in her heart to forgive him.

Chapter 19

Dirty Deeds and Deception

On the evening of the 16th June the Royal Barge snaked its way along the River Thames. Crowds had gathered on the muddy banks to try to catch a glimpse of their Queen. Dressed in fine red velvet and ermine Elizabeth waved to her devoted citizens. The flagged, gilded vessel entered the Tower of London via the Queen's private water-gate. Guards wearing scarlet and black uniforms embellished with gold stood to attention, the shiny blades of their pikes pointing skyward. Gloomy, dark clouds reflected the monarch's mood as they rolled above her. The surface of the dark water was disturbed as large chains were manned to raise the portcullis. The Constable of the Tower acknowledged her Majesty's welcome return and saluted as she passed by. A rally of cannon fire excited the French ambassador who lapped up the grandeur of royal ceremony. On entering the impregnable fortress Elizabeth felt a familiar confused mix of emotions. Her head ached so badly she could scream. Apprehension, fear and paranoia battled a strange comforting sense of security and stability. Ever on edge whilst inside the riverside fortress she sat, bolt upright and seemingly relaxed, in her regal splendour. She played her role of a powerfully masculine, yet feminine virgin queen down to a fine art. As her inner turmoil belied her outer calm, she kept her eyes peeled for the resident ravens. Since childhood, she had possessed a firm belief that, once within the sight of the great White Tower, she would somehow taste a trace of the fear that her mother had left lingering in the atmosphere.

Concentrating on keeping her breathing steady, Elizabeth felt a tingling sensation as tiny beads of sweat gathered on her forehead. Despite the crisp, cold evening air, she felt stiflingly hot. The clanking of metal on metal gradually died down behind her as the heavy iron grille was lowered trapping her inside the Royal Keep. Whether the fortress had been designed for this purpose or to keep out invaders, she could never decide. Obviously both, she admitted smartly. A leader could never be sure whether a traitor was in their midst, planning to overthrow them every day whilst feigning undying loyalty. 'In God's Name, cease this intolerable fluster and calm thyself, Bess!' her conscience demanded. She began to panic but, to her great relief, the paternal side of her personality soon re-emerged. Henry had always had the ability to crush her pointless sense of dread. At times she honestly believed herself to be possessed by her dead father's embittered, restless soul! A warm feeling filled her as she thought, 'I am my father's daughter, the lion's cub.' All at once, renewed confidence overwhelmed her. It felt as if a massive surge of adrenalin was about to burst through her arteries! Her mother's bloodline had endowed her with the uncanny ability to switch mood and character within a split second. This made her dangerously unpredictable; possibly a feminine trait.

Beaming brightly and filled with self-assurance, the Queen turned to the French Ambassador. She addressed him with unmatchable charm. Her pride was clear to see, literally oozing from her. 'My predecessor and beloved father, the eighth Henry Rex of our fair England, had our palace brightened in preparation for his marriage to my mother, Anne Boleyn', she bragged. The Royal Bargemaster held out a gloved hand to help the Queen from her seat. Trumpeters blasted a herald. Idly fingering the gold tassel trim on the rich purple drapery of the Britannia, Elizabeth was in no rush. She always waited until the visual pointer that she had memorised as a small child, was in place. Elizabeth spotted the gated entrance. When it was exactly at the tip of the barge's golden prow, she would know that it was time to prepare to disembark. From a very early age, the Queen had been used to learning and performing rituals. Every ceremonial formality had been permanently engrained in her mind, so she was able to act without even having to think anymore. It all came naturally to her now, so her mind was on her Robin, not this ludicrous formal engagement. Standing to attention, the Yeoman Warders saluted the Queen. The Royal bodyguards had been pre-warned that Elizabeth's temper would probably be on the brink of boiling. Unimpressed that she had been practically forced to host the French Ambassador, de Simier, who she referred to as 'her monkey', Elizabeth was not amused. The purpose of her monkey's visit was to ask Elizabeth for her hand in marriage on behalf of François de Valois, the Duke of Anjou. The duke had contracted smallpox in childhood which had left his face badly pock-marked. The debilitating disease had left him very weak and had severely stunted his growth. He was well under five feet tall. With a strong dislike of sport he was always ridiculed and belittled. Elizabeth's council knew that their union would help calm Catholic/Protestant conflict. The Queen dreaded the day when 'her frog', as she called him, would pay her a visit in person.

The Queen's party was escorted by the constable through the grounds of the outer ward. They reached a drawbridge over the moat. Pausing for a while for more pomp and ceremony whilst the bridge was lowered, Elizabeth's mind was still on her lover. She missed him so much and hoped to see him soon. The next few days were going to be gruelling and she had summoned her jester to entertain them all later that evening. Until then, she would have to stay as focused as possible. How she loathed the farce of formal procedure! Having crossed the moat, the party reached a gated entrance where palace guards stood to attention. Another rally of cannon fire deafened the French visitor who laughed when the Queen addressed him in French, cursing the loudness. A fine rain began to fall. Four men came out of the guardroom carrying a large canopy. They accompanied the Queen and her two ladies-in-waiting. Led by the constable, the elaborately attired party walked quickly towards the White Tower. Elizabeth took the palace official to one side and told him to 'hasten the tour'. She had far more urgent matters to deal with aside from mindless entertainment.

The Queen's party was shown the Royal Mint and armourments within the White Tower. Then they were guided through the Wakefield Tower along the Great Hall which led to the Lanthorn Tower. Elizabeth said a prayer for her late mother and father in St. John's Chapel and lunch was served. The Queen had requested that they visit her menagerie for most of the afternoon. She loved spending time amongst her collection of rare and beautiful creatures. The animals were kept in the bulwark in rows of sturdy cages behind heavy iron grills. The lions were kept in the barbican, which the Yeoman

Warders, or Royal bodyguards, had affectionately named 'Lion Tower'. Leopards, white lions, bears, an elephant and a polar bear were amongst the exotic beasts. They were all exercised daily and the polar bear would often draw a crowd when allowed out into the river to catch fish. The Queen also owned pet monkeys that were used to train bears for baiting. Elizabeth had several cavies that she enjoyed petting. She was also very fond of her white greyhounds.

The French Ambassador was not impressed when the Queen declined the proposal. Although he was disappointed, and somewhat angry with the obstinate monarch, he told her to keep the expensive gifts that her suitor had sent. The ambassador knew of the Queen's obsession with the Earl of Leicester, so he played his trump card. He told her that Robert and Lettice Knollys, Countess of Essex, had secretly married back in September, 1578. Having not predicted the Queen's violent reaction to his malicious revelation, the ambassador asked to be escorted to the safety of Greenwich Castle immediately. He was ushered off quickly but could still hear the Queen's bitter screams accompanied by the fearful sound of her wild animals' disturbed roars and fearful din. To think that Robert had organised for Elizabeth to be away on progress for her latest birthday back in September! He had wanted her out of the way so he could marry! 'How dare he!' Elizabeth roared over the din from the hysterical animals. The bravest amongst her dignitaries stayed to try and comfort the Queen but most disappeared.

On hearing news of her Robin's marriage to Lettice, Elizabeth had been livid but the birth of their son, Robert, in January enraged her beyond belief! Robert had not asked her permission to marry. As she stormed through the grounds of the Tower of London, Elizabeth gave orders for Dudley's immediate arrest. Yelling aloud, she threatened to have him thrown in the Tower. The Earl of Sussex was the only person who had stayed with the Queen. After a while, he managed to talk her into ordering Robert to retire to his estate at Wanstead under house arrest. Well aware of Elizabeth's impulsive nature, Sussex knew how deep her love was for her lover. He was sure that she would regret having him confined to the Tower. To everyone's relief Laughing Dick arrived and joined the Queen in her chambers. Her head was pounding and the only person she wanted to see was her loyal jester. They were in for a long, distressing night but, as always, Dick was prepared to entertain.

With a stroke of luck, the following day brought news from abroad that Sir Francis Drake had claimed sovereignty over New Albion. This elevated Elizabeth's mood but it was an unexpected gift that caused her fighting spirit to resurface. Lady Blanche brought her a scroll that had been tied with a piece of blue ribbon, its ends badly frayed. There was no seal so she unrolled it with a great sense of curiosity. It was an immaculately hand-drawn map of the River Thames. Every stair, pier and landing stage had been named and marked clearly in black ink. Studying it carefully, Elizabeth noticed that the Hampton Court landing stage had been ringed in indigo ink. A tiny crown had also been drawn on that spot. A red X covered the jetty at the Tower of London. There, a drawing of the Royal Barge at the head of a massive river procession had been completely blacked out. It was beyond a doubt that the Queen had her hands on a document that marked the spot of a planned assassination attempt. Taking a magnifying glass, Elizabeth studied the expensive paper. The fancy watermark was Italian. Only the wealthy could afford this type of parchment. As the Queen rerolled the invaluable document, she noticed a very faint date on the reverse; the 24th June 1579. Baring her rotting teeth in a cunning grin Elizabeth savoured the moment she had been waiting for. Patrick Culley was bound to want revenge. Her guess was that Grace O'Malley had something to do with a plot against her. She also suspected that the cowardly Spaniards, or French, or both would be involved somehow too! Both Catholic countries were strong allies of Ireland and openly against Protestant rule.

The Queen called for an immediate Parliamentary meeting. Robert would have to be summoned as one of her leading statesmen. As Master of the Horse, he planned all Royal official celebrations. Coincidentally, the Midsummer festival fell on 24th June, St. John's Eve, which would also be Robert's 47th birthday. This would give Elizabeth the ideal opportunity to invite him and Lettice to the annual St. John the Baptist festivities for a joint celebration. She would have to ensure that the deceitful couple did not find out that she knew of their betrayal. More guards would be needed at the four main landing stages marked on the map. Elizabeth was suspicious at all times and canny to the fact that this could be a red herring. She would have to take that into consideration but also strengthen security measures in case she had received a genuine tip-off. Either way, the warning had confirmed that the Queen should always stay vigilant.

Elizabeth's powerful position put her in constant danger. She only wished that someday she could live the free and safe lifestyle that her citizens enjoyed. The noblewoman had no idea or concern about her subjects, many of whom suffered extreme poverty under her rule. As her mind ticked over the many precautionary measures that she and Robert would have to put in place for the forthcoming event, a foul idea suddenly struck her. With careful planning, the assassination attempt could be used to sort out her greatest dilemma. With the most devious idea for a way to gain revenge on an enemy who she believed deserved her come-uppance, Elizabeth sat at her desk with a self-righteous expression on her bitter face. Calling for her secretary she gave orders to have an invitation delivered to Robert and Lettice's home immediately. They had been summoned to join their Queen in the Royal Barge Procession. Elizabeth could guarantee that this year's celebrations were going to be particularly spectacular. In fact, she thought, St. John's Eve would be an event that neither Robert nor his wife would ever be able to forget. That afternoon the Queen called for the main organisers to discuss the massive firework displays that were to take place at various points along the route of the Royal Barge Procession. She insisted that the most spectacular and loudest display be set off at the tower; the site of the likely assassination attempt. Guard duty was to be doubled there and at Hampton Court landing stage where the Queen and her party were to board the three Royal Barges. She was going to allow Lettice the privilege of unknowingly sacrificing her life to save the monarch. Determined to make the plot flawless, if all went well, Elizabeth would be successful in killing two traitors with one stone. Patrick Culley and Lettice Knollys would be out of her way forever.

Late that night Anthony and Patrick paid a visit to the treacherous River Thames. Dressed all in black and carrying forged papers, the two men posed as one of the firework display team so they would be exempt from curfew rules. They arrived at the landing stage the city side of London Bridge and waited. It could be guaranteed that, sooner or later, one of the guards on duty would need to take a piss. Moses and Shrimp had been carrying out regular surveillance of the area where they had found a hiding place that had been overlooked by security. When an unsuspecting guard relieved himself Anthony crept out of his hiding place in a dark nook on the embankment. Grabbing the shorter man in a neck lock, the blacksmith pressed a rag soaked with oil of vitriol firmly over his nose and mouth. The guard scrabbled blindly at his captor's arm kicking his feet in desperation as he struggled to free himself of his attacker's firm hold. The struggle went on for a good two minutes. The pyrates stripped the victim of his uniform before pulling his body to the river's edge. It slid easily down the muddy bank into the water. Taken swiftly away by the current the soldier's body was soon out of sight. Quickly pulling on the dead guard's uniform, Anthony grabbed the pike and took a steady walk over to the jetty. The other duty guard whispered urgently, 'Tha' should've said tha'dst be a while! I needs ter crap.' Anthony mumbled a polite apology. As predicted, the soldier barely glimpsed him as he rushed off to relieve himself.

Patrick waited until the guard put his pike to one side and untied his trews. The captain's bludgeon struck him on the back of his head, smashing splintered skull bone into his brain. He fell onto the canvas that the pyrates had put on the wet, muddy ground so that the uniforms would stay clean. Luckily, this guard was tall and well-built. His uniform fitted Patrick almost perfectly. Placing a heavy chain around the corpse's neck, he rolled it into the water and waited for it to be carried away by the rushing tide. Shoving their discarded black clothes into a dark bag the captain scanned the area. There was no evidence of foul play. As the church bells tolled midnight two new guards marched towards the wharf. Tipping their hats to welcome their replacements, Anthony and Patrick handed over a metal box which contained spare candles for the lanterns. The night-watchman always tried to be in an area to witness the guards change-over. He stood upright and tipped his hat, mouthing the traditional command from the old watch, 'Present arms!' The four smartly clad sentinels parted in pairs and the watchman's dog barked when he heard the nearby sound of shattering glass. 'C'mon, boy!' he shouted as he broke into a run towards the source of the sound.

Everything had gone to plan. The time had finally come. The captain was pleased with his gang who were all ready to carry out the attack the following night. They all sat in the barroom, the air thick with tension. Anthony suggested that the lads try out a different brothel. After all, this could be the last night of their lives. Creppin took the considerate blacksmith to one side, 'S'coozies me, sirrrree', he muttered, hopping uncomfortably from one leg to another. 'I's 'avin' problems wi' me pills-lick-cock.' Anthony swallowed nervously. He shuddered at the thought that Twills had passed on an unpleasant disease to the poor wretch. With a look of discomfort, the hunchback explained to the man he looked up to, ''Tis me 'ssspermsies', sire. They's all grrrrreen an' 'av blocked up me piss spout.' Anthony knew it! Fearing the worst, he took Creppin to seek Mabel's advice. The wise landlady was well-used to dealing with what she politely referred to as 'her girls' fanny ailments'. It had been the right decision. Mabel prepared a bowl of warm vinegar mixed with mead. The hunchback yelped when he dipped the end of his sore cock into the acrid liquid. 'OW!' came the sound of initial shock from a brief sting. The medicinal concoction soon numbed Creppin's pain. A feeling of pure relief spread through his genitalia as he fully immersed the swollen member. Letting out a long, 'Ahhhhh' the thankful hunchback slowly swirled his penis around in the acidic preparation. Delighted at being able to piss into the bowl, Creppin sat with his cock submerged for a full hour. He supped ale, chatting happily about the love he had for 'Twillykins'. When Anthony checked in on the patient, he was surprised to find him ready and keen to accompany the gang to the brothel. The Irishmen laughed at the hunchback's eagerness to touch some new 'brrrestibubblitts' as he called them. The gang were determined to make this a night to remember.

The group of horny pyrates approached a tall building with white-washed walls. A small metal sign creaked on rusty chains above them. It read 'Sauna'. On entering the seedy establishment a tall, skinny old prostitute was the first to approach the men. She addressed Anthony who sent her over to the hunchback. Creppin haggled confidently and they agreed on a price. Leading him up a rickety staircase into her room, the strumpet invited the cripple to lie back on her bed. Watching her undress in front of him, he felt his soothed penis harden. Picking up a pipe and two vials of opium, the elderly woman untied her client's trews. A three hour session was an unusual request and ol' Mary was desperate for returning clients.

Patrick decided to stay at the Red Lion whilst the others went out on the town. When he told Mabel he would be leaving soon, she begged him to let her keep Micken. That suited Patrick fine. The parrot had been very happy since being in her care. Shanny and Jock wanted to spend the night together. They had taken food to Jock's room where they could spend the whole night pleasuring each other. Patrick lay on his bed with his lover. The unexpected surprise that she had just revealed left him in a state of shock. Patrick Culley had never even contemplated the prospect of fatherhood. He was stunned. Like a stray cannonball, harsh reality blasted through the most sensitive reserve of the captain's mind. In a flash of pure madness, the idea of fatherhood was appealing. Violet's words should have brought a sweet sound to Patrick's heart yet they had stung like the deathly strike of a viper. Dread filled his heart. 'I am with child.' The four simple words sank in. The captain wished that he was four thousand miles away from the poor girl who he had deceived. His face must have shown his deep regret. 'Th'art nay elated by my news...' Violet stated rather than questioned.

It was too late to rectify the situation. The damage had been done. The pregnant girl had already sensed Patrick's fleeting dread. She was no fool. 'Oh my God, I ought to have known better!' Violet cursed herself silently. Feeling her body and mind weaken with dejection the actress turned her face away from her lover. How could she have been so naïve... so stupid?! Feeling suddenly angry and over-protective of her, no, THEIR unborn child, she held her belly. She spoke bravely,

'I shall bear our child.' When the proud actress said that she did not expect Peter to stay and support the baby, Patrick died inside. He was stricken with a sudden feeling of self-contempt. How could he possibly have allowed her to think that he would abandon their baby! This could all have been avoided if he, no, THEY had taken precautions. Now she was pregnant. The captain had to stay focused and get in the right frame of mind for the following day. If he could not rid his head of this dilemma something terrible was going to happen, he simply knew it! 'Bloody brilliant timing!' he mumbled. As the words left his mouth, Patrick instantly regretted them. He loved the wench but what could he do? 'Zounds!' he said aloud. Violet was crying now. This was the last thing he wanted. If only she knew what he planned to do the following day! Patrick tried to stay calm. He had to deal with this sorry situation as quickly as possible. He had to concentrate on the pending assassination attempt. It was a matter of life and death.

When Patrick grabbed the actress by the arm he knew that he had made another bad move. She flinched. A natural reaction, he supposed. The captain's mind was spinning. What was he playing at? His mother had warned him about the female tendency to over-react. Sushana Culley had been quite different from the majority of women. On the other hand, Patrick had made Violet cry and she was carrying his child. 'Oh my God' he thought aloud. 'I love thee!' he told his distraught lover. 'I have to leave London for a while', he admitted. Patrick had never been one for tact. After he had said it, he knew that he had been far too abrupt. Violet turned around and held him tightly. Her face was so beautiful, even though her expression showed vulnerability and fear. 'I love thee, Peter.' she sobbed. The lovers stood together, each fraught with the fear of losing the other. The actress broke the silence, 'Shalt tha return to me…to us?' she asked nervously. Subconsciously, Violet stroked her slightly swollen belly, concerned for their unborn child. Patrick's heart was racing, his mouth dry. He found it difficult to swallow. There was no way he could tell her that he was planning to avenge his mother's execution and kill the Queen! Now the silence was impenetrable. Violet was scared. She held her breath. Having been lost in a romantic whirlwind the idea of pregnancy had been magical. Now reality had set in.

This was all becoming a dreadful nightmare. 'I shall return. Tha hast my word,' Patrick vowed. A feeling of relief spread through Violet's soul, offering the warmth of renewed hope. Now what had he done! A false promise was not enough. He had no idea whether he would survive! All of a sudden the pyrate captain felt a desperate urge to live. A stifling dread overwhelmed him. Although he wanted to stay, hold Violet close and tell her that everything was going to be fine, he had to leave. The petite woman stood on tiptoes and kissed her man. A passionate kiss loaded with sexual longing and the deep human need for love led the couple into a wild sensual squall. Their sex was basic, needy and hurried; almost desperate. All they knew was that they needed to be one. Their brief encounter felt like a tiny droplet in the ocean; a fleeting moment in the essence of time, yet it seemed to satisfy their longing for unity. To Violet it felt like a confirmation of their bond, a gift of her trust in Peter. For the pyrate captain, it sealed their union in a pagan way.

Patrick pulled on his outer garments and secured them with Violet's help. They had nothing else to say but their actions spoke volumes. Ironically, it almost felt like she was preparing him for war. Shunning that dreadful thought, Violet passed her man a lantern and watched him walk away. Locking the door, she felt desperately sad and alone. Unable to contain her tears, she began to cry. Deciding to stay in her lover's bed so she was still able to smell him, she snuffed out the candles. Lying on top of the covers she curled into the foetal position. As she felt herself drifting off to sleep, Violet was startled by a rustling sound. The disturbing noise was coming from the corner of the small, dark room. Without much concern, she wondered whether Mabel's cat had sneaked in earlier. The moggy had a habit of making his presence known out of the blue. When she first moved in, he had terrified Violet during the night when he jumped through an open shutter and landed on her bed. Luckily, she had become used to his unpredicted nightly visits and was now far less edgy.

The tired actress yawned and lay her head back down on the pillow. Before she had the chance to close her eyes a stinking cloth was pressed firmly over her mouth and nose. The pregnant woman felt the room spinning around her. Her eyes rolled back into her head as drowsiness overtook her. The last thing she sensed was being rolled roughly out of bed onto coarse cloth. Feeling an intense, nauseating pain deep inside her stomach Violet lost consciousness before being dragged into her own costume chest.

CHAPTER 20

Royalty Snared

Rumour was that the unfathomable hatred that Elizabeth harboured for Lettice was so intense that she had banished her from court. The Queen had forbidden her return unless she was summoned. Everyone had been surprised to see Lettice and Robert at the Midsummer celebrations so assumed that they had both been forgiven. The truth of the matter was far more sinister.

Curfews had been lifted for St. John's Eve and nightwatchmen relieved of their duty. They were to join the procession with community officials. Huge bonfires had been lit all over England. Every city had organised parades that featured giants and mechanical fire-breathing dragons. At Hampton Court, the Thames was crowded with vessels carrying spectators who wanted to be on the waters as the Royal Pageant passed by. A large flotilla of barges had gathered along the stately river. Merchant ships and barges from the capital city's livery companies had been covered with banners, streamers and sparkling cloths of gold and silver. Everyone awaited the Queen's Royal Barge to collect Elizabeth and her entourage to lead the procession. Robert had arranged for two more luxurious barges to follow her Majesty's. Important dignitaries and wealthy noblemen and women had paid substantial amounts of money for the honour of being at the head of the magnificent flotilla. No less than three hundred vessels were to join the extravagant armada.

Queen Elizabeth kissed her former best friend's forehead. Lettice had been surprised that she and Robert had received such a coveted invitation to join the Queen, and a select few other courtiers, for dinner before the grand fête. Elizabeth was being been very pleasant towards Robert's wife and had lavished her with gifts of a fine tiara, set with emeralds and diamonds, and a cape that had been richly embroidered with Tudor roses. To everyone's surprise, the cloak had been trimmed with fine ermine, a fur that was usually only permitted to be worn by royal subjects. Overwhelmed by Elizabeth's generosity Lettice felt a sudden wave of guilt. She felt bad that she had hidden so much from the forgiving Queen. Thinking herself foolish for believing that the woman who had loved her since early childhood would have ever caused her harm, she felt incredible happiness. Lettice decided to consult Robert after the celebrations and propose that they confess all.

Meanwhile, over at the Royal Barge House, Anthony was pleased to gain the best position on the leading vessel. He looked very smart, immaculately dressed in one of the guard's uniforms that he and Patrick had stolen. He wore a striking red tunic, trimmed with purple and gold lace, a white lace ruff and red knee breeches, stockings and a hat with a plume. Armed with a gilded spear, a battle axe with a tassel of red and gold and a sword, he really looked the part. He wore a leather cross-belt to support the heavy butt of a long, cumbersome matchlock gun and soft buckskin gloves. When everything had been checked the two Royal Barges set off for the Palace.

Spirits were high as everyone awaited the arrival of the Queen's Barges. When the time came, the royal party prepared to gather outside for the procession. Elizabeth told Lettice that her gifts were to be worn that night. Giving Robert a secret smile, the unsuspecting woman followed the Queen's personal servants to her private chambers where they had been told to prepare her. The Queen and her guests gathered in the palace gardens where torches lit the paths that snaked their way, over the vast lawn, down to the riverbank. Tables had been decorated and set inside pavilions so the guests could see each barge arrive. When Lettice emerged from the palace, dressed like a Queen, she was met by a roar of cheers. Dipping a curtsy to her kind friend she expressed her gratitude. Elizabeth shrugged off the appreciative flattery, straightened Lettice's exquisite tiara and adjusted her cloak. 'Thou art as fair as thy Queen!' Elizabeth spoke loudly making her jester inwardly cringe. Although he loved her dearly, he feared that this underhand trick would someday backfire.

Champagne flowed and an old, wise-looking butler announced the arrival of the first two barges. The Queen's chief manservant read out the names of guests who were to follow him down to the jetty. He accompanied the eager cluster of finely dressed nobles who praised the splendid Royal Barges. Ample applause and shouts of, 'Bravo' and 'Hip, hip hoorah!' satisfied the Queen's ego. She stood against the backdrop of her Royal Palace, wearing a nonchalant look on her over made-up face. Her heavy white make-up was luminous in the torchlight. Looking old and drawn, Elizabeth announced in a rather droll manner, 'My Lords, Ladies and gentlefolk, our faithful old man River Thames beckons us'. Robert smiled. Looking down at his fine Italian leather shoes that had been made especially for this occasion, he felt glad that his Bess had finally accepted his predicament. He needed the stability of a permanent relationship that she was unable to offer.

As it was Robert's birthday he was told to join the Queen in the second barge. Neither he nor Lettice had the slightest suspicion that Elizabeth had recently learned of their secrets. Robert watched his wife board the elaborately decorated vessel. Feeling extremely privileged, she smiled with joy when she noticed that tiny bells had been sewn onto the fine cloth canopy. Their chimes sounded so pretty when they were stirred in the breeze. Glorious tapestries and flags decorated the gilded oared craft. Musicians played a sprightly air as Lettice stepped daintily aboard, blissfully unaware of the danger that awaited her further along the busy river. The well-padded and beautifully upholstered seats were so comfortable. Anyone would have believed the noblewoman to be the Queen as she sat, proud and upright, surrounded by soft silk cushions embroidered with multi-coloured flowers. To her delight, royal enthusiasts called from skiffs and gondolas on the water 'God bless good Queen Bess!' Anthony stood to attention as the oarsmen pushed the craft away from the landing stage. Oblivious to Lettice's true identity he had yet to realise that the Queen would be boarding the next barge. Crowds lined the banks cheering and waving as the impressive river parade began.

A sudden downpour of rain caught the Queen's party unprepared. Sir Walter Raleigh was amongst them and quickly laid down his cloak to save Elizabeth's silk shoes from spoiling. She was amused by her courtier's thoughtful gesture. Her group chatted merrily as they made their way over to the landing stage. Thankfully, the Queen arrived dry shod otherwise there would have been hell to pay for the servants who had not provided a litter. Everyone boarded the Jubilant, her late father's favourite barge. Twenty four Royal Watermen raised their oars, blades facing towards the sovereign as she was seated in a luxurious velvet throne. She patted the seat next to her and Raleigh stepped forward assuming that he had been invited to join her. He was mistaken. Shaking her head and frowning, Elizabeth summoned Robert. Instantly obeying, he took the place by his lover and his humiliated rival plumped himself down next to Laughing Dick. Folding his arms, Raleigh threw the jester a warning look in case he decided to mock his embarrassment.

Elizabeth felt absolute self-satisfaction as she began the journey along the majestic river with her Robin beside her. The waterway was alive with revelry and merriment. She recalled the story that her mother had told her of the magnificent flotilla that her father had organised to take her to the Tower to be crowned as his Queen. In honour of Ann Boleyn, Elizabeth had ensured that similar displays were set up along the final stretch. She felt angry at the thought of her poor mother who had stirred exactly the opposite reaction from London's fickle citizens who now greeted her daughter with exultant applause. Ann Boleyn had been cursed with cries of, 'witch!' and 'harlot!' as she was taken from the Tower to her coronation. Elizabeth could not deny that she still felt bitter resentment towards the ignorant commoners who had helped make her mother's life misery.

London's busiest highway was teeming with vessels of all shapes and sizes. The rapid river was so vast, so stately, so elegant. Great carracks and galleons, barges and all forms of boats imaginable crammed the swift flowing river. Oblivious to the Queen's evil plot to murder his wife, Robert enjoyed the spectacle as the pageant wound its way along the Thames. Laughing Dick entertained the guests with juggling, magic tricks and comical tales of the ancient river. Thousands of citizens had flocked to see their monarch in all her finery. Many had hired wherries so wherrymen were glad of the trade. Vessels were weighed down, packed with as many spectators as possible. Tough, aggressive watermen yelled obscenities as they fought amongst themselves in their efforts to gain the best place to see the procession. Robert and Elizabeth found the brutal fights over territorial disputes amusing. Dick shouted encouragement which made the hard-working boatmen even more determined to defeat their rivals.

Lettice dared not look back to seek her husband but hoped she would not have long to wait until he joined her at the Tower. How she wished they could have enjoyed this wonderful experience together. As the barge passed Lambeth Palace, she remembered playing there with Elizabeth as a child. The Queen had always been bossy but fair and Lettice had longed to be like her. As her sole role-model, Elizabeth had inspired the youngster greatly and her admiration had never since faded. Lettice waved at the crowds. She felt such pride and pure joy as she relished in the euphoric atmosphere. Enjoying the company of the nobles she engaged in small talk and felt honoured to hear them praise her husband for organising such a spectacular event. As the mayor addressed Lettice, Anthony caught his breath. How on earth could this have happened? It was unheard of for the Queen not to take her place at the head of a procession! The conceited whore never took a back seat. This was terrible! Tightening the grip on his pike the blacksmith stole a quick glance at the woman who he now knew to be the Queen's niece, Lady Knollys. Her jovial manner confirmed his fears. The pretty, happy woman who sat enjoying herself was definitely not the sour-faced Queen of England!

As the water pageant continued, fireworks were set off from platforms that had been strategically placed along the winding river. Tall ships blasted cannon fire as the Queen's vessel rowed by. Lettice noticed that the crowds had become even denser. People lined the banks, waving flags and cheering as the grand parade passed by. Their enthusiasm was addictive! The most spectacular firework displays were staged along the main stretch through London. Cannon salutes could be heard from miles around the jubilant capital. The Royal Barge procession threaded its way between hundreds of vessels along the busy waterway. Merchants had brought their wares onto the river to sell. They sang along to the melodic peal of church bells.

London's citizens were treated to a grand spectacle as the Queen's Barge led the procession along the celebratory route. As they passed tall merchant's houses decorated with banners and flags to celebrate the holy saint's eve, Anthony tried to stay focused on his guard duty. He was trying desperately to figure out a way to make the gang aware that the Queen would be following in the next barge. It seemed so soon when the leading barge reached the Palace of Westminster. The blacksmith knew that the Tower of London would soon be in sight.

As the vessel continued on downriver to pass under London Bridge, where hundreds of people crowded the piers, Lettice pressed the palms of her hands to her ears. A lady-in-waiting handed her some cotton to plug them.

By now, the warships' booming cannons had become over-bearing. The oarsmen slowed their pace as the barge emerged on the other side of the famous bridge. Actors from the Southwark theatre district had gathered on the banks opposite the city to pay tribute to their founder. Stilt-walkers dressed as giants danced above players representing Neptune, mermaids and other mythical characters. The actors gave a lively performance that would be sure to enchant their heroic thespian sovereign. Waving a huge painted banner that read, 'God Save Gloriana, our Faerie Queen' the giants danced and waved their huge hands in celebration. Sadly their efforts were missed as Lettice suddenly felt light-headed. Placing her empty silver drinking vessel on a tray she noticed a guard snatch a quick look at her. Such a good-looking man, she thought. Smirking as she chastised herself for even thinking about another man, she realised that she had enjoyed way too much red Champagne already. It would probably be served all night too, so she was regretting her greed. The fine wine's potency had already begun to take its toll.

All of a sudden, the Queen's niece felt nervous apprehension. Hearing a loud groan, she looked towards the edge of the river. In a sickeningly macabre display, prisoners had been chained to iron poles along the banks as a harsh reminder of the brutality of capital punishment. These unfortunate souls had committed the heinous crime of pyracy. Their broken bodies were now being exhibited as a warning to others who may be tempted by the sea robbery trade. The victims had been condemned to bear three tides before their release. In actual fact they had been cruelly offered a rare hope of freedom that would be impossible to achieve. It would be a miracle if any of them survived the first tide let alone all three! A Yeoman Guard thrust his long pike into the mouth of a prisoner who had dared to make his presence known. Lettice turned her head away from the sight of the wounded man whose jaw had been cut from his face. She tried not to think of the dark forms of vermin that had dived into the cold water to tear away the flesh of the dying man. The Tower of London loomed before the Royal Barge. Lettice's river trip had almost come to an end. As Anthony watched every stroke of the oarsman in front of him he dared not move an inch for fear of blowing his cover. The royal party was soon to disembark for a spectacular finale. As the vessel approached the wharf, a huge firework display began. Several flashes of white light preceded another rally of cannon fire, this time, from the Tower. Warships responded with innumerable gun salutes. Crowds surged forward as people fought to see the Queen and her dignitaries.

The Royal Fire Master of England happened to be an Italian man called Gambini. He was treated with great respect by all. Renowned for always stunning his audience with the most dazzling displays, Gambini's father had been amongst the first in Europe to use the science of explosives as a mesmerising art form. The firework enthusiast had been experimenting with an explosive compound that burned much slower than his previous mixtures. Upon ignition, he discovered that his new product produced the most delightful radiant showers of pure white sparks. Each firework composition was closely guarded and the Gambinis had vowed to only ever pass on their sought-after recipes to their oldest sons. As Europe's greatest and most successful firework manufacturer, Gambini, and his team had spent several weeks organising the most extravagant firework spectacle ever. They had built large frameworks that had been set up with various forms of explosive delights. Arrangements of fountains, roman candles and aerial shells had been fastened to wheels and lances which had been mounted onto the machines. A team manned each rig and, one after another, set their displays alight. This created a spectacular firework fiesta that would be difficult to outdo.

It was ironic that, on that fateful night, Gambini had chosen Colm and Danny to help him fill his pièce de résistance with explosives. A huge dragon covered with papier-mâché scales had been kept hidden until now. The Irishmen had packed its belly full of spinners, fountains and firecrackers. The machine had been constructed on a floating platform a hundred yards or so in front of the Tower. A simple mechanism made the giant beast open its mouth to spurt out fire. Gleaming scales came alive with spinning silver sparks. Dressed all in black Colm and Danny stood on the landing boards ready to ignite their two explosive surprises. Since their first meeting, the two Irish pyrates had made an excellent impression on the Italian Fire Master. He had entrusted the explosive experts to concoct a perfectly safe mix to be set off to welcome the Queen as she stepped off the Royal Barge. Having worked with the lads over the past few weeks Gambini felt able to leave them to carry out the simple task while he directed the main show. Gambini's instruction had been for them to 'Prepare-a a gentler displaya to agreeta Herrra Rrroyal Agghhighness.' Their moderate explosives would signal the release of the splendid fire dragon which would then be set afloat downriver.

Anthony's woollen doublet and jerkin made him uncomfortably hot. He was sweating profusely but dared not wipe his brow for fear of exposure. The blacksmith wished that he could see the progress of the barge that carried the Queen. He had a few options. Not really convinced whether any of them would work, Anthony had little time to decide what to do. Unable to comprehend the Queen's callousness, having allowed one of her closest friends to walk into a deadly trap, Anthony knew that he had to protect the innocent woman. Somehow he was going to have to warn Patrick to delay the explosion. Suddenly, it was too late. The moment had arrived. The cold, grey fortress loomed before them.

In his nervous state, the blacksmith began to count the oarsmen's final strokes. His anticipation had been difficult to hide and he felt immense relief when ordered to 'Pre-paaaaare for disembark-aaaaay-SHUN!' Shadowing his flanking officer's routine moves perfectly, Anthony was thankful to make out Patrick's figure standing on the jetty. Dressed as another Yeoman Guard, the pyrate captain had taken position closest to the barrier that had been erected to prevent the public from entering the docking area. Looking extremely serious and official Colm and Danny stood as still as statues. With arms behind their backs they waited in place, as planned, either side of the landing platform. Both men had their eyes firmly fixed on an imaginary spot ahead of them. They appeared to be in a trance-like state. Anthony envied their composed cool. Dreading the moment when Lettice was to disembark, he made a split-second decision and stepped forward. His superior officer flashed him a threatening look. His stern expression quickly faded when he realised that the guard had stooped to pick up a small box that someone had thrown into the boat. Strict orders had been given to immediately remove anything that landed inside the vessel. Nodding a quick approval the officer relaxed and continued his duty, 'Preeseeeeeeent.... ARMS!' he yelled loudly. Suddenly feeling the need to let out a nervous laugh, Anthony obeyed orders and thrust his pike diagonally outwards, at an angle that offered more protection to the passengers. 'No!' he thought as he took his position at the side of the barge, facing away from Lady Knollys.

The light rainfall had ceased. A fresh wind blew the miniature bells. Their tingling charm was drowned out by the crowd's cheers. Trumpeters wearing red and gold tabards bearing the Tudor Coat of Arms heralded the arrival of the Queen. The barge was moored. Anthony tried to catch Patrick's eye. Staring straight ahead, the captain was focusing on the welcoming guards' routine. The blacksmith's mind raced. The whole plot was doomed to fail if he was unsuccessful in delaying the explosion! Who could have predicted that the bloody sadistic Queen would trade places with a decoy?! There was no time for any pussy footing around. He had to make a move. Turning to stand to attention, Anthony stooped before Lettice and held out a gloved open hand. The tipsy woman realised his intention and accepted his offer to help her disembark. She stood up unsteadily so the blacksmith held her gently by the elbow. When they stepped out of the craft onto wet, slippery boards, Anthony positioned himself between his new ward and Patrick. This was exactly the opposite move to their well-rehearsed plan. Having already sensed that something was amiss, the captain went to lift his arm to prevent Shrimp and Creppin from riling the crowd. It was too late. As he heard Creppin's high-pitched whine, Anthony's stomach turned a somersault. Patrick turned white with dread as he realised that his warning had gone unheeded.

'Yi!' came the hunchback's phony startled cry, 'Bewarrrre! He haths pubonic plague!' In any other circumstance, Creppin's mispronunciation would have been hilarious. Acting on sheer impulse Anthony pulled Lettice close. At the thought of contracting the Black Death the terrified woman had grabbed onto her guard's tunic begging him to take her back onto the barge. A frantic mob went wild when Shrimp threw back his dark hood to reveal a hideously made-up face. He had stuffed his mouth with rags to create the impression that his buboes had become swollen and inflamed. Expert make-up artist, Valentine, had applied a tacky, dough-like mixture in lumps along the small man's jawline to create convincing fake boils. He had made a slit in each and added yellowish goo to look as if the pus-riddled abscesses had burst open. As a final touch to create a realistic victim of the deathly plague, a splattering of calf's blood had been added. With a combination of Creppin's natural, vile stench and Shrimp's agonising groans, the crowd were convinced that a plague carrier was amidst their masses.

Hysteria ensued creating the confusion and mayhem that Patrick and the gang of assassins required for cover. Danny bent to light his ceramic stinkpot and threw it to the floor leaping into the cold river as the contents hissed and crackled into life. As the taper burned, the pot burst into flames and emitted thick, heavy smoke and stinking, pungent fumes. For those still on the landing stage the smoke and toxic vapour caused further chaos as they coughed and spluttered desperately trying to breathe. It was impossible to see anything in the smokescreen. Acting quickly, Colm pulled his black bandanna over his nose and mouth and picked up a heavier earthen pot. His container had two small handles on either side to which he had attached a lighted spill. A piece of coarse linen had been pushed inside. His explosive device contained a lethal mixture of gun powder, saltpetre, sulpha, sal ammoniac, camphor, linseed oil and small shot held together by pitch. Anthony tried to keep hold of his hysterical charge but could not gain a firm grip as he struggled to breathe. The noxious fumes were intoxicating. Unable to see a thing, he tried to find his bearings before it was too late. Willing to die to save innocent pawns in the English Queen's game of death, the blacksmith used all his strength to push past panicking guards and dignitaries towards Colm. He felt sick with fear knowing that, within seconds, he and everyone in the vicinity would be blown to kingdom come.

Lighting the spill precisely two minutes following Danny's explosion, Colm hurled his explosive missile high above him. Feeling a strong hand grab onto his tunic, he wasted no time and dived into the icy cold river. Swimming as fast as he could, he heard an almighty blast. The riverbed reverberated beneath him. He swam deeper as broken pieces of timber blocked his way. Feeling a heavy weight against his legs, he grabbed onto a thick root protruding from the riverbank, to avoid being dragged down. The current was very strong. Seeing a woman whose leg had become tangled in debris, Colm tried to duck down to free her. He tore at the mass of weeds but had to return to the surface for air. Feeling the woman's nails clawing his leg he lunged back down to try to save her. It was too late. Her limp, lifeless body, still anchored to the riverbed, swayed and twirled like a macabre puppet. Colm let go of the root and let the speed of the river take him away from the corpse that waved both arms as if signalling danger.

Lettice, Anthony and Patrick had all been badly injured in the blast. Colm's lethal ammunition had shot everywhere causing maximum damage. Dead and dying lay on the banks and walkway. The cruel metal shots had caused horrific injuries. Despite the guards' efforts to douse the flames with buckets of water, the fire continued to burn. Its searing hot blaze quickly devoured the pier, leaving nothing but filthy smoke in its trail. Amidst the chaos Patrick had made his move and ran to grab poor Lettice thinking that she was the Queen. A damp horse-blanket was thrown around her to extinguish flames that still burned raw, naked flesh. Now a dead-weight, Lettice was dropped into an awaiting boat that rowed steadily away. Shanny, Remando, Saul, Abadeyo and Babatu had moored their hired wherry a short distance along the river bank. They had managed to move into position at the perfect time. A guard had seen Patrick grab Lettice and drag her away but was unable to give chase. They had instantly disappeared, lost amid the panicking mass of people. The captain passed his hostage down to Remando and Shanny, who wrapped her in another blanket. Before making an escape, Patrick had to find out what Anthony had been trying to warn him about. Pushing the wherry away from the bank, he made sure that the crew were well on their way before he turned and limped back to find Anthony.

Remando and the others rowed as hard as they could. It was going to be a big challenge to cross the congested river. All being well, Jock and Moses would be waiting in a carriage on the southern bank. Three giant, charred, black skeletal fingers were all that remained of a once sturdy landing structure. They appeared to be pointing smouldering fingertips at the stunning display above. As the pyrates made their way across the busy river a man grabbed onto Shanny's arm. Covered in filth and blood, his skin was blistered with severe burns. The poor victim tried desperately to board the wherry. In the struggle to save himself he almost pulled Shanny into the river. Remando kicked him hard in the face. Drawing back his bow, Abadeyo fired an arrow straight through the frantic man's neck. As he fell back into the rapid flow, a beautiful spray of fireworks lit up the night sky. Whistling rockets and Catherine wheels came alive in a wonderful display that most spectators watched without an inkling of the horror that had taken place at the Tower pier.

Gambini and his sons continued to light explosive after explosive, completely oblivious to the terrorist attack. Having entrusted Colm and Danny with the responsibility of lighting the simplest display, the conceited firework specialist wanted to make history with Colm's new recipe. Gambini had not believed his luck when he had met the naïve pair at his favourite city tavern. Not only were the Irish lads experts with explosives but they had been stupid enough, after he had plied them with enough spirits, to agree to join his team of experts AND give him the recipe to their new invention! Gambini was about to launch the first fireworks ever to produce orange sparks over the Thames.

When the dragon's chains exploded, the huge beast was set free. Floating along the Thames, it lifted its head and opened its mouth wide to spit out tangerine-coloured orbs for a grand finale. The Queen and audience were wowed beyond measure. Rockets soared high then exploded sending sprays of tiny sparkling orange and white lights cascading down from ink-black skies. Surrounded by pin-prick stars a spiteful, razor-thin moon slashed the midnight sky. The night scenery faded into an insignificant backdrop to the beautiful sparkling lightshow. English citizens had been firework-lovers for years but had only ever seen silvery white sparks. Gambini's new amber fireworks made the crowd further down the river gasp in awe. Cheers and applause could be heard between loud crackles, hisses and bangs. Thanks to a stolen recipe, Gambini had managed to put on another magnificent spectacle. Smiling to himself as he thought, 'a-this a-one-a will take-a long-a time-a to a-match-a!' Gambini still reigned as Queen Elizabeth's Master of Fire. Now his head swelled larger than ever.

Creppin and Shrimp had been thrown into the river during the blast. Some caring wherrymen, who had been nearest to the explosion, pulled together in a comradely mission. After taking their passengers to the safety of the shore they returned to rescue survivors. Sadly, many bodies had been washed away by the current or pulled down to the muddy depths. The Queen's Barge had continued on when her guards had seen the disaster ahead. Their sovereign's safety was paramount. To Elizabeth's frustration, Robert had tried to dive in to save Lettice but had been restrained by two soldiers. Word had begun to travel. All kinds of rumours were being spread about the city. Some heard that one of

Gambini's fireworks had back-fired and killed the Queen. Others had been told that there had been an assassination. The Spanish were immediately blamed with the Catholics coming a close second. The latter had been a concern fuelled by a few men who had heard Gambini, a strict Catholic, bragging that he had a 'big-ga sur-per-iza' for the popular celebration. Their curiosity had prompted them to take one of his assistants aside to find out more. The intoxicated man had complained that, despite many years of service under the Italian, he had never had an increase in wage. Yet he was disgusted by Gambini's recent hiring of two Irish travellers who were receiving double his pay!

Amidst the commotion, the yeomen captured a tall, dark-haired man with blue eyes. They took him to the Queen who had revealed her identity soon after the explosion. She had entered the Tower via a water gate. Everyone had been in turmoil believing that they had witnessed an explosion that had killed the monarch. Lettice had been thrown like a blazing ragdoll further along the grassy banks of the river. Raw strips of flesh were hanging in ribbons from her body. Most of her clothes had been blown off in the blast. A few remains of silken cloth floated in cinders in the air. As the ash fell like snow and settled on the victims of the blast the prisoner could hardly stand. He was in searing agony as two guards bound him roughly in chains. Surrounded by a circle of armed protectors, the angry Queen approached her would-be assassin. The pyrate sneered. He dared to spit at the woman he despised. Taking a kidney punch for his insolence, his brave defiance did not lessen his self-disgust for having failed the mission. As spangled stars glinted in blackened skies, the Queen's harsh, piercing screams amused the captive, 'Patrick Culley, thou art a murderous traitor and thief...thy...mother's...bastard... child! Thou shalt surely suffer for thy treason!'

As the broken man was shackled and led away to the dungeons beneath the Tower, Dudley stood in shock. He was beside himself with terror. Lettice was nowhere to be seen. His wife had disappeared during the skirmish when some of the assassins had escaped. Now, his only hope was that she had been taken away to safety by the Queen's Guards. Fearing the worst, he frantically began to search for any clues that might lead him to her whereabouts. Looking over at the ruined landing stage, he watched the confused mass of people. Some tried to stamp out flames whilst others lashed out in fear trying to leave the crime scene. Robert's heart skipped a beat. Spotting something that he had seen drop from the captive's shirt during the struggle, he rushed over to retrieve it. Miraculously, a rabbit's foot brooch had remained unburned, half-covered by ashes. It was lying next to a large piece of the bloody, singed skirt that his wife had been wearing. He felt sick at the thought of her clothes being blown from her body in the blast. Robert's eyes poured with tears that stung his face in the heat of the fire. Lettice's scorched, bedraggled wig floated on the river. Retrieving it, Dudley cursed as he touched the pretty bow that he had watched her pin to its base earlier that night. Falling to his knees, the Earl begged to God that the poor soul had been killed in the blast. It grieved him to ask such a thing but he did not want his son's mother to suffer at the hands of anti-Royalist kidnappers. Heavens only knows what they would do to her in their belief that they had abducted the monarch. Wasting no more time, he concealed the brooch and went to find Elizabeth. Surely she would have some answers by now! Hopeful that his lover was doing all she could to find Lettice, Robert felt relieved to see the Queen and Laughing Dick looking out of an upper storey window as they watched a breath-taking finale from the safety of the tower.

Breaking into a run so he could join them as soon as possible, Robert thanked God. His Bess had been smiling and clearly enjoying the firework display. She must have heard that Lettice was alright. Feeling a cold shiver, he heard the deep, rasping call of one of the Tower's resident ravens. The chainmail suit that he wore under his clothing felt uncomfortable. He tried to hitch it up under his ruff. It was ungainly attire, to say the least, but he was glad of it. Continuing his ascent, Robert pondered over possible attackers. He soon gave up. He and Elizabeth had far too many enemies to consider each individually. Reaching the top of the stairs, he heard the pleasant sound of his lover's sweet laughter.

Chapter 21

Something Seriously Amiss

Jock and Moses dragged their bound captive down twenty cold stone steps into an underground cellar. A brazier of hot coals had warmed only a small part of the damp storage space. The chill, mouldy atmosphere gave Saul the shivers. Although he had witnessed torture and execution he had never actually been involved before. The prospect was daunting. An assortment of carpentry and blacksmith tools lay on a small table next to the fire. One at a time, the young man picked up each to study. Shanny stoked the fire. She had been crying. Remando had died in her arms during the rough river crossing. Loathed to leave him in an abandoned wherry, she had begged Jock to take his body ashore. In the heat of the moment, her lover had pulled her away from her surrogate father. The Scotsman had wound Remando's rosary beads around his hand before throwing his corpse into the Thames. Shanny had been so shocked by his actions that she had accepted them. Jock knew that a burial at sea would be what the old pyrate would have wanted.

Although she despised the Queen, Shanny dreaded the torture. Even though she was well-used to watching condemned criminals die, she had always hated the thought of prolonged agony. Everyone present knew that this was exactly what their royal prisoner was about to endure. Unsheathing a large knife Saul cut the rope to release the motionless captive. Although still unconscious, Lettice groaned in pain as she was rolled out onto the icy-cold floor. Large pieces of seared skin had torn away from bone as it had stuck to the coarse woollen blanket. The stench of burnt flesh wafted Shanny's way. A sickly sweet, putrid smell filled her nostrils, so rich that she could almost taste it. She puked up the contents of her stomach. Luckily Saul's stomach was stronger. He managed not to bring anything up but gagged all the same. 'The wench hath a stink o' tanned leather o'er a flame', he complained, covering his nose and mouth with his hand. As if sensing her imminent torture, the Queen's niece tried to raise her hand in defence. She turned her ruined face away from the brazier. Her pain was excessive. What was left of her skin appeared to be dark brown leather. Bone and charred muscular tissue was exposed in several places. Skin on her face and neck resembled molten wax. Lettice was a monstrous sight to behold. Full rosy lips that had been painted so carefully before the celebration had been completely burnt away. From now on, her teeth would be bared in a permanent grimace.

'Awaken, Yerrr Rrroyal Highness!' Jock's voice bellowed. Lettice's shrivelled carcass twitched. She screamed as she realised that the eyelids on her left eye had fused together. Lifting her hand to her disfigured face she panicked when she saw that her fingers had also melted together. Grabbing the victim by the ankle, Jock pulled her naked body across the floor. The suffering woman's shrieks were blood-curdling. Shanny turned away, unable to watch her lover's cruelty. The amber glow of the fire allowed the captors a clear sight of the extent of her wounds. It was incredible that she had survived. 'Tough ol' harrrlot, th'arrrt!' growled the

Scotsman through gritted teeth. ''Tis tha' rrroyal blood!' he sneered sarcastically. Liquid puss seeped from damaged muscle tissue as Lettice begged for mercy. She tried to sit up. 'Ny nane…', Shanny winced at every painful word as the injured woman tried desperately to explain her identity, 'Lay…ee…Knol…' Jock struck her across the face with the back of his hand. Hitting the side of her head on the stone floor Lettice let out a horrible sound. She tried, but failed, to lift her head. Muscle and sinew was exposed on her visible cheek and her hairless scalp had fused to her skull. She still wore a beautiful jewelled necklace and several rings. A diamond earring had become part of her neck. 'Strrrip herrr Majesty clean!' Jock had uttered the words his lover had been dreading to hear.

As Shanny performed the gross task she retched and heaved until every piece of the cringing burn victim's jewellery had been removed. Grabbing the large key from Moses, she hurled herself up the narrow steps and unlocked the door just in time. Bursting out into the cold, lonely night, Shanny heaved uncontrollably. Bitter bile stung the back of her throat as she gasped for air. 'Nay mo'er'!' she spluttered. Hardly able to see the other side of the deserted street, the pyrate wench cursed the smog. Knocking back the contents of her flask, no amount of alcohol would rid her of the vile smell of charred human flesh. Reluctantly, Shanny went back inside. The scene that awaited her was gruesome. As Lettice begged for her life Jock had allowed her the privilege to explain. None of the gang had witnessed the full extent of the tough pyrate's anger until then. After listening patiently to her story, Jock refused to believe that Lettice was not the Queen. The others had agreed with him. The tragic soul sobbed whilst laughing at the same time. This nonsensical situation had driven her mad. Lettice was not surprised that she had failed to convince her captors that she was telling the truth. Even she would never have believed that Elizabeth would allow someone else to bask in her glory.

Shanny froze on the spot. There followed a brutal torture. Abadeyo and Babatu poured a cauldron of boiling water over the hysterical woman's breasts; the only part of her body that had not been severely burnt in the explosion. Jock took a cudgel and smashed every bone in both feet before all of the men urinated over her. Finally, Jock branded Lettice's chest with the papal symbol of crossed keys. When she lay helpless before him in a puddle of piss, blood and vomit, she still insisted that she was not the Queen. Finally having to accept the awful truth, Jock could not believe how this had happened. This poor wretch had been double-crossed and so had they. The woman responsible for Sushana Culley's death was still alive. Jock promised to let Lettice go on condition that she took a message back to the Queen. She was told that the Spanish were to attack the following week. Knowing that the Queen would order the immediate deployment of her navy before enemies could breech her shores Jock hoped that Grace's army could then successfully sack the city. The fight was now in the hands of the Fianna Fail. If royal blood was to be spilt then he knew no other more capable of the deed than the Irish pyrate queen and her New Model Army.

Abadeyo and Saul volunteered to take Lettice back to the Tower. Although the others objected, they insisted. Someone had to do the job. The brave men hardly spoke on the journey back to the Tower. Both knew that it would be a near impossible task to escape after dropping the victim where the guards would find her. Young Saul was terrified but glad that he would be with his African friend at the end. Both armed with four loaded flintlock pistols and two sabres, neither one was prepared to die without dragging as many of the Queen's Guards as possible down into the depths of Hades with them.

Chapter 22

A Twist to this Tudor Tale

The pyrate captain walked into the gang's prearranged meeting place just inside the city walls. To keep the original name, the landlord of the Pope's Head Tavern had commissioned a derogatory anti-Catholic sign depicting the Holy Father's severed head on a pike. The Irish pyrates had been disgusted at the sight of the crude painting. Patrick had only just managed to talk Danny out of blowing the place 'skoy hoy!' as he had suggested. A cumbersome wench filled the captain's tankard with ale. He took a seat in a dark corner next to Shanny and Babatu. Moses, Jock and Shrimp were already supping ale at the next table. They all looked desolate. Patrick noticed Jock's swollen, bloodied fists. 'Numbers ain't good. Less' n 'alf o' us present', he remarked shaking his head. Ordering another large pitcher of ale Jock delivered some bad news, 'Rrremando perrrished.' Shanny's doleful eyes met Patrick's. He blinked and looked down. 'May God rest his dear soul' he whispered, crossing himself in respect of the devout Catholic. On hearing Jock's account of the mistaken captive the captain bit down on his bottom inner lip. He could not get his thoughts straight. The metallic taste of blood awakened his senses. 'Anthony?' he asked hesitantly, then listed the other missing men forgetting the hunchback. The pyrates shook their heads, shrugging their shoulders. Jock praised Saul and Abadeyo for their act of blind courage having volunteered to return the hostage. Deep down, everyone knew that their feat had been suicidal. 'Creppin's missin' too', Shrimp mumbled into his blackjack. Moses sat bolt upright, watching the door. He stood up and signed to Patrick that he was going to take a piss and scan the street for any stragglers. With a faint glimmer of hope, the captain nodded at his loyal friend to signal gratitude.

Patrick was devastated. Worried sick, he had no clue who had been captured, maimed or killed. The latter would be favourable. If the Royal Guards had arrested anyone then their fate had been sealed in a tragic finale. Although the captain had made Anthony a promise that he would not do anything stupid should anything go wrong, he was his mother's son. Every one of the Culley clan had always done what the hell they wanted. Deciding to take a risk, he left the inn. He scoured the bustling city streets on a last frantic search to locate his friends. In spite of grave danger, Patrick was determined not to leave until everyone had been accounted for.

On hearing the town crier's bell Patrick's legs turned to lead. He had been walking for hours and was numb with cold. The announcement made his very soul burn in hopeless anguish. The booming voice delivered the tragic news, 'Oh yay, oh yay! The treasonous son of the executed pyrate captain, Sushana Culley, hath been captured!' A second broadcast confirmed that Patrick had been taken to the Tower where he would be tortured and then hung, drawn and quartered for treason. At first the information did not sink in. How on earth could they…? The foul truth hit Patrick like a shot piercing his brain. He was horror-stricken. Absolutely furious with himself, he realised that Anthony had been arrested. The valiant fool must have claimed to be Patrick Culley!

The captain should never have allowed the young blacksmith's involvement in such a perilous conspiracy. Wringing his hands in exasperation he had no idea what to do. Pacing up and down the cobbled street the frantic man tried to make sense of an impossible dilemma. How the hell had he been so stupid! Ever since he had met the friendly lad, Patrick had felt sole responsibility for his safety. Anthony had risked everything and, eventually, had been made to pay the price for honouring a dead pyrate queen. Anthony had been raised as a blacksmith and had everything going for him until he had attended Patrick's mother's execution. The fates had been cruel to the kindly man.

A skinny young beggar held out a filthy hand. 'Pri'thee, spare a penny sir?' he whined. The captain stopped and took a golden cob from his pouch. As he went to put the valuable coin into the hungry boy's cold palm he caught a glimpse of the words that both he and his mother had tattooed on their wrists; Alea iacta est. The die is cast. Not quite believing his luck, the beggar's eyes widened in astonishment. He thanked the stranger as he walked away. Patrick's mind calmed a little. As the rain began to pour down, he broke into a run. It did not take him long to navigate through the busy streets and back lanes that led to the Red Lion. When Mabel greeted him she asked whether he had seen Violet. She seemed very concerned that the actress was not in her room. Grabbing his bags Patrick told the innkeeper that he would go and look for her. 'Oh. By the way,' he said as he left, 'Have tha seen anythin' of Creppin?' 'Ay,' she said, 'Nay 'alf an hour since. 'E came back ter collect all 'is stuff.' 'Well, he's safe, at least,' thought the captain, but the hunchback was the least of his concerns as he headed for 'The Theatre'.

Deep in the dungeons of the Tower of London, Anthony lay in heavy chains. He had been confined in a tiny cell known as the 'Little Ease'. Unable to move, he lay helplessly in the four-foot square hole; the most uncomfortable hold in the prison. When he was pulled out to be dealt further torture he could barely straighten his stiffened joints to stand. Norton, the Rack Master, was the most sadistic of the commissioners who had interrogated Anthony. The blacksmith already despised the monster who showed thorough glee as he put men through agonising torture. Norton had ordered a Catholic priest to be suspended in 'the manacles' between torturous stints on the Rack. As the iron handcuffs held him suspended from the ceiling, the priest's feet could not reach the floor. Dislocated bones meant that sinews and ligaments stretched painfully as they took the strain of body mass. The pain was so intense that the poor victim often passed out, only to be roused again by his callous tormentor.

Anthony endured ten days of ruthless torture. Despite their sadistic efforts, the brutal torturers were unable to force him to reveal the identity of any accessories. Every time he regained consciousness the brave and helpless victim spat at his tormentors. They would then take great pleasure in beating him until he passed out again from excruciating pain. Anthony's fingernails and toenails had been ripped off, one by one. He felt inwardly amused at a fleeting ironic thought. A common farrier like he had once been, had probably been commissioned to make the tongs that his punishers used to butcher his body. Hell's fire, some of the torture tools were similar to those that he had used in his innocent trade.

On the 4th of July in the year 1579, Anthony Brown, a humble blacksmith's son, took the place of his blood-brother, Patrick Culley, at his trial for High Treason. Due to the horrific extent of his injuries the guards had to tie him to a board to carry him to court. Despite enduring ten days of atrocious cruelty, Anthony never betrayed any of his twelve accomplices. He had not breathed a single word about any collaboration. In their frustration, his torturers had ensured that he suffered far worse than most. Still claiming to be the son of the infamous pyrate queen, Anthony was condemned to death for his heinous crime. The judge's words merged into a fluctuating drawl as they drifted in and out of the poor man's broken mind; 'Patrick Culley, on the morrow, thee shall be led to the place from whence thee came, and from thence be drawn upon a hurdle to the place of execution, and then thou shalt be hanged by the neck and, being alive, shalt be cut down, and thy privy members be cut off, and thy entrails be taken out of thy body, and, thee living, the same to be burnt before thy eyes, and thy head to be cut off, thy body to be divided into four quarters, and head and quarters to be disposed of at the pleasure of Queen Elizabeth's Majesty. And the Lord have mercy on thy soul.' Anthony managed to discern that he would be killed on the following day, the 5th of July. Blood spurted from the nostrils of his broken nose as he let out a snort of laughter at the irony of his final destiny. It had not even been a year since he had witnessed his heroine, Sushana Culley's, execution. Now, he had chosen to be executed in the guise of her son!

As reality suddenly hit him the condemned prisoner felt nauseous dizziness. Heaving up dark yellow bile onto his filthy, sweat-stained shirt, he yelped as he felt a heavy blow to his stomach. 'Da'' he managed to mutter. Heaven knows why he had called out for his dead father in his hopeless despair. 'Battan tha' filfy maaarf afore oy daz it faaaw yers!' the guard put his face right up to Anthony's as he spat the command between rotten, gritted teeth.' It all happened in an instant. A single shot exploded above. Anthony heard the unpleasant sound of the spinning lead ball as it penetrated the back of the guard's skull. Eyes wide with shock, the man's face turned waxy and grey. When he lifted a hand to feel the gaping hole that had been blown into his forehead his body slumped forward onto Anthony as the mangled remains of his brain died. Struggling to breathe under the dense weight of the corpse, the blacksmith tried hard to raise his head to see who had fired the fatal shot.

Chaos ensued in the overhead galleys of the courtroom. A man leapt over the railings, landing only an arm's breadth in front of the pompous judge's stand. As Anthony strained to hold his head up high enough to see the barrel of Danny's pistol pointing right at him, he witnessed a quick flash as it discharged. Feeling the bullet graze his temple the condemned man dropped his head in dismay. He tasted the bitter blood of the dead guard that still seeped slowly from the fatal wound. If only he had not tried to see who was trying to help him, his nightmare would now be over. All he could see was a bright white light, caused by the flare of Danny's weapon. Danny roared a defiant Irish Gaelic call, 'Erin go bragh!' before he was run through with a rapier. Anthony realised that the dying man had flung his rosary when he heard a clatter as it landed on the polished oak floorboards behind him.

The jeers and yells from above became a muffled hum. In his semi-conscious state, Anthony tried hard to focus on the faces that made up the blur of the animated crowd. Chaos reigned. Commoners who watched from the public galleries spat down on the prisoner and the corpse of the loyal Irish pyrate who was finally at peace. The blacksmith had lost what would probably be his only chance of being put out of his misery. Danny was the last man who Anthony would have expected to sacrifice his life to help ease his comrade's agony. With his head pounding in screaming pain he lay, dumb-struck and powerless, awaiting his next plight. The blacksmith thanked God when the hooligans' frenzied cheers faded into a muffled hum. The image of the flawless courtroom blurred into a murky swirl. The petrified prisoner emptied his bladder and blacked out.

Chapter 23

A Traitor Begs for Royal Reprisal

Elizabeth felt wonderful! Laughing Dick had provided perfect company since the failed assassination attempt and Raleigh had hardly left her side. She had received every man in her court at the Tower which was deemed the safest place for her to stay until the navy had dealt with the impending attack from France and Spain. Many had brought their Queen exquisite gifts and she was determined to make the most of the latest assassination attempt. Elizabeth had not experienced any head pain in days and felt refreshed and ready to put 'her eyes' out of his misery. Feeling a rush of excitement at the thought of her lover's reaction at the revolting sight of his wife's face, the vindictive Queen smiled. Dressed in a simple gown of green silk over a high-necked chemise with standing collar and intricate lace ruff, she fanned herself calmly. Subtly embroidered silk gloves that exposed long slender ringed fingers had been scented with her divine perfume. Elizabeth was very proud of her elegant artistic hands. Her late mother's had been almost identical. She kept admiring them as she imagined Robert's lips paying tribute to their beauty once more.

Inviting John Dee, the Royal Astrologer, to walk with her in the gardens, Elizabeth fanned herself gently with an ostrich feather fan. Thankful for having been blessed with a bright sunny day, the Queen had chosen to wear a delicate French veil to protect her thickly made-up face from the warm rays of the summer sun. She looked stunning. Her ladies-in-waiting had arranged her large veil over her head and shoulders to create the impression of the finest faerie wings. The delicate silk was shot through with silvery strands to create an illusion of a constant fluttering movement when the sun's golden rays caught their reflection. Dick danced ahead of the intelligent pair as they discussed Elizabeth's latest 'gravest concern'. Dee was sweating profusely. Gloriana's cool, calm and collected presence made him feel even more stifled and uncomfortable in the heat. Elizabeth laughed at her jester as he tiptoed around the lavender maze. Slowing her pace, she spoke in a hushed whisper, 'I hath need of thy skills.' Dee wiped the sweat that had accumulated on his brow. 'Pray, how can I assist, Ma'am?' 'Elizabeth,' the Queen corrected her addressee curtly. 'For God's sake! Thou art worthy to address thy monarch by our Christian name.' Dee was taken aback by the invitation to become more familiar with his powerful friend. He nodded his gratitude, subconsciously dipping a slight bow. Satisfied, Elizabeth shared her concern, 'Verily, a death-curse doth prowl our Boleyn spirit.' She referred to her mother's maiden name, a rare occurrence. Suggesting that they continue their conversation in a safer place, Elizabeth picked up her pace. Dee strode after her. He followed the Queen into the Chapel of St. Peter ad Vincula where Laughing Dick was already kneeling in prayer. 'Our jester hath faith far superior than his fellow mortals.' Elizabeth said proudly, in subtle referral to her own divine faith. The rustle of many layers of her silk skirts and tinkling golden trinkets fitted well in the small private chapel.

The regal Head of the Church swept through the holy building with an almost celestial yet demure manner.

A messenger brought word of Dudley's arrival. Totally focused on the advice that her astrological mentor was giving, the Queen ordered that her lover be taken to the Great Hall. This was where her chief advisor, the Lord High Treasurer, had also been taken to await her presence. She had summoned the counsel of William Cecil to check on the state of her Royal Trust. There were several properties owned by the Crown that she wished to sell before they fell into too bad a state of repair. The scorned woman would make her Robin wait on tenterhooks. Elizabeth was going to prolong her faithless lover's mental torture.

Robert was made to wait for five long hours before his lover decided that he had suffered sufficient torment. Since he had no idea why he had been summoned to the Tower he felt tense and nervous. Elizabeth had purposely chosen the most airless section of the palace for him to await her presence. Lately, the weather had been intolerably oppressive and everyone was feeling the toll. Exhausted and thirsty, Robert had rung the large tasselled bell rope several times to summon a servant. Having not heard a stir in the building since William Cecil had been escorted elsewhere over three hours earlier, he was beginning to feel uneasy. Knowing his Bess all too well Robert was positive that she had something sinister in store.

Elizabeth's demeanour had changed considerably. On entering the Great Hall she greeted Robert formally, giving him little eye contact. When he bent to kiss the back of her gloved hand she did not let him linger. Laughing Dick was dressed in a fluffy grey suit complete with long tail and donkey ears attached to the bonnet. Robert could not conceal his laughter when Dick kept shaking his tail. How on earth he managed to flick it around, he had no idea. Realising that Elizabeth had asked her friend to dress as an ass to mock him further, Robert tried to stay calm and allow her the pleasure. After all, he had deserved the mistreatment having not spent much time with his mistress of late.

On many a happy occasion, Robert and Elizabeth had walked to the Queen's Apartments together. Today, the mood was sombre. Laughing Dick bucked ahead of the silent couple who had never before felt awkward in each other's company. 'Eee-orrrrr! Thoin toim is nigh!' the comedic character bayed in a creepy fashion. Sweat dripped from Robert's brow. Clutching a silk-wrapped parcel for his lover, he was reluctant to give it to her. 'My Bess…' he tried to address the Queen who walked two paces ahead of him. Gracefully lifting a gloved hand she signalled for him to keep quiet. Taking a large key that had been tied to a long pink ribbon the donkey unlocked the door. It creaked open. The ass trotted into the room where Anne Boleyn had been pampered before her coronation and imprisoned before decapitation. Robert's dry mouth caused him to cough. Spluttering uncontrollably, his eyes poured with water and he was unable to talk. Finding it difficult to breathe, the troubled man had to squat down. It took him a good few seconds to compose himself. Swallowing the smallest amount of spittle that he only just managed to produce, Robert stood tall and took a deep breath. What the hell was Elizabeth going to surprise him with? He stepped over the threshold. Laughing Dick bolted past, faking terrible fear: An extremely cruel hoax! Robert stepped inside the room.

Luxuriously decorated, the bedchamber had a four-poster bed with a comfortable down-stuffed mattress, fine linen sheets and the softest lambs' wool blankets. Averting his eyes, Robert could not bear to look at the horrific sight before him. A hideously burnt woman lay in the comfortable bed. She had been recovering slowly under the care of the Queen's Royal Physician. The bedchamber that Elizabeth had chosen for the patient had been whitewashed and painted with pink roses for her mother's pleasure. Despite the raging fire, Robert shivered. Stepping further into the room Robert felt an inexplicably bitter chill in the air. Two plain-looking ladies-in-waiting were immediately dismissed by the monarch. They whispered as they brushed past the stunned visitor. Robert was assured that they had been in constant attendance of his wife since her unfortunate mishap. The woman who he had not recognised stared at him from lidless eyes. Their eye contact only lasted mere seconds until Lettice could no longer bear the look of revulsion on her husband's face. Elizabeth had allowed Lettice to stay in her late mother's haunted room so that she could experience, first hand, the oppressively depressing atmosphere that lingered there. Anne must have sensed a constant, overwhelming sense of betrayal during her short reign. With great composure and patience, Elizabeth had explained to her house-guest that she had felt a similar sense of treachery on discovering her secret marriage to Robert. With cold detraction, the Queen delivered the same speech to her lover. No longer able to produce tears to soothe her sore exposed eyes Lettice whined a regretful lament. She was so glad to be alive and was desperate to leave the Tower.

The Queen left the couple alone for a while. She wandered through the grounds back to the Chapel of St. Peter. Entering the cold building she lit a taper from a torch flame. Taking a large unlit candle, she walked serenely over to the chancel and knelt on the cold stone slabs. Beneath one of these lay her mother's body. Melting the base of the candle, Elizabeth pressed it firmly down onto the paving. Lost in meditation, she lit the wick and lay down on the chilly floor. Ever since she had learned of her mother's final resting place, she had pressed her cheek close to the stone in the hope that she was right above her remains. Leaving the candle in its place, the saddened woman walked back out into the garden.

One of the Tower's resident ravens plucked worms from the rich earth. Elizabeth wondered if the bird was old enough to have witnessed her mother's beheading. She wandered aimlessly around to the spot where she had been told that a scaffold had been erected. Where she stood alone, William the Conqueror's great White Tower lay to the south. Her mother had only been made to walk a short distance from her Royal Lodgings to the place where she would be beheaded. The raven's caw reflected Elizabeth's lament. Had it read her thoughts? Following Anne Boleyn's early morning execution, her head and body had been left for her ladies-in-waiting to see to. No coffin had been provided. The two grieving women had placed Anne's head and body in an elm chest. This had once contained bow-staves that King Henry had given to her as a gift. The chancel paving stones were not lifted until late afternoon. Then, the loyal women had difficulty carrying the chest to the Royal Chapel. There, they had placed Anne's corpse in a shallow, unmarked communal grave. Two more ravens joined the other bird. Elizabeth studied them. The Raven Master cared for the sacred birds well, ensuring the safety of any offspring. His responsibility was immense as old English folklore foretells the ruin of the White Tower and England should the ravens ever leave its walls.

Lettice tried to conceal her face from her husband. It was obvious that her appearance sickened him. Robert promised that he would send regular payments so that she could live the rest of her days in comfort with her children. From that day onwards, they would want for nothing. Warning his wife to keep out of the public eye, and to never speak about him or the Queen, he told her that he would divorce her as soon as possible. He left the bedchamber. Returning to his Bess, Robert felt remorseful. Admittedly ashamed of marrying Lettice without her prior permission, he was told how his wife had also begged for forgiveness. Elizabeth assured him that she would allow her to live a quiet life in the country with her children, on the premise that she would never leave her home. Lettice had pleaded to keep Dudley's name and for their child, Robert, to retain his father's title. The Queen had refused to give her an answer. Having confessed his genuine deep remorse Elizabeth dismissed her lover and ordered that he be banned from court. As Robert stepped into an awaiting barge, he heard the Queen's frenzied screams. He hated leaving the woman he loved in such a state. Thankful that she still loved him, Robert touched the back of his neck. Had their bond not been so strong, he would surely have lost his head by now!

Yelling for her guards, Elizabeth tore off her veil and hitched up her skirts. She ran hard and fast. A sudden urgency to remove the burnt carcass that lay festering in her late mother's bed overwhelmed the maddened Queen. She was like a woman possessed. With venom in her heart bitter enough to rot her very soul Elizabeth cursed Lettice before ordering her guards to throw her out of the palace. Anger towards her late father scorched her veins at the thought of the brute terrifying her mother with a threat of having her burnt alive. How Anne must have agonised before she was forced to admit that her marriage was invalid. Had she not done so, she would have perished by fire. As she ran swiftly up the spiral staircase towards her late mother's room, Elizabeth decided to go against her dead father's will. She vowed to honour her mother, Queen Anne Boleyn, with a plaque to mark her grave. The inscription would tell of her nobility and bravery. Tripping on an uneven step, Elizabeth fell in a howling heap at the top of the stairs. She now knew that she could not bear to be apart from her Robin. Without 'her eyes' she was surely blind.

Chapter 24

An Extraordinary Sacrifice

Anthony woke to the sweetest sound of pealing bells. He had slept on filthy straw that had been soaked in his own, and previous occupants', piss and blood. Anyone who had known the strong, muscular blacksmith would never have believed that he was the wretch that was pulled from a damp, stinking cell that fateful morning. His eyes had swollen into globular masses of infected puss. He had to prize apart bloody eyelids to be able to see. It was all he could do to kneel, let alone stand. Laden with heavy chains and fetters that restricted his movement, Anthony could not make his weak body function. Before he had chance to focus his painful eyes, two guards unlocked his cell. One grabbed him by the hair, the other by a floppy, shattered arm. They chatted casually as they dragged the prisoner roughly along the compact earthen ground. Anthony's cold body momentarily became boiling hot. He began to sweat profusely. His bottom jaw went into spasms making the few teeth that had not been ripped from his gums chatter uncontrollably.

It had taken just under two weeks for the fit, healthy blacksmith to be reduced to a battered and broken victim. He was now unable to walk unaided. His sorry state was a sickening sight to behold. Even the dim light from wall-mounted torches made Anthony's swollen eyes sting. He winced in pain. An ever-present nauseating stench filled the torture chamber. The poor man began to heave. Everything became a blur. He could just about make out one of the other captives, the Catholic priest. His wrists had been screwed into 'the manacles'. These iron 'gauntlets' were attached to a pillar so the helpless victim was left hanging with his arms above his head. His toes could not reach the ground. The flesh on the priest's hands had become hideously swollen and his fingers had turned black. Although the unfortunate soul had been subjected to barbaric punishment, he had steadfastly refused to denounce his Catholic faith. Anthony noticed that thick, dark blood was dripping from the priest's mouth. The bastards had even extracted his teeth. Too shattered to speak, Anthony managed to whisper, 'God be with thee'. His ruined body began to shiver. He felt himself going into shock. A hot sweat overcame him. His mind screamed aloud. How the hell was he going to find the strength to cope with what was about to happen?! The time had come. No going back now. He began to panic. Trying to lift his head to look for something to grab hold of and use as a weapon, he began to sob quietly. His sight faltered. Anthony's vision blackened. All he could see were tiny silver specks darting around wildly. 'Oh my God!' he thought. Soon, he would meet a ghastly end. He was going to be the main attraction of the execution spectacle that day.

As if hearing his fellow victim's silent plea, the priest began to pray. Despite the certain prospect of being subjected to even more punishment, the prisoner blessed Anthony as he was dragged past, 'God of power and mercy, thou hast made death itself the gateway to eternal life. Look with love on...' One of the guards let go of Anthony to head-butt the defiant priest. He called for reinforcement. More guards ducked under the narrow arched entrance into the horrific torture chamber. A small, fat man demanded silence from the priest, 'Shat tha' filfy' trap, papist!' he spat through rotten teeth and diseased gums. Despite his entire body suffering unimaginable pain, the devoted man was determined to complete his prayer for Anthony. Tears flowed freely as the blacksmith heard defiant screams over each repulsive thud of bludgeon smashing bone, '…our condemned brother, and make him…one with thy Son in his…' Despite taking a nasty blow to the side of his head, the priest managed to continue, 'su-suffering a-a-and d-death… that, sealed with the blood of Christ…he may come…before thee…FREE FROM SIN. AMEN!' His final words had been screamed aloud to be sure that Anthony had heard. The tortured holy man's limbs had already been crushed and split by contraptions that had been purposely designed to inflict maximum injury without causing death. Pieces of bone protruded from the priest's gaping, festered wounds. The guards continued to beat him long after he had fallen silent. Anthony stumbled out through the damp, dripping corridor into broad daylight. Gasping desperately as sweet fresh air filled his lungs, he mouthed a silent prayer of thanks. He hoped to God that the priest had finally joined his maker.

Thrown onto the barge floor Anthony left the Tower via Watergate. Prisoners on their way to their execution were always taken via this route. As the barge passed under London Bridge the condemned was forced to look at the severed heads of recently executed traitors. Each had been rammed firmly onto a spike attached to a long pole. These were mounted on the roof of the stone gatehouse.

When the barge reached the disembarkation point, the prisoner was dragged out onto the landing stage. Heavy chains that weighed him down were replaced by coarse hemp rope. Anthony was then tied to a hurdle. Two beautiful horses dragged the blacksmith to Tyburn where the gallows awaited. The crowd in London were far more vicious towards pyrates than anyone had been at Sushana's execution in Plymouth. As the prize prisoner for the main entertainment event, Anthony was pelted with stones, rotten food and excrement. Some children even threw dead rodents. The hustle and bustle was comparable to any other market day. Vendors sold wooden puppets with nooses around their necks. One bright businesswoman had even made ragdolls with a hole in their middle. Anthony watched in horror as a dirty-faced child waved her pyrate doll right in front of his eyes. She delighted in pulling out woollen intestines for him to see! The most popular dolls were dressed as pyrates. In the capital city, they had become the most favoured criminals to watch die.

On arrival at the gallows Anthony witnessed several executions. Two of these had been dreadfully botched. As he watched a child, no more than six years old, piss himself as a noose was placed around his scrawny neck the blacksmith felt newfound rage. His heart pumped adrenalin around his veins as instinct made him struggle against his bonds. Anthony watched helplessly as the executioner lifted the malnourished child onto a wooden stool. The boy was beside himself with fear. He stood, frozen on the spot, staring at the mocking crowd as they shouted obscenities. It was obvious that the urchin had been caught stealing. No-one was interested but the boy's name was Jacob Briggs. His friends and family had called him Jake for short. A row of young lads stood right at the foot of the gallows. Their front-row position had not been due to chance. Without a doubt, they had been put there to be taught a valuable lesson. The children's eyes widened as they watched every terrifying moment of their friend's hanging, right up close. When the stool was kicked from under him, they witnessed his small body jolt at the end of the rope. Jake began to thrash his legs violently. His fingernails came clean off as he scrabbled desperately at the coarse rope, trying to release the grip on his neck.

The crowd cheered. Hats were thrown into the air as wee Jake's face became engorged. His beautiful blue eyes popped out of their sockets. The child had been caught whilst trying to cut a leather purse from a tailor. The canny businessman always inserted wire into the drawstring cord that he secured to his belt. This made it near impossible for a thief to cut through first time so they would always be caught in the act. Jake's mother was a widow who watched her youngest son's undernourished body kicking and thrashing in a frantic fight for survival. She was beside herself as he fought for his breath. 'E's a-dayncin' the Tyburn jig!' a teenage boy yelled out in glee. Everyone laughed as the victim pissed and defecated. It took his bravest friend about three minutes watching Jake suffer before he could no longer stand the trauma. Ducking swiftly under the scaffold, he grabbed onto his pal's legs. The extra weight immediately broke his neck. Blood seeped from Jake's nostrils, mouth and anus. His tongue lolled out onto his dimpled chin. The lad's suffering was finally over. His small body was cut down and dropped unceremoniously onto the ground below. In total disbelief, Jake's mother struggled through the crowd. She would have to pay a fixed price to claim her son's body.

The criminal next in line to die was an old woman. Her crime had been heresy. After continually refusing to denounce her Catholic faith she had been condemned to die. As a noblewoman, she had been far more fortunate than the Catholic priest who she had harboured during times of Protestant rule. He had been reported by a visiting clergyman who had discovered a hiding hole under the stairs of her magnificent stately home. The two were arrested soon after. Both parties flatly refused to convert to Protestantism. The young executioner, who had been hired that day, was extremely nervous. This was his first attempt at beheading a live victim. Although he had practiced many times on cadavers, he could not imagine how successful his strike would be in this situation. He was sweating so much that he could not get a decent grip on the handle of his axe. The stubborn old woman was led up the steps to the gallows. She stood before the nervous young man. Shaking her head vigorously, she was angered when a Protestant priest read her last rights. The crowd found it hilarious when they heard Lady Arlington's age. She was positively ancient at eighty two years old! No-one was interested in her crime as it was read aloud. Everyone expected this one to be boring. The quicker she went the better. Noisy boos and heckles literally fell on deaf ears as the faithfully religious old dear had not heard a thing in years. The bloodthirsty mob knew they were in for a special treat when the frail old lady refused to kneel before the young executioner. It was obvious that she was petrified. 'Hie thee, crone!' someone called. In defiance, she began to walk proudly over to the steps. What happened next was abhorrent.

When the inexperienced wielder of the axe ordered the condemned papist to stand still, she continued to totter away. The crowd erupted and began to throw rotten food. They had seen enough. Wielding his axe, the inexperienced executioner gave chase. 'Ooooo!' the crowd blared in combined revulsion when he buried the heavy weapon into the old lady's shoulder. She stumbled and screamed, horrified by the unexpected blow. Half the size of him, the condemned woman turned her head to face her attacker. He was clearly in shock as he dislodged the hatchet from her collar bone and aimed for a second strike. Falling to her knees in agony, Lady Arlington lifted her bony hands in defence. Screaming loudly, as deaf people do, she begged for mercy. The crowd roared, egging the executioner on. He struck again but this time at an angle. His heavy axe hit the victim's jaw. Panic-stricken, the noblewoman tried to hold her butchered face together. She managed to stagger to her feet. Again, the terrified victim tried to flee. With blood pouring from her wounds, she skidded helplessly on the slippery platform. The executioner was beside himself with alarm. Raising his weapon he dealt a quick series of hacks at his quarry's arthritic body. He yelled at her loudly, 'Be still!... Aggghhh!' The audience were appalled. Now sickened by the scene that they had initially found amusing a few witnesses began to cry out, 'God 'a mercy!' 'Oooooo!' 'End it, tha' fiend!' Old people were disgusted. Children began to cry. Many people had closed their eyes and began to pray.

The Queen's clergyman brought up the rich meal that he had recently enjoyed. Now he gagged on bile as he tried to get past the dreadfully mutilated woman. By now she had lost an arm. Her lifeblood sprayed the front row of spectators. Incredibly she still tried, in vain, to escape. Dragging her maimed, hacked body across blood-saturated boards, past large chunks of her own flesh, Lady Arlington finally expired. She had endured twenty five horrifying minutes of torment and suffering. The scene was gruesome. Sobbing and sickened by the botched killing, the crowd had lost their buzz. Covered in blood, the worst slaughterer that anyone had ever seen dropped to his knees in exhaustion. Begging for God's forgiveness, he threw his axe aside and shuffled over to the corpse. Sparing his victim further humiliation, he picked it up with care. Sickened to the stomach, he carried it down the steps and placed it gently on the cart that took the deceased away. The man was sobbing. The mob surged forward and began to chant. They were unhappy. The failed executioner was violently sick before he walked away with his head down.

Anthony watched in sheer despair as he waited for his time to come. He had been forced to watch the botched decapitation. He could not believe what had just happened. Now, it was his turn to face death. Terror enveloped him. Two burly guards pulled their prisoner roughly up the wooden steps to the platform where his executioner waited. Anthony froze. The hired killer wore a black hood with holes cut in front of his eyes to enable him to see. Already broken, bloody and bruised the poor young man felt absolute terror. Finding it difficult to stay on his feet, Anthony's legs felt as though they would buckle beneath him at any minute. Thankfully, the weak man managed to stay upright when forced to stand on a stool. His heart pumped faster and faster as a noose was placed around his neck. Anthony tried hard to remember how dignified and beautiful brave Sushana had looked as she stood before the crowd at her execution. Try as he might, he could not actually visualise her. Jaw clenched tightly, a searing pain filled his head. His mouth was so dry he would give anything for a single drop of water. The condemned nodded bravely at his executioner. Looking down at the pouch tied to his belt, the blacksmith signalled with his eyes for him to take payment. Containing coins that each of the gang had been given to carry, in case of situations like this, the moneybag was pulled from Anthony's belt. The satisfied executioner then knelt before a priest who gave him a blessing in the name of the Queen.

Bedlam ensued as the crowd erupted. Yelling loudly they taunted the new prisoner. The noise was unbelievable. London mobs were far more raucous than any Anthony had encountered during his spectating years. Silently he wished that he had never attended any! Who would have ever imagined that he was to become a victim! Closing his sore eyes, he did not want to see any faces in the crowd. His head ached so badly. Ruthless pain pounded his temples. Thoughts raced through his mind: What in hell's name should he think about to dispel the horrific thoughts of the suffering he was about to endure? Heaving uncontrollably, he tasted more bitter bile. He gulped it back quickly. With eyes still firmly closed, he could just about hear the priest going through the motions. Not a single word registered in his addled brain. All of a sudden the stool was kicked from beneath him and the noose tightened around his thick muscular neck. It had begun. The mob cheered. Despite urging himself not to, he struggled so hard that the rope tightened even more. After a few minutes of sheer panic, as he fought for his life, the poor man's body went into uncontrollable spasms. Shit and piss spilled from Anthony's bladder and bowels. To the crowd's absolute delight, he ejaculated for the final time before losing consciousness. Sadly, this was nowhere near the end of his brutal torment.

Anthony was cut down and revived for the next stage of his punishment. Cold water brought him rudely back to his senses and although he could see angry faces in the crowd, their yells and screams were now completely muted. The two guards grabbed the prisoner and threw him down the steps of the gallows. When his body hit the ground, he was kicked, punched and spat upon. Before he lost consciousness again, one of the Queen's Guards grabbed him by his long hair. Taking a horse's tail in his other hand, he tied the two together and yanked the knot hard to make sure it was secure. Anthony noticed how poorly shod the carthorse was. The farrier even felt pity for the poor horse that dragged him, face down, around the streets. Feeling too weak to lift his head to avoid jagged, uneven cobblestones Anthony's teeth were smashed and his lips and face torn to shreds. He tried to spit out broken teeth, mud and shit that went into his mouth as he was pulled through the filthy gutters of England's capital city. It seemed like an age before his final journey came to an end. They had arrived back at the foot of the gallows.

Warm urine ran down between his legs and he vomited when he saw that the executioner had prepared a cauldron of hot coals. Petrified, drained and in sheer agony, Anthony was, once again, dragged up the rough wooden steps. This time he was nailed, through his wrists, to a large pillar to allow the crowd the best view of the most gruesome of punishments that was ever dealt. He could feel the scorching heat of the blazing cauldron beside him. He began to freak out. Sick with fear, he managed to summon enough strength to tear one of his hands free, the huge iron nails ripping the tendons from his wrist. The power of the mind is incredible when it is faced with terror. Although he was aware that escape would be impossible, all the poor man wanted to do was fight for survival. Fuck, he wished that he could just give up! Onlookers were delighted to witness the young man put up a fight despite futile odds of survival. Punters groaned and swore loudly as they lost wagers when the victim had survived past their predicted time of his death.

As he watched his executioner sharpen a long, curved knife, the horrified victim bit down on his tongue to prevent himself from screaming aloud. Knowing what was about to happen, Anthony tried to grab the sharp blade of the executioner's weapon. His severed fingers flew into the crowd. He panicked when he felt an icy cold, digging sensation as the knife sliced his penis and testicles clean off. This time he puked blood and bile. Unfortunately, his terrible injuries had not caused him to pass out. Agonised cries further enthralled the crowd. They began to jump up and down in waves of hysteric elation. Sickening pain spread through Anthony's entire being. No longer able to distinguish whether it was hot or cold metal that carved his flesh, he felt every slice of the knife as the hooded butcher slit open his stomach. Biting off his own tongue to prevent himself from crying out again, Anthony closed his eyes tightly as his intestines were yanked out. All that he wanted was for the unbearable torture to cease. Whatever they did to him, he was determined never to beg for mercy. Patrick's honour was at stake, not just his own.

To Anthony's surprise, the executioner began to speak to him as he worked. Feeling uncharacteristic compassion for his remarkably brave prisoner he spoke gruffly, 'Shalt nay be long anon, lad'. He continued his gruesome work. Tears poured down the victim's cheeks. They soon dried in the searing heat. Anthony tried to focus on the fire that raged beside him. Strange to say, he felt no hatred towards the man who was causing him more agony than he would ever have believed possible to bear. 'Hold still, lad!' came an urgent voice from the slaughterer. 'Pain'll lessen if tha' dunna struggle!' Anthony stared in horror at his torturer. He was becoming desperate now. When the fuck was it going to be over?! The stench was repulsive; similar to that of a knacker's yard. Reluctantly, the blacksmith emptied his bowels. Unbelievably, he wished that he had not looked at the pretty young woman who was now pointing straight at him, laughing aloud. 'Why the hell should that bother him now?' he thought. 'No matter. It did!' he reminded himself with a short spurt of anger. It was the spectators' sin to force him to lose his human dignity.

The crowd cheered as the executioner finally fed his victim's lengthy soft pink bowels into the scorching flames. A small boy near the front spewed vomit. His father laughed and hoisted him up onto his shoulders. The grubby little lad covered his eyes. Anthony yelled aloud when the big man jabbed the charred intestines with a fork to prevent them from exploding. The pain was excruciating. Some children found it funny that the smell of burning human flesh was exactly like roasting pork. Laughing loudly, they taunted the victim with sick chants, 'Pay the 'angman afore 'e drops, so's 'e cooks the piggy 'til 'e pops!' Unfortunately, Anthony did not die until the executioner had already started butchering his body, a few minutes after he had hacked his way through two arms. When the victim had passed out a couple of times during the primitive amputation, the cruel crowd had thrown stones at his head to revive him. They were thrilled by the bloody spectacle and wanted to prolong such excellent entertainment.

It took an agonising four minutes for Anthony to die… after the executioner had severed the femoral artery of his left leg. Even the hardened hired killer was revolted by this merciless kill. Exhausted after finishing the final cuts, he used a chopper to hack through stubborn bone. Anthony was wild-eyed in terror as he finally faced death; the row of the mob became muffled. His body tensed. He listened to his final, wavering intake of breath. An oddly comforting sound of blood pumping weakly into his brain distracted him from the putrid stench of his own fear. The slayer shuddered as he finally chopped off the head of the bravest man he had ever encountered in over six years in his gruesome trade. ''Tis o'er now, son.' he whispered quietly, knowing that victim could still hear his words. 'May God grant thee eternal peace. Amen.' The crowd had reached fever pitch. No longer able to see, the final sounds that the heroic blacksmith heard above the raucous crowd was the baying of hounds and the toll of a distant church bell. There were tears in the executioner's eyes as he paid his last respects before holding Anthony's severed head high to face the hysterical mass. Covered from head to toe in his victim's blood, piss and, for the first time ever, his own vomit, the heavyset man prayed that he had been slow enough with dismemberment to have spared the victim from his final view of the hateful crowd. The last part of any beheaded victims' punishment was to experience more humiliation when their head was held up to face the mob. Their final sight was usually the spectator's glee as they watched them die.

Anthony Brown had certainly paid for his involvement in the assassination attempt. He had suffered an agonising death for another man's sins. He had died without naming a single accomplice. By his sacrifice, he had allowed a kindred soul freedom; the most precious gift of all. Anthony Brown's decapitated head was dipped in tar then rammed on a spike and displayed on London Bridge for all to see. Patrick Culley was officially dead.

CHAPTER 25

Hickford for the Price of a Winchester Goose!

The survivors of the assassination gang had planned to travel back to Ireland separately. Patrick knew that it would be impossible to save Anthony on the day of his execution and his friends had convinced him that a rescue attempt would be fatal. Grace awaited his return and if he risked his life, then the blacksmith would have died for nothing. Worried about Violet the captain had left messages at 'The Theatre' and with Mama Mabel in case she returned. As posters of 'Patrick Culley, infamous pyrate' were all over the city and beyond, he feared that his pregnant lover had recognised the likeness, guessed Peter's true identity and ran away to find him. Prepared to risk anything to let the actress know that he was safe, Patrick decided to stay in London for a while. He insisted that the others left for Eire.

With a faint hope that someday he would have the chance to take Violet to Ireland where she could give birth to their child, Patrick tried to stay positive. He went straight to 'The Theatre' to find out whether any of the actors knew where she was. She must have told someone where she was going. No-one knew a thing. Frantic with worry, Patrick travelled across the city and outside the walls on a fruitless search. Not knowing what else he could possibly do, the captain sat in the Red Lion awaiting Violet's return. She never showed. Mabel told him that she had been worried about the actress lately. 'I 'oped our Vi' 'ad cleared orf wi' thee, tha know? 'Andsome as th'art! Ne'er seemed roight neiver of thee 'ad told me, mind.' Without thinking, Mabel made matters worse by worrying Patrick. She kept harping on about how many times she had warned Violet about the theatre. Although Burbage was a true gentleman who looked after the actress when she pretended to be his young male star, Victor, Mabel would still worry herself silly until her pretty lodger was safely home. Most theatre-goers were 'bad sorts an' 'eathens!' as the landlady described them. Many of the plays were obscene which would stir the drunken crowd into becoming even more rowdy and horny. Patrick needed air. Land dwellings had always made him feel stifled and claustrophobic. He longed to return to the sea.

It was very late but the captain wanted to call in at Dick's pad before he went to bed. He knocked loudly at the front door. Em welcomed her late-night visitor and they enjoyed a nightcap. Violet's close friend became flustered when she heard of her disappearance. The simple girl had no idea where she could be. Assuring Peter that her friend was a decent girl and never went with punters, Em also told him that Violet would never have left without telling her. She started to cry when she told Patrick that the actress had declared that the artist was 'the one'. Unable to bear the prostitute's wails, Patrick made a quick getaway. He took a brisk walk to the next inn where he hoped that someone might know Violet's whereabouts.

When he reached the small drinking den Patrick went inside. Having chosen to sit on a bench in a dark corner, lit only by a single candle, the captain could not believe his ears. The hairs on the back of his neck stood on end when he overheard two drunken men talking. 'Olaf 'ickford 'e said 'is name was. Roight proud 'e was too o' the botchin'!' Shuffling along the long seat to sit closer to the boozers, Patrick felt a rush of horror and excitement at the thought of locating the executioner who had placed a noose around his mother's precious neck. Straining to hear the men's drunken slurs he downed his drink in one; 'E'd 'ad the nerve ter return ter Landun ter take advantage o' crowds an' beg!'. Patrick could not contain himself any longer. Interrupting the conversation, he offered to buy the men more ale. They were keen to accept the stranger's kind offer.

The two dockworkers told Patrick that Hickford had been bragging about his former position of Royal High Executioner when they had first met him. Having once been a citizen of Plymouth, one of them had recognised Hickford as 'the prat who 'ad botched that gorgeous pyrate captain's 'angin'.' Once again, the fates had allowed Patrick a spate of good luck. Having harboured pure, bitter hatred for the man who had dared to execute his cherished mother, he felt a strong sense of power. The pyrate's mind teemed with terrible ways of torturing Hickford. He hoped that the day had finally arrived when he could gain revenge on his mother's behalf. Apparently the arrogant oaf was staying at a nearby inn. Leaving a large pouch of coins for the dockworkers' priceless tipoff, Patrick headed for the place where Hickford was staying.

It did not take long for Patrick to find the hoodlum, who was boasting in his cups again. The pyrate captain eyed his pig-like human quarry with the air of an eagle owl. He approached Hickford. Plying him with plenty of strong ale, he eventually invited the arrogant fool to 'partake in a little bush-bonkin' with a 'lady of negotiable affections.' 'Huh?' the ignorant fool had responded without a clue as to what Patrick meant. Speaking in ridiculously exaggerated Queen's English Hickford added, 'Pri'thee maketh thine offer a little more plain...' 'Allow me to be blunt...' Patrick warned, trying hard to conceal his impatience, 'Wouldst tha' allow me t'offer thee a blissful hour o' crumpet... bonin'... pole polishin'... dippin' tha' wick...' Hickford's small eyes narrowed as the words registered. He sniggered into his tankard. Finally, the penny had dropped! 'Ahhhh, verily, I understand', the blubbery creep replied. Oh... how... Patrick... longed... to drive his mother's treasured disembowelling weapon... deep... into... Hickford's over-bloated gut! The captain would give his left arm to watch the oaf writhe before him as he tried to push back the intestines that spilled out of his gaping belly!

Hickford was eager for a session with the gorgeous young prostitute who the captain told him he had been with earlier. As they walked back to the Red Lion, Patrick felt hatred literally pummelling his brain. His mind egged his body on to deal a fatal blow to his archenemy. At long last, the inn was in sight. Hickford's flabby form disgusted Patrick. The spineless rapist stopped to piss. He was still blarting on about his many conquests at the top of his ludicrous voice. Mabel Brayne was surprised to see the artist back so soon. Patrick asked her for a quiet room for his companion and she offered him Twills' room which was the most soundproof. Perfect, he thought. Winking cheekily, the canny businesswoman promised to pour Hickford some mead whilst Patrick went to rouse Twills. Passing him a key to the prostitute's room, Mabel promised to send the 'gentleman guest' up ten minutes later. Hickford was more than happy to stay and flirt with the buxom innkeeper who was equally glad of his custom.

Patrick entered Twills' poorly-lit, smoke-filled bedchamber. Luckily, the sore-riddled woman was stoned on opium. Her heavy facial make-up was streaked with tears. Every now and then she let out a satisfied moan. The captain assumed that she had taken Creppin's departure badly but was now well and truly lost in a drug-enhanced erotic dream. An elaborate set-up of smoking equipment lay next to the semi-naked woman. Until now, the captain had no idea how scrawny and withered the unkempt wench had become. An air of contentment and carnal desire spread over him as the inhaled potent vapours began to take effect. Patrick shook his head and opened the window shutters wide to get rid of the lingering smoke. He needed a clear head to deal with Hickford. There was no way on earth he would allow himself to botch this golden opportunity of sweet revenge. Hiding the ornate tray and long pipe under Twills' bed next to the piss pot, Patrick crouched down low. Taking out his curved disembowelling knife the captain waited.

The drunken outcast, who had once held a prominent position in the Queen's army of torturers, knocked on the end door of the upper storey of the Red Lion. Groping his erection, Hickford looked forward to the indulgence that he was being treated to. It had been a while since he had fucked a consenting woman. Becoming more aroused at the memory of his last victim, Hickford untied the string that held up his tattered trews. The rapist had abused a young orphan girl so brutally that it was doubtful she would ever be able to conceive. As unoiled hinges creaked under the weight of the heavy ill-fitting door, the clueless whoremonger breezed confidently into the shadowy room. In his drunken state he did not care what the woman he was about to molest looked like. With his back turned to the bed, he began to undress.

Patrick regretted rushing the murder of Hickford. Turbulent rage that had built up inside him exploded in a frenzied attack. Pouncing on his loathsome quarry Sushana's son reigned blow after blow on his startled victim turning blubber into pulp as he smashed his large fists into bone. Having caused injuries more severe than he had intended the merciless pyrate could not stop his powerful punches until his knucklebones were completely exposed. Not finished yet, he bound his injured hands with rag before continuing to pummel his victim's broken face. This time Patrick used his elbows to cause grievous damage. Still high from his hyper-manic fit he stood over Hickford to admire the result of his violent assault. Both predator and prey were out of breath. Patrick panted as a metallic smell stimulated his senses into a primal need to finish his kill. Blood oozed from two flattened holes where the fallen High Executioner's nose had been. It bubbled as the beast fought for breath. Taking his disembowelling knife Patrick stooped to carve a large arc in his great underbelly. He heaved at the squelching sound when he pushed both hands inside to grab sloppy intestines. Poor little Twills sighed deeply and stirred. 'Slumber, Twillsy,' Patrick said calmly, using Creppin's pet name for her. Feeling intense euphoria, the skinny woman stretched slightly and smiled before returning to her sensual dream. Before leaving the room, Patrick wrote a short note for Violet. It simply said. 'Join me in Eire. Love always, Peter'. Leaving the message together with a substantial amount of gold with Mama Mabel, who had been like a mother to the actress, Patrick left London.

The following morning the body of an unknown vagrant was discovered by Mama Mabel. Her husband sold the mutilated cadaver to a physician who had immediately recognised the sailor's knot that had been tied in the victim's intestines. The medical professional paid much less for the emaciated body of the prostitute who had overdosed on opium. Mabel was so distraught by the incident that had happened at the popular inn that she had nailed up the door of Twills room. For years after the gruesome event, lodgers would hear unnerving giggling coming from behind the barricaded door. The smell of opium smoke was often reported by guests who stayed in the coldest part of the building. All of the girls dreaded walking along the corridor that led to Creppin's favourite prostitute's room. The Red Lion Inn was never the same again.

Chapter 26

A False Sense of Security

Elizabeth heard the cannon fire that she had ordered to begin the celebrations at the news of Patrick Culley's death. Finally the treasonous swine had been hung drawn and quartered, thought the self-satisfied Queen. She smirked as she imagined his head being shoved onto a spike that would now be in a prime position on the roof of the stone gatehouse overlooking London Bridge. A large sack of straw concealing a hefty reward had been dropped at a location that the unknown informer had marked on the map. A linkboy had been told by a mysterious person to pick it up and drop it off at a different location. The conniving creep had been sure to take numerous precautions to cover any tracks. Elizabeth was sure that it had been a cunning, well-educated person who had given her the tip-off. Possibly a woman, she reflected. She admired the informant's nerve but had no personal interest in his or her identity. As far as she was concerned, Patrick Culley was gone and that suited her perfectly.

On retiring to her bedchamber, the tall, slender Queen was sure that she would sleep soundly that night. England and her monarch were becoming more powerful as time went by. Sushana Culley's filthy rebel bastard of a son's head was now rotting on a spike. With the heart of a king, the Queen was ready to defeat any European country's prince who dared to invade her realm. If necessary, she was willing to take up arms herself. Robert had sent word promising that he would be faithful to his true love 'til he breathed his last. Bess's sweet Robin had been confident that he would be able to charm his way back into her life. He had been right. Having re-established his place in her heart as favourite, equal only to Sir Francis Drake and Admiral John Hawkins, the Queen had allowed him back to court. He had received so many death threats since the assassination attempt that he had become as mistrustful as his lover. He even started to sleep in the thin chainmail suit that he had worn under his day clothes for the past year. Having returned to his permanent lodgings at Elizabeth's court, Dudley quickly re-established a close friendship with Laughing Dick. He would often confide in the jester and seek his guidance on how to handle Elizabeth's volatile personality. The thoughtful comedian suggested that the Queen hold a masked ball to make Robert feel more settled but his hopes of reconciling Dudley with his peers were soon dashed.

John Hawkins' cousin, Francis Drake, was well on his way home. Having sailed from Guatemala he had stopped to repair the Golden Hind and restock dwindling provisions. Naming the region 'New Albion' he had taken possession in Queen Elizabeth's name. Already in possession of a Spanish map that clearly marked England's newly claimed area Drake shamelessly took the glory for its discovery. He had stolen the priceless chart from one of the treasure-laden galleons that had been raided on his latest voyage. Of course, this would be presented to his queen. Drake's account inspired an immense boost in national pride. England was rising in dominance over the vast oceans. Hawkins still felt deep bitterness towards the Queen who was responsible for his lover's and now Patrick Culley's death. Drake's popularity and ability to manipulate Elizabeth made him distrust the privateer. He never revealed his hatred of Elizabeth to his cousin who had been hailed England's newest hero. Drake was now a world-famous explorer. Grace O'Malley thought it best to keep the news of Patrick's survival from Hawkins. The admiral began to plot against Elizabeth which was exactly what the Irish pyrate queen needed. Hawkins still kept his word and regularly sent news of the Queen's plans and movements to Connaught but the Irish noblewoman still distrusted him.

In 1579, England's population and wealth were steadily expanding. Queen Elizabeth continued her outward-looking attitude and was keen to gain more profit in the wool and Eastern spice trade that Spain and Portugal had monopolised for far too long. New colonies were needed and she was determined to continue to extend her vast flourishing empire. Her greed intensified. Elizabeth's ambition was to rule as much of the world as possible. She confided in Dee who was confident that her lifetime astrological chart showed that only death would stop the most powerful woman who had ever lived. Elizabeth was happy to hear that her stars had foretold that she had many more golden years to reign.

CHAPTER 27

Return to the Vipers' Court

A few weeks after Robert's return to court, Elizabeth had sent him to Ireland to buy more horses. During his absence, she hoped that her back-stabbing courtiers would tire of bitching about her lover. Eventually the vipers would move on to demeaning another poor soul. On Robert's homecoming Elizabeth had thrown a banquet and ball. Musicians played lively music and Bess and Robin danced the Gilliard and the Volte, her favourite dances that many considered risqué. When Robin embraced his Bess and lifted her above his head, jealous tongues began to twitch, sounding their disgust. In an act of defiance to peeve gossiping sycophants the Queen had recently demanded that her skirts were shortened. Every time Robert lifted Elizabeth's fit, lithe body, the 'virgin's' dainty ankles were revealed to spectators.

The royal apartments soon became alive again with fiery exchanges between the two passionately obsessed lovers. When the Queen refused to allow Robert to visit his estranged wife and son, he challenged her vehemently. All staff disappeared when they heard the angry man yelling at his lover. Laughing Dick felt sorry for his dejected friend as Elizabeth had turned all of Robert's proposals down, including his last at Kenilworth Castle. Admitting that he had finally given in and married Lettice secretly having accepted that his one true love would never be his, Robert's plea was heart-rending as it echoed around the palace walls. 'What...in God's name...dost thou desire from me? For thine sake alone I have but hitherto forbore from marriage.' Elizabeth had Robert's undying love. She could never deny his absolute loyalty. The man was even despised for loving her! The stale-mate situation was fated to plague him 'til death. Bess screamed that she could not help loving the man who had taken her maidenhead. Trembling with anger, she roared, 'I plight thee my troth. I shall ne'er lie with another man!' In her dire state of melancholy, Elizabeth refused to accept anyone but Blanche and Dick into her chambers. Once again, Robert took her rejection to heart. Taking a huge risk, he left to visit his children.

Bubonic plague returned to cast its deathly shadow across England claiming almost a third of Norwich's citizens. Apothecaries began to employ tradesman to provide medicine further afield. Their trade became one of the most prestigious in the country. With one licensed medical practitioner for every four hundred in London, residents turned to unlicensed quacks who swindled desperate patients. Many passed off ineffective remedies as genuine medication. As access to doctors and medicines became more difficult, people began to practice herbal medicine again. Wise women used mandrake, datura, monkshood, cannabis, belladonna, henbane and hemlock in brews and ointments to aid a wide variety of conditions. Possession of any of these herbs that produced psychedelic effects was illegal.

Fear of witchcraft was increasing in Europe. The Catholic Church accused herbalists as devotees to satanism stating that 'those who used herbs for cures did so only through a pact with the Devil, either explicit or implicit.' As Witchcraft Law in England did not recognise sorcery as heresy, the Church had no part in the prosecution of witches. Queen Elizabeth was far more merciful to those accused of witchery than religious leaders in France and Spain. They were never put through torture during their trial and, if condemned, were hanged but never burned. Elizabeth continued to consult John Dee. Secretly, she feared that she too might someday be denounced as the witch whore-Queen's daughter so she had to make a point of being dead against the craft. Word had spread of the tragic plight of Lady Knollys who had become mysteriously disfigured; such an incredible coincidence, after the Queen had found out about her secret marriage to Dudley and the official birth of their child. Ugly rumours were now afloat that the Queen had bewitched Robert as 'Nan Bullen' had her father. Robert was detested by fellow courtiers who had begun to call him 'gypsy' because of his dark hair and eyes. Bess and Robin seldom argued unless the awkward subject of marriage was mentioned. Dudley enjoyed spending money on extravagant gifts for his lover and his possessions were copious and luxuriant. Many thought him arrogant and wasteful.

Dee, Robert and Laughing Dick had all encouraged Elizabeth to have laws set to ensure that all citizens attended church every Sunday Sabbath. If anyone failed to do so they faced arrest. Another law was put in place to ensure that children attended church every other Sunday to receive religious instruction. Despite the fact that Elizabeth swore like a trooper and spat and lashed out violently at people who annoyed her, she was overtly religious. One Sunday afternoon, a churchgoer found a waxen image of the Queen in a hedgerow near

Richmond Palace. Dee was summoned right away to counteract the evil spell. Rumours were beginning to spread around court that a witch was in their midst who wished death upon the Queen. No longer able to abide the venomous gossip that had been the very cause of her mother's condemnation, Elizabeth became so scared that she took to her bed. Everyone feared that she was beginning to lose her mind but she took it all in her stride and stayed out of sight for a few weeks until she felt strong enough. Then the rejuvenated monarch made an appearance to prove her mental stability once and for all. Having always preferred the company of men, Elizabeth did little to promote more rights for women. The ordinary woman was still ruled at home by the rod despite the realm being ruled by a dominant queen. Interestingly, her alter-ego sex slave, 'Bess', became even more submissive with every sweet stroke of her Master Robin's crop.

Chapter 28

Erin Go Bragh!

Back at Rockfleet Castle, Grace had heard news of Patrick's execution. She was devastated. Everyone was in mourning. The pyrate queen felt totally drained. She was so angry that Elizabeth had outsmarted their plot and was still alive. Rumour had it that the English Queen had been pre-warned of the assassination attempt and had sent her closest friend in her place. Grace wasted no time and decided to go ahead with the planned attack. A fleet of Spanish allies already lay in wait for the order to sail to England and begin Grace's war of vengeance. With Patrick dead, she had no other choice but to move in her Fianna Fail. Before she made any crucial decisions, the Irish noblewoman wanted to ensure that reports and information from her spies were accurate. All she could do now was await confirmation. Her army was ready and their spirits had been high until they had heard the awful news. Now, it was up to Grace to refuel their hatred and rouse their anger. As for their leader, she was already in a murderous state and more than ready to risk her life in a fight to overthrow the woman who had taken so much away from her.

In response to news of a foreign ship that had been spotted on her territorial waters, Grace yelled a Banshee scream. Jumping out of her window, she grabbed the thick rope that was fastened to her bedpost and shimmied down into a boat. Rowing out to a galley, she found her crew at the ready and wasted no time weighing anchor.

Very soon, the vessel's bow was slicing through the dark blue sea in pursuit of the unfamiliar craft. When she was within hearing distance, Grace's deep, threatening voice boomed aloud demanding payment for passage through her waters. When she saw Anthony standing tall and proud aboard the vessel, her heart leapt, 'Oy taaarldjers ye'd be back!' As the waves hissed and the sails flapped in a temperate wind, Grace steadied herself by gripping slippery wet boards with her bare toes. She was delighted that the blacksmith had returned to her. As her expert crew manoeuvred the ship closer, her confusion set in. 'Jaysus, Mary n' Joseph!' Crossing herself, she found it hard to believe her own eyes. Thanking God in silent prayer, Grace yelled aloud, 'Patrick! Oy tart yers were jed, me lad!' He yelled back but she strained to hear what he was saying. She watched her friend shake hands with the crew of the trade ship and waved a sign of dismissal of charge for passage. Shouting her thanks to the captain for her friend's safe delivery, she watched Patrick dive into the rough sea. When he climbed safely on board, she embraced him as a long-lost son. Ordering her crew to return to Rockfleet, Grace broke down with tears of relief and sheer joy.

The hardened pyrate queen could tell by Patrick's body language and demeanour that something was seriously amiss. She knew him well. Like his mother, he was never able to hide his feelings. When the ship had been secured, they climbed down into a boat and rowed to shore. They disembarked and embraced each other tightly. Grace's men ran out to greet the man who they had thought they would never see again. Patrick felt overwhelmed by the whole scenario and asked to speak with the pyrate queen in private. Everyone understood and began to talk, trying to fathom out what could possibly have happened.

Once they were alone, a sickening wave of dread overcame the pyrate queen. Suddenly she understood what had happened. She had been right all along when she had sensed Anthony's good heart. As Patrick explained the sad story of the blacksmith's ultimate sacrifice to save his blood-brother's life, Grace's face turned pale. She had served alongside many brave men but nothing had ever come close to Anthony's heroic sacrifice. When he was captured, Anthony had been well aware that he would be mistaken for his doppelganger. It had become obvious now that he had been planning this deception all along. Swallowing back bitter tears, Grace realised that his intentions had already been running through his head when she had told him of his uncanny likeness to Patrick. By deceiving the Queen of England into believing that Sushana Culley's son had been executed, Anthony had given them all a better chance to strike when the monarch was feeling far less vulnerable.

Grace felt sick to the stomach. What a shocking twist of fate. She grabbed a leather flask of poitín, took a good swig then passed it to Patrick. Neither felt the need for words. They just sat together and drank until their faces were as numb as their spirits. It was time to announce the news to the others who eagerly awaited an update. Patrick stayed put whilst he heard their shocked reactions in the room below. He took another mouthful of poitín when he heard Grace propose a toast in Anthony's memory. She included Sushana Culley and many other loyal souls who had lost their lives in the fight for liberty. Lying back on the rush-covered floor Patrick Culley felt the warmth of the comforting turf fire as he fell into a drunken slumber. Grace stood on the ramparts of Rockfleet and whispered into the wind. She had managed to summon renewed strength from within now that Shana's heir had returned. Determined to put an end to any English power over Eire, she vowed to continue fighting the cause until the day that she ceased to breathe. Patrick and Grace agreed that the fewer people who knew of Anthony's tremendous sacrifice the better. The heroic man had given his own life to enable Patrick to start a new life as one of Grace's pyrates fighting for her Irish cause. Together they would continue the battle against slavery and the Queen of England.

Chapter 29

Dumpish Bess

Elizabeth still felt depressed. She was sick to death of how everyone at court treated her lover. Dick entertained her for a couple of hours and then suggested that she ask Robert to take her to 'The Theatre.' She often accompanied her lover disguised as an ordinary wealthy lady. Decent women theatre-goers wore masks to protect their identity and the Queen always revelled in the excitement of anonymity. Robert would arrange for his players to put on certain plays that he knew his lover would enjoy. They would take a wherry across the river then hire a litter to carry Elizabeth to the venue. Robert's troupe of actors always made a real fuss of 'the beautiful mystery woman' during and after their performance. The Queen always lapped up the attention and enjoyed the exaggerated flattery. She was blissfully unaware that everyone present actually knew her true identity. For the Queen's safety the audience were scrupulously hand-picked by the Earl. Everyone entering the building had to show their invitation. The lovers had a wonderful night watching from the wings. Later, they returned to make love in the Queen's private bedchamber. As Elizabeth lay in Robert's arms, he comforted her as she wept. She felt safe and happy when they were together. It took a lot to make her cry but nothing hurt her more than being unable to marry her Robin.

Every morning Elizabeth would wake with the curse of the Boleyn family on her mind. Every night, her final conscious thought was of her mother's demise. She had often since tried to imagine how terrifying it must have been for her mother to face her father's wrath. Elizabeth's burden had always been heavy to bear. Ann Boleyn's greatest wish had been to give birth to a son yet in a satirical twist of fate, her only daughter now reigned as well as any king before her. The majority of her fickle citizens loved their monarch who had taken on the role of both King and Queen of England. She had brought hope and glory to a realm that had struggled under her male predecessors. In recent years, she had begun to publically refer to herself as 'prince' or 'king'. As time went by more men began to accept that King Henry VIII and Anne Boleyn's daughter had become a capable, fully empowered monarch who had earned for herself the envied position. The first Queen Elizabeth of England had broken the age-old tradition of a woman successor taking a subordinate role to rule jointly with a husband. By using cunning tactics, she had been able to appease would-be dominant princes by going through the motions of selecting a suitor but remaining single and officially childless. This had enabled her to keep the throne without fear of threat from usurpers.

A wise and worldly 'king' who regularly found inspiration during times of despair, Elizabeth took a new quill and added the final verse to her heart-felt poem. It was finished. Reading the words aloud she felt pleased with the prose that truly bared her soul.

> Some gentler passion slide into my mind,
> For I am soft, and made of melting snow;
> Or be more cruel, Love, and so be kind.
> Let me float or sink, be high or low;
> Or let me live with some more sweet content,
> Or die, and so forget what love e'er meant.

Elizabeth's words spoke volumes about her surreptitious relationship with her 'sweet Robin'. Wiping the tiniest diamond of a tear from her eye, King Elizabeth of England took to her bed.

CHAPTER 30

A New Beginning

A dark, ominous ship loomed above two tall, muscular black men who were busy loading heavy cargo. Miserable, drizzly rain always bothered the dandy character who stood on the gangplank. Captain John Clarke had given up relighting the damp tobacco that he had prepared in a long-stemmed pipe. Despite this fact, he still held it to his lips, purely out of habit. Occasionally, he shouted at the strong but slow-moving sailors to hurry them along. They paid him no heed and continued their duties at their own pace. It was totally out of character for the captain to be in such a bad mood and his two crewmembers were not going to comply. This visit had not been a good one, which was unusual for the Thames venue. John could not complain about takings but news of Patrick Culley's execution had upset the hard man. He had been very fond of the lad and their recent re-union had come as a pleasant surprise. The last thing he had expected was to hear that Patrick had been captured during an assassination attempt on the Queen.

John felt glad that he had escaped the life of pyracy. He recalled the day when he had left Shana Culley's ship with his small band of freaks. Captain Culley had been very supportive and had encouraged him to pursue his dream. Over the last few years, John had managed to build up his rewarding and lucrative entertainment business. His floating freak show had become a popular attraction. Every time they docked at a new port, people were waiting, keen to come aboard to see his macabre exhibits. John Clarke had witnessed too many young friends die during his short stint of swashbuckling on the high seas. Granted, his days of pyracy had been exciting but not worth the fear of the threat of the noose. He still had nightmares when he could actually feel the cursed hemp rope tighten around his neck.

John spotted a cloaked figure emerge from an eerie mist. He looked up at a pair of cormorants as they circled the docks. Others stood with wings outstretched like fallen angels as they balanced on spars drying their black feathers. Struggling along, pulling a heavy container behind him, the newcomer waved a hand enthusiastically at the captain. One of the black men noticed the hooded man and approached him. Holding out an open hand, he signalled an offer to help with the stranger's luggage. 'Yi!! Creppin's loud yell made the sailor back away. 'Unhand Crrreppin's crrrate, darkened one!' John signalled for his men to back off then turned to the crooked little man, ''Ast tha' brart tha' payment?' Creppin fumbled under his cloak and untied a large coin bag from his belt. He gave a self-satisfied smirk and jiggled the heavy pouch in front of his grubby face. The owner of the world-famous attraction gave the hunchback a nod and invited him to board his Ship of Freaks. Creppin returned a hideous grin and shuffled up the gangway to join his new master. John noticed that the little man was nervous, his stray bulbous eye twitched and he kept glancing back over his deformed shoulder.

The little man felt so proud of himself for getting rid of Patrick Culley. It made him snigger every time he thought of the day he watched the guards take the cocky captain away. His lucky rabbit foot brooch had not protected him from harm then, had it, he thought as his eyebrows danced wildly above cruel eyes. Before he had jumped into the river, Creppin had been delighted to witness Patrick's arrest when his late mother's stupid lucky brooch had fallen to the ground. Ever since he and Anthony had met the pyrate, the hunchback had disliked him. On the evening when he had been allowed to roam free in Grace O'Malley's castle, Creppin had accepted a cold, hard truth. He was not, nor ever would be, accepted as anything but the outcast of society he had been born to be. From now on, the little man was determined to demand respect from his peers. With Patrick out of the way, he would have Anthony's full attention once again when they met up that Yuletide. The plan for any survivors from the assassination team was to return to Ireland. Then they would all meet in São Vicente to celebrate Christmas together. This would give them plenty of time to throw off any unwanted attention. All being well, their tracks would be covered before returning safely to the paradise island. Not feeling any desire to experience the miserable, cold climate of Ireland again, Creppin planned to travel with John's Freak show before going back to São Vicente in December.

Creppin had been collecting precious things that he called his 'prrroperty' since he had first started to feel rejected by Anthony back at Rockfleet Castle. He had managed to build up quite a hoard pilfered from the pyrates over the last year. He had even managed to obtain his very own 'pretty' courtesy of Patrick Culley. The hunchback had kidnapped her the night before the assassination attempt. Creppin had convinced himself that no-one would ever suspect the stupid, loyal cripple. He had been right, 'More fools they, sez I!'

The conniving little fiend had planned to rob each of the gang the night before the assassination attempt. As he had predicted, they had all gone out and become intoxicated not knowing whether they would be alive for much longer. The hunchback had joined them at the brothel where he had made sure that everyone thought he would be spending a long time with an old whore. As soon as she was stoned on opium, he had left for the Red Lion to rob everyone but Shanny and Jock who had stayed in their room all night. Creppin had become a kleptomaniac who was ever determined to add more to his secret stash. Each member of the gang had been given a generous amount of money to use for living expenses, bribes and, most important of all, a means of escape if needed. Patrick had brought Violet back to his room which was unusual as they had always used hers for their nightly trysts. When he was disturbed, Creppin had crouched in a dark corner. He had sat still and quiet as the couple argued. After that, he had been treated to a voyeuristic show as Patrick and Violet had wild passionate sex. Stuffing his mouth with rag to prevent him from making too much sound, the hunchback had squeezed his hardened member until he came. At that point, he must have fallen asleep. When he awoke, the young actress was lying alone on Patrick's bed. She was weeping.

Creppin had stayed in one position for too long and could hardly feel any sensation in his numb, twisted legs. Slowly, he tried to kneel and, in doing so, had put his hand on a small bottle. Holding it up to the window he had seen that there was still some liquid inside. The captain had already taken enough of the potent anaesthetic to drug the guards on watch that night. Soaking a rag with the sweet oil of vitriol, Creppin replaced the cork and waited in the darkness.

The evil hunchback stood in the safety of the Freak Ship and recalled Violet stirring when she had heard a rustling sound. 'Patrick?' she whispered, suddenly aware of another's presence in the cramped room. It happened within seconds. The hunchback pounced on the bed and pressed the sodden rag firmly over the actress' nose and mouth. She had struggled a little but Creppin's weight held her down. His heartbeat quickened and he immediately felt aroused. 'Hussshhh my prrrritty! Sssslumber nowwww.' Creppin's voice had changed. It had become much deeper, rasping and more sinister. Drool dropped onto Violet's fair skin as her captor took away the rag to inspect his prize. 'Yi!' Creppin could not contain his excitement. 'Pardy me mi'lady. Shalt tha' mindst if we takes a peek?' Ugly eyes grew wide as he wasted no time untying the ribbon to release the drawstring on the unconscious woman's chemise. Filthy gnarled fingers caressed Violet's naked shoulders as he took his time inspecting her perfect form. When he had satisfied himself, he wrapped his captive up in rough blankets, tying them securely with string. He dragged her into his crate. After dragging it downstairs, the evil little man even had the guile to ask Mama Mabel to store it in the cellar until his return the following day. The landlady was more than happy to help her lodger who would soon be leaving her inn.

Mabel had not seen Skippy slip past her to follow his master down into the cold, underground room. When he caught Violet's scent, the little dog had sensed something was wrong. He had begun to growl menacingly. Creppin warned him away from his crate but the animal had bared his teeth and attacked him. In a sudden crazed fit of anger the hunchback had smashed his cudgel against the loyal animal's head. Skippy yelped as he took the violent blow. Leaving the poor dog lying in a pool of his own blood and whimpering in pain Creppin had limped back up the steps to join Mama Mabel. She wished him well and they enjoyed a pitcher of mead together before he went off to join the others back at the bawd house.

The hunchback had been the traitor who had stolen the map that gave away the location of the planned assassination. He had paid a linkboy to deliver the vital evidence to one of the Queen's Guards before joining Shrimp at a prearranged place near the landing stage. The two had been assigned to distract the crowd by causing havoc and hysteria. They had done an excellent job. The public had panicked and caused more confusion when the little men had threatened them with flintlock pistols and stabbed random people to make them run.

'Crrreppin fooled 'em all!' the little man bragged to himself as he remembered the day he met Patrick Culley. From the very start, he had detested the man with an uncanny resemblance to the only true friend he had ever known. No-one but the kind blacksmith had given Creppin a chance to improve his life and now look at him! Once a reject of society, he was now a wealthy man determined to start a life in the New World. He would search until he found a society who welcomed and accepted his kind. The hunchback was sick to death of being treated like vermin. Someday, he hoped to return to be re-united with Anthony but, until then, he had many years of poverty and maltreatment to make up for.

FINAL CHAPTER

Unfinished Business and a Foul Tale to Follow!

Many common English citizens thought Francis Drake to be above his station. Still raging his personal war with the King of Spain he constantly urged Elizabeth to back him. The Queen flatly refused to be drawn into waging warfare with Spain so Drake continued to plague Spanish ships. Elizabeth preferred diplomacy to armed conflict and was very careful not to become involved in continental issues, publicly, at least. Often secretly giving aid to allied countries she continued to focus diplomatic negotiation on possible marriage unions. Whilst foreign powers were keen to have England on their side, their primary concern was to send the right regal match to impress the supposed Virgin Queen. War was not an issue, so Elizabeth had made a clever decision in her choice to remain single. This provided an excellent means of defence. Whilst her subjects enjoyed a peaceful life in Elizabethan England, their Queen was playing one realm against another in the competition to gain a foothold on the English throne.

The Spanish were much more experienced in ocean exploration so Drake took advantage of their invaluable knowledge. Whilst sailing the Pacific he seized two charts from Spanish pilots bound for the Philippines and continued to load his small barque with plundered Spanish treasure. Enemies of Spain began to order prints of the Naval Commander who they regarded as a hero. The Spanish referred to Drake as 'el draque', meaning 'the dragon'. They despised him, regarding him as pyrate scum. The Spanish King offered a substantial reward of 20,000 ducats for Drake's death or capture. John Hawkins continued his work as treasurer of the English Navy and pleased the Queen by launching a new campaign to recruit more sailors into the naval forces. The men were promised better working conditions on board his advanced warships. In the meantime, England and Spain continued to argue over religion and trade.

Patrick and Grace still planned to seek revenge on the sadistic English Queen. With Hawkins on their side they had a far better chance of success. Now it would only be a matter of time. Clueless to their betrayer's identity, Patrick and Grace could only hope that he, or she, was not still amongst them. For all they knew the traitor could have been one of the lucky ones to escape that fateful night. They would have to be sure to choose their new gang very carefully. Patrick missed the blacksmith and so did the Irish pyrate queen. Grace already knew that neither of them would ever get over his death. Sensing the deep remorse that Patrick felt, she tried to settle his conscience.

Patrick despised himself. What in heaven's name had he been thinking!? Anthony's death would haunt him 'til the day he died. Taking Patrick's hand, Grace looked deeply into his beautiful blue eyes. They were so like her Anthony's! 'Oy've decided dat, from this day onward, ye shall be known as Pádraig MacCullagh,' she declared. Although the Queen of Connaught shared similarities to the English bitch Queen as a ruthless leader of men, an independent, strong warrior woman and powerful pyrate, there was one thing that Elizabeth would never come close to experiencing; that was motherhood. 'Oy can'ne'er replace yer mudder, Pádraig, but oy'll be here fer yers, nay matter what!' Grace promised as she hugged the man who she loved like a son. 'We'll ne'er gi' up the foyt, moy lad!' Silently, Pádraig agreed.

Grace remembered standing on the ramparts of Rockfleet Castle with Anthony by her side when she had allowed him a glimpse of her feminine vulnerability. She told Pádraig that she and Anthony had felt a connection during their first meeting and that they had experienced the wildest, most satisfying sex ever. As they looked out over Grace's land, with their long hair flowing behind them, the two hardened pyrates felt angry that they had failed to avenge Sushana Culley. The fire within their souls grew fiercer and hotter in their desperate need for revenge. Grace shuddered to the core as she remembered how she had felt when Anthony had stood on that very spot and told her that Pádraig needed to be free. She should have guessed that he planned to die in his friend's stead. Grace felt such self-denigration. Anthony's sacrifice had been unnecessary. She could have stopped him! How could she have been so blind?! If only he had shared the burden! They could have planned another way for Patrick to disappear. She stole a glance at the handsome young man beside her who reminded her so much of the gallant blacksmith. Gulping back the tears, she spoke, loud and clear. Grace O'Malley's bitter words made Pádraig's very soul quake, 'Oy swears ter yers noy, Páddy. Oy'll ne'er rest 'til we foind the cowardly barrrstard who betrayed yers arl dat sarry eve. As Gad's moy witness, oy vow dat dey'll soffer a fayat far, far worse dan det! Oy shall cast de' traitor's sorry carcass into d' depths. A heavy toid'll surely push his filty soul straight t' hell.' Pádraig took heed of the Grace's compelling words but stayed silent. Grace kissed him on the forehead and went inside her castle.

A lone merlin screeched from darkening skies high above Rockfleet Castle whilst a flock of puffins skimmed low over the water… then it happened. With a sudden surge of speed, the slate blue killer dived onto a straggler despatching its victim with a single blow of its talons. Pádraig watched as the predator wheeled towards him, carrying its prey within feet of his face. The once cheerful, clown-like face of the puffin now resembled a grotesque gargoyle and Pádraig had an awful feeling that he had caught a glimpse of himself. He stepped up onto the top of the cold, grey stone wall to look down at the water. The therapeutic sound of waves lapping the foot of the castle helped to calm the pyrate's busy mind. His heartbeat slowed to a steady rhythm… pum-pum… pum-pum… pum-pum… pum-pum… A sharp pain shot through Pádraig's head. He felt faint. An unexpectedly strong gust of wind stole his breath. Suddenly losing his footing, he frantically tried to keep his balance. His hands scrabbled for something to grab onto but to no avail. Pádraig MacCullagh blacked out when his left temple hit the hard stone wall. The pyrate captain's limp young body plummeted towards the dangerously shallow waters below.